WATER *from a* BUCKET

WATER
from a
BUCKET

A DIARY
1948–1957

◆

Charles Henri Ford

INTRODUCTION BY
Lynne Tillman

TURTLE POINT PRESS
NEW YORK

Library of Congress Control Number: 00-136359

Paperback ISBN: 978-1-885586-20-9
eBook ISBN: 978-1-885586-81-0

Design and composition by
Wilsted & Taylor Publishing Services

CUT UP LIFE

Dear Poet
Charles Henri Ford
Did the lake overturn
when Narcissus fell in
become opaque
a mad lake—
Oh poet dear
please make it clear
and let it recover
the reflected image
of that foolish lover—

Amazedly
        Florine Stettheimer

Charles Henri (né Henry) Ford made his entrance on February 10, 1908, in Hazlehurst, Mississippi, to Gertrude Cato and Charles Lloyd Ford. It was his idea to change the spelling of Henry to Henri. "I was tired of being asked if I was related to Henry Ford," he says, "and a young girl wrote me on lavender paper and in red ink and made a mistake that I liked so I kept it."[1]

Ford's parents, and his father's brothers, owned hotels in various small cities in Mississippi and Texas—Ford was born in a hotel that burned down soon after—and his early life was peripatetic. His mother, whom he compares in his diary with Hamlet's mother, Gertrude, was an artist herself and seems to have been a dramatic, beautiful, and compelling character. This primary love led the way to Ford's two great loves—Djuna Barnes and Pavel (Pavlik) Tchelitchew.

[1] All spoken remarks are Charles Henri Ford's to the author in two recent conversations. All other quoted material is from *Water from a Bucket*, unless a source is cited.

Ford met Barnes in New York in 1929, before he left for Paris in 1931, and lived with her in Morocco, where he typed the manuscript of her novel *Nightwood.* "She couldn't spell," he says. His most enduring relationship was with Russian painter Pavlik Tchelitchew. They lived together for 23 years. Ford and Tchelitchew met in Paris, in 1933, at an opening, when Ford was 24 and Tchelitchew, 35. Of the meeting Ford notes in his diary that he wrote Parker Tyler at the time: "I've found a genius." In a powerful way, the diary circles around and is about Pavlik, "his great heart," and their complicated love and long relationship.

His younger sister, Ruth Ford—the diary's "Sister"—was a well-known actor. She debuted in Orson Welles' Mercury Theater production of *The Shoemaker's Holiday* in 1938; performed in plays by Tennessee Williams; had a lead in Jean-Paul Sartre's *No Exit* (translated by Paul Bowles), and received a nomination from the London Drama Critics, in 1957, for her performance as Temple Drake in *Requiem for a Nun,* which she had adapted into a play with William Faulkner. Ruth Ford was married to Hollywood actor Zachary Scott, who died in 1965, and lives in the Dakota, four floors below her older brother.

> I loved the Blues before I loved the Poem. Somehow the two loves
> were from the same source. So it was natural I called my poetry review
> Blues.

Precocious and ambitious, the young poet launched *Blues,* The Magazine of New Rhythms, in 1929. William Carlos Williams and Eugene Jolas were two of its contributing editors and Kathleen Tankersley Young its associate editor. For nine issues, Ford solicited and published writing from Ezra Pound, Gertrude Stein, Kay Boyle, Harry Crosby, James Farrell, H.D., Kenneth Rexroth, Mark van Doren, Louis Zukofsky, Edouard Roditi, Erskine Caldwell. He was the first to publish Paul Bowles.

From Mississippi, Ford moved to New York, to write poetry and lead *la vie bohème* in Greenwich Village. Ford had published Parker Tyler, the poet and future film critic and writer, in *Blues* and was corresponding with him. They met in person in New York—"I could hardly see his face, he had so much makeup on," Ford says—and soon collaborated on writing *The Young and Evil.* Called by some the first gay novel, published in 1933, banned in the United States and England, it is, like Ford himself, unapologetic, unashamed, poetic, candid, and determinedly free of conventions.

> It's not doing the things one wants to do—even if considered a vice, like
> opium-taking—that makes one age, but doing things one doesn't want
> to do.

A kind of Surrealist free verse, the uninhibited novel was influenced, in part, by Ford's mentor Gertrude Stein, who took him up when he was first in Paris. When Ford fell in love with Tchelitchew, Stein found less reason to see him; she and Tchelitchew had had one of those famous, furious partings of the way. But in *The Autobiography of Alice B. Toklas,* Stein writes of Ford: "He is also honest which is also a pleasure."

Along with *The Young and Evil,* Ford is perhaps best known for *View,* the international art magazine he edited in New York, from 1940 to 1947. Europeans Marcel Duchamp, André Breton, Max Ernst—forced into exile during World War II—Americans Maya Deren, Meyer Schapiro, Joseph Cornell, Florine Stettheimer, Man Ray, Paul Bowles, and many more found a home in *View*'s pages and on its covers. Not coincidentally, Ford begins his diary a year after he stops *View* and ends it shortly after the death of Tchelitchew in 1957.

Since finishing the diary, Ford has produced or invented the "poem poster" (shown at the Ubu Gallery in New York in 2000); published many books of poetry, including a limited edition, unique collage book, *Spare Parts,* and *Out of the Labyrinth: Selected Poems* (City Lights, 1991); directed the feature-length movie *Johnny Minotaur* (shot in Crete, starring Allen Ginsberg among others), and exhibited his photographs, most recently with fellow Mississippian Allen Frame (at the Leslie Tonkonow Gallery in New York).

You have to enjoy what you're doing and do it every day.

Ford has made a habit of doing what he wants to do, and his life is dedicated, as much as anyone's can be, to poetry, art, and the pursuit of pleasure. He usually adheres to a self-imposed, rigorous routine, and now, just short of 93, he writes haiku poems and makes collages daily. When I visit him on a brilliant fall day, October 1, 2000, one of the day's haikus is on his desk:

Men too have a
          change
of life
didn't Marcel
          Duchamp
     have it twice

◆

I first read Charles Henri Ford's diary in the late 1970s, and again in the late 1980s, when I urged him to have it published. He didn't want to bother. He was writing poems, making collages and photographs; not one, as the reader will see, to look back with longing or regret.

Those were not the days. These are the days. My days are always these.

I find it pointless to have a nostalgia about the past.

I: "Would you like to be in Rome . . . where all the pretty boys are?" Pavlik: "Don't turn the dagger in the wound."

Poetry, genius, love, fame, friendship, beauty, family, character, sex, psychology, youth, and Pavlik, always, are variously appetizers, entrees, or desserts on Ford's menu du jour et de la nuit. His diary is riveting. As it moves from theme to theme, the reader senses a life formed consciously in the present, one lived spontaneously, interrupted and interfered with by memory and the pressure of unconscious thoughts. The reader feels the moment's vitality and presence, and the sorrow at its loss, but not because Ford insists on it. Emotion—disappointment and sadness—is there in the way he writes the day, flying from an idea, sex act, or fantasy, to a line in a poem, a report on dinner talk, a death, an argument, to a question about aesthetics, a worry about Pavlik—then it's all gone, except the memory of it, what he's written down.

A passionate schoolboy who knew what he wanted—and got it. (In the pissoir.)

A shadow falls, a fragment of night; a day goes, a fragment of death. Life and the sun tomorrow.

Many beautiful machines—Tanguy painted. But the most beautiful machine is and always will be the human body.

His diary is beautiful and homely, an epic poem about the dailiness of art and life. It's filled with insights about himself, love, sex, his illusions, delusions; there's silliness, homages to his heroes—Isak Dinesen, for one—and acerbic or reverent considerations of his contemporaries. Tchelitchew comments that Jean Genet, whom Ford finds "solemn and humorless," is "un moraliste—comme Sade"; Ford refers, less perceptively, to "messes signed by Jackson Pollock." The diary is loaded with gossip about history's celebrated, with whom Ford has had lunch or met at an opening. When he introduces Djuna Barnes to Tennessee Williams at a party, she asks Williams: "How does it feel to be rich and famous?"

Diaries confirm that life is in the details, and in its passions, all of which Ford includes, all of which are inevitably subservient to time. Ford's diary is profound not because it marks time passing or spent, but because it is imaginatively and definitively of its time and in it.

I asked Parker (in a letter) if he thought posthumous fame is any fun and he replied it might be to posterity.

Go back to music, rhythm, as Yeats did, for a renewal of inspiration in poetry. "Go back" in the sense of renewal—

Pavlik's summary of how I spend my time: "fornication and fabrication."

Like histories, diaries are accounts of the past. Unlike histories, they are not written retrospectively, and subjectivity is their central claim to truth. Faithful to the subjective, the diarist's words, Ford's eyes and ears, conduct the reader through the world he inhabits. The reader finds the way back as it was to Ford. His irrepressibility, his understanding of the power of transience—in sex, art, love—his appreciation of the ephemeral, and his desire to have it all, anyway, for as long as he can, carry us with him.

Years of work, a burst of glory, and it's all over.

Up at six and found a feather in my bed, as though, while I was sleeping, I'd been a bird.

Pavlik told me—in 1933—that I had been sent to him because his mother died.

What is called history comes to us as a transcription of the evanescent. A radio announcer's excited play by play of the Tony Zale-Marcel Cerdan fight becomes a monologue written by a Surrealist. The now-famous 1948 Life photograph of poets at the Gotham Book Mart—Ford, the Sitwells, Marianne Moore, Tennessee Williams, Delmore Schwartz, W. H. Auden, Elizabeth Bishop, Stephen Spender, Randall Jarrell—was first, in the diary, an occasion for a gathering. The photograph documents the group, contributing to the historical record—these poets were there, those not, some are forgotten now.

Ford's commentary about the group offers another record, a personal view that instantly affects the august photograph. He complains that Gore Vidal is in it, that Vidal is not a poet, and the reader can see the tension the photograph does not image. And then there are Ford's musings about Christine Jorgensen, the G.I. who in 1953 underwent the first highly publicized man-to-woman sex change operation.

Why is everyone always foolish enough to think that a sexual partner will make life happy?

I took a terrace walk and saw the most brilliant falling star. I always make the same wish: Love.

A diary tells us what its author was thinking about then and how it was thought. It is different from a history, because it is an itinerary of lived attitudes, a catalogue of attitudes. Attitude is in the air we breathe, and we don't always think about what we take in and give out. Ford's ideas are his and not his, and, as a matter of history, the expression of attitudes allows a return to the past that so-called objective accounts can't. Ford lets us conspire with him, breathe with him.

A record of himself is all any man records.

Being jerked off—if done by the right person—leaves no regrets.

Characteristic of our age (Henry James' *The Turn of the Screw* a forerunner)—more and more interest in the perversity of children. . . . to shock now, the child must be involved—Example in painting: Balthus, more shocking than Dali. . . . The child is all.

The contemporary reader may be surprised by Ford's anxiety about the effects of masturbation—"I recover from self-abuse"—or disturbed or pleased by his ecstatic evocations and lust for teenaged boys, by his openness about his desires generally. Maybe the only thing in life that doesn't change, apart from the certainty of death—though these days that seems to be changing—is desire. Only its articulations and the environment in which it is felt shift. Ford's freedom or constraints, his prejudices or lacks, gauge his moment and ours.

◆

But I look too good to ruin: I wish my twin would come along and I'd kiss him.

I don't know how my character will come out in these notes and memories, but I think we usually are to others what we are to ourselves.

The literary diary is a strange form. Was it written to be read? Maybe. Probably. Is it self-conscious? Necessarily. Ford's diary was written to examine himself and others, and in a way, its self-consciousness is its raison d'être. Preciousness is stripped from its self-consciousness by Ford's sardonic, unflinching self-criticism —he's regularly concerned with his character as well as Pavlik's. (The diary pulses, too, with the impact of psychoanalytic theory on contemporary thinking.) But Ford is unself-conscious about his devotion to the cause of aesthetics and the examined life. And is, in his fashion, devoted to love, writing a love story with its own deliberate ideas about heart.

No one will ever mean more to me—inspire me more—than Pavlik....

The fatal image: Vito's profile as he looked over the terrace yesterday. There it was and there's nothing one can do about it. I wasn't born to live alone.

Pavlik's great heart stopped beating at ten to eight (July 1957).

Ford's diary ends with questions. Does he love Vito? Does Vito love him? Anyway, what is love. Pavlik has died. Ford's days will change. His life has come to the reader in bits and pieces, a collage, or, like his poems, a cut up. It ends the same way.

"This ravaging sense of the shortness of life..." (V. W.) I don't have that. I sense, rather, that life will be long—too long.

Charles said something, on that brilliant fall day, about being fortunate or having had good fortune. I teased him about becoming soft. He said, I think a little sheepishly, "Well, it's the right time, isn't it?"

I shall continue this document until the end of next year, then I vow to continue it no longer. It's a secret vice. Vices should be public.

Lynne Tillman
January 27, 2001

1948

SEPTEMBER

NEW YORK CITY [360 EAST 55TH STREET]

Poem (from the Insurance Policy of the Automobile Club of New York, Inc.):

FOR LOSS OF

Life
Two Eyes
Two Arms
Two Hands
Two Legs
Two Feet
One Arm and One Leg
One Arm and One Foot
One Hand and One Leg
One Hand and One Foot
One Leg and One Eye
One Hand and One Eye
One Foot and One Eye
One Arm
One Hand
One Leg
One Foot
One Eye

◆

There is an Alexander the Great Service Station on First Avenue.

Pale city sun, as pale as the desire to write poetry, when one first comes back to the city.

"Fourmillante cité, cité pleine de rêves," I quoted to Pavlik* as we drove down Park Avenue. "No dreams," he said, "—except for making money."

*Pavel Tchelitchew

I stopped in at the "Men's" at the subway station, Third Avenue and 53rd Street. Mutual masturbation does not leave the aftermath of depression that the "solitary vice" does.

That poor little lonesome bird on the terrace opposite our terrace (across First Avenue)—making the most hideous noises.

At Alice's they were discussing Denham Fouts and his opium taking. Denham is Peter Watson's ex-boyfriend and was staying at Peter's former apartment on the rue du Bac in Paris. In spite of his dope addiction, said Alice [Delamar], Denham still looks so young, not over 28, no lines in his face, hasn't got a gray hair. I pointed out that it's not doing the things one wants to do—even if considered a "vice," like opium taking—that makes one age, but doing the things one *doesn't* want to do.

The talismanic titles given to race horses:

Problem Child
Touch Control
His Nickel
Jet Power
Cold Brat
Pink Tights
Swing Me
Blow Me
Gunners Mate

◆

If I weren't so fucking lazy I'd give an account of my trip to Tennessee last July— to see Mother and Daddy [Gertrude and Charles Ford].

All right. I got off the bus in Chattanooga, Tenn., right in front of the Tourist Court, found Mother in the "Residence" and looking very well. But poor dear Daddy on the side of the bed, in his white nightshirt, sitting up to greet me, looking so thin, so pathetic and weak. He grasped both my hands and clung to them, as if wanting to draw strength from them.

Then I think Tim came in, or somewhat later, carrying food on a tray. Tim is the boy who takes care of Daddy, gives him the shots of morphine (Daddy doesn't know it's morphine, nor does he know he has cancer). Tim gives him alcohol rubs, keeps his room straight, etc. He didn't strike me as good-looking but pleasant looking, good-humored and well built; not ugly either; reddish hair and big nose.

Daddy smoked his cigar and I sat in his room and we talked. He spoke about his early life and I learned family history I hadn't known before. My Grandpa Ford's family lived in Alabama at the beginning of the Civil War. Grandpa Ford, enlisting before he'd reached the age of sixteen, fought four years with the Confederate Army, and when the war was over decided to settle in Mississippi. After he married Lizzie Fore (my father's mother), he bought timberland and developed a sawmill on it. Later, he sold the place, moved into town and built the Hazlehurst Hotel, where I was born (Hazlehurst, Mississippi).

I also got straight the blood relationship between Mother and Daddy—I'll see if I can remember it. I was shown tintypes of the father and mother of Lizzie Fore. Her mother was first married to a Cato, by whom she had a son, my mother's father. That would make my Grandma Ford and my Grandpa Cato half-brother-and-sister. So that Daddy would have as half-uncle Mother's father, and Mother would have as half-aunt her mother-in-law (my grandmother). Thus Mother and Daddy are half-first-cousins.

◆

"I looked at myself in the mirror the other day and I was absolutely terrified—an old mad face."—Pavlik. He has discovered that the second vertebra (in the neck), on which the head pivots, resembles the Sphinx, "secret of life."

Seurat: "the last Frenchman," says Pavlik. "With Cézanne came 'analysis.' I am doing analysis too."

◆

In sex, there are all sorts of "side dishes" that one discovers, which add to the enjoyment of the "main course." ... A letter from Tim in Garnett, Tenn. "Hurry home again I am anchous [sic] to see you." Well, as I wrote here yesterday, in July I was in Tennessee—on the 27th. Tim said maybe we'd go swimming the next day. I stayed in the room while he gave Daddy the goodnight alcohol rub. Daddy joked beforehand about the way he'd look undressed: "I'll break the camera." His skin hung in folds over his stomach. Mother asked me later if I had seen the navel, where the pus is coming out, the cancer is eating through there. No, I hadn't. He said how well he had felt for three hours ("three hours is a long time") after one of his shots.

That night, after Mother had gone to her room and Daddy's light was out, I went to my room, followed by Tim who said, "You're not going to bed now, are you?" and I said, "No"—I was only getting a sweater. Outside I asked him if he'd like a drink of bourbon and Coke and he said yes and I went back in and got it. He continued in the storytelling vein of the afternoon: a fat girl made a bet with his brother and another boy that she could stick a quart milk bottle up herself and make it disappear. She won, but they had to make a hole in the bottle (big end) to get it out. When we finished our drinks Tim said, "Let's go listen on the radio." As soon as we got in the "Doll House" where he slept—originally a kind of play-house built for children—he turned the radio on and I turned off the naked light bulb and we lay down on the bed. He asked me why I didn't spend the night in his bed, but later I went back to mine ... The next afternoon there was time for Mother to have her nap before I left, so I went out to the Doll House with Tim. Mrs. West, the maid, and her husband were around the grounds, in and out of the cabins, cleaning up. I eased my cock up towards Tim's face and he said, "Let it die down." "I'm about to come," I said. "You won't," he said, "if you let it die down."

When it was time to get ready to leave, I went in to say goodbye to Daddy. I thought to myself, this may be the last time I'll see him alive.

◆

At a quarter to eleven last night: I conquered the desire ("let it die down") and then as if against my will started feeling myself again and it felt "too good to stop." As an argument against stopping I thought of all the pricks in the world being masturbated at that moment—mine was a symbol of them all—it belonged to someone else.

◆

The Poet by Isak Dinesen. I do not know why this story makes such an impression upon me—probably because I see in it my Myth. Both Francine and Anders ("the poet") become passion-sick—the infection begins with their first meeting—the play (adaptation of which I'm working on) will be like the progress of a disease—worse, worse, crisis. (Another example of the passion-sick: Phaedra.)

We must depend less than Shakespeare on arousing *pity through rhetoric*. Character and situation and simple dialogue are our means. And even in Shakespeare, his characters, in their most passionate *moments*, talk in very simple sentences. And then they are at their most moving, as characters.

Othello: "I kissed thee ere I killed thee; no way but this, killing myself to die upon a kiss."

In *The Poet* there is the tension of *waiting* throughout: waiting for the lovers to get together (they never do); waiting for the marriage of Francine and the Councillor (it never takes place). The *anguish* will gradually grow (in the spectator) until the *release*: the shooting ...

◆

The "art boom" is off and Pavlik is in a continual panic over his finances. He thinks there's no chance to make a success in Paris with his new paintings until Picasso (monstre sacré) and his influence no longer exist.

When he is upset like this he begins to talk against America in general, where "there is no such thing as friendship," and New York in particular, says he would like to leave and go to Italy but we have no money. He told me I'm a parasite ... then something nice: that I probably didn't know when I put a cow in a poem dedicated to him that the cow is the symbol of Isis. His formulation of what his present work means: Magic formulas operate sometimes even when the one who executes the ritual is unaware of their working. His theory is that the human being—in art as well as in life—has been broken to pieces. To put the pieces together, reconstitute l'être humain, not merely the surface must be painted but the entire man, transparent. And if all the parts painted transparently are painted *flatly* enough, the figure will seem to "turn," i.e., sometimes it is looking one way, then the opposite way. To "put together"—Pavlik says he's always done that, says he did that to me, and *holds* me together too—that I would fly off in a thousand directions if it weren't for him.

He's really tough, to be as sensitive as he is—"the Butterfly and the Bull"—an image I used in a sonnet to him in 1934 (Fuengirola, Spain):

One moment you are stabbed with a white flag,
snow-blind, pissing with fury, fence-leaper,
the next no flower is too frail or fair
to keep your terrible delicacy intact.
Quicker than intellect, evil for good,
intends to disembowel the strong and gentle—
sensible wings, transparent, good for evil,
forgive the autumn for the end of summer.
How defy a red sword and flee from sparrows,
endure opinion's cuts, be worn by zephyrs!
I see you from my boat that plows the mountain,
its prow lit up with fireworks loud and sudden:
your fame I trust, your actions I descry,
nor reconcile the bull and butterfly.

◆

The Sitwells (Osbert and Edith) are arriving in about a month. More headaches for Pavlik! But Edith is his dear friend . . .

◆

Pavlik called me to his studio where we talked about his work. He said he's bored with working over anatomy charts so many years (six) in order to learn the position of nerves, bones, muscles, veins and arteries, and that he still does not know them or see them simultaneously, which he must do in his mind in order to paint them simultaneously. My advice was for him to simplify his pictures, that is, use economy in what he paints, now, not try to put everything in at once.

The tree in "Hide-and-Seek" (his big picture at the Museum of Modern Art) is sometimes, he said, like a flowing green river, seen from above.

Today, the 21st, is Pavlik's birthday. On my wishing him many happy returns, and before I could give him a present, he said, "All I want you to give me is courage." He's reached the half-century mark, looks rather more rested and less harassed than yesterday—perhaps the tension of "waiting to be fifty" is gone.

◆

The Tony Zale-Marcel Cerdan fight for the middleweight championship of the world is on the air. Second time tonight I've heard the "Marseillaise." Pavlik says it always reminds him of "war." Now someone is wailing "The Star-Spangled Banner."

Announcer: "Introducing, from Casablanca, Morocco, wearing white trunks . . . Marcel Cerdan . . . His opponent, from Gary, Indiana, wearing purple trunks, the middleweight champion of the world, Tony Zale . . . Packed to the rafters, eager avid humanity . . .

"Round 1 . . . Zale snaps Cerdan's head back . . . Both were going mostly for the body . . .

"Round 2 . . . There is some blood showing now on the forehead of Marcel Cerdan . . .

"Round 3 . . . Both boys right now are waiting for the other to make a mistake . . .

"Round 4 . . . that beautiful, effective way he has of tying up Tony's punches . . . Tony is not opening up like the wildcat we have known of old . . . Zale has the quality of desperation about him . . .

"Round 5 . . . He's found out that he can hurt Cerdan and he wants to do it . . .

"Round 6 . . . Marcel seems to have no respect for Tony Zale at the present time at all . . . Tony comes plodding in flat-footed . . .

"Round 7 . . . Which man is going to shoot his bolt in this round? . . . a left uppercut that was a thing of beauty—a terrific left hand that had Tony Zale on Queer Street for just about thirty seconds . . . Cerdan beats a little tattoo on the chin of Tony Zale with his right . . . Tony wiped off his nose with his left glove . . . Tony is anxious to grab both of those fiery gloves . . .

"Round 9 . . . —a remarkably clean fight, very savage . . .

"Round 10 . . . —rips his mouth and almost took his mouthpiece out . . ." (Cerdan the aggressor.)

. . . (Zale) "ineffectually flapping around . . .

"Round 11 . . . leans his weight on Marcel Cerdan . . . Zale is just looking around as though he doesn't know where his opponent is . . . Zale falls forward." End of Round 11. Then: "It's definitely over . . . Tony Zale unable to come out for the 12th round . . . A new middleweight champion of the world . . . Marcel Cerdan from French Morocco! . . . This ring is a madhouse . . . it's a regular bedlam." Cerdan "now being embraced by Gorgeous Georges Charpentier."

◆

Must write on my play every day. "Writing callous" on my second finger increasing. The reality is the work—all the rest is apparition. One's "gift" consists in taking what belongs to one. Not for the asking, but like wresting gold from a stream.

Pavlik came home yesterday quite excited over having seen in a doctor's office, to which George Balanchine took him, a transparent skull—a real one, put in an acid which rendered it translucent when certain lights are turned on—"like made of dragonflies' wings," said Pavlik, and it showed him how right he was in the drawings of his transparent skulls.

Racehorses picked this morning: First Nighter, I Did (have a wet dream last night), Blunt Remark, (about a little boy holding onto "mine," and I came in my clothes like an) Irish Oyster, Noble Impulse, Night Sound, Roman Slave, My Good Man, Bug Juice, Blue Peter, Slam Bang, Surrender (you know what I'm thinking), Rush Hour, Curtain Time.

◆

The masculine type of simple boy, who goes with girls and yet has something passive about him ... The incredible-looking gymnast who appeared in the weight-room yesterday at the Y: face of a soap-sculpture athlete (baby face), expressionless; corn-blond hair contrasting with double-thick black eyelashes which gave the final artificial touch—what can you do with a big doll like that? Why, it's too heavy to pick up.

◆

Last evening: to the Paris Opera Ballets at City Center. Tamara Toumanova in audience looked pale and rather shrunken and sad—eaten by Hollywood, there's a certain look... Christian Dior with Marlene Dietrich, who looked rose and white and gold. Pavlik recalled how he was helping pose La Dietrich for Cecil Beaton, put his hand on her waist and she removed it, saying, "Please," and he replied, "You are mistaken."

We were sitting on the front row, someone pinched my ear from the back, I turned around and it was Carl Van Vechten. Carl is editing some works of Gertrude Stein. I sent him recently this quotation from Jung: "... only when we have found the sense in apparent nonsense, can we separate the valueless from the valuable."

Gertrude Stein told me, in 1933, after she learned of my liaison with Pavlik: "Americans are strong but Russians are stronger. You'll come out the little end." And when she couldn't "break it up" she stopped seeing me.

◆

"How difficult it is to write a play!" ... Lyric poetry—not difficult: it's either possible or impossible.

Pavlik read my hand: "... très paederastique ... succès, carrière ... three love affairs ... I am the biggest ... putainique ... genius ... but you did more for yourself than you were born with—because I came into your life."

OCTOBER

Dreamed I was carving up the sex of a cadaver, cutting it off until it looked like a celery stalk. Then it occurred to me to violate the stiff body.

> Beating around the bush.
> Biting around the bitch.
> Butching around the bitte.
> Pushing around the butt.
> Butting around the bite.
> Pissing around the puke.
> Passing around the punk.
> Now I know I'm not sick, the hard comes on—
> Drive yourself to work, you slut!

◆

One day last summer, on Block Island, Pavlik and I were walking near the golf course of Vaill's Hotel. In the distance were the golfers—with their caddies, who, remarked Pavlik, were busboys from the hotel. "Now," I said, "instead of lugging to the sinks, they're sucking on the links." Said Pav: "That's like a line from Auden's poetry!"

Two words coming together may make another kind of poetry:

B e l l
M O V I N G

—sign painted on front of a truck.

"Mother, may I go out to cruise?"
"Yes, my darling bugger.
Drag your ass down 42
And see what you discover."

♦

Yesterday we went by the School of American Ballet where George Balanchine was rehearsing "Serenade." On the sidelines: Maria Tallchief (George's wife), Marie-Jeanne [Pelus], whose dancing I admire, and Nicky Magallanes. Nicky looked very well, with his dark skin and hair, set off by a dark blue sweater. He is to be featured in the forthcoming New York City Ballet presentations at City Center. How his destiny was changed—by my getting off a Madison Avenue bus! I get off a bus—a boy's whole life becomes something other and undreamed of.

I met Nicky when Pavlik and I were living on Christopher Street, spring of 1936 (or it could have been towards the end of 1935, perhaps it was around Christmas time). I often went to Sportland on 14th Street, where there were all sorts of machines for fun and chance—pinball games, nickel-operated derricks that picked up gifts if manipulated right, etc. Crowds of men and boys used to stand around watching. I found myself standing just behind dark, attractive Nicky, aged 16. When he left, I followed him out to the street, where he waited and I walked up to him and started talking, made a date to meet him the next day. But at the cafeteria on Seventh Avenue the next day there was no Nicky. Months later—yes, it was the early spring of 1936—I was in Union Square, listening to the haranguing, when along came Nicky in a white shirt. Again we talked and he said he had been at the cafeteria rendezvous. I was planning to go almost immediately to Tennessee, to spend Easter with Mother and Daddy—so I made a date with Nicky to meet him at a certain place when I got back ... He wasn't there; so this time I thought I had lost him for good—I didn't know his address.

Then—soon after—I was riding up Madison Avenue on a bus with Sister [Ruth Ford] (she lived at the corner of Madison and 73rd) when—I saw Nicky walking in the opposite direction in which the bus was going—putting handbills on automobiles. It took me a minute or so to collect myself enough to give an excuse to Sister and get off the bus. By that time the bus had gone far enough to make it necessary to catch another bus going downtown. So when the bus caught up with Nicky, as it did, I got off and accosted him. Again he said he had been at the rendezvous and that I hadn't shown up; perhaps it had been a misunderstanding. In any case, from that time on I saw him regularly until Pavlik and I sailed for Europe a couple of months later.

Pavlik knew nothing about Nicky until the following fall and winter (1936–37).

I invited Nicky to a party at Anna R.'s and introduced him. At later parties there, with charades, Nicky was partly undressed by Pavlik in order to be dressed up in improvised costumes and Pavlik asked him to come to our studio-apartment on East 73rd Street and pose for him (Pav was working on "Phenomena" at the time). Between sittings, Nicky and I used to shag and shuffle to the Victrola music and Pavlik got the idea, since Nicky was such a good dancer (would Nicky have been a dancer now if we hadn't danced together then and would we have danced together if Mother hadn't taught Sister and me to dance together as children—and what started Mother herself dancing—ad infinitum), to get him a scholarship in the American School of Ballet—where he made progress slowly but later became a professional with the Ballet Russe de Monte Carlo.

◆

Iolas came to dinner, just arrived back from Paris, brought us Lanvin perfume, socks and ties, raves about Paris being the only place to live, gave us news of plays he'd seen: by Nerval, Pichette, Merimée; tried to run down Léonor Fini and build up Bébé Bérard; we weren't impressed.

The other night, coming home across 55th Street, says P.: "Woman are happier when they're fucked."

"So are men," I replied.

We laugh out of sympathy. We cry out of sympathy. We care.

Acting what? Acting emotions. Is that all? No. Acting guile, acting something we don't feel, but mostly emotions—acting cruel, acting jealous, acting hurt, acting excited, acting angry, acting humble, acting proud, acting fond, acting foolish, acting kindly, acting crazy, acting mad, acting calm, acting happy, acting dumb, acting like you're in love.

Masturbation is all right if you have *nothing else to do*: such as in solitary confinement in the dark.

"Lord we know what we are, but know not what we may be" —Ophelia.

"He slept many long hours, like a child"—Djuna [Barnes] in the unpublished short story she wrote about me (1932).

When I was ten a man gave me a dollar to suck him off.

◆

"This country is nothing but obscenity"—Pavlik, when I repeated words of a blues singer which came in over the radio:

"I like a man that takes his time.
Control yourself, Daddy,
You'll like it better if you do!"

Ice-cream cones, hot dogs, soda pop in bottles—all of these are identified with America—and symbolic of what we like in sex too.

The time is long past when a Tolstoy would be shocked by a Wagnerian display of "elbows and knees." Our epoch is nearer to the workers' cabaret in Madrid (to which a taxi driver took Pavlik, Cecil Beaton and me, summer of 1934), where the female performer thought it not enough to show her bare cunt, but brought out a magnifying glass.

◆

Wrote a note to Bert, the sailor, that Blanchard and I gave a lift to from Newport (Jamestown, rather) to New York, on the way back from Martha's Vineyard last May. He's stationed now in Philadelphia, gets his discharge from the navy in November.

Do you love this person or don't you?—a question that *always* comes up. One doubts—and the only proof is in the endurance.

Dropped by to see Frances Steloff in her Gotham Book Mart, after making last payment on *View* debt at National City Bank where a barber, Italian, in white coat with sleeves rolled up displayed his powerful forearms—which I should have liked to have had for dinner, served raw.

I am holding my prick tight and down at the base, pulling the skin tight. I was doing this in Italy once in order to get it to stand out nicely while I photographed it in a mirror, when lo! it shot—sort of crept up on me without my meaning to.

Here lies Charles Henri Ford
Sleep is his reward.

◆

Sylvia Marlowe and Léonide [Massine] invited us for dinner—Vittorio Rieti (composer) was there too. After dinner Léonide brought out a little album, "Souvenir d'Ischia," 1925. In one of the snapshots Léonide was standing in a group on the beach, all in bathing suits, holding a rather pretty boy on his shoulders; it was hard to believe that the boy, who looked 18 but was 21, was Christian Bérard (Bébé). Léonide said that Bébé was doing some of his best painting then. Now Bébé is enormously fat, with a bushy beard. He's still painting well, according to Iolas, but I'm afraid his talent has been dissipated—between the fashion world and his opium-taking. On his visit to New York year before last, he came to lunch with us here, and was having his "tapering off" opium in the form of clear drops in water. "Do you think I've changed much?" he asked. Well, he hadn't changed much since the last time I'd seen him—1939—but I hadn't seen the 1925 snapshot then!

◆

This afternoon, sorting MSS and letters, came across a card headed "Babys Record" (mine) and filled in by Mother:

> Date of Birth: Febr. 10, Monday night 11:55
> Weight at birth: 8 pounds
> " " 3 mos.: 14 "
> " " 6 mos.: 20 "
> " " 9 mos.: 26 "
> " " 12 mos.: 26 "
> Cut first tooth: 6 mo.
> Commenced to creep: 8 mo.
> Commenced to Walk: 10 mo.
> " " Talk: 12 mo.
> First Words: Bye-bye—Tata
> *REMARKS*
> *Laughed when six days old.*

◆

"I'm full of nostalgia lately." (Pavlik.)

"For what?"

"For life—you Americans are so cold . . ."

I *must* add a few pages to my play. Go profoundly, go movingly, understandably, fearlessly, into the subject I have and it will become more than the subject.

The world is filled with petty personalities. It is also filled with charming, beautiful, simple people—or at least a lot of them look so.

The play *must* approach before one catches it—though you can always meet it halfway.

◆

Edith and Osbert [Sitwell] due on *Queen Elizabeth* day after tomorrow.

Haircut at Plaza, 3 P.M. yesterday afternoon (Philippe), then bought some petits-fours at Longchamps to take to tea with Paul Bowles, staying at Libby Holman's house, East 61st Street. I talked to Paul about playwriting, urging him to try his hand by learning the technique—he says writing music is "all technique." He gave me the MS of his novel, *The Sheltering Sky*, to read (New Directions is publishing it).

Heard from Mother, first news I've had since she phoned three weeks ago. "C. L. (as she calls Daddy) is just getting weaker and thinner each day. His urine all comes out at the navel now as the tumor has completely stopped up the other passage . . ." Tim quit. "He was the most *unreliable* person I've ever known. Just a common uncouth uneducated mountaineer and dishonest with it."

Started the MS of Paul's novel ("Don't be too hard on it," he said when he lent it to me). What a letdown after the short stories! One would not recognize the same author whose first stories I published in *Blues*. How could such a thing happen? I must ask him. And the [James] Laughlins were raving about it.

◆

The Sitwells arrived last night. Mrs. Vincent Astor sent us her car at 7:30 (her secretary had made an error in ordering our dock passes—they were made out to meet "Mr. Oscar Sitwell and daughter") and we drove to Pier 90, West 59th Street, where the *Queen Elizabeth* loomed, her two red smoke stacks, like huge gas tanks, lit up. We watched the covered gangplanks vomiting passengers and crew, loaded with luggage, then someone, a friend of David Horner (who arrived with the Sitwells) told us they (Edith and Osbert) were already off and we found them. Pavlik embraced and kissed Edith, so did I, surprised to find her looking no older, a real youthful expression shining in the virginal pale face—her eyes do not seem separate features as they do in other people's faces, but a part of the whole mask of the face. She carried a stick, wore a green felt hat with feathers leaning over towards the front, furs and cat-skin mittens. Osbert had around his neck a black and white large-checkered wool scarf.

Then came the ordeal of waiting for all their baggage to be brought from the hold and placed under the letter S—this was done in the most haphazard way. They had 16 pieces of luggage between them, and by the time everything got there and was examined by the Customs Inspector (Edith had to pay 85¢ for importing a few copies more than 6 of her book on Shakespeare!) and we got to the car, three exhausting hours had passed. We left them at the St. Regis.

◆

I'm drunk. It's night: 12:40 A.M.

We've just returned from the dinner party given for the Sitwells by Mr. and Mrs. David Bouverie—I never knew before how difficult it is to write while champagnized. Bonne nuit!

I've just vomited . . . now I'm drinking buttermilk.

◆

I think it's rather absurd the way Edith insists on calling herself Dr. Sitwell, merely because Doctor of Literature degrees were conferred upon her by two of the lesser British Universities—Leeds and Durham. If everyone in the United States who received a Doctor's degree in Literature or Philosophy began calling themselves Doctors what a sick nation we would appear! (We are anyway.)

Paul Bowles phoned last evening and I couldn't resist telling him the truth as to what I thought of his novel—MS. He wanted to come over and take it back immediately!

◆

Lunch with Osbert and Edith at the St. Regis. Edith looked well in a red velvet turban (though Pavlik found it too "fixed," said the ones she used to make herself were much better, didn't say this to her, however). We discussed, among other things, the dinner party of the other night (guests included Lady Ribblesdale—Alice Bouverie's mother, Monroe Wheeler, Pauline Potter, Fidelma and Lincoln Kirstein, Mrs. Nelson Rockefeller and several Mr. & Mrs. Somebodies). I said today, "The drinks were passed as though for an orgy," and Osbert said, "I rather liked that, didn't you?" Edith gave Pavlik and me a dozen Liberty silk ties, and Osbert, seeing me look over the books on display, said, "Do you see any you would like?" and I said, "I'd like the last one, *Laughter in the Next Room*," but he ignored the request and picked out *Miracle on Sinai* ("a satirical novel") and inscribed it to me.

◆

Pavlik's always telling me I'm in this world for the "first time" and that he's been here many times before—that he's the end of a "race," and I'm the beginning of one.

Edith's company is witty and pleasurable—she hasn't become the "fatuous old woman" that Gertrude Stein, according to Virgil Thomson, became in her last days—or years.

After the lunch yesterday Pavlik and I took Osbert to the Museum of Modern Art to see Pavlik's chef-d'oeuvre, "Hide-and-Seek." I suppose he was properly impressed, though P. says that he doesn't know how to look at pictures; and besides, says P., "Hide-and-Seek" withdraws its images from the Sunday crowds. Pavlik is bored with Edith's preoccupation of who is a lady, who is well-bred and who isn't. He says he's going to tell her that in America there are two classes, those who are rich and those who aren't—"and you aren't."

◆

WESTON, CONN.

We're in our white cottage at last, lent us by Alice Delamar. And what a beautiful morning to greet us, blue sky as backdrop for the branches losing their petals. Happy to be in this particular house, where we spent the winter of 1938–39—the winter Louis Jouvet telephoned Pavlik from Paris, asking him to come and do the décors and costumes for *Ondine* by Jean Giraudoux. So we crossed on the *Normandie* (early spring of '39), the play broke box-office records at the Athenée, mainly due to Pavlik's sets, costumes and lighting (how many designers can "paint with light" as Pavlik can?), then (early summer of '39) went to the Lac d'Annecy, where we found a house for the season, Villa des Tilleuls, once a pension-hotel—three floors and the rooms still with numbers on the doors. It was right by a railroad station which no longer operated, hence there was no business for a hotel, hence its being on the market as a villa for the season. That summer and that place (St-Jorioz) produced Claude, age 15; he was expelled from the summer camp for boys in St-Jorioz but returned triumphantly from his home in Lyons, and with his parents, and then he was 16. He was to return again and spend a weekend at Villa des Tilleuls but before he could do that the papers informed us of how hot other things were getting and we just had time to reach Paris (Mother was with us) and get on the *Champlain* before war was declared between France and Germany (we were on the high seas then and continued the voyage with darkened portholes in case German submarines were on the prowl).

Pavlik was talking to Edith on the phone before we left New York for the drive here and I heard him say: "I was so tired that night I didn't notice *anything*" and then he impatiently said goodbye. I asked him, "What was it Edith asked you if you'd noticed at Alice's dinner party?" "Oh," he said, "she wanted to know if I had noticed that she was crying when we said goodnight—because she had not been able to speak with me enough"—! Pavlik is very irritated with this "romantic" attitude of Edith. "She considers you her 'old flame,'" I said.

Where do those two white hens come from, scratching in the leaves? I should be scratching at my play.

My books of poetry:

1938: *The Garden of Disorder* (earth)
1941: *The Overturned Lake* (water)
1949: *Sleep in a Nest of Flames* (fire)

So to complete the four elements my next title should correspond to the element of air (which Pavlik says is *his* element).

The leaves are falling like swift yellow birds going to the ground: they disappear there as if swallowed up.

NOVEMBER

To Lincoln Kirstein the other day when he said Jean Genet's new book (laid in Brest) would upset me: "Nothing upsets me except not being able to write like I want to."

Balanchine's instructions to a dancer in teaching him a certain attitude in choreography: "Go down on her!"

◆

Pavlik is full of complaints about the "disturbing" atmosphere of the Sitwells, thinks Edith's admiration for his work too closely connected with his personal attraction for her ("She sat like a big white worm"), finds Osbert well-disposed and "willing to learn" but basically snobbish and interested only in himself. We took them to the ballet last night and, during intermission, much to their amusement, Pavlik turned his back when Harold Acton fluttered up. We had been talking about Poulenc, who came to lunch at Renishaw, the Sitwells' country estate. I: "Was he amusing?" Osbert: "Not a bit."

Monroe Wheeler suggested that Edith go for her scheduled lecture at Smith College, Holyoke, Mass., in a sirened ambulance, when she mentioned that she hates trains and detests flying. "Our theatrical stars, such as Tallulah Bankhead, do that when they're late for the theater." Edith unimpressed.

◆

With Sister to Town Hall, where we went for the Sitwells' "performance," as Osbert put it. Crowds of old ladies with feathers in their hats—the one on my left didn't know whether it was "Oscar or Oswell." Osbert came out first and recited poems—in a flat uninspired manner; the poems themselves were the sort of Georgian verse that the Sitwells are supposed to have revolted against 25 years ago. His second group picked up when the verse became frankly light and satirical. Edith read beautifully and looked wonderful in a long black dress and dark red cape, with the silver necklace and silver bracelets ("my Lady Macbeths," she calls them). One heard all the letters of her words, she took deep breaths like a trained actress. Her hair was pulled tight and flat which made the small head on the small neck stand out—the bulging brain in the small forehead. Much applause for them both—though many (not too many) people had left when they found out it was to be a poetry reading—at least that's what Sister said—"Some people can't listen to poetry"—just as some can't listen to what Virgil Thomson calls "art music." Pavlik went backstage to congratulate them and was annoyed by Edith's "Well, I don't suppose I shall see you again—you're avoiding me."

◆

"Tamed madman," Pavlik called himself in a letter to Alice Bouverie which he wrote and let me read. There was also a wonderfully poetic letter, which he read to me, written to Edgar Wind, in answer to a telegram saying his (P.'s) telephone had not answered for ten days—Edgar must have phoned in the morning, when we do not answer the phone—and hardly hear it, covered as it is with an overcoat in the hall closet.

Went out before lunch this morning to buy two books for Alice Bouverie: *Diaries of Tchaikowsky* and Parker [Tyler]'s *Magic and Myth of the Movies*. Corner of 42nd Street and Broadway: meatmarket in the rain: a seaman wearing tight light blue jeans and dark blue knitted cap. If I had gone up to him and said, "How much?" and he'd have said, "For what?" and I'd have replied, "You know for what," would he have told me?

Where there is no mystery there is no life—

◆

Yesterday from 5 to 7 was the tea-cocktail at Gotham Book Mart for the Sitwells. I arrived at 5:30 and found the *Life* photogs and editors making preparations for the group photo of poets. One of the editors, Mrs. Feldkamp, let me see the list and I asked what Gore Vidal's name was doing there. "He never wrote poetry," I said. "He said he had," she said, so there he was by mistake, and will be. Others in the group were Auden, Spender, William Rose Benet, José Garcia Villa, Marianne Moore, Marya Zaturenska and Horace Gregory, Randall Jarrell, Elizabeth Bishop, Delmore Schwartz. Osbert and Edith sat on a bench and I was asked to sit at their feet between them and afterwards Brion Gysin came up to me and said, "You were in the Sitwells' lap," and I said, "That's the way it should have been—in the lap of the gods ..." Tennessee Williams also got in the photo—some of the poets who were supposed to come didn't, or didn't show up until too late; so Tennessee could be squeezed in—he loved it, holding on to his whisky glass.

Marianne Moore, to whom I had never been introduced, came up to me and spoke, said she'd asked someone, "Who is that pretty girl?" and was told, "Charles

Henri Ford's sister," and she said, "But Charles Ford isn't here?" and I was pointed out and she came over to thank me, she said, for various things, how kind I had been to her, etc. I think she has had a little guilty conscience ever since I sent her a copy of *View* with a card (it was the big Paris number) saying, "For Marianne Moore, this 'unimportant little magazine' "—the words Cecil Beaton told me she had used about it one day at his Plaza suite when she was there for tea. Anyway she made up for everything yesterday and I complimented her too, saying something about "the modesty of greatness" and she called me "incorrigible."

◆

WESTON, CONN.

"O delicious pleasure! ... That utter self-abandonment, that delirium of joy, where pleasure is purified by its excess..."

"Edith is a vampire—like you"—and now I am quoting Pavlik, not Laclos.

He says he will go with me to New Haven to a matinee of Sartre's *Red Gloves* (*Les Mains Sales*) starring Charles Boyer. He also says that the reflections from the earth "derange" his painting out here—he will be able to do only drawings. "I definitely cannot work here and will come on Saturdays and Sundays to relax... I am getting worse and worse and begin to understand Mr. Gorky"—the painter [Arshile Gorky] who committed suicide last spring. I laughed and he said, "Will you for once in your life not laugh—look at my face." I said, "It changes like the weather." Then he said, "I had an uncle who went mad, you never knew that"—but I did.

From Chekhov's *Notebook*: "Viciousness is a bag with which man is born." What bag—but that which carries the testicles. Speaking of organs, a dwarf of a man, with well-proportioned body, whom I saw at the Y last Wednesday, had the most classic cock I've seen in a long time—nicely sculptured, the head in proportion to the rest of it. He also has one of those flat stomachs with the skin of the navel stretched tight as a Chinese eyelid.

◆

Pavlik, as he went to bed last night: "I don't love anybody." "Not even me?" "Not even myself." His work is at a point where he can't go back and cannot see his way forward.

Yesterday afternoon we went to New Haven to see the Sartre play. Jed Harris' "restrained" direction is more strained than directed. The casting is abominable —Boyer no more than a voice. The play has been disastrously cut and mauled— it's cheap with a cheapness even *Edward, My Son* doesn't touch. If this is the theater, take me away from it.

◆

NEW YORK CITY

Pavlik had dinner with Edith last night: "She doesn't eat anything at all—she only looks at me . . . She only thinks of herself . . . What are you writing down?" He's watering the terrace plants while I sit bundled up on a garden bench.

"Something I dreamed."

"What was your dream? Somebody fucking somebody?"

To give a well-rounded portrait of Edith, as presented by Pavlik after his tête-à-tête dinner with her: he said that fundamentally she's a "good" woman, that she confessed she's at a loss for words when she goes out "in society"—because she does not have that sort of facility—she's bored with most of the conversation around her and has cultivated the writer's (poet's) habit of using the right and precise word—feeling for it with her mind . . . Lincoln thinks she's only interested in "gossiping about personalities," but Pavlik explains it by saying she's sensitive to hurts, having suffered so many. "You remember," Pavlik reminded Lincoln, "Florine [Stettheimer] also talked of her slights, etc.—she and Edith are alike in that respect; both virgins, too and wonderful artists."

Pavlik has recovered from the nausea he said he had when looking at his work depicting the internal organs, because he's re-imagining them—in an unrealistic, crystalline form.

Theater note, after seeing *Edward, My Son* (you can have him), to which Alice Bouverie took us all (including the Sitwells) the other night. I must think of the majority of my lines as being *shouted*, with emphasis given by *lowering* the voice, sometimes to a whisper. The critics like it obvious—they're no better than the audiences they write for—that's why a critic (such as Mary McCarthy) who writes for the élite (such as it is) would be out of place on a daily paper. (Likewise a special criticism such as Parker-on-movies is suitable only for a so-called "intellectual" audience.)

Perry Embiricos took me to dinner (filet mignon and champagne) at Le Martinique to see Gypsy Rose Lee and her show. The nightclub itself looks like something out of a "B" picture and the "acts" other than Gypsy's are tawdry beyond belief, without the old spirit that gave Burlesque its vitality. Gypsy looked pretty enough, is always charming to hear and watch—but she's unhappy in that joint—we learned in her dressing-room after.

Perry said he'd like to go abroad in early summer. "Will you go to Greece?" (his native land). "Yes." "And to your island there?" "No—it's been lent by my father to the King [Paul] and to go there we would have to ask the King's permission—so we won't disturb him—he wanted to buy it but my father wouldn't sell, it's two and a half hours from Athens, the King goes in a motor boat and likes to walk 2 or 3 hours a day—he's afraid to walk in Athens . . ."

◆

There's always a point beyond which we can't go—or it becomes unconvincing. Well, that's the artist's problem—

Life creates its own circumstances, and acts out of them.

Why is a play more interesting than anything else? Answer: because it's about human beings.

Scientist of the emotions (a dramatist should be).

Alexander, personification of poetry: he *lived* what the poet projects—and sometimes aspires to be. Glory, I'll wait . . .

◆

Found in the weightroom the boy who gave me handstand pointers some weeks ago and who said he works at Macy's. We went to steamroom together and swimming. He asked me about my occupation, I told him I was a writer. What subject? Sports? "No," I said—"crime." He said he liked a good crime story, that he was no longer working at Macy's, was "lining up" something else and going to school two nights a week. "What are you studying?" "To be a policeman."

◆

Hug it tight, boy!

Induce that special concentration which brings the angels down.

◆

All faces have: two eyes, a nose, a mouth, etc. Why are some attractive, some not so, some divinely beautiful, etc.—? The dictionary is full of words: when put together in a certain way, why are they so ugly, unattractive, etc.; when put together in another way, why so divinely beautiful? A keyboard is full of notes: they may be struck anyway, but what happens when a Scarlatti is inspired to arrange them in a certain pattern, with time-spaces between them? Then they're divinely, etc. . . .

Pavlik still going on about Edith: "I have very little feelings for her, except that she's a good poet. For the rest, seulement pitié . . . I'm going to tell her: I'm sick because you arrived here. I wish you'd stayed where you've been!"

◆

WESTON, CONN.

First snowfall. Pavlik announced it when he woke me up: "We're snowed in." But we're not.

He says one of my symbols is the Sphnix and Edith is Isis—and that it's very appropriate that she wrote the introduction to my *Sleep in a Nest of Flames*. Edith is "earth," he says. "She drags me down, I drag her up because I'm air."

DECEMBER

We went to the Museum of Modern Art and there met Edith and Osbert. The "bee" film was being especially shown for Edith, Pavlik had asked Iris Barry, Curator of Film Library, to procure it, because of Edith's preoccupation in her poetry with bees, bee-priestesses, the bee-keeper, etc. Also convoked: Lincoln and Fidelma, George Hoyningen-Huene, Mrs. Vincent Astor, Alice and David Bouverie, Sylvia Marlowe and Léonide, David Horner ... The film is Soviet-made, soundtrack in Russian, Léonide and Pavlik translated where needed. A lovely and dramatic film—like a Ballet of the Bees. A bird (Private Enterprise) ate one ... and a rat (representing the Germans) intruding in the community's tree-trunk was stung to death.

◆

Viola came to clean yesterday for the first time in a week (she's Stewart Chaney's maid)—said she'd been sick—arriving at almost 4:40 so I told her she had to be out in an hour; she put on speed and was out in under an hour; Pavlik left too. Bert arrived at 5:30, apologizing for being half an hour late. First time I'd seen him in civilian clothes. Naturally the sailor suit was more attractive—he looked like a child then, dressed up as a sailor. Now his hair is somewhat longer but cut up too short in the back and slicked down. His eyes are large, blue, surrounded by thick lashes and dark shadows (he had masturbated three days before). When he saw that I received him in my shirt sleeves he immediately took off his jacket (after taking off his father's topcoat) which left him in bright yellow sleeveless pullover and brown pants. He began talking at once about his recent hunting trip, during which his ass had been almost frozen—"still cold," he said. "I'll make you something to warm you up," I said. So I fixed him an "old-fashioned," which he had never tasted before, and then another, and he felt them and we ate some roastbeef and salad, had vin rosé (he wouldn't drink over two glasses—"You're not going to get me drunk") and coffee and then I was changing records on the phonograph and he said put on the radio so you won't have to get up . . . He avowed that on ship the cook had "taken care" of him and I said what do you mean by "taken care" and he said, "He used to blow me," and I said, "Did he do a good job?" and he said yes . . . that he liked to be blowed . . . He showed me some playing cards he was carrying in his wallet and said I could have them, probably because he didn't want his father or mother to come across them—part of them made a striptease series of eight and when I remarked that numbers were on only two of them he asked for a pencil and put all eight numbers in correct order, on the backs. He's of German descent.

"If you ever meet my father," he said, "be sure not to give a weak handshake—he hates that." "So do I," I said.

He's like a piece of nicely seasoned meat—not tough, not tainted. The Navy did it.

◆

Yesterday when Pavlik asked me, "Do you think Osbert is intelligent?" I said, "He has the intelligence suitable for his function, which is enough . . . Many people may be *more* intelligent but still not intelligent enough to fulfill what they're trying to do or be . . ." We dined with him and Edith last Thursday in their sitting-room at the St. Regis. During the dinner Pavlik said, "I think alcohol is very good for you at times," and Osbert put in, "I can't get along without it," at which Edith added, "And to think that at one time I had it for toothache only!"

Pavlik said: "When we are between lions and tigers we can say things that lions and tigers say . . ." Edith recalled something that Pavlik had said on a former occasion about Mrs. Cornelius Vanderbilt: "She's acting a part which has never been written."

◆

Bert told me of the women he'd had in Milwaukee, Philadelphia—and in Newfoundland, where they wanted to go out and fuck in the snow . . . "And when you jerk off do you try to make it last a long time?" Bert: "No, I like to get it over with as soon as possible." He told me of how they used to extract the alcohol from shellac, on board ship, by straining it through a loaf of white bread . . . And he said, "It's been so long since I had a woman it's pathetic."

The human, being there—one is moved, that's all.

1949

JANUARY

Pavlik and I had intended going to bed early last night even though it was New Year's Eve. But we were still up about 11:30 so I took down the bottle of port and P said he'd have a glass too so we had a couple of glasses and some slices of brioche, and we talked awhile. Pavlik remembered his first New Year's Eve away from Russia—in Constantinople in 1922—"I was so happy, I felt life was just beginning for me—I was quite drunk"—with happiness and wine. When he told me this such a sadness seized me—I became inhabited by the Muse of Sadness. I thought it would be too painful to lie in my bed, being so sad, but then the sadness left—I was released—and in its place a kind of serenity—as if achieved because of the sadness. And I thought, I shall never be afraid to be sad again.

Pavlik has just pointed out to me that the circular field of wheat behind my head in the Red Portrait he painted of me (in 1933) corresponds to the Wheel of Fortune—my card, number ten, in the Tarot. And he counted tonight the red spots of the poppies (some whole, some with petals missing and others separate petals) around the field of wheat and they totalled: ten. The Guardian of the Realm of Waters, the Mysterium Magnum, the Isle of Mothers, wears a red cloak (he discovered from a book of fantastic stories): which corresponds to my astrological sign: Aquarius . . . And of symbols which apply to himself: Merlin lived in the Enchanted Forest (the "interior landscape") from which there is no return.

◆

Telephoned Jean Cocteau at St. Regis yesterday morning, he said he was glad to hear my voice, which Pavlik says was a subtle reproach for not having telephoned sooner. Jean said he was free for lunch today and I said I would get in touch with la grande poetesse Edith Sitwell and find out if she were free too as she wanted to meet him. Wasn't able to reach Edith until almost 6—after her lecture at the Colony Club—and I suggested either her having us to lunch in her suite (Pavlik, Cocteau and myself) or my getting Alice Bouverie to arrange the luncheon for us all.

Edith was undecided, first thinking it would be too exhausting for her to play the hostess, then calling me back later and saying she'd prefer to have us at her place if I would come early and help her to order, etc.

When I arrived at a quarter to one, Monroe Wheeler was there. After a little while, Edith announced that there had been some confusion about the lunch, that Monroe had been about to arrange for her to meet Cocteau and he got her on the phone and said he would arrange it for that afternoon whereupon she told him that she was lunching with Cocteau that day, whereupon Monroe said, "May I come, too?"—so of course she said, "Why, yes." Monroe was surprised when I came in, having thought that Edith was lunching alone with Cocteau so I explained to him how it was I who was bringing them together and he said he hadn't understood, that Glenway [Wescott] had left him some "garbled message" and he thought he would be helping out by "assisting" at the lunch, etc. "Well, it all had a happy ending," I said.

Pavlik was late but not as late as Cocteau so I finally decided to go down in the lobby and wait for him (it was twenty-five to two) and there I ran into Gala and Salvador Dali. Dali said he'd had a "triumph" in Spain and that he was doing sets, etc. for a production in Rome of *As You Like It*. Then Cocteau arrived and was telling the Dalis something about "Pierrot" before I took him upstairs where I learned he was talking about Greta Garbo who had told him the night before that she'd like to play the part of Pierrot. In what?

◆

"If you would wash your ass, you'd be much happier," said Pavlik to me when I protested scrubbing the bottom of the pot that the fish was boiled in.

"Should we have another lady?" he asked the other day. Ollie Jennings is taking Edith, Osbert and us to see *The Madwoman of Chaillot*. "No," I replied, "Edith is lady enough for two—with her 'Plantagenet blood' all over the place." And then we thought of inviting Djuna.

◆

Where does sleep go when we get enough?

We float on a cloud of sleep through a landscape of dream.

Is sleep, like the sun, always there even when we don't see it?

And if I married a girl, I'd want to sleep with her—both of us naked, in a double bed, the lights would go out and we'd begin to fuck. Sex would be no problem. The problem would be: would she bore me the next day?

◆

WESTON, CONN.

"They're green when I wake up," said Bert about his eyes when I said, at breakfast, "Your eyes are green!"

Bert is shaving, Pavlik's raving.

◆

NEW YORK CITY

On arrival in Weston Friday before tea, Bert jumped into his Levis, looking more sexy than ever, and we three took a walk. Vorisoff, our neighbor, came to dinner. Shortly after dinner Bert and I went upstairs, he wanted to look at the porno-graphic playcards and since there was nothing else to do he suggested we go to bed so I went back downstairs and said goodnight to Vorisoff and Pavlik (9 P.M.)—Bert was going to spend the night in my bed ... "Fuck me between the legs," he said—and hollered when I hit the piles which seem to be practically *out*—because the next afternoon even my tongue hurt them (I had taken him in his bathrobe down-stairs and washed his ass for him). So after we had both come (I sucked him after shooting between his legs—I can see him now in bed lifting one leg to wipe the come off his crotch with the towel I tossed him), he said he was hungry so we had scrambled eggs, then he said he felt "jumpy," that he wanted to take a walk and wanted me to get dressed and go with him. We had Scotch after we got back. I shall make a list of "what's beautiful about Bert." Not now—it's too long.

◆

Cocteau (at lunch the other day): "Any actress can play Jeanne d'Arc—any actress, except—Ingrid Bergman ...

"Russia has the Iron Curtain, America a rideau d'ôr ...

"Garbo also told me she'd like to play Cyrano, with a false nose, etc. ...

"L'amérique n'a pas du luxe ..."

◆

Bert: (after his asking to be told about Vorisoff and my saying, "He's another mad Russian") "Are they all that way?" While I was doing the dishes he came in the kitchen and wanted to know where my "pictures" were. "Same place," I said. "Middle drawer?" "Yes." So he went back in my room and when I came in he was sitting in the chair gazing at his favorite (the man going down on the woman) and I said come on over on the bed. I felt in his pants and he had $3/4$ of a hard on and he said, "Lock the door." He didn't want to take off his pants at first but he did at last ("If I take off my pants you'll want me to take off my shirt"). His feet stank so I

asked him when he'd washed them last and he said it was the medicine for the athlete's foot he caught in Panama that smelled. "Does it smell like cheese?" I asked.

I told him, "I'm not going to Canada with you unless you learn to suck—this
jerking off business is boring"—he didn't say anything. He may have those piles
all his life—so that part of his anatomy won't do me any good ("I'd like to come in
you and then suck it out").

"Make me come, Charlie, I'm hot as hell—" so I made him come—"I'm coming," he said, and began to jerk me at the same time as if it were his own prick he
was jerking off—he wanted me to suck the last drop out—then I lay on my back
and shot all over my stomach and chest—a fountain of come—he liked looking
at that.

◆

Cocteau has begged Garbo on his knees not to play "George Sand" in the movies.
"George Sand was a cow," he told her—"Chopin and her lovers were cowboys—
you should play one of the cowboys, but not the cow." She promised to do as Jean
asked ... Jean: "America is the only country where passion is considered psy-
chotic."

◆

I was in the shower when Bert arrived yesterday, he opened the door to the bathroom and said, "Don't fall in." Later we left for Peter's, he carrying the bottle of
whisky Peter had begged me to bring to the party. After we got off the bus, I tried
to squeeze a small pimple on Bert's face but it wouldn't squeeze. Then I told him,
"But no one will notice it unless they get close enough to kiss you," and he said,
"Do you want a bottle broken over your head?" At the party I discovered that Peter was hiding sufficient liquor, just wanted to get a bottle out of me—I didn't
mind as he went to a lot of trouble to give the party at my request so Bert could
meet some "eligible" girls.

One of the girls Peter had picked out for Bert—Jane someone—I didn't like.
Was glad I had invited Georgia Rikers, who came in a New Look cape and haircut—she was fun, joking and cutting up—a dozen or so bores were there. At the
very end Truman (no, Bert, Capote, not the President) came in, lay flat on his back
on the bed, in his overcoat, and I said, "Someone, kiss Truman!" Some little phoney ex-sailor was hanging around Georgia, pretending to want her and I found out
later he'd asked Bert if he was ever without me—meaning could he see him alone.
Georgia said she'd take us back to her room ("Dinner?" I asked; Bert said, "It's better on an empty stomach") so the three of us stopped in to buy some bottles of beer
at the delicatessen (the clerk with a half-smile as if he knew what was up) and then
climbed the stair to Georgia's little skylight room and bath. Both Georgia and I

were higher than Bert, who takes the precaution to drink little when he knows a fuck's in store—even then it's not always as stiff as it could be. So we all got undressed—Georgia with a very young body until the breasts were untrussed. So we were all naked and mixed up, Bert and I took several turns, and several combinations were made: Bert went down on a woman for the first time and, he told me later, didn't like it as much as he expected to. While I was in Georgia I said to Bert, "Let her suck you." "Huh?" he said and put his cock up there and she took it in her mouth (first time he'd been sucked by a woman). At one point I had to suck on him to get it hard and soon as it was hard he wanted to get in her again. So things went on like that (at one point Georgia seemed to come but I don't think Bert did then). There was an intermission (I hadn't come yet) for beer and a series of Bert's dirty stories, some of which were funny, some awful. Georgia: "Where did you find this one?"

Finally Bert came in her with me looking on at the balls flapping and he got out and I stuck mine in and came in his come which felt good. Then Bert and I dressed and Georgia put on a kimona and gave us more beer and cheese and crackers. Bert said, "I feel like fighting, beating someone up." "Is it me?" I asked. "No, not you," he said—but I'll bet it could have been. After the fucking session he had begun to talk about his girlfriend Dottie and also put in that after he got married he wasn't going to fuck on the side.

◆

I phoned Georgia at noon and woke her up—she said she couldn't get to sleep before six A.M.—I got home at midnight. So I told her to phone me back when she woke up, so about 2 P.M. she did and I asked her, "What did you think of that number?" She said, "Well, I was so drunk—" "Do you think he's beautiful?" She said, "Well, part of the skull got left out ..." "I wondered what your intuition was," I said. She said, "Well, I think he's the type that would break down a door." I got a new view of Bert as he was on top of her—the sweeping line from underarm, tapering to waist—like the line of a seashore or a bay—then the broadening and rounding out of the ass below the smooth waist.

"Projecting ears are common ... to sexual offenders." (Lombroso.)

"He's a Momma's boy," I said to Georgia as he was fucking her, and Bert said, "This is my Momma!"

◆

And it's ten to eleven before I get to my desk because it was an evening out last night with Edith Sitwell and Osbert, Ollie Jennings and Djuna coming for dinner (Ollie had two bottles of champagne sent around, he was also host for theater and had a car and chauffeur for the going and coming). The play: *The Madwoman of*

Chaillot by Giraudoux, Bérard sets (Bébé could not forget the opening up of entire stage in *Ondine*, and his second act looked like Léonor Fini's flat in the rue Payenne with a chair stuck on the wall from Pavlik's ballet *Magic* for good measure). Martita Hunt, though too young to give the part of the old folle its full pathos, was good to listen to, Estelle Winwood very fetching as another woozy biddy. Sokoloff's thick Russian accent got in the way. Carradine's part too long for his talents. The play as a whole full of wit—more wit than play. We all enjoyed it more than Djuna who always sours up on one point, forgetting the sweetness of the rest—she didn't like the end of either act and all she'd say going up the aisle was how unbearable the last part was—no praise for any of the cast—that's like her. When I took her to a preview of *No Exit* she began to execrate the play without *one single word* for my sister Ruth's performance—I was going backstage and didn't offer to take her (I was so put out) and she merely said, "Give Ruth my love," and I let [Henri] Carlyle Brown (who was with us) take her home.

And though Djuna is "for" good manners she's naive about what constitutes them: for instance, as we left my room to go into Pavlik's studio for dinner, she went through the door first when the polite thing to have done would have been to let Miss Sitwell, visiting English-lady and the elder, precede. And she did the same thing leaving the apartment and at the theater. American manners are a lack of manners. Man in the men's room at theater: "Good evening, Sir Osbert. I met you in Buffalo."

◆

Bert came by looking sweet all dressed in brown, in my room immediately went over and turned on the radio to what he called "Shit-heel music"—hillbilly, cowboy ballads and such—"I like that kind of music," he said. It was about to rain and he went to the window to look out—I stood behind him and felt of his muscles and we went into a clutch, me still behind. "You don't think you're as strong as I am, do you?" he asked; nevertheless, couldn't keep the hold he tried to get and sat down again in the chair rather winded and surprised me by saying he didn't want to wrestle because "I don't play fair—I play dirty"—and I got out of him what he meant by not fair. He said when he got in a fight he would hit with the back of his hand instead of his fist and that he could break two ribs that way. "Why don't you fight fair?" I wanted to know and then he confessed that he'd gotten the worst of it too many times by fighting fair and the other guy fighting dirty. "Would you with me?" I asked. "I might forget myself," he said.

◆

"J'ai un grand fatigue," Pavlik says, sitting in my room, sewing on a button while Carrie (so slow, sent by Viola who may be back after next week) cleans his studio. "How I'd like to have a quiet life ... All Lincoln's ideas of explaining—such stupidity—things that nobody needs, all this explanation ... Listen to me, if you want to be great ... Recurrent image of repetition: is that what Time is ... ?"

Not doing what one wants to do eventually makes one afraid to do it.

"Man's inhumanity to man" is the only thing we should be shocked by—not by accounts of pleasure-giving activities. Anything that brings two people closer is, theoretically, good—even to eating each other's excrements.

◆

Sometimes, one has to empty out oneself to feel the world's fullness. "Je suis un pauvre coeur, sensible idiot"—P. He prefers the company of women but I prefer the company of men: to have a ranch in the West and live among cowboys, or to be a merchant seaman, or live with lumberjacks—or in prison—or be in a boys' school or "home" (how soon I'd want to be out!). "You're just a whore, that's what you are," Pavlik tells me.

FEBRUARY

WESTON, CONN.

Masturbation is such a low form of pleasure—a bare prick staring you in the face, wanting to be stroked like an animal—

Pavlik told me a dream he had, cursing out an old auntie who'd gotten herself up en travestie; then a dark young man came along and took Pavlik away—"there was the boring dream of poursuite—and the young man said, 'When you get to Venice you will be shot in the bowels.'"

Laughlin asked for the place and date of my birth, to be put on the contract for my book of poetry, *Sleep in a Nest of Flames*, so I told him. "You're not so old," he said. "Who said I was?" I asked. "I always think of you as belonging to the generation before me," he said. "And I always think of you as a contemporary, late in getting started," said I.

◆

NEW YORK CITY

Last evening just before bedtime Pavlik had another of his crises, in which he unloaded his feelings about our relationship. The most terrible thing he said was that he had the feeling that I was waiting for him to die and that when he did die I wouldn't shed a tear: "Americans are the hardest people in the world . . ."

He said that when I was away from the apartment, then he "bloomed," that there were other people who "calmed" him when he was nervous, but that I drained him—"I feel your pulling, pulling all the time, that's why you look so young, you eat me, if you were to stay away from me one year you wouldn't look like you do now, like your portrait, just look in the mirror after one year, you'll see!"

I told him: "If we are only staying together out of convenience and cowardice, then it's pathetic, a break should be made . . ."

◆

"I'd like to have that."

"Take it."

"In here?"

"Yes . . ."

"Don't you know this place is hot? They sit out there in the change booth and watch everybody that comes in."

"Then we'd better not take a chance."

"Do you live around here?"

"No."

◆

With the light out at eleven I began to think of Bert and stroke the butt of my gun, like a nurse soothing a child, and the gun went off accidentally but no one seems hurt this morning. Gave Pavlik an enema before 9 ("tout pour toi est un prétexte de rire"), preparation for his X-ray at 10:30 A.M.

◆

When I came home after yesterday's matinee performance of *Richard III*, Pavlik was in the bathtub and said, "You know what's happened yesterday?" "To whom?" I asked. "You know what's happened?" "Happened to whom?" "Bébé Bérard died." He had a heart attack during a rehearsal at the Theatre Marigny with Louis Jouvet and Jean-Louis Barrault. Iolas had telephoned Pavlik the news earlier. Bébé: *une* rare personage, full of charm and wit and talent—the thought of Paris is less gay, with the thought of his being there no more. We sent a telegram to his friend, Boris Kochno, with whom he'd lived for as long as I can remember— since before 1931. . . . This morning Dougie [Allan Ross Macdougall] phoned and announced in his vulgar gross way that "Miss Bérard" was dead.

Last night at dinner Pavlik said he had "no more feelings" for me. I said, "I feel about you now as I did towards Djuna just before I left her . . ." He said, "I suppose you wish it had been me instead of Bébé who died."

What should I do? The thing I *want to do* is what he wants me to do—how can I tell?

◆

Pavlik, looking very bad, tired and pitiable, has just told me, "Don't think I don't appreciate what you have done for me . . . I'm too old for you, you need to be free and I need someone to take care of me . . . my sister. These rich people wouldn't care if I died tomorrow . . . The death of Bébé must have been more of a shock to me than I knew." He'd told me, "Let it be a lesson to you," and I didn't get what he meant at first, then it dawned on me that he was reminding me that death might happen to him too, unexpectedly. "I'm sure, though," he went on, "Bébé is happy where he is. He was meant to be a great painter and his life would not have grown any happier, he died at the height of his theater and worldly success—maybe next time he will be a great painter."

◆

With Edith on phone conversation led to Norman Douglas, of whom she doesn't approve because of his "affairs" with "eight-year-old girls"—I didn't correct her as to which sex was involved. When she wanted to know if I didn't disapprove too, I replied, "I don't approve of any form of torture . . ." I asked her if she'd like to see Mae West's play but she said, "No, thank you," that she didn't think Mae West would be her "cup of tea." Then Osbert rang up, after Edith told him about Pavlik's complications, wanted to know if Pavlik needed any money and that he thought Pavlik was "looking like hell."

"Pavlik's complications," according to Dr. Garbat, consist of anemia, gallbladder inflamation and colitis. He will need three injections a week. "How upset I am, I'm so upset I could cry and scream and yell"—his mood before lunch today. At breakfast he'd said that he was sure that Bébé would "be reborn on the Indian Reservation and become the Great American Painter."

◆

Talked to Sister on phone and she said, "I wanted to tell you the last time I talked to you, I think you should go to Tennessee now and see Daddy . . ." "I should go for Mother's sake." "You should go for Daddy's sake." "I'll talk to Pavlik about it." "He talked to me an hour on the phone the other day and said he wanted you to go . . . Anyway—you should go—I'll help take care of Pavlik—I can do that—I would go myself if I could . . ." So I told Pavlik that Sister said I ought to go and I thought I should go and he agreed. But, he said, "I warn you—you're in for a terrible time—you'll see what decay is . . ." "I should have the courage to face it," I said.

◆

WESTON, CONN.

Having read about the "insertions in the urethra" in the Kinsey book I'm about to make an experiment: a pencil covered with a condom—the eraser end—greased with vaseline—is it too large and what will it feel like? . . . It goes in the head all right . . . it doesn't want to go in far without hurting . . . Pavlik has just come in and interrupted me. "Pavlik, I'm writing." . . . He said last night he had heard of the urethral insertions in Russia—an instrument with a little sponge on the end of it—I think this pencil is too big . . . (reminds me of my treatments for gonorrhea in Paris)—I got the pencil in about three inches with no hard on—when I start to get hard then it starts to hurt a little . . . the pencil's half in—seems to hurt only near the head: the further in it gets the better it feels! It's practically all the way in! . . . Now it's out—so what? Is the pleasure something one can cultivate for increasing pleasurability? Let's try again . . . It's in again—hurts less, feels better? I'm not sure . . . If I lose my load instead of saving it for Bert I'll hate myself . . . I'm fucking myself in the head of my prick with a pencil!

◆

JASPER, TENN.

I went straight in to see Daddy without Mother's going first to tell him I'd arrived. He was sitting up in the rocking-chair (where he sits day and night now, the pressure on his bladder not allowing him to lie down in bed). I squatted at the foot of the chair and took his hands and said, "I'm here"—he'd been in a doze and came to and didn't know who I was at first. Then he remembered and was very happy and I squeezed his hands too hard and he said I was hurting him. I sat with him awhile and he told me of how he has suffered and paid his debt and said, "Of course we all must pay the debt of death." He said "Gertrude" (Mother) had been awfully sweet to him but that the man, Mr. White, who waits on him in the daytime had been "so mean"—so mean he couldn't sleep at times—but that at other times he took care of him well. However, "If I sent him after corn he'd get peas."

It's like Mother described it in her letters: the urine comes out the navel, which has opened, the cancer having eaten through, and Daddy sits there with it covered with cloth pads, or wipes it off with Kleenex and toilet paper—the odor is almost overpowering. Daddy says, "Your mother can't stand the sickroom." He said that though he suffered and felt "the sap, the very soul" going out of him, he still loved life too much to want to die.

◆

The high point in Mr. White's career here—Mother's version—is his bringing back a 16-year-old wife, a preacher's daughter (he's forty)—without warning anyone. Daddy said, when she had left his room after being presented to him: "I didn't know they came in the world that ignorant." Wanda is her name. Mr. White has had her in Daddy's room "singing hymns." This afternoon I asked her what she had been doing all day. "Just settin' around," she replied. Mr. White, Mother says, "is religious, prays with C. L." (Daddy). "The religious kind are the meanest. I understand now why people commit murder, they can't help it."

Daddy: "Like when you pass out, in two days you're forgotten—it's good night."

MARCH

"Lord how I am suffering, oh Lordy Lord. Nobody knows but me, oh Lordy Lord"—he's saying this with the cigar in his mouth . . . Now Daddy's dozing and the cigar may fall from his mouth at any moment. He told me, "Your mother would jump over the moon with her hat off for you . . ."

Now he's awake and telling me about the country girls in the hospital at Chattanooga. When he was there last year they were complimenting his hands and skin—"so soft." "Do you like it soft?" he asked them. "Most girls like it hard!" "I've got to get out of here," they said. Daddy said, "They wouldn't have sense enough to get back in the room after they got out."

I've just helped him to the toilet in his room and he's standing in front of the bowl urinating painfully. "Lord, Lord. Lord, Lord have mercy on me, good Lord. Help me, oh good Lord, how can I stand this, oh good Lord, oh good Jesus help me now, how I'm suffering nobody knows, oh Lord, Lord have mercy . . . how I'm suffering, suffering, suffering, help me won't you, help me this afternoon. Oh Lord, I'm suffering so much, suffering untold agony that's what I'm suffering, help me, won't you please, oh for Jesus' sake, help, oh I know you will . . ." He's praying now: "Show me how to go, I'm ready good Jesus . . . Jesus suffered death upon the cross, to save the sinners of the world. I happen to be one of the sinners . . ."

Mr. White is in here now preparing his shot. "Take a good aim," says Daddy.

"I'm just about ready." (Mr. W.)

"I'm ready's brother—I live right next door." (Daddy.)

Then: "I thought Gertrude was coming in."

I: "She'll be back."

"She's like one of those little black fleas—you think you've got him and you haven't..."

He gives a big belch and says, "Oh"—he pretends sometimes to be more pathetic than he is. "You see that poor old arm, I've whipped 4000 niggers with that ... My Daddy used to run a gin mill and I whipped 15 niggers every week"—this was in Mississippi... When I mentioned to Mother that the character of the community here was determined by the poverty, she said well you can be poor and not be like these "mean and stubborn and ugly" mountaineers. "In Mississippi the *Negroes* were poor but they were never like this!" She said she'd never lived in the midst of a "poor white" class as one does here in Tennessee.

She reminisced a bit about her early life—we were looking at the map of Mississippi. Daddy was her senior by 18 years and when things seemed to be getting serious (before they were married)—Daddy taking her for buggy rides but no kissing—Mama Cato (her widowed mother) had numerous visitors telling her how awful it would be if Gertrude got married to someone so much older than she was. But Mama Cato didn't interfere too much and one day "Loyd" as she called him took Gertrude to the fair and proposed to her in the ferris wheel (my "wheel of fortune"!) and was accepted. "I thought I was madly in love," Mother told me. And if she thought she was she was. They had a big church wedding with crowds of people, so many the church wouldn't hold them all ("Negroes out in the back"). "I was considered very beautiful," Mother told me as if speaking of someone else. "I used no make-up, was just beginning to fill out, had such fresh skin and rosey cheeks and beautiful hair." Daddy weighed only 110 pounds at the time and wore a number 4 ladies shoe.

◆

10 P.M. Daddy was awake when we went in to see him, grabbed our hands and said, "Oh, love me," said it had seemed so long since he'd seen us. "He's just a skeleton," said Mother over the phone to Sister the other night.

When I told him that I had postponed going to Florida he asked if Pavlik took the train to meet me there as he'd planned and I told him No, Pavlik had cancelled his trip. "And you cancelled your trip to Florida to be with me?" "Yes." "That was sweet of you," he said, "but I'd cancel a trip to anywhere, anywhere..." He asked Mother if she were praying for him and she told him she was, every night. "I'm praying," he said. "Precious Jesus, save my soul, pardon my sins." He spoke of the crucifix on the wall facing his bed: "Every time I look at that cross, I think of Jesus who died, to save the world … Son, I'm dying, I'm dying … Can't you stay all night … do you have to leave me?" "We'll be back tomorrow morning." "If you get up at six, you can leave at seven, how long does it take you to drive here? … Jesus keep you both, take care of you, my son, my dear wife, my dear son … Son, you look so good, so well." He said he hated the Brothers coming in and telling him he looked well, "but that's their hobby."

◆

I talked to Dr. H. on the phone. He thinks Daddy won't live more than a week or ten days longer. Daddy is taking a new medicine in capsule form every six hours—a prescription which will hasten the end by a day or two. Dr. H. said that Daddy would go into an "eurethmic coma," and this sedative would relieve the "mental anguish." I told him that Daddy had told me that no matter how much he suffered he loved life so much that he wanted to live out every minute of it.

Brother Benedict told me how the old care more about clinging to life than do the young.

Dr. H. has a very impersonal attitude about the uselessness of the old and incurable—said he thought the sooner they were over with it the better it would be for us all.

Daddy did look terribly, painfully wasted today, came alive enough to try to cry when we said we had to go. He's so dehydrated I don't think he has any tears left.

◆

A little after 3 I took my car across the road to the filling station for the oil to be changed and a grease job. Hal [Plunkett] took over, and out popped Shorty—a friend of Jack's—who was ready to go fishing but we didn't go for quite a while, finally I said, "Do you want to go and see if that colored man has caught anything?" Shorty said, "Let's go" so we hopped in the Mercury and went by his house and he got his fishing pole, a hoe to dig for worms and some matches, then we walked up the road to the river. We gathered some wood for a fire, the sun had almost set, and Shorty hoed up a couple of red worms and I baited the hook and he concentrated mostly on watching it and we warmed ourselves by the fire. He'd said something about "suck your dick" at the filling station and mentioned a deck of playing cards with "pictures"—so when the conversation turned on girls, etc., he said, "I wish I had those cards down here," and I said, "You wouldn't want to go home with a hard on, would you?" and then suddenly someone from the river-bank above us said, "Come on, you know it's time to get home"—and it was his Daddy! So we put out the fire and his Daddy waited for us and we all walked back to the house and his Daddy asked me in and I said I'd come in for a minute. Five little children were on the sofa in the front room of the poorest type of log cabin, with a coal-grate. I was offered a chair and took it and gave the children pennies and a dime to Ula, Shorty's sister (6 years old) for a hair-ribbon. She had one tooth out and her father said she looked funny with the tooth out and I said, "She'll have a new one maybe soon," and Shorty said to his toothless father, "She look as funny as you," so I had to say, "Maybe he'll be having some new ones too!" so the father said he had some "made by the government" but the wires in them hurt.

◆

I told the little boy at the filling station that I'd like to see the two billy goats he bought for five dollars. Hal Plunkett, who runs the filling station, was kidding the boy about buying two billy goats and no nannies—inferring that a nanny would be good to "rock," as they say down here. "I wouldn't know what to think of a fellow who had two billy goats," he told the boy.

Daddy cuts in, "Son, I hate to disturb you but I'm going to need a little assistance—my butt's a-burning me up . . ." I've helped him to the toilet.

Poor, poor Daddy is turning himself around—the most wretched human sight I've ever seen—lower legs swollen, upper legs so thin one can see the thighbones.

Daddy to me: "Why don't you trim your nails? That's the first thing I notice in a gentleman's dress is the nails, then I go on down, the second thing is the feet."

◆

"It's a good thing Jack doesn't mind being teased," I said to Hal last night—Jack is his stepson, is tattooed on both arms—had the work done in Pearl Harbor. Hal was teasing him about going to bed with Mamie, the roadside whore—and Jack hadn't. She used to hang around the coal mine where 200 truck drivers came and went—"she was always off in the forest with one of them." Then Hal teased Jack about his mule: "Can you see through him?" "If you get close enough," said Jack.

Hal the other night telling about the murdered man found on the mountain with his pants down and a big hard on that had to be tied to his leg. "As the nigger said, 'they was just about to do's it.'" The woman with whom he was just about to 'do's' it was put in the jail for the night and her husband came down to the jail and spent the night with her. "He was low as she was," said Hal.

◆

The crisis and climax of my stay here has passed—arranging for Daddy to go to a hospital and getting him to agree.

◆

We got off this morning with Daddy in the car at about ten o'clock after Mr. White dressed him and both of us helped him into the front seat. Jarred Daddy a couple of times so had to go slow towards end of the trip, sometimes he would holler before he was hit. (Daddy had his hat on when he was ready to leave and Mr. White told him, "You look like a cranberry salesman before Christmas.") . . . Parked the car around to the side of the Alexian Brothers Resort—which is more of a place for retired elderly gentlemen than it is for sick cases—they are taking care of only 15 hospital cases at the moment, and accommodate 20 at capacity, whereas 60 "guests" can be taken care of in the "hotel" part. Daddy was shown to his room by one of the younger Brothers, all very pleasant and talkative (on the sissy side). I promised to send them a copy of my book of poems for their monastery library.

◆

2:30 P.M. Mother and I went to see Daddy this morning. When we got to his room I smelt, very strongly, the cancer odor of which Mother had spoken—but here at the Court it was so mixed up with other odors, urine, airwick, burnt matches, incense, cigars, that I couldn't distinguish it. He was being fed by a young Brother from St. Louis (with only one eye, I think) vegetable soup. Daddy opened his eyes for us but they were rather glazed and half-seeing, he would lie there and masticate his soup with his eyes closed. He drank milk through a glass tube and had some chocolate pudding, couldn't speak much or plainly, later asked what was new, Mother said, "Nothing."

◆

10 P.M. At the hospital this afternoon we found Daddy moaning and groaning and only fully conscious by fits and starts. He was given a shot shortly after, it didn't help him much. He kept complaining of his heels killing him and said, "I'm going to die . . . Don't leave me here . . ." Then he would go into a half sleep and not know we were in the room.

After dinner I went over to the filling station, matched nickels for Cokes and Hal lost. He said he'd refused to let a Negro man use the men's room and had gone out to head off two Negro women from the "Ladies." Brother Benedict said one day a group of the Brothers were out driving and stopped, I suppose in their long black gowns, at the Cafe in Garnett, they waited and no one came over, finally they called to the waitress and she came over and told them that they didn't serve Catholics there.

Hal telling today about how he acted when he was Shorty's age, riding to town on one of his daddy's horses, stopping when he met a "nigger," tying up his horse then tying up the "nigger" and "beating the shit" out of him, until one day two "niggers" got at him first, "as I come from under the horse's neck," and beat him up and from then on he didn't bother "no more niggers."

Morning-glory blue, Shorty's eyes are—with bleached lashes—the eyes seem those of someone caged inside his tow-haired head—like those of Jean Marais in *Beauty and the Beast*.

◆

SARASOTA, FLA.

9:40 A.M. I'm in Chick Austin's house, 232 Delmar, in the "baroque" room, still in bed, the sun shining in the window but not as many birds singing and calling as there were last evening just before the sun went down.

7:40 P.M. I drove out to the Ringling Bros. & Barnum & Bailey Circus Winter Quarters and ran into John Murray Anderson immediately who greated me cordially as always. We went to the Big Top where Murray directed rehearsals through the mike—giving nicknames to everyone, some of which stick: Gangster, Dorothy Lamour, Miami . . . He calls me Little Ford and I thought I heard him call for me over the mike but I wasn't quite sure but he did for when I saw him later he asked where I'd been—said he wanted to work me into the elephant routine (he was only kidding). Such a beautiful white horse led the elephants in, the elephant boys seeming to beat them brutally, and in the semi-light of the tent, with the false moons in the web hanging around, and the holes in the tent like stars, and the music of the circus organ—that horse, so white, so unreal in his fabulous form . . . There was a poignant moment, I thought, when one elephant was elevated by climbing up on stools and another big fat elephant got down on its knees and crawled under and through—as if it were a human being in another incarnation.

◆

PALM BEACH, FLA.

Arrived here at Alice's yesterday about 6:30 P.M. after leaving Sarasota around 2.

I wrote to Léonor in faulty French: "This morning I shall go in the jungle, aboard Alice Delamar's little boat, to see exotic tropical plants and alligators, those grotesque prisoners (human prisoners one sees working the roads—more beautiful and more sad than alligators) . . ."

"Here's old Fanny Ward," said Alice to me as we entered the terrace of the Miramar—and Fanny turned around to see who was talking about her—and spoke to her friend, Alice Delamar.

It's after lunch and I'm naked in bed. All this sunburn burning arouses the skin everywhere—and what would the penis be without its skin? Skinned, I guess.

APRIL

Back to 360 E. 55 at 3:30 yesterday afternoon (the 7th) after an exhausting and maddening drive through too much traffic, near-accidents, getting lost in Washington, and arriving to find a wreck of a station wagon blocking the parking entrance here. Found Pavlik smiling, thin but younger looking ("because I had no one to eat me")—I was glad to hear his voice and he was glad to see me ("black as an Indian").

Carrie on Pavlik during my absence: "He was so upset—the way he was acting I thought you wasn't coming back ... He didn't want to eat alone ... he was so a-scared he keep the front door locked during the daytime ..." "But he got adjusted?" I asked her. "Well—kinda."

◆

WESTON, CONN.

Morning of the 9th. Just talked to Mother—Daddy died at 6:25 A.M. She was crying over the phone, said the burial will be in Brookhaven Monday; must find out train schedules now.

The feeling of *impatience* that rises in me with Pavlik as with no one else. Perhaps I've overstayed my "apprenticeship." Buddha said ten years is enough.

◆

BROOKHAVEN, MISS.

Mother and I went first to the Funeral Home to see Daddy—I was surprised to find the casket open but Mother said everyone would be disappointed if they didn't get to see "the body." "It's not him," was my reaction. And I said to Mother, "The soul is somewhere else." He was so painted, for one thing, and the transparent net they let fall over him made him look even more unreal. Banks of flowers, and the white satin upholstered casket. Mother, crying, "I'm glad they put the rose there"—a red rose in his lapel.

A dozen or more relatives came, one recalled holding me on his knee and my singing, "I Wonder Who's Kissing Her Now"—loud. Aunt Mamie told me that one day when I was a child at table I finished before everyone else did, pushed my plate away and said: "Now I'm ready for my *tee-DIRT*!" She said I sure could talk a lot then, too. "Can you still?"

At the cemetery the pallbearers (there were six of them), after the short words of prayer by the Methodist preacher, came by one by one and dropped the white flowers from their lapels onto to flower-covered coffin.

◆

WESTON, CONN.

Mother, Pavlik and I are here, having driven out in the spring weather before lunch.

In New Orleans, from where we took the plane back to New York, I left Mother in her room at the Roosevelt and walked down Bourbon Street to Toulouse— never had so much soliciting from pimps before—"hot spots" they call their joints. I had been told that the real wild gay bar was Tony Pacino's so I went there. Sign tacked up on wall in one corner: THIS PLACE IS OFF LIMITS FOR ARMY AND NAVY. Continuous singing going on at piano—when one Negress stopped another would take her place—one sounding like a false Billie Holiday, the other an imitator of Nellie Lutcher. Saw only one boy in the place who was really attractive—but he was with a "friend" ("two beers for two steers") . . . A man took the stool beside me and we got in conversation—he told about his first wife and his daughter and how he has to pay $15 a week alimony, and the other women he's lived with, etc. Seemed to be a completely masculine type, with moustache, in white shirtsleeves. We got to pushing legs and ended with his asking me if I'd like to go to his place ("that might not be a bad idea") so he took me in a taxi—a pair of women's high heel shoes on his kitchen table—what for? . . . It was a sordid little place and his feet needed washing (he had a shower bathroom there too) and I think I saw a black crab crawling on his belly.

◆

It's sympathetic having Gertrude (as Pavlik calls Mother) here—there's been less tension between Pavlik and me and he seems more at ease—falls back into a pattern of reaction that he knew years ago when Mother used to stay with us—but it's only a surface pattern—underneath he's tense and bitter.

> I have not from your eyes, that gentleness
> And shew of love, as I was wont to have . . .

He laughs little—this weekend ... Solemn, depressed, grave ... "I suppose I have to prepare myself for the Trail of the Lonesome Pine," he said at the breakfast table and Mother gave me a look.

Then sometimes he's like a river without a dam—unharnessed power—flooding it all over the place is wasting it.

No delight in life means no delight in art—Pavlik's an example.

◆

NEW YORK CITY

So after we drove in from the country I was lying on my bed with a half-finished or ¹/₄ finished glass of milk and Pavlik got in one of his hysterical abusive states, "Why are you lying there? Why don't you get a job, make some money," etc., so I threw the milk in his face. "That's my answer," I said. "I'm sick of you! Sick! Je n'ai plus d'émotion pour toi." (Damn it, I splattered my settee) ... It all came up with his saying how extravagant it was to take the car to Europe. So I told him he could go to Europe alone, that I'd spend the summer in Weston: "C'est fini!"

"You have more emotion for me than I have for you," he said.

"I left for Tennessee to get away from you—I couldn't stand it any longer."

He listens to everything his friends in New York say—especially about me. How I loathe trivial, gossipy, mischief-making people.

◆

His attitude this morning: nothing happened. He doesn't want any more trouble.

Carrie still carrying on about how lonesome Mr. Tchelitchew was while I was gone: "Sometimes he couldn't keep his mouth closed, he'd just holler: for Mr. Ford ... I hated to leave him, sometime ..." She says he's looking better than when I left: "He's picked up ... would have picked up quicker if he hadn't been grievin' ..." How heartless I am!

"Ruining is very simple, creating is very difficult—" Pavlik on seeing the spots on my settee, left by the milk.

◆

We made applications for passports this morning.

◆

The invisible becoming visible: the amaryllis in my window blooms every year—grows like an erection, the flower sprouts, opens wide and drops off, the stalk dies down (like a hard—"let it die down")—and the bulb is left for next year's performance. What I'd like to know, is next year's bloom-potential "trouvable" even under the microscope? Perhaps not—the potential alone may be there, like a work of art in an artist.

◆

WESTON, CONN.

Some people just can't handle the mob (of facts)—retreat in fantasy—or, get torn to pieces.

"If you can't afford me, you'll have to give me up . . ." (me to Pavlik).

Lady Precious Stream: "You should remember what our sage said: 'I examine myself three times every day to see whether I have done truly and loyally my best to my friend—' "

My friend says, "L'humeur est toujours assez noir," and I believe him. Because he tells me, "Tu vendrait mon cadavre si vous ensez de gagner dix cents."

MAY

WESTON, CONN.

We are back from lunch at the Tanguys. [Yves] Tanguy told the story of Eluard's "Elle a chouché, elle a couché!" Tanguy: "Qui? Qui? Qui a couché?" "Nusch!" (Eluard's mistress.) "Couché avec qui?" Elated Eluard: "Avec Picasso!"

The Beadles, Ernst and Gina, are going to take our apartment while we're in Europe.

P. says he's dissatisfied with his work—"too dry"—and that one day he's going to "open the doors" and let everyone in (to a world of poetry). I said, "If you've lost your way, as in the fairytales, you'll refind it." He said, "I need a hunchbacked horse—*you* have one—" (meaning himself).

◆

NEW YORK CITY

I took corrected proofs (*Sleep in a Nest of Flames*, poems selected by Edith Sitwell and with her preface) back to New Directions. Laughlin seemed fatter-faced and at the same time more wrinkled—gets a sort of embalmed look at times, the blue eyes unmoving. He was amiable, though he didn't encourage me to submit any excerpts from my journals to the next ND annual.

When Pavlik returned from his chiropractor (Dr. Van Rumpt) he greeted me with "I've got varicose veins."

♦

The first rose opened on the terrace. "Ils savent que nous partons." (P.) The chrysanthemums are not doing so well. "They know I won't be here," he says. Brooksie [Jackson] told him that Tanaquil Le Clercq will be with us on the *De Grasse*. Lincoln told him, "You and Charlie hide yourselves because you do not surround yourselves with the right milieu." There is no right milieu in America. P.: "Perhaps the academic world?" No!

♦

"Did you sleep well?"

"Je ne sais pas. Je me reveille avec le dagger dans le heart."

"Well, it's of your own manufacture, you'll find the trademark to be Tchelitchew."

At dinner I told him of my plan to do the book on Alexander the Great. "A shooting star," he said.

♦

ABOARD THE *DE GRASSE*

Did I use good tactics with Bobby?

♦

Bobby made his appearance just after I wrote the above sentence as I sat in my deck chair, so I could not continue. The first time I saw him was yesterday, sailing day, at a distance, while I was waiting in line to be assigned a table. He was wearing a pistachio (says P.) colored suit. Il est trés vivant, joyeux, has lovely fresh skin and curly hair, is rather short.

After lunch (I'm still on yesterday) I decided to take a nap. So I told Pavlik, "If you see Bobby send him to wake me at 2:30." I dozed a little and there was no Bobby at 3:30 so I got up and then Pavlik came in the cabin and said he'd seen Bobby and told him to wake me up. He also said Bobby told him I had played with "des choses defendues." How did it start, that conversation? Bobby was scratching himself or adjusting his fly and Pavlik said, "Vous jouez avec des choses defendues?" and Bobby said, "C'est votre ami qui joue avec des choses defendues," and Pavlik said, "Où?" and B. said, "Dans le cinema hier soir …" Did he seem mad? I asked and P. said, "No, he was laughing—he wanted to go and wake you up immediately when I told him you were sleeping, but then I told him not to, that it was too early, so he went to the afternoon picture with his cousin." Anyway, there was a life-saving drill and I put on my life-saving jacket and went to the appointed place and passed Bobby and we spoke but didn't stop and when the drill was over he lagged behind as if avoiding me but I waited for him to catch up in the corridor, and asked him, "Tu te sent sauvé?" and he replied, "Je me sauve toujours"—which

I thought didn't bode well for my future rape (active), and that's why I started yesterday's entry with "Did I use good tactics with Bobby?" He answered the question for me by appearing and seating himself by my side, taking out his pack of cards. When I said I'd have to go to the cabin for my cards if we were to play Russian Bank he volunteered to accompany me. I gave him candy and sat on the bunk and he sat on the chair but got up when I said let me see the back of your coat then I gently pulled him down beside me and caressed his hair and said, "Vous avez des jolies cheveux," and he said, "Non," and I said, "Vous avez un peau joli," and he said, "Non," and I said, "Comme une fille," but then he got frightened and said, "Let's go." (He'd told Pavlik he's never kissed any girl excepting his sister.)

So we went back upstairs and played cards all afternoon and after dinner he came again to our deck chairs and was falling all over me with hands and face close—having drunk wine at dinner. So I had some pretext for going to my cabin and he followed but when I took him in my arms and half kissed his ear he said, "What do you think I am?"

He's just come on deck, dressed in white flannels, red sweater and tweed jacket, and made so much fuss that he caused Pavlik to move to the writingroom. Bobby's hands are large, but not too large, with round wrists; good legs. The shape of his face is classical Italian—he has an Italian mother, also Russian and German blood—but he's French. His nose looks as if it had been broken. He has brown eyes and good lashes, a sweet, fresh, red mouth. His teeth need cleaning, however. He has a delicate neck.

◆

6:10 P.M. in my bunk before dressing for dinner. Pavlik has talked to Jimmy Savo, the comedian everyone loves. Tanny Le Clercq knew him from Balanchine's television show, *Cinderella*: "He was my fairy godmother" (Tanny to Pav). "He's like a priest," says Pavlik.

Bobby told me he didn't jerk off at all, then said, "Two times a month." I said, "At your age it ought to be two times a day." "I'm not American," he replied.

◆

After dinner last night when Pavlik and I went to our deck chairs there was Bobby, saying he had drunk a bottle of wine at dinner. I'd had three glasses and told him I was drunk too. I suggested we go to my cabin to fetch the cards—or bonbons—and he agreed so quickly I thought he was kidding but he followed me down and the moment we got in the stateroom I bolted the door (the room steward is always peeping in for some reason or other). Bobby sat in the chair and closed his eyes as if sleepy from too much wine—I embraced and kissed him on the mouth and he didn't resist too much, then I sat beside him. He jumped up and made for the door but I stopped him. Then he fell over on Pavlik's bunk, and wouldn't get up, seemed half passed-out . . . We did what we did and then he lay tossing and kicking on the bunk and I couldn't get him to sober up—once he got up and started falling on the floor and sliding out of the chair onto the floor so I dragged-carried him back to the bunk—he fumbled for a cigarette, I got him one and lit it, asking him to try to get up, that the steward would be in to make up the beds, etc. "Quel garçon! Tu est impossible!" etc., and he would cover his face with the spread but I uncovered it and ran a damp towel over it—I couldn't tell how much he was drunk and how much putting on an act—but anyway I was glad when he finally decided to come out and he came staggering down the corridor after me—I went on ahead and to the open deck where I found Pavlik walking with Luke Bouchage and P. said, "Where have you been?" and I said, "Looking for you!"

Then we three walked down the deck and there was Bobby in the distance and when he saw us he went inside but he was standing there when we passed again and we stopped and Pavlik kidded him about being drunk on too much wine. I asked him if he'd like to play deck tennis and he nodded and we played in the twilight—the rubber rings were easy to see against the light sky though it was dark where they hit the deck.

Then we stopped and walked and Tanaquil passed and I stopped her and kissed her on the cheek and she said she'd had so much sun she was almost sick but promised to play cards later.

Bobby and I started down and he told me at the top of the stairs, "Je ne rapelle rien," and I said, "Je vais te rapeller un autre jour," and he said, "Fuck you."

◆

Bobby sat in front of me on the same deck chair holding my ankles and I caressed his hand with a finger. He said, "You thought I was drunk—I can tell you everything that happened." Then he got up and disappeared. I went to look for him, found him in the doorway of the dance salon, wearing a paper hat and throwing paper balls at the crowd—I gave him a French sailor paper hat that Tanny had given me, said, "Bonne nuit," and he threw a paper ball in my face.

◆

Bobby's carrying around a box of rat poison because he's got a penchant for fishing and he puts a bit of this poison in the water and it attracts lots of fish.

"I'm very very bored, I'm very very tired, I'm very very frozen"—Pavlik's announcement on coming in cabin just now. He says deck stewards are very unpleasant because we ate lunch in chairs without being seasick. "Funny that I see so badly, I don't see anything," says Pavlik—so I fix the link in his keychain for him.

"Dix ans on pris beaucoup de moi"—it's ten years since he's been in Europe.

◆

The first time Bobby got his nose broken he fell from baby carriage. The second time was with boxing instructor. Last night he rushed across the cafe-terrace to get to the less crowded door, slipped and sprawled. Then came back and stood with one foot in the chair I was standing in (to see over heads), other foot in other chair. The boat swayed, we both lost balance and fell together back on table, glass fell from table and broke, Tanny saved her crème-de-menthe.

Such a one for bumping his head. Adolescence exploding, kicking, bumping in all directions. Has never shaved upper lip and chin—fuzzy like a girl's. I told him that for his birthday I'd send him to a dentist for a teeth-cleaning! He'll be sixteen.

Last night after dinner I told Bobby I was going to my cabin to shave. I did, then decided to take a nap. I did, and was awakened by Bobby and the first thing he did was pour a jigger of bourbon for himself, and one for me—so it was eventually off with his shoes, pants and—about that time a knock came on the door and it was Pavlik screaming, "Charlie!" so I opened the door so as to let him in and Bobby, not wanting to be seen, flung himself against it to close it so I tried to pull it open and Pavlik tried to push it open and was hollering, "Charlie, what is it!" so I had to say in a loud whisper, "Bobby est la!" so then he understood and went away and I was saying, "Quelle manque de savoir-faire de tous les deux"—so we dressed and went out and I came back for some money and Bobby went on and I went up on deck and found Pavlik and Tanny, walked on Promenade with them, and Pavlik said he had come to a "decision," etc.

Bobby had wanted to know if one got completely undressed when going to bed with a girl. I told him: "Le peau contre le peau, c'est l'amour même."

JUNE

PARIS (2 RUE JACQUES-MAWAS)

I'm upstairs in the little room where I used to sleep. Pavlik's sister, Choura, and Kola Kopeikine met us at the Gare St.-Lazare. Driving through Paris everything looked petit or mignon and rather shabby, people shabbily dressed on the streets, lots of little cars and bicycles. "It's as if one were dreaming of the past," I said. "On ne peut pas recommencer." Pavlik agreed with me. "Non," he said, "çela doit être autre chose." Orange and yellow poppies waiting from Léonor [Fini]—asks us to phone on arrival—there's no phone in the apartment (two flights below this chambre de bonne).

Bobby has that typically French peau—when it's typically nice—peaches and cream. "Comme une pêche qu'on voudrait manger," I told him last night, as he lay sprawled in Pavlik's bunk—before Pavlik came in. "Papa est en colère," the steward had commented earlier, when Pav chased Bobby out.

How pretty Pavlik's marble fireplace is—he says he's used it in his paintings. There's a small unsigned oil of an oversized egg on his wall—he did it about 25 years ago. "That's how it all started," he says. He also says the ocean is still between him and Choura—that what he told her about himself and his work didn't make any effect—"she doesn't listen—has no idea what I am."

Even the hurry in Paris seems hurry for leisure's sake—the hurry in New York for the sake of business.

◆

The voice of Léonor over phone—soft, and low-pitched, very seductive.

I like the idea of liking girls and going to bed with them but I'm afraid I'm much too conditioned by boy-loving. On the boat, in the group Tanny-Bobby-Betty (latter a dark-skinned ballerina traveling with Tanny), it was always Bobby who set off the sparks and whom I liked to look at, touch, listen to—I'm made that way, that's all.

◆

I was at least half an hour late for lunch, first went to Léonor's fantastically furnished and decorated apartment—no one there—went back down and asked concierge where Mlle. Fini was lunching and she said the floor beneath—apartment of Count Sforza, friend and I suppose—or one supposes—lover of Léonor. So I rang and Léonor appeared and I was surprised to embrace a brunette instead of the blonde I left ten years ago. Her hair unwashed and in disorder, face unmarked, almost, by the ravages of ten years, draped in a dark red silk robe, genre Japanese kimono. So sitting at table, besides Pavlik—Stanislao Lepri, painter, Sforza, and Léonor's third gentleman friend, the writer André Pieyre de Mandiargues. Saw Léonor's portrait of Jean Genet (he looks like a middle-aged criminal). André talks with dead-pan insistence; Sforza is sensitively bored. Léonor said she hadn't remembered my eyes being so blue ... The illusion of being inspired by the "group of Léonor" has probably been dispelled from Pavlik's mind by this luncheon.

◆

Pavlik was told by a Russian friend that Paris is very anti-paederast at the moment—orgies in the baths no longer take place; no "dancings" with boys only; no entertainers in drag. Choura said someone called the police to arrest two boys together in a hotel room! I still think the pissoirs are working overtime.

◆

One sees on the streets here: individuals; and the reality of great paintings is the marvelous reality they impose—hallucination of art as real as the real.

Pavlik thinks Paris has lost her pride, she's no longer the elegant Queen of Cities. German and American influences in evidence: knapsacks and hobnail boots—Esso signs and American-influenced fashions in women's clothes. He says, "I wish I could sleep for 10,000 years."

The excrescences of the body: garbage of the emotions. Saliva, piss, sweat, tears, jism and shit.

Epoque des solitudes. Dans les mains des dieux, on se sent libre. Pas autant souriantes—que sensibles—les figures de Paris.

◆

Neither P. nor I find Choura sympathetic. She screams when she talks, tells boring anecdotes; never wants to leave us alone—but is bitter and resentful underneath (P. thinks).

One gets a number from a machine on the street to show the order of one's getting on the mostly crowded buses. Une dame a voulu entrer avant un monsieur, even though her number did not have priority. She carried a cane and said she limped—but the monsieur was not moved. Nor the conductor—"Tout le monde peut botter," he said. No one sympathized with the lady, apparently—who showed the bottom of her built-up shoe as the bus pulled out. Suffering does not make people more kind, "mais plus dur"—according to Pav.

Who is loveable and who isn't? No one is loveable to everybody. (Chick Austin quoting Osbert: "We are all someone else's bore.")

I think Europe will change my handwriting ... "Monstre d'égotisme" (P.)—is that why I keep this diary? I can do nothing against reality: who can?

◆

Looking without participating is like pressing one's nose against a mirror where images go by on bicycles. A bird or butterfly against a windowpane, caught in a room—the world they want outside. Where is he? The ideal companion doesn't, perhaps, exist—one makes up the ideal from many: something from this one, something else from that one. So if I found an attractive French boy, I'd be amused with whatever he wanted to do.

How gently it can rain in Paris—one walks along, bareheaded, not caring.

◆

"Her seul raison d'exister is her maladie," he says of his sister. Then again, he'll make excuses for her. "With only one lung she can't work, she must rest," etc. So he resigns himself to her being his "Cross."

"Risquez! Risquez!" sings out the petite dame in the booth selling lottery tickets.

Some little French boys have older faces, like little men—horribly exciting.

"Humain, mais triste"—Pavlik was describing Paris ... "D'être humain est d'être triste," I said.

◆

Why did I jerk off? Because of the exciting memory of a night spent with a Scout (pronounced "Scoot"), chez lui—Jacques Stettiner (painter friend of P.'s) introduced me and it was somewhat like the answer to my prayers—twenty years old, nez retroussé—thanks, Jacques! ... His tiny room was très drôle—photos and prints and paintings pinned on the walls—a charcoal drawing of himself thumbtacked between two of his grandfather's swords and an enormous watercolor which he, the Scout, had done of an Indian Chief.

Faces. The substance of life. French lips get in a kissable position when they speak.

◆

Léonor's éclats de rire after hearing Pavlik's: "Quelqu'un a pissé dans la source de la poésie à Paris ..."

Henri Michaux on the Chinese: "... and he detests water (excellent for the personality, in fact, is dirt)..." Paris is bursting with it.

◆

Exhibition of Impressionist painting. "Comme si c'était fait par la nature," I said about a Cézanne. "Untouchable, unbreakable," P. said about a Seurat.

◆

Pavlik thinks maybe I should not give up Noël (my "Scoot") just because he doesn't hold his chest up and lets his stomach stick out. He does have a charming nose.

Some Arabs like to come every day, and the expression one gets on one's face by coming seems to be permanently worn by them.

◆

Paul Bowles' "Concerto pour deux pianos, trois instruments à vent et percussion" (1947) had the biggest success at the Fizdale-Gold concert. During intermission Pavlik went to talk to Alice B. Toklas, he told her he had been thinking a lot during past 15 years, she told him that he never thought, that painters never think.

I went by the Librairie where Raoul Leven works and suddenly over my shoulder I recognized Jean Genet (from photos and Léonor's portrait), asked Raoul if that were not he and Raoul said Yes, he'd introduce me and did. Genet couldn't believe I was the editor of *View*, said, "Vous êtes beau! Je ne savais pas qu'un editeur peut être beau!" Said he had quit writing, is building a house in Cannes for a young friend of his (the one to whom the poem in *View* was dedicated). He's very short, gray close-cropped hair, feminine expression in the eyes, the crushed nose of a boxer.

JULY

"Have you ever been to Geneva?" I ask Pavlik.

"Never been to Switzerland and never wanted to . . ."

He has a room reserved at Dr. Junod's Clinic in Geneva and may stay there 15 days—Choura told me he'd be confined and I wouldn't be able to see him but I doubt it.

◆

GENEVA.

I'm in my room at the Hôtel Residence and about to go to see Pavlik at his Clinique Générale Florissant—the doctor won't be seeing him until 9 tomorrow morning.

11 P.M. Hell I'm back. Absolutely nothing to do in Geneva, not even in the pissoirs. It was raining by the time I had finished dinner—rain having fallen on a framboise lake (red sun behind the mountains)—boys on bicycles passed, there was one holding an umbrella, another holding an ice-cream cone. The waitress phoned for a taxi and I set out with the driver to find the Bar Max, which turned out to be a private apartment where Mr. Max Bar lives. I spoke to the driver about the lack of amusements in Geneva—in comparison with Paris—he was an old red-eyed man, began to hint that he knew of amusements in Geneva too—though

there are no "maisons"—tried to get me to come out with what I wanted—
"une femme?"—"partous" with "hommes et femmes?"—finally—"un jeune
homme?"—and *finally* he proposed himself but I didn't hurt his feelings by refusing bluntly—told him I didn't want to go straight to a bed, rather wanted to find a
bar where there was a choice of acquaintances. Then he asked me not to speak of
his proposition; I said, "Oh, je suis discret"—and we shook hands and he drove off.
(Anything can happen!)

◆

5:15 A.M. I'm on the train which leaves in a few minutes and a passenger says we
change at Lausanne for Italy. The taxi ordered to fetch me at the hotel at five
turned out to be the driver who made me the proposition!

◆

MOLVENO (TRENTO), ITALY

Cabled Pavlik a nightletter yesterday: "MOLVENO CHARMING FOUND
SUITABLE APARTMENT TELEGRAPH WHEN TO MEET YOU IN MI-
LAN BEST LOVE."

It doesn't take me long to fall in love with a really enchanting place or person—
and I think I've fallen for this Alpine village. I've never seen any mountain lake
as beautiful—just as water—and the surrounding mountains themselves are of a
variety in shape and color that is inexhaustible—I saw them at their best and most
varied from the lake this afternoon where I rowed for an hour.

◆

Telegram at last from Pavlik; still at the Clinique: "ESPERE PARTIR SAMEDI
TELEGRAPGIERAI [*sic*] DEMAIN AMITIES"—it was written yesterday.

I've been wanting to say: I asked a question about connections, of a Swiss on my
train from Geneva, and when we changed at Lausanne we were in the same com-
partment (3rd class, very comfortable). He asked me if I were a musician (probably
because he thought I needed a haircut) and when I told him I was a writer he said,
"intellectual ..." and that he would show me the hill where Rainer Maria Rilke
was buried; it was by a church in a beautiful setting before we reached the Italian
border. "J'ai coupé des roses sur sa tombe," the man said.

◆

I'm back in Molveno with Pavlik, we spent night before last in Milan. A telegram
just received from Léonor wanting me to take for her the little house here, about
which I'd written her. Pavlik, on my showing him the place: "She will probably
be aghast, like me ..." But he did seem pleased with certain aspects, its newness,
the beds, views of the lake from bedroom windows ... As to our apartment, he

finds it "on the depressing side, like all peasant places"—and our landlady is the soul of stinginess, supposed to furnish all towels but won't buy any bathtowels and gave Linda, our maid, only two extra-small kitchen towels . . . P. says one can't organize one's work and working hours until the household routine is organized, and I guess he's right . . . "The doctor says I musn't have any contradictions." The gloom and pessimism which he can exude is unbelievable—Russian, I suppose—everything is disastrous before disaster—the water will be too cold to swim in, the house will be too far to walk back to, etc. It's true that his bed is too short and we're going to exchange it for one of the iron ones which I'd had taken downstairs. "The sand in my gallbladder changes like the Arizona desert."

"Je suis exalté pour Molveno," Léonor writes.

The climax of Pavlik's arrival in Milan (alone, from Geneva) was his jumping off the moving train with the last and heaviest suitcase—the porter had the others. Passengers were yelling at him not to jump (he didn't know that the train was only changing tracks) but he jumped and sprawled over the suitcase and bruised his ankle and it all seemed like a nightmare when he told me about it.

◆

A man in the morning passes here at seven, blasting a bugle, a sound for everyone who has a goat to graze to bring it out and he takes the whole flock "like a black sea" (P.) to the hills and pastures.

The lake, so still, had marvelous reflections in it which we saw from above on our walk—Pavlik "took back" his statement about these mountains being depressing and said he'd said it only because he himself was depressed in general.

The importance of air: we can go without food for days—without air we die in minutes. Intangible life-giving substance—or spirit.

◆

Concentration is like an animal or a rare plant that must be hunted—I'm on the road. "My shitting is of a completely different kind now," P. announces, on the road to recovery.

◆

The cheese woman came and tried to cheat Pavlik by saying the piece of cheese she cut for him weighed more than it did. I weighed it again and Linda said if she tries to say it weighs more than it does then we won't buy from her anymore. Pavlik quoted Lao-Tse to the effect that we should believe those who tell the truth and also those who lie because that is real kindness. Yes, that's true, I said, but children and poets are cruel. Cruel Dante!

Pav is pathetically thin still, when I see him on the beach and remember how he used to look. "You think I just had a nervous breakdown? New York drives me crazy."

The air in New York excites without supplying the necessary energy to enact the excitement—hence the tiredness and enervation which comes from living there.

◆

Morning noises: goats, bells, bugle-notes, cows, cats, babies, cars, voices, hammering, birds—but all at a distance, until that cur starts his yapping—he has the biggest repertoire of unattractive noises that I've ever heard from one animal.

Isak Dinesen has a charming way of placing and spacing her adjectives: "The long, wet, and fragrant grass."

So what should I discover on the beach but a crab—not in the water but on the outskirts of my pubic hair.

◆

I also like Dinesen's unabashed awkwardnesses of style: "—that same moon—turning the white-washed wall milk white where it struck it." That woman is a genius. Here is how she presents (in *The Poet*) Anders' confrontation by the Councillor, at the end of the Temple of Friendship scene with Francine: "He (Anders) only grinned, when he set eyes on him, as if he had been shown the solution of a crafty riddle." The crafty riddle was his life.

◆

Another letter from Léonor—they're arriving the 6th or 7th (of August)—she hopes there aren't too many "villegianti" and babies here. Well, there are, but we avoid them.

Pavlik and I took our longest walk today, along the west bank of the lake, beyond the peninsula, where we sat in a rolling field above the water with a background of mountain-top emerging from a cloud-wreath—when one looked away from the water awhile, then back, its blueness was startling. Returning, ran into three singing boys—they'd been masturbating out on the peninsula, one supposes.

AUGUST

The Poet. Only now have I reached a satisfactory understanding of the story and characters—that is why I've instinctively postponed further writing on the play. Try, try! my muse is saying. What torture, not to begin.

My god, begin! That dog's anguish adds to my own.

◆

Baudelaire changes, after the White Goddess, to the Black: "C'est Elle! Noire et pourtant lumineuse."

The other side of the moon.

The bell is tolling, Linda says someone is dead. Who? An old man. From what? His heart.

◆

Still no Léonor . . . But a new tenant in the lower floor: a pig; never heard anything scream so much like a child except a child.

I see beyond the calm lake, enclosed in its mountains, another mountain, sunlit; between the lakeside mountain and this sunlit one a white cloud lies, as if it were still in bed.

◆

Léonor, Stanislao Lepri, Edalgy Dinsha and Sherban Sidéry (friend of Léonor's) arrived yesterday afternoon in Lepri's Pontiac. Léonor looked tired in the car but at table she looked better, suntanned and young with that strange cat-girl's face and purring voice. However, as I told Pavlik, Léonor's tragedy is that she doesn't like her face, that's why she invents all those masks, paints pictures of herself in an idealized way, etc.

After dinner we fooled around in the piazza, Léonor dressed like a gypsy, with bright colors and a shawl, hair all messed up and sticking out in every direction. She insists, at least for the present, on wearing high-heeled wooden slippers which force her to advance in small slow steps. "C'est de la blague," I said to Lepri, "—c'est pas une promenade."

◆

Léonor confessed that she suffers from her physiological defects—often—but doesn't let them bother her in other ways or at other times: "Je suppose que c'est un signe de la santé," she said.

"—de la liberté," I suggested and she said, "Oui, c'est çela."

Linda is singing, not at the top of her voice but half-way up.

◆

"To let go the emotions through impulse is called assertiveness," wrote Lao-Tse. Léonor does this. She should be more like water, and simply flow over people— and give way like water when they intrude upon her—she would still be the sur- rounding element. She feels like a "chevalier," she told Pavlik. The maiden she thinks she's rescued, at the moment, is Edalgy.

Léonor is greedy for everything—success in the monde of fashion, in the the- ater, in art, among the literati, she wants to eat and see everything, rushing around from one château to another—like a "knight errant," Pavlik told her when she said she felt like a chevalier. As if she hadn't *time* . . . "That's her character!" said P.

"Léonor is not a walker—but a rider—dans tous les sens," I said. "I know," Pav- lik said. "Je sais ce que vous voulez dire."

She needs to be continuously *reacting* to something—places or people. "Elle a peur de rester seule avec elle-même," says P. He thinks her pictures need to take on fresh color—she wants "nuance," but, he said, "too much nuance makes a paint- ing look the same color all over."

◆

Before lunch, around eleven, Léonor and Lepri came by. Léonor looked lovely, soignée for a change. "Vous êtes belle aujourd'hui." "Parce que je suis coiffée." She had on a black tight sweater showing busts as prominent as an African's. Pavlik told her that we've remarked how in Italy there's always a female voice one hears calling another female who doesn't reply. Léonor said, That's true and told Pavlik an anecdote. An Italian girl was sucking a man's cock, and her mother was calling and calling her, "Angelina!" or "Maria Rosa!" or whatever her name was. Finally the girl took her mouth away and hollered, "Subito!" and started sucking again. The man said to her, "Are you using my prick as a telephone?"

I went to the beach ahead of Pavlik this morning, the sun was out bright so masses of people were there, more than ever. I chose a fairly isolated spot covered with pebbles and along came Lepri and we stripped to our bathing trunks and stretched out for a sunbath. In fifteen minutes or so I spied Léonor coming alone down the beach towards us and I waved and she waved back. "Elle a l'air furieuse," said Lepri. She was in her high heels, as usual, so couldn't jump the little stream separating her from us, stepped smack in the middle of it, the shoe sank in the mud and she lost her balance and fell forward. I helped her up after she found her shoe, people were looking on and she didn't like that—said the place was awful, smelled of "pipi," as bad as Ostia, etc. I told her we had chosen the best spot unless one rented a small boat and the boats were all taken. Anyway she took Lepri to search for a less crowded area—I thought they were going to look in the rocks along the lake but I found them later, with Pavlik, who came down afterwards—they had decided to sit in the worst possible place, where the sawdust washed down from the sawmill collects and is damp. Léonor began to rave against the people and children, saying one bambino had felt their hate radiating, drew closer and closer and finally called Lepri a cow ("che mucca!"). She ranted about having foregone a much better endroit by the sea where she could take nude sunbaths, that the doctors had recommended the mountains but she felt no better here than by the sea, she ate too much and felt gonflée, etc. I said it wasn't because she ate too much but because she didn't rest ever—that her nerves manufactured the gas.

I told Lepri, after he came along with us to his garage, which is next door here (Léonor went on back to their house), that I'd go mad were I to live with as many friends as Léonor had around—that I could stand strangers on the beach much better than friends in the house. Léonor had said how she'd like to murder some of those children. Thinking we were shocked, she added, "You don't know in how corrumpu a milieu we live in Paris . . ."

Il faut respecter la monstruosité des autres.

◆

"It's so boring when one starts to make école de soi-même," says P.

Léonor perhaps thinks of herself as one of those perfumes of Baudelaire, "corrumpus, riches et triomphants." She says she must leave for Venice around the 10th of September.

◆

Like Genet's Spanish gambler who went into a pisserie to jerk off before joining the cardgame—I do feel more calm, less irritable.

Simple people (like Linda) thoughtlessly imagine that "writing" Italian is something as difficult to learn as speaking it. When she saw a letter addressed to Lago di Garda, she said Oh, you write well in Italian.

A blue mountain of green trees.

A dreamed sentence: "Your life will hang over where you hang the sense."

◆

Linda is howling—with song. I told her to ask her friend who plays the accordion to come by Léonor's after dinner and he did. Léonor and I danced the polka (though she has *two* abscesses and has to sit on a cushion).

Genet thinks he can force a legend from literature—as one forces a door. But is glory stolen or conferred? If taken by violence it's conferred by destiny—as in Alexander's case—but it was not the legend that interested Alexander, it was the act: the legend was conferred by history.

◆

Dr. Junod, in discussing Pavlik's work: "There's a difference between a dead bone and a living bone." Pavlik says his bones, in his paintings, are living, "a hymn to life."

The cloud, child of water and air, that caresses the mountain—tender and chaste caress!

Bunch of mountain-hikers we met on the road, returning from the Brenta Dolomites, a priest among them, gayest of the lot, red-faced and smiling. "They smell high!" said Pavlik. "Whew!" "Aphrodisiac," said I.

A shadow falls, a fragment of night; a day goes, a fragment of death. Life and the sun tomorrow.

SEPTEMBER

Up at six and found a feather in my bed, as though, while I was sleeping, I'd been a bird.

◆

They all came by to say goodbye, they're leaving this morning for Venice—Léonor with freshly curled hair. Pavlik showed some of his drawings, the spiral heads and a beautiful out-of-this-world lake-colored head. I found a half-mask for Léonor in the forest—a hole in a piece of wood which may be looked through with one eye; the shape like a feather.

◆

Little girl with long hair pulled up her dress to take a piss or a shit in the garden—saw me on the terrace, let skirt down and walked a bit through the beans, squatted again, half-hidden, and, doing her business, turned her face around to see if I was still looking at her. I was.

I'm sitting here, having stupidly induced a hard (imagining what my feeling would be showing the German doctor here the mole hidden in my pubic hair—on the pretext of asking his advice as to whether or not it should be removed)—I'm feeling of the animal now, so nice and pink and warm—and *lonesome*. But I look too good to ruin: I wish my twin would come along and I'd kiss him.

The rocks are like clouds in the green black body of the sky-mountain. Darkness cures all.

◆

"Let's go back to America," Pavlik whispers on our cloud-lit (the moon was behind them) walk ... but he couldn't have meant it because before we got back to the house he mentioned our buying a French car. I told him one reason I'm enjoying Europe so much is that I feel I've escaped from the prison of America, where I was confined ten years. Europe, America—poetry, prose.

Bought masses of postcards, silent cinema stars—and a nun coming out of a rose for Joseph Cornell.

"Be not afraid of absurdity; do not shrink from the fantastic. Within a dilemma, choose the most unheard-of, the most dangerous solution. Be brave, be brave!" The Baroness (Blixen) speaking.

Pavlik says some old people have an old smell, not because they're not clean, but because they're old—like an old house.

And resist the weakness of letting myself be spit at—by myself (the white spit of the prick).

◆

Work in progress: *The Imaginary Theater* (poems in prose) ... allegorical. Emblematic. Symbolical. Fantastic. Marvelous. Sublime. ("The sublime is not everyone's climate"—P.) Supernatural. Mystic. Enigmatic. Mythological. Legendary. Heroic. Violent—tender (by turns). Incomprehensible. Startling. Surprising. Enchanting. Magical.

Pavlik at my instigation drawing geometrical faces which give the trompe-l'oeil of reversibility—the mask that looks forward, convex, and backward, concave.

OCTOBER

The French have no talent for the casual acquaintanceship—there's something stiff, formal, inflexible, unresponsive about them—in contrast with the Italians.

Pavlik says he feels like a "broken doll." We returned to Paris by way of Venice—having been invited by Peggy Guggenheim to be her guests. She was at the station to meet us, having come in her motorboat, with Philip Lesell. Mary Reynolds was also staying, Peggy said, and we were pleased. So we loaded all the luggage in the motorboat and set out for her white marble palazzo on the Grand Canal—built in the 17th century but with only one floor (besides the ground-floor "basement"). "It's called the unfinished palace," said Peggy. The exterior is attractive with silver-lace vines on the roof-terrace and huge (stone? marble?) lions' heads on the front—Mary Reynolds bumped her head on one and nearly fell in the canal one day while disembarking. The house is modernized inside, walls painted in not-quite-right solid shades, a Calder mobile hanging in the foyer, and in the garden a couple of Brancusis; otherwise her art collection is hard to look at, especially the messes signed Jackson Pollock.

Peggy gave us her big bedroom and bath, walls and floor of green marble. The second night she had told me to ask for dinner Léonor and Lepri, and they came and the dinner was dominated with Pavlik's and Léonor's animated conversation—I saw Philip make a moue to Mary because of the noise. At 3:30 in the morning Pavlik was seized with a return of his dysentery, and it continued for twelve hours, he staying in bed all of Saturday (our third day). The next day being Sunday, and we having our wagons-lit reservations to leave Monday, we thought it would be a good idea to call Peggy's doctor, and he came and prescribed a medicine, which did stop the dysentery, and also strongly advised an examination for the amoeba, after hearing the history of Pavlik's illness.

◆

When I left the library yesterday (I'm doing research on Baudelaire), I stopped in a pissoir and took the middle stall, looked to my left and saw a man furiously masturbating. As he masturbated he looked towards the street and I couldn't understand at first what his behavior meant—then I found out. I was having my first sight of a "satyre." He would stand brazenly at the entrance to the pissoir and masturbate in front of the eyes of passing women. His face looked rather faun-like, long; he wore sandals and had a bicycle leaning against the pissoir wall.

◆

Yesterday I met Max Ernst and Dorothea Tanning for lunch, they have a nice little room with a view, Hôtel du Midi, 4 rue du Parc Monsourris. Max looking fat—the fat in various lumps when he smiles, Dorothea on the plump side too. They're not too gay, not having too much money, no apartment (though the offer of one in Antibes—but Dorothea hasn't had her fill of Paris yet); said Breton was depressed—"He's been depressed for years," said I, and they said he's even more depressed now.

Last night Pavlik and I went to the ballet—saw Tamara Toumanova do *Les Sylphides* and she gives that ballet a modern raison d'être. Before the houselights came up we got up to go backstage and were pushing past a young lady who looked like a ballerina and who cried out, "Charlie," and it was Tamara. She said she'd be back in her dressing-room as soon as she spoke to [Marquis George de] Cuevas, so Pavlik and I went with Johnny Taras to the bar and on the way ran into Truman Capote—he gave the impression, while climbing the steps to the bar, that he was climbing them like a short caterpillar—and also at the bar, which he hung against as if holding onto it with caterpillar legs all along his body—clinging. When I introduced Truman to P., P. didn't say anything but looked at him with high disapproval—and changed his place to stand beside Johnny, at which Truman said to me, "Why did he look at me so strange?" and I said, "Perhaps he thought you look strange. Don't you like to look strange?" Truman had said, after I'd introduced them, "We've never met before!" Taras said to Pavlik later, "Truman said you were rude to him, and you were!" ... We went to the door leading backstage but it was locked, then spied Tamara and Cuevas talking in a baignoire so we went over and Pavlik thanked Cuevas for giving us Tamara, who is so beautiful and dances so divinely—"with divine madness," Pavlik said. Her face is unlike any other in the world—or any I ever saw—I mean so many women may look "vaguely" like Garbo but no woman looks vaguely like Toumanova—her nose is quite long and rather flat, yet retroussé in profile; huge eyes with lids like hoods; very little chin yet the jawbone line is firmly defined; hollow cheeks held up by visible cheekbones; a girlish smile that may disappear in a flash.

◆

Paris a small labyrinth—not only do people whom I know appear and reappear but people whom I don't know.

I ran into Carl Van Vechten on the Boulevard Haussmann, reeking of white wine—gentle and sympathetic in spite of all.

The appeal of Paris: I feel chez moi and at the same time in an exotic city—this "double action" is irresistible.

"Wild blue"—color of French eyes.

We invited Carl to come to tea today, after his letter saying how glad he was that I'd sent him to see *Ondine*. He made an observation about Jouvet's acting: "He listens so well."

This morning at 6 A.M. began the Drame du Cabinet in the hall outside—and it continued all afternoon. Two women were accusing each other of making a mess in the toilet, with the concierge chiming in. Finally the concierge decided that a little girl who didn't know any better was responsible—so she was telling her in a loud voice to hit the hole and not leave a mess, etc. Her parting words to one of the women: "Madame, ne vous faites pas de bile . . ."

When I went down for breakfast I found Pavlik with a fever of 101 and $^3/_5$. He told me—for some reason, suddenly—of three pictures he remembered painting in very early youth: one, Venus and Adonis, rose, in a sea-shell; then a forest scene with "fairies"—slim young boys with "dragonfly wings"; then a night scene with strange dark flowers.

"Don't sit on my soul," he says, when he thinks I'm impatient to have us leave.

Verses I wrote in Peggy Guggenheim's guestbook:

Water, my element, makes a dream of air.
Venice, gold phoenix, rises from fire.
Her veins of sunset never know night—
Narcissus of cities, hold tight, hold tight!

The whore (a new one) in next room is called Madame Rossignol (Mrs. Nightingale). According to Choura, she had a German aviator as lover during the Occupation. When there was an air-raid by the British, he'd go up to chase the raiders off, and Madame Rossignol used to show her concern. After the Liberation, she was having lunch one day with the (former) concierge, decided she wanted some mustard, went out to the charcouterie for it and didn't come back. The concierge, who was her friend, went out looking for her—and found her at the Préfecture de Police. Some woman had denounced the Nightingale as having consorted with the Germans. When the concierge explained that her metier was whoring, she was released.

◆

I went to see Léonor and took her a dozen large shaggy flowers, like purple and white cat's fur. She said that Max and Dorothea had been there yesterday and she met Dorothea for the first time, found her sympathetique. Léonor told Max that he ought to buy himself some teeth (only the two front ones seem intact).

◆

Choura coughs, and smokes, constantly—though she has only one lung and a bad throat besides. P. says she tells him she stays alive only for him—little she knows what a burden he considers her. It was rather ludicrous when she said, "Je ne demande rien de vous—" Merely her living. Poor thing is a moral and physical— and, Pavlik thinks—mental wreck. Her scalp eczema doesn't seem to be getting any better.

"The end of a family," comments Pavlik, "isn't very pretty."

NOVEMBER

After an excellent lunch of bleeding beef I made my prick bleed white blood . . . in honor of all the adolescents jerking off at the same moment all over the world.

Americans: big bony children.

◆

I dreamed of black centaurs. Their pricks were quite thick at the base and rosy-black on the head; they were peaceful. Further down in the rocks, a black seal boy—as if his arms had been cut off. I ran back up the hill from him, borrowed Pavlik's binoculars to look at the pricks, close-up.

◆

"Tu est d'un humeur de chien?" (Me.)

"Oui, un peu." (P.)

"Alors, dit 'bow-wow'!"

◆

Foolish sensation: letting a man of gross appearance jerk me off (in the pisserie) at seven after jerking myself off at 2:30.

Cecil said Truman was very insulted at the way Pavlik ignored their introduction. I told him that Pavlik acknowledged the introduction but had no reply to make to Capote's "We've never met ..." Cecil: "He's so young." I: "Sa voix n'est pas faite!"—as Jouvet says of Dominique Blanchard who has replaced Madeleine Ozeray in the revival of *Ondine*.

◆

At 4 A.M. I awoke—my wet dream was with Pavlik—he lay on his stomach et je l'ai enculé (I didn't tell him). But the hole I went in was not the ass hole: another one above it from which the prick came out—but the prick was pushed back in when I entered—certainly the trick of the week.

◆

Saw Breton walk past the Deux Magots with an old-fashioned long bob hanging down his neck, a pipe, and a woman; didn't stop him. "Vous êtes assez malin ..." (as he told me in the *View* office when I proposed that we publish a book of his poetry).

◆

Many souls make up The Soul, just as many parts of the body—liver, heart, lungs, etc. make up the body—when they function in harmony, all is well—sometimes they are in conflict. When all is well with *our souls*, then there is spiritual harmony.

◆

Drove my new Peugeot (with the mechanic)—rides real nice. And for the rodage it seems I can go as fast as 80 kilometers an hour—so we won't have to stay in Paris for that—we can go any time Pavlik feels like it!

◆

Les Ballets des Champs-Elysées. Jean Babillée made his appearance in his own creation, "Till Uelenspiegel"—first time I'd seen Babillée whom I'd heard praised by Boris Kochno as being such a wonderful dancer. He has boyish charm in his movements and looks—but he has no legs from the knees down! ... Finally came Bérard's much-praised ballet, *Les Forains*, with pleasant music by [Henri] Sauguet; Roland Petit's best choreography (with *Carmen*); Bébé unable to escape from impression Picasso and Tchelitchew made upon him—souvenirs d'*Errante* in particular: the figures of the acrobat and woman projected by shadows. Then a memory of Loïe Fuller—a term of criticism which Bébé flung in 1933 at *Errante* (which was not "Loïe Fuller" at all)—when those yards of white Chinese silk came tumbling down from heaven. In *Les Forains* Bébé dressed a little ballerina in the very model of Loïe Fuller's costume and dance—but on the "pathétique" side, expressly ... Still!

◆

Les Fourberies de Scapin. Barrault extraordinary—more commedia dell'arte than the Italians! Pavlik and I went backstage afterwards and instead of being shown into the little salon adjoining Barrault's dressingroom, where there were people waiting for him, someone indicated to Pavlik (after his "Je suis Tchelitchew") the door leading directly into the dressingroom—Barrault peeped out and then admitted us, seeing that it was Pavlik, whom he was expecting to meet for the first time. He was naked except for jockstrap (very well built—as one could judge, even with clothes) and being given a rubdown by masseur—he really gives a ballet performance and this athlete's treatment is very wise—an exhausting métier, and he looks worn but with much reserve strength. He told Pavlik, very amiably, that the theater was his (Pavlik's) anytime he wanted to come for any play. I thought Pavlik said many wrong things—against the theater (for being so ephemeral), and that he'd been ill for eleven years and that he wasn't staying long in France—"Je rentre bientôt" ... Pavlik is still like a shy child when it comes to meeting new people —but I shouldn't have reproached him (on the way home in the taxi) for his gaucheness.

◆

I saw the hole in the head of the bald animal, out of which its brain (the sperm) flowed.

◆

Dinner last night at the Mediterranée with Peter Watson. They gave us a table in front of the door and Pavlik made a fuss to have a screen put at his back, which the patron, very obligingly, arranged, also gave us cognac all around but all this did not persuade Pavlik to do a drawing in the guestbook—where we saw pages by Bébé (coffee-and-ink wash), plus Picasso, a portrait of Truman Capote by Cecil, a smeary Léger, Chagall, Miró ... Balthus, who was there, has a big picture (a Puss-in-Boots) on a wall, and Cocteau a pastel over the bar ... The range of Peter's sensibility is like a company of cripples—things missing here and there. When he said he was bored with "clever people" I said, "I should think you would be, after all these years with *Horizon*"—the magazine edited by Cyril Connolly and supported with Peter's money.

DECEMBER

"Whether one says gods or Buddhas, there is no difference between the water and the waves." (Nōh play.)

Me to Pavlik: "You take what you get; I get what I take!"

"One day I will be gone," he says.

I was putting on some kind of theatrical show—Gypsy Rose Lee was one of the entertainers—she held an umbrella on which I turned a hose from the wings. When I looked out at the audience there was no one but a few rows of nuns. (Dream of yesterday morning.)

1950

JANUARY

We have found and leased for six months a house we like at Grottaferrata, twenty or so kilometers from here; moving tomorrow.

◆

GROTTAFERRATA

We took the Signora Sereni, our landlady, to dinner last night at the trattoria across the road—the owner has four sons, two of them, at least, good-looking—Franco and Corrado. Corrado served us, went into half a dance when the radio let out American music.

"People sleep bad when they have dirty necks"—Pavlik.

I bought a little coral dog for P.'s charm collection but he seems to have lost it, which upsets him ("that means I have no wisdom").

What a beautiful wide view we have from the terrace (which runs all along the long dining-livingroom and my bedroom—southern exposure, sun all day)—with Rocca di Papa on the mountainside changing in detail as the light changes. From the front terrace, and from Pavlik's north window, may be seen the pine-crowned hill of Tusculum, where Marcus Cato was born.

Such good wine Domenico (the caretaker who lives down below with his wife, Bice) makes from the grapes he grows on Signora Sereni's little tract of land.

The wind doth blow.

"Bitch energy"—P. calls mine.

◆

We're wondering if we shouldn't send for Linda—she's working in Florence, having left her home in Molveno. But I guess we'll see first if our present maid, Regina, won't do—she nips at my cognac so I've locked it up.

Germans took over this house during the war—Signora Sereni came out one day to find some of them dressed up in her clothes, a party going on; she said she laughed. Then a bombardment started; the Germans fled to the fields and hills, she stayed trembling and crying in the garage—they came back and found her and told her to take the paintings which she'd come to ask for and which they'd refused—just before the bombardment started.

◆

Yesterday in Rome, Gaspero Del Corso of the Obelisco gallery amiable without being dull and he's proposed Pavlik a show in the spring. We came home to find the kitchen ransacked (in small amounts but detectable enough). Today I write Linda asking her if she'd like to come work for us.

These beautiful January afternoons like summer with a chill. The more one works the more one has the feeling of using time as it passes, instead of time using you. "The stars pull the strings," says Pavlik.

◆

Insomnia's an eerie room in which you find, sometimes, something you've been looking for.

Corrado brags but—

P. says when they have a big one they show it.

Staring at my standing one, I say, "If I like it so much—then get yourself one not your own!"—and put its unbloody, unbowed head back (in my pants).

◆

Corrado came by, bringing cheese, and sang after vermouth, in a sweet girlish voice.

I'm about to come again—I'll count the strokes one two three four five six seven, 8, 9, 10, 11, 12, 13, 14, 15, 16, 17, 18, 19, 20, 21, 22, 23 I'm coming!!!!!! Carlyle Brown sucked off seventy boys in Ischia last summer—said he threw rocks in a hole to keep count of them. I'd rather find one who pleased me enough to go to bed with seventy times.

Domenico: "Rain and death come suddenly."

◆

Driving in Rome is something like house-to-house fighting! We picked up Linda at the station.

A new road on our walk before lunch led to a marvelous surprise: the Villa Aldobrandini; courtyard décor embedded with statues, Atlas in the center, his world running with water.

The forests of the mind have fears as formidable as the snakes and tigers of the mountains. Sleep, sleep, Minotaur . . .

There was a tremendous circle around the moon last night ("like the ass-hole of the universe," I told Pavlik).

Ghyka (*Le Nombre d'Or*) points out that the words "number" and "rhythm" in

Greek are derived from the same root, "je coule"—(I flow, or, "I come"). Little boy, keep your hands where they will do most good: grasping pen or pencil, tapping typewriter keys, scratching symbols (words) instead of scratching your balls (you'd think the cats had been at them).

Even the sun can embrace but half the world at once.

FEBRUARY

"Maybe he's a hermaphrodite," Pavlik says about Corrado.

"No such luck," I say.

Edith sent Pavlik three huge rubber hotwater bottles—we'll all three—Pavlik, Linda and I—use them tonight.

Can one learn to be a poet? Could any other flower learn to be a rose?

The limitations of the lion.

"Snow!" yells Pavlik—and it's true—but it won't stay on the ground.

◆

Carnival at Frascati. A lady midget in a box, a hole for her to breathe through, two other holes for her hands to stick out—fingers with red nail-polish and one hand holding a cigarette in a holder; the barker referred to her as the "principessa." Boys hitting the girls over their heads with rubber cocks.

◆

Valéry's ideal in poetry: to combine "unembodied objects of pure intelligence" (a phrase I found in Plutarch, describing Plato's conception of geometry) with *sensation*: sensation as distinguished from sentiment. And he compares the "sensation" produced by poetry to that produced by music: through sound.

Wonderful description of a "neurosis" in Plutarch: "For the soul . . . being born to love . . . inclines and fixes upon some stranger, when a man has none of his own to embrace. And alien or illegitimate objects insinuate themselves into his affections, as into some estate that lacks lawful heirs; and with affection come anxiety and care . . ."

Dreamed Edith sent an enormous special edition of one of her books, as big as a bed, and one page was bordered with fresh roses and inside the next page were all kinds of fresh fish, dressed to be cooked.

The milkboy, about 13 or 14, comes by and rings the gate-bell, pulling on the bell-rope as if he were jerking off a man . . . Pink-headed, dark-balled, hairy-based animal—it swells. Its face is red as someone's palate.

◆

The Dutch photographer (25) who came for tea with Lepri, Del Corso and Fabrizio Clerici. He wore a dark leather glove over his left hand, but the stiffness of it indicated there was no hand there. I asked him, "How did you hurt your hand?" and he told the story of his accident in the darkroom, on the top floor of his house in Haarlem, two years ago. There was an explosion of acid due to contact with electricity, not only his hand was wounded but his thigh, near where the appendix would be if it were on the left. He lost most of his blood before they got him to the hospital—had a pint or so left—the surgeon cut off his hand and sewed up the other wound. He couldn't walk for months and when he did start to walk the wound bled every ten days or so, there had to be another operation and a part of the artery was cut away. Surgeon predicted that he would either lose his leg or be a cripple, but he mended and here he is with an iron hand which he used once to bang over the head of a Negro—whom he'd seen gouge out someone's eye—in a jitterbug joint in Amsterdam.

I heard him talking with Pavlik—which means that Pavlik was doing most of the talking, and I was startled by hearing Pavlik say, "I look exactly like Hans Christian Andersen . . . we have the same hands . . ."

MARCH

It's raining on all four sides and in the middle.

Pavlik, reading Edith's *The Canticle of the Rose*, insists that he doesn't want to visit the Sitwells in their castle at Monteguffoni. He says she dotes on death and doesn't know who Venus is.

"Il professore" he was referred to, respectfully, by the electrician yesterday, so Linda and I call him professore now, he's half teased, half pleased.

Jung (in *Modern Man in Search of a Soul*): ". . . as long as we are still submerged in nature we are unconscious, and we live in the security of instinct that knows no problems." In 1932, in Madrid, Carlos Enriquez gave me one of his drawings, of my own selection, a portrait of Hamlet, and inscribed it, "To C.H.F., who has no Ophelias to mourn and no problems to solve."

Pavlik says Derain was against his lighting the white decors of *Errante* with colored lights—saying how beautiful they were, simply white. Pavlik told him a white canvas is beautiful too but one puts paint on it.

◆

My Siamese twins (as Jung says the testicles are "vulgarly" called) are beginning to feel rather lonesome.

I just returned from a walk in the landscape which I see from my window: the long valley many shades of green, touched with the pink and white of flowering trees like wisps of cloud.

Pavlik asks me who I saw on my walk.

"The only one I saw was fuckable Franco."

Pavlik: "I'm sure his father fucks him—"

I: "I hope so."

If sperm has eyes—how it must blink when spilled in one's hand in the daylight; but if it goes directly into another's body—then it goes from dark to dark.

Linda looks this morning as if she'd masturbated *too* . . . That manhandling of the Siamese Twins won't do—one of them's sore (the one that swelled when I got the clap which hit me on my first voyage to France, 1931).

I suppose I'm *equally* active and passive when it comes to sex—the final choice, had I to make one, would be *active*—I.e. if I had to choose between the manly wood-carving creature (at Grottaferrata fair) and the tender milkboy (whom I should treat as if he were a girl).

> Therefore, brave conquerors,—for so you are
> That war against your own affections,
> And the huge army of the world's desires—
> (*Love's Labors Lost.*)

At the street fair in Grottaferrata I had my fortune told twice—buying slips of paper, one from a blond bearded man with a turban and a marmoset—another from a man who had a little theater with a gypsy queen doll that moved. There's going to be a "separation" and I'm going to be "rich." There was the usual village drunk, and the beggar showing his truncated leg, and the father beating his son until he cried. Pavlik marveled at how I enjoyed mixing with and rubbing against the crowd . . .

The milkboy's first name is (in Italian) Warrior and his last name Peace! (Guerrero Pace.)

In bed at bedtime: I've just shot what looks like a white sea of come.

◆

Under the influence of Bachelard's *L'Eau et les Rêves* I dreamed of trying to fathom the origin of human life. My conception amounted to this: disembodied forces of the unconscious (Jung's primeval chaos) pouncing upon the drops of sperm which engender the child. These forces being limited by the form of matter, as the embryo grows (encouraged by these very forces *seeking form*) more and more "forces" grow with it—until a whole army of them are in the child and, as the child grows, in the man. When the body dies, these forces return to the disembodied, from where they came: they are immortal.

APRIL

"All day long she plays with her cunt," says Pavlik about Linda. "That's why sometimes she's so dumb."

He said the milkboy looks like "an animal that bites."

Childhood—the Underground Movement which always takes over—with Time.

◆

Age: 21, teeth perfect, eyes rather as if he'd had a Chinese grandmother (Italian father), height medium, hair black as coal, smiling always, talking, lonesome, makes 200 lire a day (32¢) besides room and board (he has a roof over his head)—but what board—bread for lunch, soup at night. No work, he said, in his little town— he's the second oldest of four brothers, has four sisters, will work here as a shepherd three months, then go elsewhere. One of his brothers is a carabinieri in

Rome; he doesn't know how far his hometown is from here—he came in a truck at night, with six others, they've all scattered. Sisto is his name.

He gets up at 5, I don't know if he's finished work until nine or ten at night; said he quit his last shepherding job after 40 days, didn't like the way the wife of the patrone fed him. Since he doesn't smoke, I gave him some candy (he wanted to refuse the second piece). I asked when the sheep would make love and he told me Saturday (in large numbers, apparently)—so the young ones will be born in September.

Sisto is by far the prettiest thing I ever saw in the world—to be so lonely! How to make him fond of me? By giving him presents, of course.

> ... there is no evil angel but Love.
> (Shakespeare.)

Anyone who has such a pleasing pleasant and smiling face knows what a charming effect he has on people. The ugly little shepherd, on the other hand (met the other day on the road to Tusculum), has a miserable life because he *is* ugly—he feels no one wants to pet him ...

◆

In the market-place: a little girl's pushing a littler girl's screaming face in the placid face of a munching sheep ... A trembling white duck being weighed in hand-scales: part of the trembling world, part of me.

◆

As soon as we returned from Rome yesterday (where we went to take Del Corso the drawings for Pavlik's show) I set out to find Sisto—having brought him a couple of picture-papers and a chocolate bar. I saw his flock before I could find him—he was up on a hill and lying down, with a paper cap on his pretty head and a bunch of wild asparagus in his hand. We wandered about and he showed me a grotto. When I pissed, he didn't—but waited until he was further off where I couldn't see him. We talked of girls and he said he'd never made love with a sheep but I don't think he was telling the truth. I'll suggest we take a sheep to the grotto and screw it—while he is screwing the sheep I'll hold its head and when he starts to approach the climax I'll kiss him! ... The rams now have their stomachs shaved, all around the cock, so as to be prepared to take on the ewes when they arrive in heat.

Sisto has strange ideas about the English—said an Italian prisoner of war, who'd been interned in England, told him the English laugh and dance when someone dies, cry when a baby is born ... His ewes were calling their missing young ones, which had been taken away to be slaughtered for eating; he said they'd continue to call for a couple of days.

◆

Easter Sunday. The day is clear as clear. We've chocolate eggs for all the children around—and I've a sugar sheep to give the milkboy to suck.

◆

Contessa Pecci-Blunt (Mimi) gave a large cocktail-buffet for Pavlik in her Rome palazzo. I met, among others, the poet Ungaretti—face of an old Satyr. Janet Flanner was there, and told me that when she saw that lovely Man Ray photo of Djuna in the April *Flair* she thought of me, my cap and cape in Paris, 1932, when I was living with Djuna at her rue St.-Romain apartment. I said, "I thought of Djuna!" Mina Loy lived on the floor below, one morning came up while Djuna and I were having breakfast, saw an empty vinegar bottle in the kitchen, picked it up and waved it about, saying, "Did you have a night of love? Did you have a night of love?"

Then Janet, sex-gossip-loving, mentioned something about Djuna's pregnancy, when she had to return from Tangier in 1933. I said, "That wasn't me!" and since Janet had always thought it was, I told her the man's name (whispering it in her ear) and that she shouldn't tell Djuna ... Then, as Janet was going ... "Not that I didn't try ... Goodnight!"

Pavlik, re Mimi: "Her actual life is like a cobweb which she wants to tear off and know what she is ..."

◆

Wind and rain all night—but after tea it was nice enough for walking. Pavlik turned back at a fork on the hill and I went on to seek my shepherd, Sisto. I found him roping barrels of water on a mare and I helped him (he asked me to)—his face across the pack-saddle was like a young Buddha's. We walked back with the mare and a young horse to where the sheep-milking pen is, meeting on the way his patrone, Vincenzo. The mare was in heat and the young horse tried to get on her, his long pink and black thing standing like a baseball bat held at the wrong end; the mare kicked up and he didn't succeed in getting in her so Vincenzo haltered both their pairs of front feet and sent them down into the field. Enter another shepherd, whose name turned out to be Fausto—the opposite physical type from Sisto: tall and blond, with a faun's mouth and nose. He gazed over the fields and said there were three couples down there—fucking, I suppose—so were the sheep—some of them—I went into the sheep-pen to look on. Then I went back to the row of stalls, where Sisto and Fausto were milking—the ewes crowded in one by one, without being herded or called. There was room for only one at a time to take its place, where it was held with a wooden halter while Sisto, by whom I squatted, squirted milk with both hands into the wooden tub. When I got home at past 6:30 Pavlik was having visions of my being murdered in a cave.

◆

Parker prefers my sonnets (in *A Pamphlet of Sonnets*)—1936—to all my other poems—finding a certain "grandeur" in them. I wonder if I should not return to that
form to see what violent metamorphoses may be managed now—within the sonnet's metrical strictness and circumscribed space. The attraction of the sonnet for
me is the fact that it may be *completed* in fourteen lines—the *satisfaction of comple-
tion is enormous* . . . Here I go, jumping from Baudelaire back in my own bed—of
poetry. The waters of dream recede.

◆

"You know why the lights went off at my exhibition yesterday?" asks Pavlik and I
say No, and he says, "Florine came." He says she (Florine Stettheimer) always
comes to his exhibitions (I can't remember what year it was, in the mid-forties,
that she died). No fuse was blown, and the lights came back on after a minute or so.
"That's why Del Corso was terrified—he knew," says P. . . . We arrived at the Obelisco around 4:40 and no one was there. Princess Colonna was one of the first to
wander in. Del Corso whispered to me that she'd been a big friend of Mussolini
and doesn't buy pictures. Later the gallery was packed. Pavlik says the reactions of
the Americans were the dumbest.

   We heard a nightingale's "coloratura" (as Pavlik called it) on our pre-lunch
walk. "The voice of nature," he said—"better than all the other compliments."

◆

Finished the sonnet begun yesterday ("What kind of poem would I like to
write?"). Pavlik suggested I change the word "eye" to "ear"—so I gave it to him—
he was pleased as a child.

SONNET
(For Pavlik's exhibition, Rome 1950)

What kind of poem would I like to write?
One in which the images are new
and yet fill one with pleasure, like a face
that's strange but which we recognize with joy
mixed with nostalgia. When the thick blood
of winter's cut like a cake by the sun's gold knife—
have a piece! It's the birthday of the world.
A lamb may sing like a bird, a bird may bleat;
flowers smile as though no one were poor,
oxen make an inarticulate
music as if no one were too rich.
One ear is not less awesome than a pair.

What kind of poem would you like to read?
What kind of life is there still left to lead?

◆

He was so *displeased* with Kirk Askew's letter saying the drawings looked "arbitrary" (in the photographs sent to him).

◆

Art is form but inspiration comes from Chaos.

◆

"What do you know?"
It's midnight, or daytime.
"But have you lived a lifetime?"
That I don't know.

◆

Lorca's "Green, green, I love you green" could be extended into: He had a heart shaped like green.
    "A country cursed by dying bulls"—Pavlik's words on Spain.

◆

Edith is at Osbert's Castello di Monteguffoni near Florence and is expecting us to come and visit them the middle of May. She writes: "I had a perfectly *hideous* time getting here. I had no food excepting four small pieces of ham, and some dry bread, from Friday to Sunday night. I had a fearful row with Italian customs at 8 A.M. in a blinding snowstorm, having not been given time to dress properly, so that I was drenched. Finally, I arrived at Pisa to find all my luggage gone, and no motor waiting for me. I waited for one hour in the midst of a giggling crowd staring at me. I can't speak Italian, Monteguffoni is a 2 and $^3/_4$ hours drive over the mountains, from Pisa, I don't know the way, and expected to spend the night in the taxi on the mountains . . . I am still feeling a little battered, and have very bad filiositis (?) as a result of my battle in the snow."
    Sade: "You will know nothing if you have not known everything, and if you are timid enough to stop at the natural, it will always escape you."

◆

I saw a mad dog shotgunned in the piazza at Frascati—by a civil guard—a crowd gathered around it—I wouldn't have approached except that I took the opportunity to speak to a boy in a beret, on a bicycle, whose looks, legs and buttocks appealed to me—but he didn't pursue the opening so all I got was the sight of the relaxed ass-hole of the dead dog oozing a big piece of shit.

MAY

I'm making a list of words found by going over the dictionary systematically (i.e., one letter at a time), words which strike me for one reason or another: for freshness, or familiar words which might seem strange in a poem: yesterday, for example, I extracted "acetelyne torch" and "billiard cue" and they fit perfectly into my hommage for De Chirico.

And to mock. Use words in a favorable or complimentary sense which have always been used in a derogatory sense, and vice versa.

All of Edith's highly plumaged, witty early poetry was like a mating call—which was never answered.

A proverb in the candy box said sex, like death, would come without being called.

◆

Experience in fabricating . . . Here's my method: having made a list of dictionary words, words which struck a spark in my fancy, for one reason or another (reasons I do not stop to define), I make combinations of these words into phrases which may be used, as the subjective or objective parts of a sentence. After the phrases are made I divide them into two groups, object and subject. This morning there were twelve in each group; I laid the typed slips face down on the table. I also had a list of verbs, mostly active, which I typed and put in a box, all shuffled up. Next I proceeded to form my sentences—"Superstations of Grottaferrata"—by choosing blindly, at hazard, a subject-phrase, then the verb, then the object-phrase. Example results:

"Irresolute gamecocks provoke Lesbian uprisings."
"Indoctrinated electricians cradle emasculatory emotions."
"Three equilibrists in a turret presuppose forthright
    lasciviousness."

◆

MONTEGUFFONI

I spotted the castle (who could miss it?) as we turned a curve on the dusty gravel road out of Montagnana. (Osbert's father imposed a Gothic affixation onto the simply medieval tower which ruins it.) The castle isn't pretty from the outside (nor is it what I would call handsome on the inside). Edith met us in the courtyard in black dress and heavy black coat and wide-brimmed green straw hat. We sat in the garden, where there's a covered terrace, and had tea. I remarked (to myself) how smooth, unlined, Edith's forehead still is. Then Osbert came back, sweating and red from a walk, wearing a loud blue-plaid American jacket. He showed us our rooms, after going through endless others, mostly bare, one with a fantastic gold-carved four-poster bed (no one sleeps there). Osbert said the castle was a tenement when his father bought it, with 280 people living here. There's a nicely proportioned courtyard which my room overlooks, a well in one corner—long long ago a woman drowned herself in it, her husband was let down by ropes to fetch her body, attached her body to the ropes, but as his friends hauled the corpse up it became unattached, or the ropes broke, and it fell on the poor husband and killed him. I said to Osbert, "Don't tell Pavlik the story, he'll imagine the place is haunted."

At dinner Edith told us again about the trouble she had getting here. There was no "motor" to meet her in Pisa. "I am known in Pisa," she said, "for the way I walk up and down, wringing my hands." After dinner we walked to the terrace (everyone but Edith, who started looking ill-at-ease during dinner, whether because she had drunk too much, or was feeling ill for some other reason—or whether she was displeased because the conversation wasn't going the way she had imagined or hoped it would)—and there were fireflies, a new moon, and a band practicing somewhere (sounding like a small circus). At eleven Edith said goodnight and that she'd see us this morning at 10:30. "So late?" I asked, and she made it ten.

When Pavlik started to insist that I sleep in his bed because he was "afraid" to sleep alone, I had no intention of doing so, then he began to blackmail me by saying he'd never design a play of mine if I refused to do as he asked. I tried to get him to go to bed alone, saying I'd come to his bed if he were still awake at midnight, but he wouldn't do that, so I said, "All right, I'll come to your bed, but if I'm not asleep by midnight then I'll return to my room"—and I left my bedside light on. I dropped off to sleep very quickly, but was awakened by Pavlik's snoring, so I decided to make my escape. Very quietly, I slipped from beneath the mosquito netting, quietly opened the door and made my way to my room. Pavlik didn't discover I was gone till almost dawn—he says I must come sleep in his bed again tonight, however.

◆

GROTTAFERRATA

Our second and last day at Monteguffoni consisted, among other things, of being taken for a tour of the castle and gardens by Osbert. There's a grotto with clay statues (frog-men), where the water doesn't trickle anymore, a chapel crammed with the bones and skulls of saints, in glass and gold boxes—one with the bones bound and decorated with coral beads and rosettes … I should like to believe with Krishna that one should not mourn, either for the living or for the dead.

On how many shoulder-blades have you wanted to cut your throat?

◆

Mountains change, even the bare rock ones with their melting leaves of snow.

Pavlik is absolutely as wild as a domestic cat—always ready to be petted or frightened.

◆

As unlikely as the broadcast of the song of the fly hovering about the urinal of the men's room at the 3rd Avenue and 53rd Street subway stop.

No longer than the time it takes to see an egg fall from your hand to the kitchen floor.

◆

Sitwellian theme-song:

> I've never been a crashing bore,
> I never hope to be one,
> But I can tell you anyhow
> I'd rather be than see one!

Pavlik: "I'm ready for the nursing home."

JUNE

The highest-headed wheat is always empty—a Russian proverb (as reported by the Professore).

The most charming picture: Sisto leaning on his shepherd's staff, on the right, with his head inclined to the left, making such a pretty curve of the neck.

Miss Filth of 1950 (Linda). Women in general are terrible bores: Aeschylus was so right in his continual railing against them.

"I wish I could have a character like yours—that's what my sister said."

"Why?"

"You don't care about anything." (P. to me.)

◆

When I went in the car to fetch Sisto I found him with Fausto, each with a bowl of long green beans (their breakfasts). He changed from his pants with leggings to long khaki pants, which made his legs look shorter, somehow, and off we went. Stopped in Albano to complete supplies for picnic—I had brought only a liter of red wine, cheese, and tea and chocolate bar, so we bought bread, prosciutto, olives and cherries. Arrived under the pines, no one on the beach, Sisto apologized for his dirty feet, so I suggested we go in the water at once and wash them. That was at 11 A.M. We enjoyed our swim, came out and applied Nivea suntan oil to our faces and to each other's backs. What I'd guessed about Sisto's legs was confirmed when I saw him in bathing trunks: he practically dwindles away. Quite (too) narrow shoulders, wonderful back, breast and nipples, fine arms, non-muscular stomach. After sunning about an hour we had another dip, I took some photos of him, then we set off to find a place in the shade, to eat. I selected a spot which seemed secluded enough, though near a path, under a spreading pine tree. I spread my beach towel and we ate everything in sight and drank all the wine as well as some cognac which I'd brought in a little bottle and it all went to Sisto's head and he talked and talked and we both felt quite good. Started looking at the map to find out where he lived and our bodies got sort of entwined. The map away, I suggested that we take a nap—he turned on his stomach—but I got him on his back and my hand found the place it was after because my wrist had been pressing it and it was more than half hard and he asked about mine and I brought his hand down to it and he commented on how much bigger mine was than his (all with the birds singing) . . . Then he said he didn't want to, that he'd done it ("sega" is the Italian word for masturbation) the day before—said *if he'd known* he wouldn't have done it—but before he'd hidden his prick's head, there upon it I spied what was undoubtedly a round sore. He got off the beach towel and I got to my knees and he stood by me and looked at my gun firing its white load.

The sun was half-clouded but it was hot enough to make me want to go in the water again—he thought it would be too cold with the sun not out full blast so I went in naked, alone, and came out with a hard on, saying It's hot and he said, "Se vede."

ENOUGH TO MAKE A ROTTER TOTTER

My marrow's mistreated,
My turpor's tormented,
Narcotics exhausted,
And I need a manicure.

◆

I was saying to Pavlik (he corrected me on the "ideal" form of earth—I was citing marble and he said No, crystal, which makes the diamond) how the four elements resemble each other: earth as crystal resembles air, also water—and fire, in its highest form, la flamme blanche.

Rimbaud's so young discovery of his unconsciousness, and his natural moving therein: I am reminded of it by Gide's description of the new-born lizard: he saw it come from the egg, then "It trotted with a surprising agility, a sureness of movement as perfect as that of an adult and not at all astonished by the sudden discovery of the exterior world." Rimbaud's baby sureness, not at all astonished by his discovery of the interior, unconscious world.

◆

I'm not going to smoke this morning though I've a whole pack of cigarettes (those nasty Nazionales) to tempt me—the pack was bought as a present for Luigi and I didn't see him when I went to the beach yesterday. Luigi is a goatherd I met day before yesterday. At the beach I'd taken a walk up towards the 600-year-old ruined tower of San Lorenzo, saw a khaki-colored figure moving among the pines and scrub-oaks, on the other side of the dunes; then I lost sight of him, then he emerged over the dunes and I made my way towards him from the water and he came towards me, looking as though he wanted to ask me something and he did— if I'd seen two horses, and I told him No. He was young, not handsome but masculine-looking with thick black lashes. I asked him if he'd like a cigarette and he walked down the beach with me to where my things were. Then I invited him to have lunch with me (share my picnic)—he accepted, though saying he wasn't hungry (bread for breakfast, bread for lunch). So we ate, and drank a liter of wine between us, and he loosened up a bit in conversation (having been shy and mono-syllabic at first), said he wanted to bring me some goats cheese next time I came down—he owns the goats himself, lives for them, he said, taking them to the mountains in the summer, returning to the warm sea in the winter. We were both feeling good with the wine and I felt as if I'd like to feel of him but didn't know quite how to start so I suggested we go in for a dip and took out of my zip bag the blue latex trunks for him to wear—to change he moved shyly apart but I said there was no one to see him and went over to show him how to put the trunks on—reached down into the trunks and showed him how the cock and balls should be placed—placing them in the sex supporter so they'd be pulled up, com-plimented him on the size of his thing and he was pleased and asked if I had a big one too—to which I didn't reply but moved towards the water. We took a very brief dip and came out to sun in the hazy sun, I sat on my beach towel and invited him to do likewise when he wanted to sit apart on the sand. Then I took my trunks off and told him to do likewise and he did. I asked him when he had last made "la sega" and he said that morning—twice! We 69'd. Such unabashed simplicity and uninhibited impulse! . . . We made a date to meet yesterday for another picnic and I don't know why he wasn't there—living for his beasts again I guess.

But someone else was there—swimming all alone and looking very bronzed in the incredibly blue water. I (deliberately of course) went in exactly where he was and was surprised to find a "fairy" voice coming out of this masculine-looking curly-headed creature. He turned out to be a goatherd too (aged 17, Luigi is 19) and I finally made up my mind to invite him to eat with me (since Luigi hadn't shown up) and we went to the shade spot where I'd been with Sisto. He turned out to be very sweet (Francesco by name), and after lunch we had a masturbation party—he said, Let's see which one will be the first to shoot. Then he told me practically the whole story of *The Count of Monte Cristo*, which he'd read recently. I gave him a gold-foiled covered big piece of chocolate, like a coin, with the head of Caesar on it, to take back and share with 20-year-old Marcello, with whom he shares a hut. They never masturbate together, he said.

◆

Pavlik's working on a beautiful pink gouache of a head like a rose: he's discovered that the muscle-pattern of the head corresponds to the original five-petaled Damask rose.

"We lose our hair but not our vices"—Domenico quotes a proverb.

P. admitted at breakfast that he woke up with such a hard on at 4:30 A.M. that he jerked off—hard like a 17-year-old, he said.

Some Italians have the most endearing way of smiling: with both eyes and both lips.

We're getting ready to leave for Lévico, to see what's there on the lake. No place in the world I'd like to stay for more than six months at a time.

◆

LÉVICO

Tonight we're undecided whether or not to settle down here for the summer. I found an apartment in a peasant's house and Pavlik liked it but there are drawbacks. However, the owner's son, Gino, is beautiful—a peasant-poet, says he has a passion for literature, loves Leopardi. He's brunet, with light eyes, sweet expression—he wants us to take the apartment and would reduce the price but I doubt if we shall—the altitude here is not what Pavlik needs, too low. Besides, the lake's water is not too clear, a cloudy darkish green, gravelly bottom in the beginning, then it turns to mud. Gypsies camp nearby, in bright-colored costumes, with bright pillows and stuffs—they have half a dozen strong handsome horses. A gypsy woman asked me for 10 lire for bread for the child then proposed to read my hand and I let her—she said I had an amico who wished me well from his heart but that an end would soon come to our friendship.

◆

MOLVENO

Before leaving Lévico I went to find Gino and said goodbye—He's angelic and accepted my invitation to come see us here in mid-July. He vows that one day he will throw over the work of contadino, leave everything and devote himself to literature. He said he has suffered much, not physically but morally, and thinks he looks older than his twenty-five years—that's the age I guessed he was. (His father gave me twenty-two years and when I said Yes, he said he was never mistaken in guessing people's ages!)

Today we went to Italo's and found him and his wife Gisella and we agreed to take the top floor of their house—with the provision that they add a studio room for Pavlik.

JULY

Our house is at the mouth of what would be called a canyon in America, and the sound of the stream and waterfall (which may be seen if you stretch your neck) comes up; pure blue-white water. Impossible to imagine a place more peaceful and romantic, pastoral and undepraved. Pavlik thinks this lake, because of the satiny sapphire, but darker than sapphire, blue this morning, must be (one of) the most beautiful in the world.

Performance below dining balcony: charcoal besmudged boy and his blonde sister Agnese. He's drunk and declamatory ("Lavoro con mia vita!"), was wallowing on the ground, his feet in the flowerbeds, now he's staggering and up ("Avanti!"), with a bleeding elbow. His lips, quite thick and pink, stand out from the blackened face: Linda tossed the two of them a couple of candies, now I've asked if he wants coffee and he replied, "Molto!" . . . He's singing and smiling now, holding out his beret ("Jesu Cristo" is all I understand from the song, plus, "Avanti, avanti . . ." This beret will be respected, I think he sang . . .) Now he's dancing, holding his arms as if with a partner. Then he argues with his sister about the satchel, then sings again.

Linda made the coffee and poured it into a small milk can, mixing some ashes in (which she said was good for sobering up drunks)—I took it down to him but he was insulted when I said it was good for an "Umbriaco"—so I left it down on the tiles. He went to the road, talking to his sister, now he's back up on the lower terrace. Linda is urging him to drink the coffee but he says he won't drink it. Now he's singing the song about "questo beretto" again—"Who knows what will happen to him who wears the beret?" the song goes (in Italian) . . . Now the boy is singing around the corner of the house—I'll go see if he's decided to drink the coffee . . .

Yes, he drank most of it. Suddenly fell down by the gravel-pile and seemed to sleep—I went and got my camera, took the little sister by the hand, led her near him and got a picture of them both, he in a picturesque curled pose. He woke up immediately after.

◆

Our second twenty years is merely a struggle to fulfill and gratify the ideals and appetites of our first twenty years.

Pavlik says the specialty of the German doctor here is taking care of all the cunts and cocks. "Women love to show their cunts," says P.

Giuliano, the Sicilian bandit who captured the heart and imagination of so many, is dead—machine-gunned by the police. He still had beautiful eyes, though he was getting fat. Looked rather like a Greenwich Village Italian gangster—one of those who went to bed with me at 28 Grove Street (1930).

Baudelaire wrote (in a letter to his mother, 1861): "Quant à bruler les livres, cela ne se fait plus, excepté chez les fous qui veulent faire flamber du papier ..." Edward James and Edith Sitwell ("fous," etc.?) burned *The Young and Evil* in the fireplace at West Dean (Edward's country estate) ... soon after it was published, 1933. Little she knew that in another fifteen years she'd be writing an introduction to another of my books.

◆

Go back to music, rhythm, as Yeats did, for a renewal of inspiration in poetry! "Go back" in the sense of renewal—say one proceeds in a horizontal spiral, one seems to be going back, even as one goes forward. And what, in the infinite sphere of the universe, is horizontal and what is vertical?

◆

The riff-raff of the marrow, summoned by self-abuse—and the Italians are so *naturally* friendly—unlike the reasoning French who must have a reason.

How can one doubt the hierarchy of beings when one hears the noise chickens make? And they have hearts like humans!

◆

That snake-headed thing, why do we worship it so? Because it gives us a little pleasure? Pleasure is something no one can resist. The thought of Nirvana is the hope of uninterrupted pleasure.

"Thus Psyche became at last united to Cupid, and in due time they had a daughter born to them whose name was Pleasure." (Bulfinch.)

Dear Jung is so sensible about sex: "A direct unconstrained expression of sexuality is a natural occurrence and as such neither unbeautiful nor repulsive. The 'moral' repression makes sexuality on one side dirty and hypocritical, on the other shameless and obtrusive."

◆

Telegram from Giovanni wanting me to meet him at a hotel in Verona tomorrow—in reply to my note saying I'd like to come to Garda (where he lives) when he takes his vacation!

◆

Giovanni left this morning after spending three nights with us. The story of Giovanni I'll tell tomorrow.

◆

"Giovanni creates immediately a whore-house atmosphere," said P. this morning. "Yes," I agreed. "I suppose that's why you like him," he added.

Giovanni with his over-smoking, over-driving (himself as well as car)... It all began, with him, the summer of 1935—and, when he arrived the other day, we hadn't seen him for fifteen years. He asked how old I was and I said, The same age as you. What year were you born? 1919. What month? February. What day? The 10th. What hour? Five minutes before midnight. Then, he said, you're three hours older than I am.

That summer, in Garda, Pavlik and I were at the Albergo Terminus, wanting to find a house on the lake for a couple of months. We met Giovanni at the swimming spot—pretty, slim but large body, tiny nose, very gay, smiling and agreeable in every way. When we finally found a house in Malcesine he came over on his bicycle several times. Giovanni told me this time that he hadn't known "anything" at that time (but he did it so naturally)... And the jacket? I asked (the other night)— I wore it three years, he said. How can I ever forget his asking for it almost at the moment of climax (mine, I was inside him). Pavlik did a charming portrait of him, in green straw hat (he did one of me, same summer, in pink straw hat).

A year or two later, an appeal for money came from him and we wired him some, from America ... After the war (1945?) I got in touch with him again and sent him some packages. He sent me recently a photo and I was shocked at the change, he'd lost most of his hair and looked unrecognizable. But when he appeared here unexpectedly the other day he was very recognizable: same nose, same spontaneous laugh, same body too though everything had grown larger. But he has aged, getting a double chin, and the thin hair (on top) makes him look a vigorous 41 instead of 31. He said he'd have recognized Pavlik but not me! Said I looked thin and where was my curly hair (he remembers the waves P. put in the portrait-in-the-pink-hat).

He was most affectionate and the last time we were in my bed here, said he was *perhaps* in love with me, how he's never forgotten, etc.

His job is representing textile manufacturers, they gave him a car (which he has to pay rent on—so much that he could buy it for the same amount—except he hasn't paid up all he owes). He says he feels he can't go forward any more and wants to go to America (Venezuela). He owes money to all his friends and is in a spot with his boss, having accepted and spent money from a customer, thinking to be paid by another so as to even accounts, etc. (same old story of "embezzle-ment")—had a check made out to him for 25,000 lire which he hoped to get us to endorse—but who knows whether it was any good. When he left, day before yes-terday morning, I had the garage put on my bill 10 liters of gasoline for his car, a liter of oil . . . and he made a last (desperate) request that I endorse his check at the bank but I told him there was no bank in Molveno.

He'd brought along a pack of obscene photos and a booklet with pornographic illustrations—some of them funny—he left the lot in my custody, saying he'd give me some of them next time he visited us . . . He was in my bed for the second time, in the afternoon, and when I came in his mouth he left the jism there a while and then before jumping out of bed spit it all in my pubic hair, laughing about it.

AUGUST

A day of heaven. The ruffled lake leaves a mirror-smooth area in the middle . . . Oh the blue trees . . .

The highest point of the Nōh art (of acting and writing) is called "the flower." Seami (according to Arthur Waley) says "the 'flower' . . . consists in forcing upon the audience *an emotion which they do not expect.*"

Telegram from Gino saying he will arrive tomorrow afternoon from Lévico—he has an invitation to stay with us several days, or a week—I don't know how long he'll stay or what to expect.

◆

Gino is here. He is unbelievably sweet and pure. We took a nap together after lunch and he was very affectionate and caressing but—"If you were a girl . . ."

He kissed me goodnight but wouldn't let me sleep with him.

◆

Gino's asked me never to say again that I'd like to sleep with him. I'd kissed him on the lips and he'd responded with the information that men never kiss men on the lips.

◆

Alors ... G is the most poetic companion imaginable, quoting Virgil and Dante, taking my hand, giving me flowers ... he kisses me goodnight on forehead or cheek. "... a tongue unpractised in pleasure." (Mallarmé.)

He showed me a postcard which he said he was sending to his "fidanzata"—then admitted that he had none—asked me if I were "displeased" at the idea of his having a fiancée and I said No. I asked him if he never went dancing in Lévico with girls or to the movies or walking and he said No, that the walk we took that day gave him more pleasure than any walk he might take with a girl. But he explained very convincingly why he couldn't make love with me—giving as an example a woman who was in love with him but for whom he didn't feel anything. This woman had kissed him, etc. but he was left cold—so it's not simply that I'm a man, but that he can't *pretend* with his feelings.

He thinks that he's aged beyond his years, saying that he must look 30 or 35 but I said No, your eyes are those of a child—now he insists that he *is* a child—"bambino"—insofar as experience of the world goes. *This is the first time in all his life that he's spent even one night away from home.* He's never had a vacation, never ceased to work since he quit school at the age of twelve. His reading tastes—for Dante, Leopardi and other poets—came out of himself. His first night here he wrote 3 short poems—first he ever wrote—quite simple, charming—and a 4th (inspired by the lake) the next morning. I told him I was sure he could write a book—autobiographical. His mother died when he was five.

He says he dislikes his own face, thinks his cheekbones (which I told him were photogenic) and head, too large. I tell him he's beautiful—he says it's too late to arouse his vanity.

◆

We took a rowboat down to a little pebbly beach opposite an island (quite small) of rocks. We sunned and swam. What was I to expect? He played with my hair, took my long hands in his square ones, put his arms around me ...

Back at the house I showed him the obscene book of Giovanni's. He seemed shocked, and, after absorbing it at length, threw it on the table (mentioned the danger connected with its falling into a young boy's hands!) ... He went to Mass on Sunday.

He thinks his mouth is too big too—I told him a big mouth indicated sensuality, he admitted the possibility.

Four of five years ago when the Germans were in Lévico one of their cars ran over him—broke no bones but he was bloody from head to foot on one side of his body—his back was wrenched. He says that this accident took away almost a third of his strength. Before, he could work all day in the fields, but now a half day does him in; if he does work all day then he's half-dead at night. Two years ago, in an osteria, some man or other made him mad. He picked the guy up bodily and threw him out the window. This morning, he's smoking a pipe, the stem of which must be almost as broad as his penis.

◆

Gino began his autobiography this morning. I wish I had more power to help him towards happiness or at least fulfillment, there's something extraordinary there to be fulfilled.

In his hands, very few lines ... Speaking of which, he told of having his hand read by the gypsy in Lévico—the same gypsy woman who read mine. Somehow she brought up that she'd read the hand of a young man (the day before) and this young man (me) would have much "fortuna"—because he walked so lightly, like a hare—"un lepre." Robert Graves speculates: "The hare was sacred, I suppose, because it is very swift, very prolific ... and mates openly without embarrassment."

Gino wishes his teeth were bigger, his lips smaller, his eyes larger, his forehead higher, his neck less thick. His face the way it is: remarkable for its combination of sexual beauty and spiritual purity.

◆

I was taking some exercises, nude, when Gino came in my room this morning to wake me up. He said Hey, looked straight at my cock and went immediately out.

He's now writing a poem to me.

◆

Gino insists that he has the legs of a donna, that his thighs are too big, I tell him they're white, that's all—if they were suntanned then they'd go with the upper part of his body. I said, en plus, that every physical sign means something in relation to the soul. I pointed out to him the sensuality signs of his face: the thickness on either side of his mouth (a kind of ridge, Venus's parentheses), the square bones of the jaw ... He added to the inventory the square pillows of flesh at his fingertips and the full neck. When will all this sensuality burst out? I asked him. For burst it will one day. He says he'll never allow it to burst out. You'll put it all in your poetry, then? I asked and he said Yes.

Pavlik came and sat on my bed and asked me if I were "fallen in love" ... I said No, how can I fall in love with someone who refuses to go to bed with me? And Pavlik said, "That's exactly when one falls in love!"

◆

Yesterday Gino thought of a really beautiful title, which proves all the more that he's a real poet: *The Nomadic City*—*La Città Nomada* (or *Nomadica*, I forget) ...

Gino I'll remember when creating the character of the Poet in my play based on Isak Dinesen's story.

He told of the time during the German occupation, men were rounded up in the streets, Gino was caught in the net and questioned. He lost patience with the questioner, a tough member of the German police, and told the man that if he continued to question him he wouldn't say a single word more. This made the officer furious, Gino was choked, beaten with a club on his back (he had blood-colored welts, after, for days), finally thrown against the wall (all the time he was silent, with a slight smile on his face), then out the door, with the remark from the officer that in twenty-five years experience he'd never come across "a piece of granite like you" ... Gino didn't hate the man afterwards (says he's never hated anyone in his life) and when he had a chance to revenge himself for the treatment he received (when the Germans were withdrawing, etc.) he didn't lift a finger to touch a hair of the man's head.

When he first came to see us he thought we were "living in a dream." What does he think now? He says horizons have been opened that he never knew before. Angel of the Night I called him—in the light of twilight. "I'm not a god," he said.

◆

Gino tells me: You're different today than on other days. I tell him: I change like the lake, not only every day but every hour. He asks, Why? I say: I'm water ...

He's leaving this morning on the 10:20 bus.

He says he came here like a baby and that I took his hand and told him how to eat.

◆

Gino has gone ... gave me a goodbye kiss—on the mouth. "Very clever of him not to go to bed with you," says Pavlik.

The night before he left he picked me up to carry me to my bed, afterwards, his taking off my socks (the day before he'd refused to let me remove his mountain shoes), then crossing my arms on my chest before pulling up the covers. I asked him if he knew why mothers crossed the arms of their children before tucking them in and he said Yes, to keep them from touching something lower.

We are all of us children, some guided, others misguided.

◆

Robert Graves (*The White Goddess*) illuminates Pavlik's spiral heads: "... the spiral as token of resurrection ... This spiral-symbol is ante-diluvian: the earliest Sumerian shrines are 'ghost-houses,' like those used in Uganda, and are flanked by spiral posts."

There are so many ways one goes back to the Mother without going back to

Mother. I tell Pavlik that his explorations in the "interior landscape" were a sign of "regression" (a dangerous period for him, during which he spoke more than once of suicide)—but which ended in the "re-birth," symbolized in his new period of non-anatomical heads (begun in Grottaferrata, the seeds already there in a spiral head done in New York).

◆

I showed little Agnese my prick from the window—at least, I intended for her to see it.

The attraction of obscenity—a substitution for the incest-wish.

The things we do in the night, in the day seem dreams; sometimes the things we do in the day seem dreams when night comes.

◆

The moving immobile afternoon.

"Forget your body and spit forth intelligence," advised Chuangtse (through a character he called Great Nebulous) ... To transform the spitting sperm of the body into spiritual spit.

And clouds float close to the surface of the lake.

And the lake's beauty stays ...

SEPTEMBER

August died in the form of a snake, September arrived in the form of a spider.

As we looked at the waterfall by the lake yesterday on our pre-dinner passegiata, I said, "Fringes and tassels and trains of crystal ..." Pavlik asked, "Where is that from?" and I said, "Nowhere, it's my description ..." and he said: "That's the sort of costumes I'd like to design for a play."

◆

PARIS

Two days in Paris seem like a week. Last night we took in Jouvet's *Tartuffe* with very ugly décor and unexciting costumes by Georges Braque. Backstage afterwards we talked to Jouvet (still in costume). When he asked, What did you think of the decor?—I chimed: "Quel decor?" at which he laughed—and agreed with me that Braque is not "un homme de theatre."

◆

On the road from Molveno, we reached Spotorno the first night. The next night we arrived, after dark, at Léonor's summer house near Toulon—at Le Brusc. Dinner was waiting for us, as was Léonor (Goyaesque hat, eyes of Raphael), Lepri and Léonor's lover Gilberto—the half of whose face is paralyzed. We stayed at a little hotel, five minutes walk from her place.

Our last lunch at Léonor's, Monday the 18th, she made a terrific scene because of Lepri's criticism (pre-lunch) of a painting she was working on to change certain compositional elements at Pavlik's suggestion. She was furious at Lepri's telling her, in the midst of the changes and before everything was finished, that she was wrong to change the picture, that it was better before, implying (or perhaps saying outright) that she shouldn't listen to Pavlik, should paint the way she feels, etc. She broke a plate, threw another at him, burst into tears and approached him with a bottle in her hand as if to hit him over the head. She told him he wasn't qualified to judge and that Pavlik was, and what a swinish thing to do, after she'd made the effort at humility to listen to Pavlik with intuitive faith. She told Lepri to go home to his mother!

◆

Dream: I fled, but with not enough speed (I felt) to put a safe distance between myself and three black horses wildly dashing in my direction.

"There are two people in you," Pavlik told me, "and the bad one is very strong."

OCTOBER

It's painful to me to walk down the Boul' Mich' and see so many pretty ungraspables—so what pleasure is greater than sex? Art—if one creates it oneself.

"The Muses give but they take away."
"Take away what?"
"Your youth."
"Nothing for nothing."

When Pavlik was a child someone asked him why he didn't draw (or paint) a tree. "No!" he replied. "I could never draw all the branches and leaves." But, he says, in his recent anatomical work, he *was* drawing (painting) "all the branches and leaves."

"I look like an old wild thing," he's just remarked, peering in a mirror over the mantlepiece. "That mirror is in a spot where it's not very flattering to look into—it should be moved!" I say. Then: "Tell me something for my diary." And he says: "We are like plants, some are annual, they bloom their best and go, some are like perennials, they must grow deep roots and stay."

We sail tomorrow.

◆

ABOARD THE *ILE-DE-FRANCE*
Masses of amorphous Americans . . . Pavlik heard one refer to Truman Capote as "that saintly being."

Now that Picasso is making pottery, Pavlik calls him "Pot-Cassé" instead of "Caca-Pisse."

◆

The sense of freedom which enabled Henry Miller and Jean Genet to write their so-called obscene works. They wrote without shame, as if talking to themselves—

one has shame only in the presence of others (whether they are there or not in the flesh doesn't matter—the shame may come from imagining them there, or their reactions when reading what you're writing). Sade achieved that sort of release— where may one be more shameless and alone (rejected by society) than in prison? Baudelaire's ferocious anti-social feelings made him feel so apart that he said what he thought and shocked his contemporaries. The isolation of Lautréamont let him live (in his writings) uninhibited—it was only *after* (this word nearly became "fa- ther," symbol of authority, author of guilt-feelings in the son) his *Maldoror* was published that reactionary qualms set in.

"Obsession is part of the world of love," says P.

NEW YORK CITY

A sunny terrace but a wrecked apartment ... Edith S. sent us baskets of fruit for "Welcome home" and told me when I talked to her on phone that she has bronchi- tis but has been rehearsing for her reading of the part of Lady Macbeth. "Do you have a partner?" I asked and she said, "Yes. But I'm afraid he's not a friend of yours ... Glenway Wescott." "Well," I said, "he should know better than I whether he's a friend of mine or not."

To dream, and start anew ... It's been fifteen days since I wrote here. The reason: because the apartment has been in a continual state of disorder due to our packing for Weston, to where we are moving on the 31st ... Only one exciting session with Bert that went on pleasantly for an hour or more: he's just as pretty as before, still looks sixteen; stomach flatter.

Virgil Thomson: "Everybody likes men. Women like men and men like men."

NOVEMBER

Here we are in the country at last—everything moved and 360 East 55th vacated. Pavlik remembers that I said, when we took Penthouse C, that we'd have it for ten years—and ten years it's been, exactly.

Bert suggests I get a "fixed" skunk for a pet—says they are very affectionate.

◆

"Mortals who flee Aphrodite too much," runs a fragment of an early play by Euripides (on Phaedra and Hippolytus), "suffer a malady no less than those who too much pursue her."

This animal engine called my body—a true "infernal machine"—whom will it spring upon next?

One summer my grandmother, Mama Cato, took Sister and me visiting kinfolk in the bayou country of Louisiana. I had a cousin named Dell, who was fifteen, much older than I, he seemed like a grown boy. One day sitting under an apple tree he said, "Jack me off." And he promised me some of those red apples, too high for me to reach.

> Don't give a damn if I do die, do die.
> Just so the juice fly, juice fly!

As the radio ad man for Life cigarettes says, "Not too long and thin, not too short and fat—but Life size."

◆

Dougie to me after the Macbeth rehearsal, "Introduce Djuna to Tennessee!" "Does she want to meet him?" I asked and Dougie said, "Yes," so I took Tennessee by the arm and introduced him. Djuna's opening line, "How does it feel to be rich and famous?" did not inspire me to assist further at the rencontre. Poor Djuna looked worse than I've ever seen her—sallow and stooped and withered—a real ruin, compared to what she was twenty years ago—the dashing, red-headed, handsome, admired and courted Djuna Barnes—living in a grand apartment on Washington

Square. "Two little birds on a branch" (she told me later) were the words she used to describe Parker and me after our visit—she'd received us, after a letter from me, to confer about a MS for *Blues*, the magazine I started in Mississippi. The next year I saw her again, she came to a party I gave on Eighth Street. After the party, Djuna and I went to Harlem—that was in April, 1931. Returning to the Village that night, in a taxi, she kissed me. Two days later, when I stopped in to say goodbye to her on the way to my boat—I was sailing for Le Havre—and to pick up a copy of her novel *Ryder* that she'd promised me—she kissed me again ("You looked rather surprised," I was informed in Paris the following summer)—just to show she meant it—i.e., this time sober, as compared to the intoxicated one in the taxi.

She no sooner arrived in Paris than she had to go to the American Hospital, Neuilly, for an appendicitis operation, and when she came back to her Rue St.-Romain apartment (from the hospital) I slept in her livingroom and fixed food for her. This went on for about ten days. When she was well she told me her plan to set off on a Middle European tour and invited me to go with her: to Munich, Vienna and Budapest. I told her that I wasn't sure I was going and had gonorrhea (she'd not known about it before). I, too, had been in the American Hospital, Neuilly! ... Back in Munich Putsy Hanfstaengel gave us the name of his doctor, who took a smear, but didn't find anything. But when we returned to Paris I had a few more anti-clap treatments just to be sure. I was installed in the maid's room of Djuna's apartment, two flights up out the kitchen door. At that time Peggy Guggenheim came across with a thousand francs a week ($40) and both Djuna and I managed to live on it.

In the spring of 1933 our "romance" was quite worn and I left Paris to join Carmita in Florence. But absence made the heart grew fonder and in the spring of 1933 Djuna came to Tangier to be with me. But this move on her part didn't turn out well—she discovered she was pregnant and had to hie herself back to Paris for an abortion; Djuna and I were completely on the outs by that time. Carmita had already left Tangier for Spain, I was alone, suddenly got fed up, telegraphed Gertrude Stein, asking if I could visit her on my way to Paris, she wired yes—"si vous venez seul." I stayed a week with Gertrude and Alice at Bilignin (having taken an English boat from Gibraltar to Toulon), then to Paris where Dougie immediately "arranged" that Pavlik and I meet for dinner which took place on Bastille Day. Dougie told me later that he'd warned Tchelitchew that he wouldn't be able to afford me, that I was too expensive.

◆

At the Museum of Modern Art *Macbeth* reading, Edith was bad (except in the sleepwalking scene)—no sense of theater tempo or characterization—the whole performance was embarrassing, painful and a ridiculous mistake.

◆

Squirrels as if covered with frost, like the ground they spring upon ...

To understand the mystery of our being in time—the body's reason and the soul's future—enough for a lifetime's meditation, without bothering about the stars, space and infinity. But to understand ourselves would be to understand everything.

◆

Parker worked on the principle of: originality before knowledge.

Originality *is* knowledge ...

DECEMBER

I come across some notes jotted down in 1932 (at Carmita's little villa near Florence). Remembered from a remark of Djuna's (or was it copied from one of her letters): "I was brilliant, no one was saying a word and I had them screaming all evening." Beautiful, brilliant Djuna: she's no longer young and handsome but she's still got the bite that makes you bleed with laughter.

Did she write me this or tell me this (and it's still true): "You become irritated when everything isn't going just your way."

A note I made about her as a character I wanted to portray in a novel: "Nothing hypocritical, affected or false in anything Cressida said."

Yes: notes written on Tangier Continental Hotel paper (1932–33): "Although he loved her he didn't want to be controlled by her, was too foolishly proud, too stubborn, too already spoiled and pampered by her first attentions, her first adoration ... I think I must have wanted to do all the things that oughtn't be done and get them over with."

Some sayings of Djuna, while we were together (1931–32):

"If it's going to be just family life I don't want it!"

"With a hangover it's inevitable that one chooses the most reckless cab driver in Paris ..." ("We were living our comedy then—now I want to write one.")

Djuna said, "I don't know why I give the impression that I'm wealthy when I haven't a sou to my name ... People are not much good in bed when drunk. You are, though—as a matter of fact. That's because he's shy and doesn't really like girls." Then I said, "I don't like girls in general but I like you." Then Djuna asked, "If I were a boy would you like me better?" and I replied, "No! I wouldn't like you at all."

"Such a goof ... I think you've set me back ten years."

Djuna and the comic spirit: "I've decided that the solution to everything is ribaldry. But one can't be ribald alone ... If one could only be alone for five minutes!"

She asked me, "Who's going to take care of you now that your money's gone?" and I answered, "I don't know. More will drop from heaven."

One of Djuna's wisecracks: "She can't sing but she's such a soprano."

Djuna told me, "I think I'm bad for you. You should be with people of your own age. I'll make you older. You'll know more and be sadder and won't fall in love easily again."

I noted: "The times when he hated her voice, her face, her movements, hated her completely and to the point of tears."

At other times: "... her face was like a child's, innocent and uncynical." Djuna told me once: "I consider myself more important than you. You're nobody and I'm somebody ... A lot depends on what you make it, not what other people make of it for you."

◆

Perry Embiricos repeats to us sailors' expressions. "Love is where you stick your dick." In Turkish bath, semi-darkness, voice telling sailor, "Stick it in." Sailor answers, "You stick it in, I ain't got no map of your goddamned ass."

◆

The people called indefatigable are usually struck down by fatigue all of a sudden. Pavlik never stops talking except when he sleeps. He can talk while painting and even when reading—between sentences!

◆

Oppose your own kind of magic to any other reality, event, charm or horror in the world: that's the poet's way.

To write some new poems, with grandiose images in very simple words—such as

And all the leaves that have ever fallen
Resurrect a wall around summer's wide bed.

To use simple but musical words and musical combinations of words to achieve a *grand strangeness*: simple means, enigmatic meaning of the whole, achieved by juxtaposition.

I must simply be content in doing the thing for its own sake.

Mother arrives in New York tonight and we expect her out here tomorrow.

◆

One feels one's way—though the general direction is usually always there: when not there, then it's like turning around in the dark; but one is moving, nevertheless—

Pavlik is sweeping up a glass I just broke in the hall—throwing it against the bookcase after he told me I could leave the house when I showed displeasure at the prospect of someone whom I don't know coming for tea on Sunday.

"When you want to break something, that means you want to break yourself." He demands that I kneel and kiss his hand in order to be forgiven.

I do so—but am I forgiven?

"We are as much as we see." (Thoreau.)

◆

Mother says she'll buy a cattle-ranch or angora goat farm in Arizona if I want to help run it. I'd already told her I'd almost decided not to try to write plays but to continue with my poetry and perhaps make money in some other way ... Pavlik doesn't oppose the idea; his one apprehensive thought: the Indians might revolt one day and start taking back their land from the white men!

A "mysterious" nostalgia—I don't really know what the feelings of longing made me long for.

My mother, too, Hamlet, is named Gertrude.

◆

"La fatalité" is not, as Antonin Artaud implies, "the materialization of an intellectual force"—but the result of millions of things which happened independently of each other but whose combinations and conjunctions cause what seem to be single occurrences. One thing at a time is never one thing.

◆

It's the desire to go to new *extremes*: either down (like Sade) or up (like Rilke). Baudelaire embraced both extremes: crime and the sublime.

◆

I tell Pavlik: "—So that's what you're painting—the Psyche"—after I quote to him Jung: "... everything pertaining to the psyche has a double face. The one looks forward, the other back. It is ambiguous and therefore symbolic, like all living reality."

◆

"The more we *have* the less we can *be*—" the truth of St. Francis sets up a conflict with my dream of an Arizona ranch!

As to the poet's participation in war—it's not a question of his poetry's being more important than the national fate—but, as Jung puts it, "his work means more to him than his personal fate."

◆

A big egg-truck came down the hill with a sex-beast of a truck driver at the wheel who smiled at me, saying, "Kind of slippery, ain't it?" I smiled back and then knew he'd set the mechanism going which would end in my jerking off.

Why not have children instead of continuing in pursuit of the *deformed image*?

1951

JANUARY

The diamond spattered trees this morning—and Pavlik says, "That's the way I wanted to make my Interior Landscape."

Bert's opening line: "Hey, Pavlik, do you know how to ball a bush?"

"Sounds obscene," I said.

"But you got to do it," replied Bert.

"Fuck 'em all," called Pavlik.

"All except seven," answered Bert. "Save those for Sunday."

"And there reigns love and all love's loving parts ..." (Shakespeare in the Sonnets.)

Of particular importance in the understanding of love is to understand its degenerate, perverted and disguised forms ... "secrets of love."

Around Bert's eyes: the darkness left by so much "coming"—he's masked with a lightly dark mask, somewhat like one of those small masks Western outlaws wear in movies. And he illustrates another line in the Sonnets: "... lascivious grace, in whom all ill shows well"—WS speaking of, or to, his lover.

◆

George Balanchine ("hardly ever smiles"—Mother) and Tanaquil Le Clercq here yesterday for lunch and dinner, I asked George if he wanted an idea for a ballet which would be "comic—American folklore," and he said yes. I gave him the book of short stories, *Bowleg Bill, the Sea-going Cowboy* (Cape Cod legends)—he said it might make a ballet for Harold Lang, choreography by Jerome Robbins.

"She's there and yet she's distant—a great ballerina—" Pavlik on Tanny Le Clercq's dancing.

◆

Art and culture (music and architecture) as forms of love—even when distorted.

Love: Oscar Wilde's hidden strength.

Pavlik himself, who radiates love in every direction, is probably not completely conscious of what motivates him.

I have certainly tested Pavlik's love—to the breaking point—and it didn't break. Let me strengthen my love now—and his for me will be strengthened—for life.

Venus is Pavlik's goddess. His mother told him that his mouth, shaped like a crescent moon at birth, was because Venus smiled on him.

The purchase of the new oldsmobile (in my name) has eased a lot of the tension between us. When I'm impatient with him now he calls me "ungrateful."

We went by Hunter's shop to pick up cushion for the car. Pavlik mentioned backache and Hunter asked, "You know what's good for the backache?" "No," says P. and Hunter gives with: "A good sweat over a live corpse!"

FEBRUARY

I am a little boy kicking a beer can down a misty road. A man walks towards me and stops to piss. I would like to stop and gaze upon him pissing, I keep on kicking the can down the road.

Squirrels, half rats, half cats; the phalloi of winter.

Lincoln brought Auden by for coffee and cognac, Auden looking like a shy old clown. The talk was literary and Auden brought up the name of Emerson, saying he didn't like him. "Grandiloquent," I said. "Thoreau is simple but with an equal grandeur." Auden agreed. But I didn't agree with him when he said *Finnegans Wake* is a book doomed to go unread.

"Toujours nu," Pavlik observes (about me)—"vous êtes né cocotte."

Drove into New York to see *The Rose Tattoo*. It's funny, without being a good comedy. I told Tennessee during the first intermission, getting a laugh out of him: "My only criticism is that you don't bore your audience enough."

Perry's sailor-friend, when he saw the drawing from Pavlik's recent show, hanging on Perry's wall: "It's worth a fortune—it's one of them goddamn optical illusions!"

"Il y a trop de ducks dans 'Swan Lake,'" Pavlik tells Perry—re N.Y.C. Ballet's (Balanchine's) idea to do a long version of "Lac des Cygnes."

◆

Dear Pavlik, giving Mother a painting lesson. Mother: "Well, I'll tell you—that's the most difficult butterfly." "Make it one line"—(Pavlik)—"without interruption. There are lines that go, without interruption: you're making lots of hairy lines . . . Like that, like that, like that. You see? . . . Well—you work." (Pavlik leaves her at her easel.)

◆

Pavlik has agreed to appear before the students at Yale University and give a talk on Gertrude Stein. He thinks he'll be too moved by his own lecture, and cry in front of the audience! I tell him he'll be less moved when he gets on the podium . . . "So it will be very unusual, very strange . . ." He's talking on the phone to Mrs. Griswold, wife of the President of Yale, who has asked us to dinner afterwards. "I'm in a nervous state . . . I hope it will be all right."

Our cook, Mrs. Turner, tells him he shouldn't be nervous about giving the lecture—because "you're a well-educated gentleman."

◆

In spite of Mother's being a practicing artist and surrounded by artists—with a son and a daughter who are artists—her ideal of success is a *commercial* success—she's never developed beyond this ideal—typically American. To posthumous glory, she'd choose present riches . . . Anyway, as Pavlik says, she's a "great dreamer."

Pavlik very pleased at the effect produced yesterday by his lecture at Yale—tremendous applause, concentrated attention, lots of laughs. I sat with the Sobys (James Thrall and Nellie)—Nellie said she thought the lecture was sensational. I turned around to the Carlyle Browns (Henri and Margie) after it was over and Margie's eyes were welling with tears. Pavlik had quoted, at the end—which brought a sigh from the audience—my lines from "Ballad for Baudelaire":

A wingless horse heard the story one day
Of a horse with wings, and flew away!

Pavlik's after-dinner remarks, in President Griswold's study, about Henry Moore's "useless holes"—destroying Jim Soby's admiration somewhat—unless Jim is more stubborn than we think he is.

◆

Bert is here—we just went up in the attic … He, standing smilingly said, "Let's wait till after dinner." I said, "I just wanted to see if it's still there."

"Yeah, it's still there," he said.

Auden's new poems (according to a review) satirize "actuality." The actuality will pass, but will the poems remain?

MARCH

SARASOTA, FLA.

Here we are at Chick Austin's, having arrived yesterday. Mother rode with us as far as Ocala, Fla.

Water the color of green fire … My balls are full of lava but I refuse to trigger an overflow with none but me to witness the inundation.

We stopped by the Ringling Hotel yesternight to see John Murray Anderson and there he was, talked away to us on the veranda—whether the voice-drowning buses went by or not—and he took me in to the bar to introduce me to some of the current boys, "Nine Blankets," one of the elephant boys, I think, and to one he called "Knock-on-Any-Door." Miles White had a showgirl in tow dubbed "Hamburger Mary" (by Murray).

I called Mother in Panama City. She's found a fishing camp of thirty cottages on 15 acres—for sale, and she may buy.

◆

PANAMA CITY, FLA.

9:35 P.M. Pavlik's lecture (a repeat of the one he gave on Gertrude Stein) is just about over now—at the Ringling Museum—and here I am, 400 miles away. Mother's 15-acre Baywood Park Motel is attractively situated on the Bay of St. Andrews—and I think she's going to make a deal for it. In Sarasota I got up at 4 A.M., started out in the car under the stars, ran into a fog and got lost, found my way again and, after it was daylight, hit a hog on the road, when it ran in front of the car—but didn't kill it, saw it running across the field.

◆

PALM BEACH, FLA.

We arrived here at Alice Delamar's after lunch.

"Oh how I loathe my face," I say to myself en pleine figure—but the glass will have a pleasanter story to tell when some of this red sunburn changes to tan—and I recover from self-abuse.

A door which doesn't latch tightly and rattles from the wind is much less annoying when one finds out *which door it is.*

◆

From Tom Lea's documentation on bull breeding: "Daily each bull gets a little more than an ounce of saltpeter mixed with his corn, to quiet the natural urges of bullhood. Bulls will masturbate, you know."

And here comes the 40-year-old housepainter, in front of whom I wanted to masturbate yesterday. He waves and grins through the glass panes (on the upper half of my door).

I'm already getting excited at his being out there—perhaps I'll wait until he gets to the bathroom window before undressing. Yesterday the effect of a dream was produced by the salt's having made a mist over the windowpanes (the salt ocean air)—plus my looking at his dimmed image in the door mirror (of my bathroom). He has a cigarette in his mouth now and is squatting to paint the wood on lower part of door. I can see only his forehead and curly hair (receding). He's suntanned and dressed in white T-shirt and white pants. It's silly to get excited because nothing to remember with real pleasure can come of it—or is likely to.

I have now pulled off my shirt and am sitting by the window. I wonder if he noticed my shedding the shirt. I can see his face when I stand up. I doubt if he's conscious of any monkey business on my part—though he may be ... He could certainly have seen me naked yesterday had his eyes looked in the window, penetrating the salt-mist.

There's too direct a view from the windowpanes of the door—the subtle thing is to have a semi-veiled view such as window screen on bathroom window will give—then he can see me and pretend not to—here he would be embarrassed with the direct unobstructed sight—a naked prick is always startling—even to a man.

"Il est assez gentil ce petit peintre," says Pavlik (in my room now)—but I shake my head. Pavlik's near-sighted.

Painter's job at door now finished and I didn't finish the job on myself.

◆

Alice has been confined to her room with fever but she was better tonight and we all saw the rising moon like an orange-pink Easter egg and talked of plans to give a big Hallowe'en Bal Masqué this year for Léonor—"Demons and Angels" motif.

APRIL

Bees in the pussywillow.

Reading Jung does not help to calm sexuality—on the contrary stimulates it . . . "The Phallus is the son, or the son is the Phallus . . . The vulgar designation of penis as 'boy' was remarked even by Grimm and others."

Which makes me want to look at my "boy" at least. To look at him—feeling him as I am at this moment—is to love him. Yes, he's quite an upstanding lad. Go back to sleep, boy!

I've just pulled off. The prostate ache was unbearable.

In spite of all Bert says about his longing for the female, I think there must exist in his unconscious a "resistance," caused by his mother-complex. As Jung puts it, "If there exists a resistance against the real sexuality, then the accumulated libido is most likely to cause a hyperfunction of those collaterals which are most adapted to compensate for the resistance, that is to say, the nearest functions which serve for the introduction of the cat; on one side the function of the hand, on the other that of the mouth."

Jung is aphrodisiac, with his apology for onanists: "One must in fairness, however, consider that the demands of life, rendered still more severe by our moral code, are so heavy that it simply is impossible for many people to attain that goal which can be begrudged to no one, namely the possibility of love, under the cruel compulsion of domestication, what is left but onanism—for those people possessed of an active sexuality?"

Juenger's line—"the joyous feeling of safety in the burning heart of danger"—is that not a symbolical way of speaking of onanism? Then my title, *Sleep in a Nest of Flames* . . . (from Rimbaud).

Aren't we right ("we" meaning humanity) not to be terrified by time rushing by as it does?

It's tonight again.

◆

Bert arrived at 3:30 P.M., in white coveralls with Manhattan School of Typography embroidered in red on back.

After dinner I put him on his knees so as to lick his ass the better, asked him to "let me get in"—he agreed and I came in his ass for the first time—he said, "It hurts but it feels good," and asked me to push it in as far as I could, after I came.

◆

Yesterday after breakfast Bert was all ready, on hands and knees, to let me go in— but when I got the head in he yelled with pain and kept on writhing for a few seconds, shamelessly, moaning and groaning after I took it out, said it had given him a "shooting pain," it had never hurt that bad, etc. The anticipated pleasure of both of us shot to hell.

◆

Freud illuminates a corner, Jung a universe. (Of course from that corner, Jung set out.) The basic difference: Freud is corporal, Jung spiritual.) ". . . the neurotic always renounces a complete erotic experience, in order that he may remain a child." (Jung.)

◆

"What do you do when you're with your girl?" I asked Bert. "Just sit and make mad passionate love," he said, and added, "That's the bad part." (He doesn't fuck her.)

◆

To get back to poetry: it's leaving the world in order to find it. To write: grasp the magic wand (phallic symbol) and trace your words with it—after the trance is induced.

Nostalgia for my domain! Inside the magic circle, which may be drawn almost anywhere.

When Hart Crane perceived that he had exhausted the exhilaration derived from drink and sex and poetry, he drowned himself. He had lost contact with the thread that leads up, Poetry, and took hold of the Whirlpool and didn't let go.

MAY

I've started a Dada farce (which will have hidden seriousness): I'm calling it *A*—taking as my motto, and first spoken line, a sentence from Gertrude Stein's "A List"—in *Operas and Plays*: "I have also had great pleasure from a capital letter."

I find compiling a magical vocabulary (going over dictionary, systematically, and picking out words which I write down in lists) indispensable: songs and sayings are suggested by them.

◆

"The comic spirit, which is at least older than folk games or any drama however primitive—" (from an introduction to the pre-Shakespearean comedies) . . . Such notes bolster my spirit to continue on *A*—which I have re-titled this morning *The Man in the Moon*. "We present neither comedy, not tragedy, not story, not anything, but that whosoever beareth may say this, Why here is a tale of the man in the moon." (Prologue to *Endymion*.)

◆

The weekend with Bert was super-pleasant. When he arrived on Friday we took a walk through the woods, he said he had to piss, stopped and took his prick cut, couldn't piss, I took hold of it, said, "Let's find a place." He was excited and rather nervous and trembly and told me that his piles hadn't been bothering him lately and that I'd be able to get it in that night. "I'll try," I said.

◆

I restrain myself from talking about the house I want to build at Panama City Beach. P. drops ideas about it every once in a while but he pretends it bores him ("drives me crazy") to hear me talking about it.

JUNE

"Never marry," Pavlik tells me, "or you'll be bound to the earth for thousands of years more." He says he wants to be loved by someone, and pounces on Bergson's view of "laughter" as being devoid of "emotion" as characteristic of me: he says I laugh at everything.

I asked Parker (in a letter) if he thought posthumous fame is any fun and he replied that it might be to posterity.

◆

Must man's grandeur be measured only by man? Thoreau wanted to measure his with nature—he felt that contact with man depraves and diminishes.

No one will ever mean more to me—inspire me more—than Pavlik. But now is the time to inspire myself. I do not like being his "satellite"—that's why it's perhaps more satisfactory to live with him in the country—or in a foreign country—as two human beings—not one famous artist and one obscure poet. I say, "J'aime la nature"—and he says he doubts it. He says he feels the need of young people around him—to inspire. In inspiring them, he says he "feeds" on them. The old problem of art's not being enough, we want "life" too.

◆

"The individual constantly wants to carry out this action (the act of touching one's own genitals), he sees in it the highest pleasure . . ." (*Totem and Taboo*.)

"Save it for tonight," Bert said, seeing my hard which I showed him from my bed when he woke me up (or thought he did) from an afternoon nap. There his lips are and I can't kiss them—though he lets me go in his ass (when his piles aren't "on fire" as he says). The morning sun directly in his eyes made them the color of Capri water. Why go to Capri when the color of Bert's eyes is here?

◆

The moon was shining. The valley was full of mist. "Nice night for a murder," says Bert.

◆

Bert said he let me come in him this morning more to "Satisfy" me than the pleasure he got out of it ("I didn't get too much")—but said while I was doing it, "Will you make me come twice tonight?"

But tonight after he came once he said it was sore, jerked me off, said, "You come a lot, don't you?"

An insect describes a circle of about an inch in diameter—so fast it looks like a circle moving in space.

"There are as many ways to wither love as there are stars in a night..." Deirdre speaks.

◆

"Don't scratch the emotional ulcer—I hate you all—" Pavlik after tea. Seeing him so sick and frantic at the idea of my leaving him to build a house, I know that I cannot. My house will be built to console me after I've lost him forever.

◆

Pavlik on our moonlit, lightning-bug-accented walk tonight was in a mood to go to Canada for 3 weeks in August.

JULY

If "we" are more important than giant stars, because we *think*, why, if the sun went out, would we die?

Criminals are our teachers. Criminals and saints.

My life at the moment is upset because my typewriter suddenly got out of whack because I pushed something in the wrong manner. And so with human beings as well as machines: one pushes something in the wrong way—and things don't run smoothly suddenly.

"Il y a un cadavre entre nous—" (Pavlik.)

◆

I call Bert's asshole my "lost paradise," for he told me I can't get in again—he called me in the toilet to look at his piles.

Let me be a writing instrument—a finger of the Earth—and write whatever I feel like.

Bert told me I was "very careless" when I squeezed one of his balls by mistake.

I licked between his toes and he liked it, wanted to know if women like it. "I've got to have a woman soon," he moans. "I can't go another weekend without a woman."

". . . for the ocean, as well as the human form, is Vishnu."

◆

Lunched with Pavlik at Stark Young's little Victorian house near So. Salem, N.Y. Stark told of Mei Lan Fang's holding a small bouquet of flowers in his right hand during the receptions given in his honor (N.Y.C. in the Twenties)—to save him from shaking hands—he needed to keep those expressive fingers and wrist in perfect working order.

William Inge got me out of a dark bed at 10:30 last night, phoning to say Miss Claudette Colbert was not permitting an audience at her dress rehearsal of the new Noël Coward play on Sunday at Westport Country Playhouse.

"Her characters are unreal," I say to Pavlik, talking about Carson McCullers' *The Ballad of the Sad Café*. "She's unreal herself," he replies.

◆

The garbage boy: arms like a man and an Italian face. If I were King he'd be in my bed tonight.

So I went for a second dip in the afternoon—instead of wringing the head of my prick.

The sperm of space forms stars. We may not be known to God until we *become*.

The fire of hell: unsatisfied longing. Poets turn this fire into poetry. Poets sleep in a nest of flames.

"Why?" is a question not to be asked too often or it becomes stupefying. *What is* is why.

◆

The three C's of (novel or) dramatic writing:

Create Character Continuously

◆

P. writes Léonor that he'd like to learn to cook and to drive a car—the two daily activities he depends on me to do.

I seem to have degenerated into a real "jerk victim"—like Bert. I went to it after lunch like a dope fiend towards his kick—not even trying to resist.

The insidious thing is that disgust passes away.

◆

How Pavlik's "morale" has been changed by my change of heart (re the house-building idea). He's working with more inspiration, feeling better, looking better, is gayer: he is highly conscious of the change in me, glad about it and probably can hardly believe it! His gloom has been dissipated as if by magic—his gallbladder ("my emotional organ") doesn't hurt him any more—il a rajeuni. And so he's more in my power than ever.

◆

Coral (my ten-year-old niece) tonight: "You ought to get married." I reply: "Why should I get married when I'm happy the way I am?" She said, "That's just what I'm afraid of—you're happy and may never get married!"

AUGUST

NEAR MAGOG, QUEBEC, CANADA

"Those mosquitoes aren't going to bother you ... They're not underneath the bed!" Bert has just told Pavlik, who was up with a flashlight, thinking a mosquito or a snake was underneath his bed. "I'd like to pack my luggage tomorrow and go," says Pavlik. "It's hot here, hotter than in Connecticut." And Bert says, "This bed is almost impossible."

◆

I've been lying in bed 45 minutes this morning waiting for Pavlik and Bert to get through having sex before breakfast. They're up now and I'll get up.

We're at the Fiacre Inn, on a lake a couple of miles down the road from Magog, and have a completely separate apartment above what was once a barn—with an astounding view—the most beautiful we've seen in Canada.

◆

Bert has his fishing license and caught a nice mess of rock bass the first time we went out in the rowboat.

Pavlik has just come in my room saying he just felt someone push him in the back and he's afraid and wants to change beds with me—so that's what we'll do!

◆

Bert asked me if I were going to pay him a "visit" last night and I said, "Not for a fist," and he said, "Give them a chance to cool off—" (of his piles).

◆

Bert surprised a skunk when he went to empty the garbage night before last, called me down to "smell" him. I turned my flashlight into the garbage room and there the little creature was, feeding peacefully. The bellboy, Serge, a runt, commissioned Bert to buy him a couple of shotgun shells when we went to town and they planned to shoot the skunk last night. But when Pavlik heard of it he told Bert if he took any part in the shooting (such as holding the flashlight for the runt) that he (Bert) would find the door locked and he could get home the best he might. So Bert withdrew from the collaboration.

◆

WESTON, CONN.

Arrived exhaustedly home yesterday, after spending almost twelve hours on the road for a distance of 410 miles—from Magog. We sped Bert on his way, thoroughly disgusted with the sight and sound of him. Peau d'elephant, humorless, stupid, rude, coarse and most of the time boring, I've decided to drop this German friend of mine—though he doesn't know it.

No travel to beautiful places, no children, no lovers—none of these can give "consolation"—only my work—poetry—can give me the pride in existence that seems so important.

And so I wrote a prose poem ("The Visitation"). That feeling of being lost in creation—a forgetting of self—is one I haven't felt in a long time.

SEPTEMBER

The will of the sperm to be doesn't mean that it wills to be us: we are accidental. If you make yourself empty, sometimes your genius will occupy you.

"O Ego, what ails thee?"
"This dress of flesh is killing me."

◆

"—like women cooking some kind of fantastic cake in which all the ingredients are put in the wrong way—just something too awful—" Pavlik on Dali's drawing.
I've just touched my tongue to the head of my prick.

OCTOBER

I meant to copy here the letter I sent to William Carlos Williams on the subject of his *Autobiography* but I sent my one copy of it to Djuna. "A ghastly excretion—" I wrote to E. E. Cummings.

◆

When the flowers go, the trees glow, when the butterflies die, the leaves fly.
Pavlik's Russian proverb: If you look too often or long in the mirror, one day the mirror will bite you.

"You're completely out of all control," I hear him telling Coral.

"I thought you didn't like the Fords," I hear Coral telling him.

She told me that he told her that a black animal lived in me and went roaming at night. "The panther of my libido," I explained.

◆

Coral: "Bubu, you have to see that baby!"

"Where is it?"

"In the nest . . . It's almost as big as the mother and she not only put something in its mouth but took something out of its back end—something white."

◆

Pavlik says I'm not ambitious enough.

"What do you want me to write?"

"A play that you think no one would want to produce."

◆

I had the idea to get together an anthology of THE POEM IN PROSE and to apply for a Guggenheim Fellowship with such a project. E. E. Cummings, Marianne Moore, Meyer Schapiro, Eric Bentley and Carl Van Vechten have agreed to recommend me.

Cummings postcard from Silver Lake, N.H.:

> am a poor recommender; but if you like, shall try
> > in the volume miscalled 'Collected' Poems exist five poemsinprose,
> I. E. 27 64 79 97 155
> > & please remember me cordially to your tiptop sister
> > > > C's

And Marianne Moore:

> The Guggenheim Foundation seems rather stern in its predilections and I don't know how it might feel about THE POEM IN PROSE but I think you would assemble a real one—a real book; name me as liking the idea, if you care to.
>
> It is I so far as I can see, who am indebted and needing to express gratitudes. I hope you and your sister are well.
> > > Sincerely yours.

◆

Pavlik said that Bert sensed, like an animal, that everything was over.

"I prefer the primitive tribes to the ladies; the boys and girls of the fields and forests," I say to Pavlik, leaving him at the breakfast table.

"Oh yeah?" says he, licking his cereal spoon.

◆

More on the subject of W.C.W.'s *Autobiography*—in which he says I rewrote his introduction to my book of poems, *The Garden of Disorder*. I've complained to a few people. Marianne Moore writes me in reply:

> I think you do not but incline to take things hard whereas we must feel optimistic and comfortable, I have come to think. Do not let this trouble you too much—about the introduction. I am constantly a "victim." However,—we must get what we can out of dilemmas; I mean, we should be hardy enough to learn; we can usually deduce a warning from injudiciousness on our part (and are foolish to gloss over anything we did which we had better not do again, no matter how innocent). I infer no ill will (or discourtesy even) from your receiving no answer (from W.C.W.) to your letter of protest. When a man is over-taxed—disabled, that is to say, he is a coward to feel he *must* write letters when he knows he must not make exertion.
>
> As for the book [*The Autobiography of William Carlos Williams*] there are splendid things in it and things which are the opposite—passages which I find saddening—indeed inexplicable . . .
> . . . the careless world when misinformed, is no serious enemy; the truth finds its level so do not let accidents disturb you.

◆

There's no escaping one's own devil, he's there because we create him.

A frog the color of flesh-colored leaves (jumped from our path on pre-lunch walk).

Leaves color of yellow-jackets, *peaches* and bull's blood.

Useless as a leaf caught in a spider web.

◆

Balanchine and Tanaquil came out night before last to stay in house across the road, which we had asked Daisy (to whom it belongs) if they could have for weekends. Pavlik finds Tanny "already disappointed"—as he says all of Balanchine's wives are eventually. Tanny is completely wrapped up, however, in the ballet and the ballet world is all she knows or cares about—aside from childish pastimes such as playing cards, doing crossword puzzles or reading best-sellers.

The sun is coming out and I'm going to polish the car and meet Virgil Thomson at the Saugatuck station—he's arriving for lunch to ask Pavlik's advice on what to do about décor for *Four Saints in Three Acts* (Gertrude Stein opera for which he wrote the music) to be produced in Paris. Pavlik will tell him to use the Florine Stettheimer set from the original production, premiered by Chick Austin in Hartford, Conn. (when Chick was director of the Wadsworth Atheneum).

◆

Virgil is amusing to watch—up to a point—with his Frenchified facial expressions (gaping with eyes or/and mouth, shooting the head forward, sudden thrusts of the hands); his face has grown in dignity with the years—an occupational development one might suppose—people in public life, like senators and newspaper critics, begin to look dignified, I guess. Also Virgil has worked with his mind, which gives him a professorial look. His squirrel's face bulges in unexpected places, as though he were hiding nuts in his cheeks. He says he likes to work in contrasts—if the subject is intrinsically comic he'll treat it gravely, etc. That explains his matter-of-fact approach to music—the most ineffable of the arts. He looked city-spruce, enjoyed the lunch and the spectacle of the trees and returned to town the successful ambassador: Pavlik agreed to "supervise" Florine's set when *Four Saints* is recreated in Paris in May.

◆

"... the waters of the psyche ..." (Jung.) ... *the overturned lake*: the psyche revealed, the unconscious discovered. "... our unconscious conceals natural spirit, which is to say, spirit turned to water ... the treasure lies in the depths of the water."

◆

A letter from e.e.c. with a P.S.: "Tell Pavlik that the oversigned hasn't forgotten that fabulous fireworks soirée high-in-la-Tour Eiffel." He refers to a dinner, during the Paris Exposition—'37?—when Edward James took us to the restaurant located in the branches of the Eiffel Tower—we had good food and good wine and talked a lot. Cummings asked me afterwards if James was "intelligent"—I knew he meant, "He's not intelligent, is he?"

◆

"I think Balanchine's desire for ballets with no décor and costumes is just egotistic, Charles Henri"—Pavlik from his bedroom.

◆

The "anima" when it appears as the figure of a veiled woman (Jung's anima, the feminine nature in a man) has turned into its opposite: the symbolic representation of the phallus—to which the man is attracted when dominated by this feminine being of the unconscious. A homosexual may marry his anima, thus identifying, allying, himself even closer with it.

Pavlik has had neurotic fears ever since he was a child and blames them on an aunt of his coming in all draped in black to scare him into taking castor oil. I've just asked him about the incident and he says she was not his aunt but one of the chambermaids, who covered herself with a greatcoat. "You're writing of the origin of my psychopathy—most kind of you!" he adds.

"I'm a very strange bird," he's just said to the housepainter.

◆

The annoying, symmetrical flies.

What a lot of fun we'd miss if we were born wise. We wouldn't run the risks.

Well, there are dreams we do not remember: but they exist, nevertheless.

NOVEMBER

Stay there, blue sky.

November rains.

Plain rain.

Many are the things which we do not desire—until they are offered to us.

◆

When Joseph Rocco said to me (1930, I lying on a bed on the balcony of a Strunsky studio-room, on West 3rd St., below the elevated track—one could look up to the non-curtained part of the windows and see the lighted trains, with their passengers, roll noisily by—Parker lived with me there some of the time—how furious I was when he and Lionel Abel would be in bed below—I slept on the balcony—and talk endlessly when I wanted to sleep; we never went to bed till after midnight, slept most of the morning away, our one commanding pastime was to find enough money to buy gin or wine, and get high before going out—pre-spring, a dead Greenwich Village, a naif, learning, wild, young devoted-to-Parker me)—Joseph R. whom we admired for his brilliant paradoxes (he's one of the characters in *The Young and Evil*)—when he said to me, "I'd like to walk with you through terrible things happening—" I did not know entirely what he meant.

◆

So we shed this body like a chrysalis: butterfly, ancient symbol of the soul. Towards experience of after life: drugs, losing oneself in music—or in anything else where the body is forgotten; Nirvana.

Young men of the year 2000 will call their "little review" *Psyche*. Fashions in poetry will change—my poetry will be recognized, my name will be exalted. And so at this point in my history I must not betray my heritage to be.

The word, a flesh that lives on, as spirit, after we are gone.

◆

During intermissions at the New York City Ballet on the 21st, saw and talked or spoke to Dean Faucett—he said the big tree at Derby Hill had been blown down; Elsie Rieti and son Fabbio, he delighted about the Panama City lot that his mother wants to buy; Dorothea Tanning with her midriff doing a peek-a-boo ("Why can't she dress like everybody else?"—Sylvia Marlowe, who sat with Alice, Pavlik and me); Russell Lynes (who has become a well-known humorist) and wife and 11-year-old daughter. I went to find Coral, told her I wanted her to meet a little girl, when we saw the unattractive child before we reached her, Coral drew back but I pushed her on; Lincoln continuing to talk to George Tooker instead of coming over to talk to me; Esteban Francés reeking as usual of garlic—I told him how much I liked his costumes for *Tyl Ulenspiegel*—but that's more than I could say for Jerry Robbins' dancing or Balanchine's choreography.

◆

I: "Would you like to be in Rome . . . where all the pretty boys are?"

Pavlik: "Don't turn the dagger in the wound."

◆

I was going to a sermon to be delivered by John Peale Bishop, swarms of people were on the way, I stopped in the men's room of the basement of the huge auditorium, a man stood by the door, at the urinal next to me was a little boy, to whom I didn't pay any attention until I suddenly found him trying to bugger me with a prick larger than one would have expected from someone his size . . . I told Pavlik the dream and asked (mock-seriously), "What does it mean? What would be your interpretation? What do you think the meaning is?" . . . Pavlik only said, "I'm not surprised."

◆

Human bêtise when concentrated on the appetites: like a dog running across a field to get to a garbage can.

"Comme une peasant woman—rather a peasant some kind of grossness—" P. describing Edith Sitwell—"no elegance whatsoever"—in contrast with Isak Dinesen (Baroness Blixen) about whom I read to him aloud, after dinner, from *Denmark Is A Lovely Land.*

Mother arrives from Panama City tomorrow morning.

"*Charlie!*"

"What happened?"

"I found a spider—I threw him out."

◆

A record of himself is all any man records.

"I have no enthusiasm for anybody or anything" (Pavlik). "Something broke down."

DECEMBER

Swedish worker yesterday in the house, weather-stripping the doors. I invited him to have coffee with me at the kitchen table and I brought up Isak Dinesen and the fact that she married a Swede, which made her name Baroness Blixen. "Blixen," the man said, "—I'd translate that as 'lightning sun.'"

◆

Pavlik dubs "Comic Strip" several of the prose poems in my MS, *The Forest of Lost and Found*: "Nostalgia of the Chinese Paederast," "The Pleasures of the Table," and one or two others.

Henry Miller and Conrad Aiken write to me, agreeing to my inclusion of prose poems of theirs in my anthology. But no chance of anything new from Miller at the moment: "I have been through so much trouble lately that it's hard to think of literary matters. My mind is a blank. I don't read. Or work . . . Hope things are well with you. More another time."

"Honey will fall," I tell Pavlik when he asks me "what the paper says" about the weather.

"Those farmers are so healthy—like bloody potatoes! Don't you think so?"— Pavlik re the Honicutts, father and son, at the apple farm where we went for cider and Macintoshes today.

And what is day but night illuminated?

"A good time to go ice-skating. I'll tell Bert to bring out his skates when he comes."

P.: "You want to *drawn* some place?"

Many days ago I sent Bert some photos which were taken last summer—and I told him I'd be in N.Y.C. on a certain day and to give me a ring at Sister's apartment if he felt like coming in to town. He did, and came in—and we had sex. I asked him if he'd missed "doing that" with me and he said, "Very much."

◆

Mother told me of the night Sister was born. She left the dinner table, where there were guests in the middle of a meal, went in the kitchen and told the cook to put more biscuits in the oven, 45 minutes later she had her baby girl, the doctor arriving only 20 minutes before the delivery. The guests couldn't believe it was true!

◆

Are not the winter trees nude? They are not skeletons—but "undressed," says Pavlik.

The image I want to catch is harder to capture than a butterfly with bare hands.

I mean: "it's the end of a year" becomes meaningless to me if I imagine it's being said by everyone in the world.

To be what you are—infinitely.

1952

FEBRUARY

PALM BEACH, FLA.

NEITHER

Which had you rather be
A black, sensitive monkey
Chained to a tree,
Or a stone insensitive cat
Staring at nothing?

◆

As the poet outgrows his naïveté, he will be as the child, bitter unless he can love in spite of his person's being less smiled upon.

MARCH

Should I go out in the windy night, where the moon is being blown about (she may be angry and mean mischief), or stay in, philosophically, and have my bourbon in bed? The magnet drawing me out is a 24-year-old with "Airborne" sewn to his sleeve. He was at the Melody Bar three nights ago (and may be there tonight).

One rides down the street, stops by a walking soldier, he accepts the invitation to get in, you take him to your room, and he enjoys being fucked. The only thing he asks in return for your enjoyment is a lift back to the base.

◆

We are sitting in the Virginia Restaurant, Allmett, Virginia, about to order dinner, our last night on the road towards "home."

Pavlik is startled that I've begun my diary again, after telling him that I was giving it up "forever." "C'est fini—je n'en peux plus," he says. "Who gets the soup?" asks the waitress.

APRIL

WESTON, CONN.

The child born on your doorstep will live to throw stones at your windows.

"I'm absolutely so miserable I just feel, good heavens, that heaven should help me—" (P.)

Are the frogs singing because of the dawn or have they sung all night?

MAY

"I'll be sent to a concentration camp and you'll be executed near Paris," Pavlik's apocalyptic vision of our future fates—because my mind is so set on going to Europe.

We go into New York to hear Dylan Thomas read on Thursday, 3 nights from now. He usually reads drunk, but they say splendidly. In looks he is unprepossessing—eyes seem "burnt out"—with drinking.

An example of Eleanor Clark's vulgarity of style, she couples "homosexuals and dope addicts." In the end, all vulgarity is a kind of provincial snobbery.

◆

Who wants to be safe and inconspicuous? As of today, we're taking the Olds on the boat.

Dylan Thomas's poetry reading at the YMHA a great disappointment—he's a ham actor—because he lacks judgement in his interpretation. A theater director with taste, etc., might be able to do something with him, for his voice has range and variety and qualities of melody—but he misuses it too frequently. And then his choice (for May 15 evening) not good—Victorian sentimental Yeats, unfunny O'Casey, Wilfred Owen. His most wholly successful item was Hopkins' "Golden Echo," with parts of Djuna's *Nightwood* (from the chapter "Watchman, What of the Night?") second. Least successful: the last speech from Marlowe's *Dr. Faustus* —perhaps the liquor was wearing off too for his voice was cracky and mawky: dreadfully bad acting; he's probably not meant for the stage, in any case, and would be inaudible without a mike.

◆

Master of the poetic quip—Auden (in *Nones*).

Because I respect Auden more (after reading *Nones*) I envy him less! His poetry's sharp-mindedness pricks one with the efficacy of the word, reminds one of the word's uniqueness—for whatever purpose it wishes to serve.

Poetry is born in the effort.

Card from Cummings: "can't believe Conn is so base (or Ischia so fine)" ... Maybe he's right!

Rimbaud turned his waking nightmares (some of them) into sweet dreams (of poetry).

But ... "a wild animal is never tamed ... only trained." (*Circus Doctor.*)

◆

I copy this news item here before sending the clipping to Cummings pasted on a postcard of Little Red Riding Hood:

> It was by landing on his head during a fall from an extension ladder that a Dutch housepainter discovered his gift of a sixth sense—divination. Having regained his senses, he noticed that he knew in detail the intimate life of his doctors, could translate a Chinese text, was able to drive a car at full speed through the thickest fog, answer questions that were about to be asked, and read a sealed letter after having touched the pen that had been used to write it, according to *Pour Tous*, Lausanne, quoted by North American Newspaper Alliance.

JUNE

I wrote to W. C. Williams asking for a prose poem for my anthology (which New Directions will publish); didn't expect such an effusion (in the way of a letter) in return: "It is pure happiness to be reconciled with you again ... I never realized what a hell it is to have to do without one's friends ..."

◆

I asked Coral: "What's the name of the song you're humming?" (I knew.)

"You know—"

"I don't, what is it?"

" 'The Kiss of Fire.' "

Pavlik's mouth and throat are inflamed, but still he talks non-stop.

Plans are progressing for the Fourth of July party Alice will give in the black barn—as a bon voyage send-off—"Fireworks on the Fourth—a Goodbye Party for Pavel Tchelitchew" ... It's all my idea. We're to have a jazz trio and have people come in red, white and blue—about 300 will be invited.

◆

The nonsensical notions held about the "fantasy" life of the child. The truth is that the child has very little interior life; it must always be doing something, playing something, acting something—and this very obvious acting is mistaken for imagination and fantasy. I've already remarked (through observing Coral) how *literal*-minded a child is. Their play-fantasy is another aspect of their literalness.

"Come promptly!" Coral calls out, after informing us that tea is ready.

"Tea!" she sings out.

"Charlie, she howls for tea," Pavlik says, going down the steps.

◆

Cummings on a postcard (June 2): "And thanks for the cheering news about divination."

◆

At tea Pavlik said he was in a bad mood.

"Pavlik's in a bad mood," I said.

"At least he knows it," said Coral.

◆

A dream in which Bice grumblingly (retardedly) called my attention to Pavlik's having fallen (at the foot of a—fallen?—tree) with a heart attack. I ran back with grief and terror, picked him up: he was a large fish whose muscles I felt as he wriggled somewhat in my hands.

JULY

I write this on the eve of our sailing for Europe.

The costume ball (with Mary Lou Williams Trio) was a great success. I wore my blue coveralls pasted up with red words cut from *Life* magazine advertisements, making sentences *Life* never thought of:

Look! the
RED HEART
of the Desert
to name all its
MAZE
of
MONSTERS
You need a
Book of
ICE

and:

When you go in a Hot Egg it's Quiet . . .
Only the lighted champion wins *all*.

AUGUST

FORIO D'ISCHIA (ITALY)

I know I am on the right path, the great path, the good path.

SEPTEMBER

Auden came to dinner and I smoked his Alfas (cheapest of Italian cigarettes) which were so awful I feel cured of all desire to smoke *any* cigarette.

The Carlyle Browns are giving a dinner party tonight for Pavlik's birthday. We will have been here two months tomorrow. Pavlik decided this morning that the time hasn't been lost after all—he feels he's made "un petit bout de chemin."

Cartier-Bresson arriving end of week to take photos of Ischia and the milieu.

Never enjoyed killing flies so much anywhere. It's because there are so many. But—"No more islands," says Pavlik.

◆

Last night listening to Cartier-Bresson expound his ideas on photography. Brian Howard's pedantic presiding was intolerable—but I tolerated as long as I could and then left. Henri (C.-B.) had appeared at our house (Via Casa d'Ascia, 12) before dinner. "You haven't changed," he told me. He's grown fat, blinks a tic at you continuously—later he had on glasses. Hard to reconcile the two pictures of him: now and the way he was twenty years ago when he stayed with Sister and me in the apartment on Eighth Street. Carl Van Vechten said then, "He looks even younger than you do."

It thunders. I think of a title for a detective novel, *I'm Going to Kill You, Dear.*

OCTOBER

GROTTAFERRATA

We're back in the Villa Sereni, where we spent the winter of 1949–50. It's marvelous to look upon—the valley leading up to Monte Cavo. At the moment, low clouds against a blue sky hide the morning sun—the low rays make all the mountain's bumps stand out.

I begin this little cahier on the day that Pavlik begins his treatment for the Lamblia discovered through a Naples analysis. The Rome doctor, Simeons, a German refugee (English now), said he knew these intestinal parasites in India, and Pavlik has perked up considerably with the prospect of being rid of what may have been draining his strength for years.

◆

Frankie, 17, still waiting on table at his father's trattoria down the road, soft-spoken, taller and heavier than I, has a pretty face. He says that at carnival time he will dress as a girl, as he did last year, and I won't be able to tell he's not a signorina: he will have a blond wig, falsies of wool. Under his skirt he will wear one of those big banana-shaped rubber soft clubs, which boys use to beat the girls on the head. He'll show the girls what he's wearing under his skirt—and make them scream.

◆

Just below Monte Cavo, as though perched on her shoulder, is Rocca di Pappa, a village like a handful of stars, at night.

◆

"The principle of life is white," says P., looking at a vine leaf held up towards the sun. "It's very funny," he says about the leaf, "it's like an enormous town, some of the streets . . . you can follow them."

He who has admirers will always have lovers, I told him when he said that no one cared how ugly and old he looks. Anyway he's pleased with the immediateness of his inspiration here in this house, has started a picture with a brand-new idea: "Toys . . ."

I took a walk towards sunset up to where Sisto used to work—the whole set-up has changed—new people, no sheep.

". . . Because you really don't have your own life—you're living on somebody—" Pavlik to me. But he's the one who can't face living alone!

◆

I return from a walk to Frascati and Pavlik greets me from his window with the news that I have a telegram from Gino saying that he's arriving tomorrow. I had Margie (who knows Italian) write him from Forio that there would be a guest room for him here till Nov. 1, after which the room would be occupied by the donna di servizio.

◆

I got up at 6:15 so as to take the train from Frascati into Rome to meet Gino. I didn't drive in because it was rainy and foggy. I was waiting for a second train to arrive from Milano when Gino spied me. He looks very well, pink, and nicely dressed, only a little older, not changed otherwise. He can stay a few days, then goes back to Lévico, which he left around 8 last night.

Gino said he trembled after he got off the train—then started smoking to calm his nerves, though he hadn't smoked in fifteen days. We took a nap together after lunch. I think it would be as fruitless now as it was two years ago to try to start any sex-play with him. He's not *quite* as beautiful as he was, but still compellingly attractive. I hold his hand, kiss his cheek, feel his hair and neck . . .

◆

Gino would have spent the night in my double bed but I decided not to let him— he said he could feel friendship for a man—even imagine sacrificing his life for that friendship—but it's the woman whom he feels made to make love to . . . if he makes it at all.

He's a pleasant friend, nice to have around, handsome to look at, true-hearted, and I'm glad he came on this visit, though he is less a poet now and admits it.

Pavlik: "He just thinks you're a selfish American bitch—he's not very far from the truth—if you think you're something else you're mistaken."

NOVEMBER

Maria, our new housekeeper, who was working for the Leslie Fiedlers in Forio, phoned yesterday afternoon from Rome and we went to meet her at Frascati. She nearly talked my ear off while we were having our risotto but Pavlik thinks it was from nervousness at the newness. I told P. that we must spoil her a little if we expect to be spoiled. He said she's going to cost us "lots of money," finds her full of "oil." Relationship with a servant is a vicious circle: you're not happy unless she's happy and she's not happy if you're displeased.

◆

Frankie asked me when am I going to get married, I said, "During carnival time when you become a signorina, I'm going to marry you."

◆

"That face has done everything," I said to Pavlik about Maria, "a real Moll Flanders."

"The moment you speak to her it's like an open faucet," says P.

◆

Gray Foy and Leo Lerman came out to lunch. "I'm an impossible man," Pavlik is saying to Gray, "you have to know that. You have to see what I'm doing now—the space is dancing—space moves on a spiral line—the form moves on an oval round thing . . . they walk, they dance . . ."

"Not like Duchamp?" asks Gray.

"How not like Duchamp! You think I'm a damn fool? I'm myself, not like anybody else. That's why I want to go to Paris—people get up . . ."

"Doesn't it make you uncomfortable?"

Gray is saying all the wrong things. " . . . Scholarship . . . intellectual . . ." (about Uccello's drawing of the chalice). "Not art but science . . ."

Pavlik says: "I give you one advice"—Gray is an aspiring painter—"look at all the past—don't come to the past with your little American ready-made ideas . . .

go on your knees ... very humbly. You come now from America with all the one-track mind. Look at everything and wait till everything turns over and clicks. If nothing turns over and clicks, pack your luggage and go back home ... I feel so near to Egypt, I feel so near to Etruscans ..."

◆

"I suffer when I see dirt"—Maria's line. Pavlik says she makes "emotional chan-tage" on him, like his sister, Choura: "Wipe my bitter tears"—Pavlik applies this phrase to Maria's habitual expression.

Leo Lerman asked me yesterday, "Would you like to hear something de-pressing?" I said, "No," but he wanted to tell me so he told: "Truman Capote is making $500 a *day* in Rome working on the script of a De Sica movie." I told Gray: "My cynicism is gay."

◆

Bice comes in to tell us that Maria is leaving in a week, will return to the Fiedlers. Said Maria didn't want, or was afraid or ashamed, to tell Signor Paolo herself. So she's taking the old job back in spite of there being seven people (5 children) to work for instead of two. She'd already told me that she felt as if she were in prison out here—that one had to be born in the country to like it.

◆

"Arachne, Arachne, you are the queen of the world."—P.

DECEMBER

Pretty people pass by, pass by, in carts or on foot or bicycling—I'm like a cat who watches the birds and butterflies out of reach. "In a cold climate one makes more mistakes than in a warm climate." (Pavlik after working this morning.) One is given a little genius but one has to work for one's talent.

Lincoln is always saying how "professional" Cecil is. He (L.) doesn't know the difference between commercial and professional, I told Pav, who replied, "In America very few people know the difference."

◆

The hill covered with velvet draperies of dark plum, with highlights of blue . . .
Huge yellow roses, deepening to orange on the outside petals, still bloom below
the bathroom window. And with a perfume deep as the South. Birds singing—and
being shot to be eaten with cornmeal.

Pavlik's done a lovely new crayon drawing. "Like a Christmas tree ornament?"
he asks. "Christmas tree ornaments try to be marvelous—your drawing *is* marvelous," I tell him.

◆

"Ready to fuck the world"—rather surprising descriptive phrase applied by Pavlik to me (yesterday on a walk). He insists that I should pull my animal nature
"up." I say it has to be satisfied, like an appetite, before I'm left in peace to work. "I
was much more animal than you," he said. "I learned how to pull it up."

◆

He says he doesn't quite understand the principle of "turning" in his new pictures.
I told him: it's the eye that turns; a movie camera, moving, can make things seem
to turn: the eye can do that too.

"Yes, it's true," he replied.

◆

"I'm sure I was Adelina Patti"—Pavlik has often said. He says her mouth was
shaped as his is shaped.

"If Hannibal came from Africa in weather like this, I'm not surprised that he
went back"—he puts on our New Year's card to Mary Rodgers.

◆

Monte Cavo now: between it and the dark blue background (the dark blue of rain
clouds) there is a huge white cloud slowly coming up and crawling over its back.

Islands of Night.

Islands of night in seas of eternity.

1953

JANUARY

I sometimes think of Pavlik as a monster of egotism, enveloping, smothering, crushing my own ego. But that is not the whole truth. Neither is Pavlik's sometimes expressed idea of me the whole truth: someone who drinks his blood, lives on him, remains young while he grows old.

Leonardo Cremonini is here, young Italian painter whom we met in Forio through Margie and Carlyle Brown. He is amazed that we can go to bed so early here, night after night—it's not the life he could lead, he says.

"C'est la pierre precieuse qui decouvre soi-même"—Pavlik describing his own painting to Leonardo. "Le merveilleux est quand l'expression n'a aucune expression," P. continues.

◆

Leo Lerman, who came out for lunch, had an enchanting, fascinating picture to paint of Baroness Blixen (Isak Dinesen) whom he visited at her house near Copenhagen. He said she had many kind words for me. I said, "She's the person in the world whom I'd *like* to meet and haven't met."

◆

"Une chose noire qui tourne"—Pavlik describing a whirlpool (to Leonardo), which he says is more frightening to him than a precipice.

It was a moment of agony: Pavlik struggling with mattresses, just below me on a terrace without a railing, I calling out to him to be careful. Suddenly he falls over the edge, and was dropping as if from a great height . . . and I awoke.

"Moi, je suis l'executeur des ordres inconnus," he's saying to Leonardo.

◆

"Je commence de manquer du courage," he says to me this morning, on account of the cold. He works in his room with the blinds of one of the windows down and a car-rug around his shoulders. The thermometer on the wall says 52.

◆

Nancy Cunard just phoned, says she'll be at the Albergo Flora working on a book for the next two weeks, wanted us to come in to Frascati and have a drink. I told her it would be better if she called us the first sunny day and came out for lunch or tea.

◆

A sympathetic, but not beautiful ruin: N.C. She came to lunch yesterday, walking the thirty-minute uphill walk from Frascati. How can anyone look that old? Poverty can enforce shabbiness, but a taste in hair arrangement does not depend on money—Nancy's is grotesque, with hairpin-held curlicues on each side. Pavlik's chief criticism: she lives in the past. Nancy rolled out names of the Twenties: Man Ray, Kay Boyle, Réné Crevel (though P. might have mentioned Réné first, Réné was his lover and he painted several portraits of him); and Norman Douglas (on whom she's doing an "appreciation"). She said he was referred to as Poet Norman Douglas in *The Rome Daily American*—"and if there was one thing he couldn't stand it was poetry!" [Miguel] Covarrubias, Jean Cocteau, Brian Howard (she was not aware of Brian's Dr.-Jekyll-and-Mr.-Hyde present personality).

"Like a sewed up sack," P. described her face. "Like a pulled up Lady Cunard," he described her body . . .

The three of us took a drive followed by a walk in Rocca di Pappa. Then I dropped her off at the Flora.

"She looks like a whore," was Pavlik's comment when I returned to the house.

"I know. And a poorly paid one," I reply.

People laugh aloud when they see her—as they did in Rocca di Pappa.

◆

I could write a comedy (but would I want to) with three main characters, as follows:

A young writer.

An older painter.

The young writer's mother.

The "plot"—as made by the characters—would be the mother's attempt to get her son away from the older man—and her failure.

The setting: a New York penthouse.

One of the subsidiary characters: a balletomane (based on Lincoln Kirstein's personality), who is a close friend of the painter's, and would also like to see the "household" broken up.

The pathos would be in the mother's failure. But her son would be the hero—for he would have won a "moral" victory.

The tension and suspense could easily be built around whether the young poet—not too young, but younger—will leave his friend of ten years or not. The poet is now thirty—still looks twenty—a kind of modern-day Dorian Gray.

"I look like a 75-year-old man," Pavlik has just said, ". . . because you have eaten me to pieces."

Pavlik has kept me, protected me like a father, all these years (twenty in July). That's why I've remained so like an adolescent—in looks and achievement. I'm not adult yet. I've told him that I'm psychologically "crippled" by him—retarded. I also have told him that our breaking up is inevitable—but he doesn't want to believe it.

◆

"Grande tristesse et gründe désastre . . . One can do nothing about it. She looks like the poorest prostitute . . . something not to be believed," Pavlik again on the subject of N.C.

He went on to remember a Russian expression, "It's impossible to sneeze with a cunt." He remarked on the similarity of the French and Russian insight into reality through grotesque expression. But with the Germans it's different, he said, "Because [with them] the *absurd* is on the level of possibility—that's the tragedy of the German character."

FEBRUARY

"Writing is one long rewriting," I say to Pavlik (speaking of prose).

"Painting is one long repainting," he echoes.

I told him I was writing a comedy. "You'll have to find some kind of frightful fairy to play in it," he said.

He said he once thought that he'd never give up his looks; then one fine day he decided to hell with them—painting was more important. "I've really given my life to my work."

"Are you a poet?"

"I'm nothing at all. I'm an old fool, that's what I am."

◆

From a Notebook of '51: Understandable that the symbol of God should be the phallus, since what comes out of it is formless creation, sperm: chaos of potential universes.

◆

I watch the skies, hoping it will clear up this afternoon—we're expecting two carfuls for a cocktail-buffet.

◆

The party went off well and I don't feel like working this morning. Channing Hare's car—with Stevie Hensel, Ben Morris, Stark Young and friend Wales Bowman—first to arrive, Channing generously loaded with gifts, a shirt which he'd brought for my birthday, a bottle of Martell brandy (none left this morning), a bottle of Haig & Haig 5 Star, and a huge box of Perugino chocolates (for Pavlik, he said) wrapped, each one, in bright colored shiny paper. Then came the second car with Thad Lovett and his friends Albert and Francis and their Italian friend Amadeo who was attractive and spoke English. After martinis we had the buffet dinner which was very good. Then about 8:45 came Corrado and his friend Mario, plus Franco's friend Claudio who said that Frankie was getting dressed up in masquerade and would be along soon. So I told Ben to go in my room and start putting on *his* make-up and a Japanese-looking black wig which he'd decorated with pearls from the ten-cent store.

Arrives Frankie (Franco) in a silk street dress, a turban and high heels—and with a *purse*—looking like a real streetwalker (also had on a small black mask). When he saw Ben's wig he immediately *wanted* it but I said let Ben make his entrance first, which he did, with black slacks, black sweater, and black ballet slippers. We forgot to give him breasts! ... When Corrado (Frankie's brother) learned that Frankie was wanting to be taken to the carnival in Frascati in his get-up he was horrified, sought him out in my bedroom (where he was trying on Ben's wig) and gave him a piece of his mind (in dialect). Frankie didn't come back in the salon—I don't know if he went home and took off the drag or went on to Frascati alone (he borrowed Ben's mask, velvet with pearls, in any case).

Stark drank too much whiskey (the last I poured for him he insisted on its being triple), went to sleep in chair, then when he woke up went out and pissed in the hall ... The last to leave were Claudio and Corrado, charlestoning to the end.

Frankie looked *huge* as a lady.

MARCH

"Can't you realize what you're doing? You're slowly killing me," says Pavlik, after my telling him to "Hurry" and let's take a walk before the sun goes down.

◆

"J'ai perdu beaucoup le côté humain, parce que j'ai cherché le mouvement"—P. to Igor Markevitch, who was here for dinner, together with his wife who is the niece of Princess Caetani, editor of *Botteghe Oscure* who has just sent back everything I submitted to her for the magazine (Pavlik, with his sense of retribution, said, "Put it in your diary!")...

Prior to bedtime Pav painted with iodine the soles of my feet and bound my head in an old handkerchief, remarking what a big "minotaur" head I have and what a little head he has.

◆

"Le Midi [Mississippi] est brutal et positif comme un sculpteur dans ces compositions les plus delicates; le Nord [Russia] souffrant et inquiet se console avec l'imagination . . ." (Baudelaire.)

APRIL

The arrangement here is no good—the time and routine of one is too imposed upon by the needs of the other. We must live in a place where each can come and go—or *stay*—as he pleases. I feel I'm not "my own boss," and Pavlik feels dependent on me for transportation. Won't do! He's *always* going to be running into Rome, more often than I will need to.

"Seeing that his talents were so little appreciated at Naples, Polidoro [da Caravaggio] determined to leave a place where they prefer a horse that jumps well to a clever painter." ([Giorgio] Vasari) . . . Pavlik is still searching for the security that a proper evaluation of *his* works would bring. Certainly the place, the market place, is not Rome. He hopes to find a dealer in Paris, even if he has to sell his work for less than N.Y. prices.

Polidoro is not even mentioned in Baedeker's *Italy (From the Alps to Naples)* although Vasari wrote: "I could fill a book with the performance of these two [Polidoro and his partner in painting, as well as, one assumes, his lover, Maturino Florentino] alone, as there is no apartment, palace, garden or country-house which does not contain their work."

◆

Easter Sunday. "The closer I get to Paris, the more excited I get about Paris," I say to Pavlik. He says to me, "I must tell you frankly, I feel the same way . . . Tanguy didn't want . . ." Tanguy's show was a flop in Paris—critics' general tone was: Tanguy has been painting the same way for twenty years.

La poésie de Paris: I shall look for it.

"Poetry should be made not by one but by all," wrote Lautréamont. At least, all should be poets—each in his own way.

Paris will be a pretext for reminiscences of twenty years ago: 1933, the year *The Young and Evil* was published, the year I returned to Paris after having left Djuna for Carmita the year before. Adventures in Italy with Carmita. We went to Spain, where we met [Félix] Pita [Rodríguez], a poet from Cuba who became her lover in

Madrid. The three of us went to Tangier where we shared a house from November 1932 until the spring, when Carmita and Pita left for Galicia (and Carmita died there of typhoid). I was in Tangier until July—by that time Djuna had come and gone.

◆

PARIS, 2 RUE JACQUES MAWAS

I am moving day after tomorrow to 1 rue Gît-le-Coeur. Alice Delamar says we can have her apartment there for two months—until her arrival in June. Pavlik was undecided whether he'd move or not, is still going to let me get installed first (but he's going to follow). Choura is the same Choura: talkative, cooks, knits, smokes and plays solitaire.

Paris is the aphrodisiac of cities—even tops Rome.

◆

Today, all alone in the upper floor apartment Rue Gît-le-Coeur (it's a duplex), the impulse came upon me to do a drawing—just any drawing, copy what was before my eyes (the window-frame, etc.). Before it was finished I heard the phone ringing downstairs so I went down and there sat Mrs. Merde, Alice's housekeeper, letting the phone ring on as she continued knitting by the window—but she jumped up to answer it when I entered. It was Bobby. He had received my letter sent to him in Meudon, said he was on the rue de Rivoli but not alone, I asked him when he would be free, he said 2:30, I asked him where he would like to meet me—here at Gît-le-Coeur or at a café and he gave me a rendezvous at the Dupont Latin. He was not on the terrace when I arrived, I looked for him inside and he saw me before I saw him. I could see the sixteen-year-old Bobby in him but the change (he'll be twenty in June) is still being "adjusted" to on my part: he looks like a young man, yet the boyishness is still there.

We came to my room here and had an Italian brandy (there wasn't much left in my flask—the flask I had on the De Grasse and which Bobby recognized—he asked me if that liquor which I had in it then wasn't a specially strong liqueur which I'd had made for me—I told him No, it was just bourbon).

We talked, and Bobby told me a lot that had happened to him since I saw him last, and he told me of some of his sex affairs. I asked him if he was in love, he said No he stopped himself from falling in love whether with a girl or a boy. So I started kissing him and he lost no time responding. His body now is lean and white, skin like a beautiful white woman's, as though it had never been exposed to the sun. He told me he'd never forgotten me and repeated several times I love you Charlie.

◆

Thank heaven Léonor's friend Monsieur Wild (the rich Swiss) has bought several of the new drawings of Pavlik's, otherwise his mood about money would be disastrous—given the difficulties with the galleries—he doesn't know where he will show or *if* he will show this spring. He's seen *no* gallery directors, the only one he had an appointment with didn't turn up!

As to my drawing, which I've been persisting in, Pavlik's being a bitch and a bastard—says he'll withdraw from my life. I told him he could go fuck himself.

◆

During intermission at the Markevitch concert Ned Rorem asked me if I knew Jean Genet and I said Yes. (Ned is eager to meet him and to see his film, *Un Chant d'Amour.*) "What's he like?" "Solemn," I said. "And humorless—and that's disastrous." That humorlessness is what's responsible for parts of *Chant d'Amour*'s being unconsciously corny and funny—the chase sequence, specifically. His books too have unconsciously vulgar-funny parts. "He's a very primitive person," Peter Watson told me . . . "anyone must be primitive who could sit in a Cannes bar night after night and jump up and run out every time a bevy of bicycle boys—or even one—slowed down at the curb."

◆

Oh it's gold, that little Gothic tower I see from the window directly in front of this writing table.

MAY

Pure Literature—with her pants always unbuttoned.

◆

Paris was a garden of lilies-of-the-valley yesterday—on practically every other corner were vendors of this sweet flower—millions of Parisians wore it, gave it, received it—for good luck.

Léonor told Pavlik that she didn't get him and Jean Genet together (she sees Genet usually every Saturday) because she didn't think the meeting would be a success. He's a very "primaire" person, she told Pavlik, and would immediately sense Pavlik's superiority. She said it's all she can do not to explode sometimes, and has often to put herself on a lower level in order to communicate with him.

◆

Peter Watson showed up while Perry Embiricos and I were at the Pergola, and when Perry mentioned that some "beautiful" (according to Peter) queen who did a drag performance at a boîte in Cannes had been put out of a job because the U.S. Navy had been told not to *go* there, Peter began spitting: "How dare they! Americans are ruining everything . . . and such awful people are doing it." Then I said, "Power always ruins. Everyone in his turn." And just to give his pro-British chauvinism another pinch, I added: "Osbert Sitwell used to call America the garbage can of Europe, but now he's eating out of it."

◆

Black statues in black niches.

During tea yesterday chez Henri-Louis de la Grange, Francis Poulenc heard some church bells ringing in the distance, stopped talking to listen, said he couldn't go on, the sound gave him such "volupté." Pavlik was so bored, finally, with Poulenc's hogging the conversation, that he shut up like a clam.

Everyone is desperate for friends to love.

"Je veux que tu me pose," I say to Pavlik.

"I never heard anything—!"

◆

At the Louvre, exhibition of stained-glass windows from French cathedrals. I was struck once more with the power which simplicity can have: not because it's *simple* but because the intention and intensity are communicated, though the means are simple: Matisse thought (thinks) his own work has this power but it doesn't.

◆

Pavlik and I took a post-dinner walk and ran into Jean Genet—I stopped him and introduced him to Pavlik, who immediately started covering him with compliments (on his work) to put him at ease. Léonor was afraid he'd be "arrogant" with Pavlik but he wasn't. He was leaving by plane for Rome in five hours, took out his ticket to show us (perhaps so we'd believe him!), was dressed in blue suit with pale blue tie, very neat looking. "Are you in love with Italy?" I asked and he said no but that he was in love with an Italian. "Vous avez toujours votre jolie visage," he told me. "Merci," I replied.

◆

Around midnight in the cup behind the Pantheon stood a policeman—he was alone there, in a niche near the exit. I took the middle stall and knew almost at once that the flic was cruising—if he'd been there to arrest someone, I figured he'd have been in plainclothes. It was only a few seconds before he looked around the barrier. He was not good-looking, but his policeman's uniform, and the idea that he was a policeman, excited me. He wanted to go; I said, "Ici," but he left. I left, not intending to follow him especially, but I found myself walking down the street he took, and he was waiting for me and started a pleasant genteel conversation. He said he lived with his parents, I said I lived with my uncle, had no place to take him, and at the corner I said, Goodnight. But he wanted me to go with him, saying something about the courtyard at his house, so I followed along. At one moment, as we approached a schoolhouse with the French flag hanging out, I thought he might be taking me to the police station, then I saw it was a schoolhouse and we continued and reached his street, he hesitated until a passerby disappeared then took me into a courtyard, we went by the concierge's loge, lights behind curtains, and voices, then into the building. There was a baby-carriage in front of a door leading to the cellar; my flic pulled the baby-carriage out and we went through the door and he held my hand in the dark and led me down some steps and then down some more steps and we stopped in pitch blackness. He asked, "Que veut-tu?" and I said, "Tu veut me sucer?" and he murmured, "Oui . . ."

When we were back up he took me across the courtyard to the front entrance, where we'd come in. On leaving I said, "A samedi prochain, peut-être," and he said, "J'en serai ravi."

JUNE

The radical way of seeing. Radical philosophers (Krishnamurti, Jaspers) see the meaning of life anew: as though for the first time. Bergson: fresh vision: a sloughing off—very close to the way an original artist suddenly sees. He sees less in order to see more.

◆

René Crevel (in *Le Clavecin de Diderot*) reminded his generation that sadism is characteristic of the male. It is also characteristic of the male to be buggered. I would say that where sadism in the male exists, there exists likewise anal eroticism: the more sadistic, the more masochistic.

◆

Here we are back at 2 rue Jacques-Mawas. Fat-assed Madame Merde thinks we're moving tomorrow—and she's planning to pass by Gît-le-Coeur in the afternoon, supposedly to continue putting the apartment in order for Mademoiselle Delamar—we decided to move this evening so we wouldn't have to see her mug tomorrow. She gives no respite.

◆

Big Bill Tilden is dead. I could write an elegy for him. He served two jail terms for sex-acts with minors (boys). Many men serve jail terms for that sort of thing, but I am moved by the combination of what Tilden was: a great champion, unorthodox personality—and, finally, a pathetic figure, whose glory was only a memory.

Christine Jorgensen's transformation from ex-GI into woman has captured the imagination of the public. She is a living dream: she corresponds to some unconscious desire in everyone: the desire of the woman to have once known what it is to be a man, the desire of the man to sleep with his own sex. With Jorgensen, that sex has become another but there's still something of the androgyne hovering about the personality of Christine.

O adolescent boys of Paris, why do I continue to dream that you have something to give me?

Out in the hall a ladder led to the rectangle opening which led to the roof. I went on my balcony, looked up towards the right and there was a young man with his ear pressed to one of the clay chimney pots. I asked him if there was a nice view from where he was—after he got up higher and looked over rooftops which I couldn't see. Then I went out in the hall and up the ladder and onto the roof and saw the view. It was time for him to leave but he wasn't in a hurry. He was a chimney-sweep, with a blackened face and blue eyes. He said No, he wasn't alone, he'd already been called to come down (I saw a fat man going down the steps as I came up). So I went inside and down the ladder and he came down the ladder and hung it on the wall and I asked him into my room to have a cognac and he came in and had one—but he was in a hurry to join his boss by this time so nothing happened.

◆

Little boys, little boys, leave my balls alone.

◆

The Rake's Progress (Auden-Stravinsky), in ununderstandable French, bored me to unseen tears. Ennui mortel, a pastiche that has nothing to do with our time, a work which, at one's most indulgent, should be heard and not seen. Nicolas Nabokov was shocked at my saying aloud most of the foregoing, after last night's performance. This morning he telephones to Pavlik that the "consensus of opinion" is much like mine. Nicolas has to write something about it for the *Figaro Litteraire* and is in a quandary—but he'll get out of it, with praise for the master. Florence de Montferrier, in a dark blue gathered-silk dress by Dior, took us back to her hotel for a bottle of champagne. Knowing that we're at a loss for a summer house, she told us of a 16th century château with a dirty little swimming pool which she "nearly" took, above Grasse, said it belongs to Lady Juliet Duff's estate, and said she thought we might like it but Pavlik says No. I said, If we don't take it maybe it would interest Léonor. "I don't want Léonor," Florence speaks up.

"Too much competition," I say.

"Too much competition," echoes Florence. "Léonor is a chasseuresse."

"Not now," I say, "she's had a steady boy friend [Kot] for a year or two."

The other night at dinner (chez elle) Léonor began to tell about her pregnancy at Beausoleil. She said she was frantic to get rid of the embryo (fathered by Lepri, though André de Mandiargues was on the scene at the time—during the war). She called on a Javanese doctor there to bring about an abortion. The doctor pleaded with her to have the child because he had an intuition that one of his own dead children would be reborn in it. He said his children's voices came to him, wanting to be born again. Léonor said the only time in her life when she felt she wanted to commit suicide was at this time, when the *possibility* of producing an infant hadn't been squelched.

◆

P. still infected with his "black hysteria"—a name I made up for it. He says he's *always* felt in Limbo in Paris—so he's not surprised at his mood. But still, he thinks he's never been treated "worse" by the French than in 1953—during these two months he's been looking for a gallery.

◆

In the hall, there's a continual stream of hard heels hitting the uncarpeted floor. La Maison des Bruits.

The legs of the French aren't so good, in comparison with the Italians, but their faces are more piquant. They're mysterious, even when sweet, even when dangerous. Americans don't have much mystery, they just don't.

If that mystery man in the hall will get away from the tap, I want to get a drink of water.

◆

Dorothea, as I guessed, is simply waiting for her dog, Katchina, to die. (Unconsciously, she identifies Katchina with Max.) She said, "Katchina is twelve years old which is equivalent to eighty-four in a human." "She may never die!" I had said earlier. "Oh, don't say that!" said Dorothea. "She's practically blind. She's the albatross I carry through life." (The albatross ... isn't it white like Max's hair?) We've talked, Pavlik and I, about Dorothea's being Max's "prisoner"—his "victim." And the fact that she mentions the dog's age, comparing it with a human's ... She wants someone younger!

It's the opposite of the "Come Back, Little Sheba" complex; it's "Go Away, Old Katchina."

◆

He who hesitates, in drawing, is lost! The same with the writing of poetry ... The Neurotic is Hesitant: can't do anything. Call it indecision or wavering or inconsistency or lack of will or confusion. The passion is perverted, diluted. Love's goal is indistinct, blurred, indefinite ...

◆

"What does Charles Henri do to stay so young?" Peter Van Eyck asked Pavlik.

"Nothing!" Pavlik replied. "Like the Chinese—just nothing!"

JULY

I've just told Pavlik that he's got an ego like a sick sea-anemone—receiving wounds on dozens of antennae, that he should ignore what he calls his "humiliations" and since he has the means to exist for, say one year minimum, work during that year and forget about everything else. If he'd only concentrate on the essential. He creates spectres, problems, where they don't exist—*problems* are always imposed or invented: abandon them and they don't exist.

"... nothing to move to rapture ... nothing to excite anguish." (Southey in Portugal.)

◆

Fourteen, fourteen, is any age more charming? None. That was Mauro's age last summer. At fourteen he had that balance between a child of thirteen and the full puberty of fifteen.

◆

Light streamed from a wound of gold. It was a medal hanging around the neck of a boy coming towards the sailor and me—the sun was going down behind our backs.

◆

"Santa Claus," I replied to the man in the movie house on whose lap I sat, as he fingered my penis, he'd whispered in my ear, "What's that," and simultaneously a slide with the image of St. Nick was flashed on the screen. My earliest memory of sex.

My experience with Negro Nurse came later (by then, I was four)—I remember her brown belly, at the bottom of which black hair grew, and my getting on top of her and making fornicating motions.

This time twenty years ago I was visiting Gertrude Stein at Bilignin. The first thing she asked me was if there'd been sex between Carmita and me in Morocco. Raspberries were in season. A big fresh bowl of them, and a generous serving of cream, arrived on the breakfast tray. Alice B. Toklas had picked them that morning. Gertrude let me read a MS-copy of her book, *The Autobiography of Alice B. Toklas*, to be brought out in September. "I've given you a boost," she told me. I read it and was amused and Gertrude, as usual, was amused. It turned out to be an even bigger success than both of us together had expected. One night, by lamplight, I complimented Gertrude on her looks. "You look very handsome in that light," I said, her profile being towards me. "Yes," she said, "we're both very handsome." She predicted "success" for me in Paris—warned me that I should work, work, not let personal success spoil me. She said I showed a "three-year" development in character and maturity since she'd seen me in the spring of 1932—when I'd gone to her to repay a small loan. That repayment fetched me a line in the *Autobiography*: "He is also honest which is also a pleasure."

◆

Last night to see a film program at the Cardinet, a couple of USSR fantasies (one puppets, one animated cartoon), for children. In the grotesque fantasy of the animated puppet film, figures in a forest metamorphosed from plant life, had a kinship with Pavlik's *Hide-and-Seek* period. In the animated cartoon, a slender stream of moonlight made spirals, made egg-shaped forms in space, the intersecting lines shining as in Pavlik's new (colored crayon) drawings. Strange that Russia should produce likenesses in her sons, though said sons are far distant one from the other—and the ideals behind each production are even further apart than the individual producers.

◆

Twenty years ago tomorrow was the beginning of what has resulted in a twenty-year relationship, constant association, with Pavlik. I wrote Parker then, "I've found a genius."

Summer of '33. I visited Pavlik and his sister (Choura) and Allen Tenner at their little country place near Lagny—Guermantes, the village was called. Pavlik did, or began (probably he finished it in Paris, I don't remember now) the Red Portrait of me—in the red shirt, with the background of wheat like a strawhat, and the poppies flying through the air. Before the summer was over, Gertrude had me at Bilignin again. The afternoon I arrived, and she found out I'd been visiting the Tchelitchews, she rudely told me, "If I'd known that, I wouldn't have invited you again." She and Pavlik, who had once been such good friends, were not speaking to each other.

Before I left Tangier I'd met Henri Cartier-Bresson. He dropped in at Claude McKay's one afternoon and I was there in a bathing suit, having swum over an inlet which separated Claude's house from the beach. Again by chance, Henri and I met in Paris, at one of Marie-Louise Bousquet's Thursdays. He was just breaking away from painting then—he'd wanted to be a painter before he took up photography. I went to the big bourgeois house which his family had and he showed me his watercolors and paintings—I have no memory of any particular pleasure in these—but his photographs opened my eyes: no photographs had ever affected me like his did. That was the spring of '35. When Henri came to see us in Ischia last summer, I told him that he'd always been and remained the poète-photographe of our time.

I spent the fall and winter of 1933–34 in a little hotel on the rue de Javel, writing a novel (still unpublished), *Life of a Child*. The summer of 1934 Pavlik and I went to Spain. In beach towns around Málaga we searched for a place to stay, finally settled on the upper floor of the mayor of Fuengirola's two-story house. We were there six weeks, eating uneatable food which the mayor's wife cooked in the restaurant she ran ... It was hot, hot, the water was cold to swim in, the nights were hot, suffocating, but we both "produced": Pavlik the series of Bullfights (three big gouaches), and I continued on a series of sonnets, begun at Guermantes (later to be published, *A Pamphlet of Sonnets*, with a frontispiece by Tchelitchew).

◆

I paid an unexpected visit this hot afternoon in Paris to Dorothea—found her combing her dog's hair, dog would give a squeal from time to time when it hurt.

An "earlier" Paris came into the conversation. Dear naive Dorothea is impressed by all the talk she hears about the Dada days—thinks they must have been marvelous. I told her that the best of what was good in Dada remains and that I find it pointless to have a nostalgia for the past. Max Ernst came in with wine and provisions, couldn't help manifesting a spontaneous smile when I told him of Pavlik's illness. I was shown a recently completed painting hanging in the next room—painfully bad composition, sponged-on forms and that hideous off-coral-red he spreads all over the place. But word goes around Paris that Max is having a comeback.

◆

When I told Pavlik of another poet who had devoted himself to the "art of draughtsmanship"—Goethe—Pavlik said, "But he continued to write." I said, "I continue to write too." "You haven't written your *Faust*." "My journal is my *Faust*." Pavlik is curious and appalled at the same time at my drawing propensities.

Everyone in Paris looks loved out (plus ou moins) rather than worked down.

◆

I saw Mayo last night—a Greek, born in Egypt, he knows Paris better than anyone—first time I've seen him since 1932 when we gave what I call La Dernière Fête de Montparnasse: we took over the top floor of a deserted apartment house, lit the place with hundreds of candles, word got around and masses of people surged in, bringing wine. A phonograph was blaring, I danced with Lee Miller, then there was a police raid but no one was arrested—we were making too much noise in the middle of the night so the party had to break up. I left to join Carmita in Florence the next day.

Mayo has the same soft voice and melodic laugh, now as then. I used to be very much attached to him in those spring months of 1932, when I was living with Djuna. After I left he gave Djuna a portrait he'd painted of me, but she burned the canvas in the fireplace of the apartment at 9 rue St.-Romain—said it looked as though I'd been "under opium" for weeks.

◆

Ben Morris and I sat on the bench outside the Bar Montana last evening and watched the people pass, the pimps play. Anne de Bièville sauntered up, I got rid of him by asking him to buy us beers: "You did it gracefully," said Ben. "If one is not gracefully rude, one makes oneself unpopular," I said. Then I spied Jean Genet at the entrance, talking to some uninteresting queens. I went up to him and spoke, told him I'd seen Mr. Wild (who gives him money and whom he's visited several times at the Wild Villa on Lake Como). I told him that Wild might arrange a dinner for us all—"avec Tchelitchew—ça va?"—and Genet was d'accord. He stood for a while longer on the street, the neon-tube lighting from above giving him that death's-head appearance which he has at times.

♦

It's as natural for a poet to want to draw as it is for an eleven-year-old boy to want to masturbate a man.

AUGUST

"My sister is a ruin . . . I am a ruin . . . and I think you are ruined."
  "I'm homesick for the Alban Hills," I say.

♦

A handsome, auburn-haired soldier was jerking all comers—reached over and grabbed mine—then pulled my arm over so I'd take hold of his. The cup was full.

♦

How I shall enjoy leaving Pavlik one day—how free I shall feel. But everything must be set first—both for him and for me. It will be like leaving a parent—but the time must come.

Babies are no more impossible than human beings.

Pavlik's arrogance, childishness, infantilism, narcissism—all combine into his personality, take a personal form—as does my arrogance, childishness, infantilism, narcissism.

♦

Irony of *The Flowers of Friendship* (Letters Written to Gertrude Stein): Stein, most intimate of writers, had hardly one intimate correspondent.

♦

Recent news item: the jealous wife who took her husband's mistress for a taxi ride and tore out her pubic hair. The wife sang loudly during the attack, to cover up the screams of the pêcheuse. A piquant note: the wife took her own mother, as well as her young son (10), along in the vengeance ride.

I had better luck, in Cannes, when I jumped out the window of the hotel room in which I'd been locked by an American sailor.

◆

In *The Flowers of Friendship* there's a letter (1945) from Carl Van Vechten to Gertrude Stein in which he says: "I went to a cocktail party for (of all things!) Marcel Duchamp last week and in the middle of it a man got up and yelled: 'I can't stand another second of this. It's just like 1912!' And of course it was except in 1912 cocktail parties were a novelty." Carl failed to mention that it was *View* which gave the party, celebrating the Duchamp number, and that he was the man (who didn't yell, however) to whom it all seemed like 1912.

◆

I go out now to have the car insured against fire and theft. Pavlik has gone, without breakfast, to deposit his stool for examination.

I shall be happy to be on the road to Italy, a country I saw first in the spring of 1932, when I borrowed the money from Djuna to get there (and never paid her back). I arrived in Florence at night and Carmita took me on a carrozza ride through the streets lined with palaces. Carmita had loved Italy from the beginning, being Spanish had picked up the language easily, took a small villa in a little town near Pisoia, Procchida, had a devoted maidservant and was happy to have me come and stay. In November we left together, by boat from Genoa, for Barcelona, thence to Madrid. Carmita was being kept by an American Jew, who had been, and was continuing to be, very nice to her, sending regular checks on which we lived modestly but well. I began another novel, *The Acts*, which was never finished. (This was during the summer, between swims in the reservoir pool.) There were too many characters and too little plot. My "hero" was a mixture of Carmita's brother (about whom she told me stories of their life together—drug taking and making love) and José—about whom Richard Thoma had told me stories and whom I knew and had fancied myself in love with. There was a chapter, which I thought very tenderly written, in which the girl (Carmita in fiction) is taken to bed by her brother for the first time. I read it aloud to Carmita and tears started to roll down her cheeks, silent tears, the face hardly changed its expression. Carmita was one of those girl-women—and I'm sure many men have known one—who come along, and you seem to have known her always, but when she goes, no one takes her place. She seems eternal while she's there, inevitable, and yet she's the very one to go, while others stay.

◆

"I feel like Djuna," Pavlik tells me this morning. Djuna, from whom I ran away, whom I *wrecked* according to Pavlik (as he thinks I've wrecked him).

◆

Writing is writing, nothing else. Gertrude Stein was convinced of this, it was her chief conviction, that's why she used so many words trying to convince others.

◆

I am not free free free. Only comparatively free. Chains formed over a period of twenty years are hard to break: they can be broken—but the impulse must be both violent and sustained, and founded on more than the caprice of a day.

◆

To walk like an Egyptian is to carry a ladder across Paris.

Who will hold out her apron to catch an old man's beard?

"Knitting threads of light . . ." Pavlik speaking of his work. "One ends, one does not begin, with simplicity . . . What I shouldn't forget is that Everything is Everything."

◆

Ben Morris, who is working with Givenchy, has been telling me of a "sensational" American model, and I meet her at last—really a beauty, tall and with beautiful blue eyes set in almond shapes—Ivy Nicholson by name. When she said we'd already met, I said, "Yes, we're street acquaintances," but then she said, "Didn't you live in Connecticut?" And then it was revealed that I did know her—*almost* intimately—she'd been brought by the photographer Milton Greene to the Red, White and Blue 4th of July Bon Voyage Ball at the Black Barn, Weston, 1952. She came in a short red costume, representing someone's idea of a red cat; lightly pencilled cat's whiskers were on her face; she won a prize for best costume. Bert and I, at one period during the night's antics, led her from the barn to the White Cottage, she was like a somnambule . . . But no coaxing could get her to go very far—I was for undressing her, but I didn't get rough. Bert's hopes of having a woman that night were not fulfilled.

SEPTEMBER

Our tentative date of departure—Tuesday, a week from today.

Paris has no charm, anymore, says Mayo. You should see New York! I tell him.

Pavlik said to me that my heart can't cry, and that's why I can't write plays. You and your "irony," was the gist of his mocking. Oh, his Russian heart. It's an organ of a kind so foreign to Americans.

◆

Now that I've progressed to wanting to buy gouache paints, Pavlik says I should (instead) continue to draw!

And what will be the moral? To be immoral . . . Society—any society—is nothing but organized mediocrity.

◆

I went to Harlem, the Cotton Club, one night with an extraordinary woman: beautiful, famous, elegant, witty, worldly. To her I was a naif, pretty, bright little boy with a Southern accent. But if I had been her, I, too, would have kissed that little boy, in the taxi returning from Harlem to Greenwich Village. The next day I was in another taxi, on the way to the French Line Pier, but I stopped by the lady's Washington Square apartment, to pick up the gift of a book—her own—which she'd promised me. "To Little Charles—With love," it was inscribed—and the offering was sealed with a kiss. She told me later—in Paris—that she'd wanted to kiss me sober, so as to show that her drunken kisses were meant. Her name was Djuna Barnes.

Last night, high, I disclosed to Mayo the three types of females who attract my imagination: the little girl, the somnambule, and the cavader.

. . . Let my inspiration roam—it will take the path of least resistance which is down—down into the unconscious. " . . . thoughts create a new heaven . . . and from it the work that he desires to create flows into him." (Paracelsus.)

◆

BELLEY (AIN), FRANCE

Hotel Pernollet, where Pavlik was Gertrude Stein's guest twenty-seven years ago. An image from Pavlik's memory of his stay in Belley (before Gertrude and Alice found the house at Bilignan): he and Allen (Tanner) go up to Gertrude's room to tell her goodnight. There she was in a white wool robe, red scarf about her neck, her long hair (it was still uncropped then) being brushed and combed by Alice, who was all in blue.

◆

LADISPOLI (ITALY)

The way you look will influence your character . . . Cacti and palm trees are here. I'm waiting in the sun, on a terrace, for Pavlik to finish shaving, then we'll have breakfast and hit the road to Rome.

◆

FRASCATI

I am sitting in the garden of the Hotel Flora. Just as I got installed, hoping to catch up a little on our odyssey (we've been to Amalfi, not attractive enough for a long stay), Pavlik returns from a quick haircutting, distressed, "They cut me all my hair." I reassure him, "It looks neat."

◆

This morning I took the bus to Rome, called Mlle. Soardo, telling her that, en principe, we're taking her mother's villa at Valle Violata for six months—it's a house we saw before leaving Grottaferrata last spring; and whose caretaker, Tonino, I went to bed with.

◆

The Sirocco is blowing, wind of vice. "Il n'y a pas de vice dans Ovide, qui pose en principe la fraternité de toutes les substances." (Jean Dutourd, *Une tête de chien.*)

   "I'm not going to buy you any more socks, Charles Henri, that's finished"— Pavlik has just come up and discovered a hole in the toe of a pair left to dry on the radiator.

   The wonder-legged Italians . . . Mirages of flesh and blood.

   Cable from Mother: "September 23 . . . Mama passed away this morning at seven o'clock." Mama being my grandmother, Mama Cato. When Daddy was a grown man he used to dangle his baby cousin, Gertrude (my mother to be), on his knee. All the relatives came to Mama Cato and advised her not to consent to the marriage—when Mother was eighteen. Yes, she thought she was madly in love. But she was certainly out of love when she took Jonesie for a lover. I was ten years old then. I can't say I enjoyed the sight of his kissing Mother. We'd all three be together and he'd hold Mother's chin in his hand and ask me if I didn't think her the most beautiful thing that ever was. Then he'd kiss her on the mouth several times. His lips would be wet after that; I was slightly repulsed.

OCTOBER

During dinner Pavlik dropped me a drawing hint: "Let your hand wander like a drunken fly."

◆

VALLE VIOLATA

We're in. That is to say, we're in the Soardo house at 34 Via Vittorio Veneto—with rent paid until Jan. 7, 1954.

The caretaker, Salvatore, and wife, Conchita, are full of willingness and we've engaged her to do for us what Bice did on the Via Anagnina: that is (when winter comes) to start the heat and get our breakfast in early morning, and cook a light dinner in the evening. Pavlik's studio has wonderful north light (double French doors leading to terrace) and he thinks, in general, the apartment (we've only the top floor of the house) is a good "working" place. I raise the blinds of my window and there is Rocca di Papa sparkling in the night—nearer than it was when we looked at it from the terrace of Villa Sereni.

◆

The lower floor is inhabited by a French family. Their baby has been squalling all afternoon—first it was under my window in the baby carriage. I wanted to try to nap so I moved to the diningroom, then the baby was moved! I've never heard such screaming—I'm back in my room—one can hear it from every room upstairs. And the new caretaker's little daughter, Angelina, runs around and around the house raising hell. Masses of boys are chunking at the appletree in the backyard of the next door villa, which belongs to the Church.

A quoi bon? as the French say. (I was thinking about the Art of Poetry.) Mightn't Bérard have asked himself that question about the Art of Painting? Many people have answered it for him (if ask it he did): "Pour nous!"

And he might have answered it for himself: "Pour moi!"

That's one of the paradoxes of art: the "pour moi" becomes "pour les autres." So much done expressly "pour les autres" (and not from the artist's deepest desires) becomes "pour personne."

Not the shadow but the word is "the stillest and lightest of all things"—the word unspoken, unwritten.

Henri Cartier-Bresson, a primitive poet. I told P. I get more pleasure out of Henri's book of photos (which he gave me in Forio) than I do from a book by T. S. Eliot.

Thomas John Marsh, "whose body is heavily tattooed with the emblems of death . . ." Poetry is poetry, and not 'subject matter.'

◆

Rosa, Tonino's widow, came to see us, with the idea of working for us, but the Soardos don't want her here. Tonino was caretaker last spring when we looked at the house, but he died from a hit on the head, which happened when he stumbled one drunken night. After his death, the widow was paid many visits by the men in the neighborhood—that's why the Soardos don't want her around anymore. "She's a fallen woman," Pavlik said, at dinner. I said, "So am I!" He said, "Unfortunately."

NOVEMBER

Ape's face on a bird's body.

What I had forgotten about poetry: it's the *working* at it that's fun. Auden finds this "working fun" in forms. I find it more in expression.

"Italian women never know how to make the beds"—Pavlik from his room. We have Peppa housekeeping for us now.

◆

Drawing was a way of getting back to writing. You have to enjoy what you're doing, and do it every day. Now I can peck at a poem-in-prose as though it were a drawing.

Where is the Equinox: the day of the conscious, the night of the unconscious? "Rhymes, too, come from the unconscious," a poet (Auden) told me. "They should stay there," I said.

DECEMBER

Auden was here for lunch on Sunday (this is Tuesday). I told Pavlik last night that he doesn't seem to be human. "He's inhuman. He's not there." Pavlik thinks such a personality is English. He's also prudish, and so enjoys obscene stories, both to tell and to listen to.

◆

Symbolic image: the sack, or bag, full of something. What's in it. Sometimes it's light enough to be held with one hand; sometimes it's so heavy it must be carried on the back. Is it gold or sand; a sack of potatoes or—?

From my window: the little shepherd boy seemed wading, knee-deep in his flock.

I've invented—or rather engineered another name for myself: Ghondi Cato. Ghondi is the anagram of Higdon (Mama Cato's maiden name).

"My piss is still dark, means my bile doesn't go where it should go—" Pavlik from the bathroom. Ghondi Kato is a better spelling.

◆

... All a question of a balance between too many details, which water-clog the interest, and too protracted an exposition—the elastic sags. *Style*, at all times, is a safeguard, a high-performance gasoline. "Genius points to change ... hence it is immoral." (Samuel Butler.) "Geometry teaches us to bisex angels." (A schoolboy.) "I think I should tickle the ass of the stove"—Pavlik, shaking down the ashes with a poker, at bedtime.

And what about the bats not yet out of hell?

To Krishnamurti: You would have me remember by forgetting. Thank you for all you have undone.

1954

JANUARY

We laugh at the childish, the inappropriate, the unfortunate. At this point, 1954, the United States is much too full of its own enjoyment.

◆

Our friend Nino says there are three "wolf-men" that he knows of, in Valle Violata, and that a few nights ago he met one on a back road, near a fountain—it's water they seek, he says, for they are burning inside, they will jump in a fountain and sit with water up to their chins. They avoid people, and if a person meets one of them face to face, the wolf-man, out of shame at being seen, being recognized, will attack the person who sees him, and that person may be murdered. Has anyone ever been found murdered by a wolf-man? Nino said No. And is the wolf-man never caught and put in prison? No, they're "sick." Do they know they are wolf-men, in the daytime, when not subject to seizure? Yes. Nino has played cards with them. They wander like wolves, especially on moonlit nights, howling. The next morning their faces are all torn and scratched. Some have families, Nino said. He was scared the other night, stopped still when he saw the "lupo" (uomo-lupo) and let him pass. Then he ran home as fast as he could.

◆

In the garden there are the caretaker's two snotty-nosed brats, one beating a tambourine. I'd hoped the tambourine had been split when Little Angel (Angelina) whammed her screeching sister, Francesca, over the head with it.

A flock of birds passes like a veil between here and snow-patched Monte Cavo.

◆

"You should show it something," said Pavlik, of the new moon, as we walked on the starlit, moonlit roof terrace.

"I show my eyes of silver blue."

◆

"Charles Henri ... Why is it so bad? ... Nothing passed this morning."
   "Nothing passed from where to where?"
   "Breakfast didn't pass from stomach ... it all remained there."

◆

Alice Delamar sends me a clipping from *The New Yorker*, complete with her own big question mark in the margin, of Dwight Macdonald's review of *New Directions 14*, in which he takes crass cracks at my Little Anthology of the Poem in Prose. He mistakes for parody things which were meant to be comedy of an intellectual order. Parker, in his introduction, quotes my saying, "One more rhyme and I'll vomit!" which Mcdonald requotes—the sucker. If I didn't already know him, this review would warn me what kind of a mental frump he is. Eat your words, you literary quack—duck soup to you.

◆

Creation: something is where nothing was. Balls are but snakes wound up   the Gordian Knot!

◆

Afro is coming to lunch today. I haven't seen him since Dec. 21, the day of his wife Maria's funeral—a week, to the day, before that, Pavlik and I visited Maria in the hospital. We walked up to the floor her room was on, the door was ajar, I pushed it open quietly, and Afro got up from the other bed, where he had been lying with his clothes on, covered with a blanket. Maria opened her eyes but did not move, she looked so thin and suffering and pathetic, but she tried to smile, and her eyes moved about with an expression as if to apologize for the *subdued* state she was in. Her hands were outside the covers, she lifted one from the wrist, and Pavlik went closer to the bed and took her hand and then I did and then Afro took us into the corridor. He explained that Maria had just been given a shot to make her quiet; besides, she was not supposed to move—a blood clot in the veins could go to her heart and cause death. The doctors were waiting until the blood condition cleared up before starting treatment on the lung. Afro did not mention cancer, but that's what Maria had—cancer of the lung. The next Saturday she was dead.

◆

"The barber wanted to know if you were my nono."
   "I'm your grandfather now? That shows how much you have eaten me ... You find it funny? ... If I look like a nono that means that I'm on my way out."

◆

Léonor has been commissioned to design a new production of *Phèdre*, and wrote to Pavlik, asking for advice (ideas). Pavlik: "I wrote Léonor about *Phèdre* ... *Phèdre* is simply the story of a woman who wants to be fucked." He told Léonor to create for the stage enormous bases of columns, whose tops one can't see, and barbaric costumes.

P. has remarked that my drawings are full of animals, which, he says, are symbols of my soul. ". . . les animaux sauvages et voluptueux qui sont les emblêmes de leur folies," wrote Baudelaire.

"Someone will give you an exhibition," he now says. "Il y a beaucoup du monde qui fait ça pire . . ."

♦

When the Allen Tates lunched out here not long ago (they're guests at the American Academy in Rome), Mrs. Tate (Caroline Gordon) quoted Jacques Maritain, as though she agreed with him, to the effect that "surrealism is madness."

"Madness is surrealism," I countered, "but surrealism is not madness," and Allen agreed with me. He told me during lunch that Spender had written him about our friend James Laughlin that he's the "Barbara Hutton of our milieu—always wanting to be loved for *himself*."

FEBRUARY

My birthday. At the next post-office, made of rocks and rills, there may be a package, postmarked Eternity (that inconceivable town), addressed to one of us, tied with strings that meet at a touch, wrapped in the skin of a transparent creature, holding an egg to explode the magic tooth which shines when the moon shines, only.

♦

The landscape is covered with a blanket of snow. All this whiteness adds to the sense of being isolated, enclosed, one feels stimulated sexually.

I've just returned from the next door villa, where Don Giuseppe is in charge. It's a huge pre-war place where Don G. lives with a younger priest and a 40-year-old caretaker Antonio. I leave my car in the garage of the villa—Don G. kindly offered to let me leave it free of charge. He's coming to lunch with us day after tomorrow. He's lonesome over there in that gloomy big house.

◆

When desire has had time to return, our mourning is over . . . "Charles Henri, listen, do you remember last year, did I have vertigoes or not?"

"Maybe."

"It's not a question of maybe, you have to say yes or no."

◆

The Italians lie to and about each other—they live in a mist of lies, so they're used to such an atmosphere—they find it their natural climate.

A horse escaped. It has just run along the path behind our house. Now a man runs by, after it. Not often does that young horse get such a chance to gallop at will! (Neither does my horse.)

◆

Don G. was telling us how in the winter season the Italians make love less—even among the peasants—their sexual nature sleeps, likes trees and such, wakes up again in the spring. And that's why, he says, an Italian man of sixty may still appear young. I know one thing: I'm sex-starved. Any age is the vicious age.

◆

We're at intermission time of a radio concert broadcast from Torino directed by Igor Markevitch. Pavlik was criticizing his conducting all the way through (less for the Mozart than for the Pergolesi)—"Kasha . . . doesn't know when to make stops . . . doesn't know how to dance or he would know when he has to pause to take breath." Pavlik's kindest comment: "Extraordinary thing, you hear every instrument." He's said before that Igor's "sonority" is good, his rhythm bad. I think the Britten selection tonight was the same we heard in Paris, after which I said to Henri-Louis (de la Grange) that it was "circus music" and he replied: "but good circus music." And when I saw Marie-Laure (de Noailles) afterwards and described it as a "show piece," she misunderstood, said, "Quoi? Chaude-pisse? Chaude-pisse?"

◆

To lunch yesterday, Giancarlo Menotti and Tommy Schippers. I asked Giancarlo whether he had ever considered working as music composer only, with someone else doing a libretto. He said the only poet whom he'd ever thought he might like to have worked with is Lorca. If ever he collaborated, he said, he'd have to have someone completely passive, obeying his least wish. He's going to give Peppa tickets for the Rome production of *The Consul*.

◆

Auden raves about a new poet, David Jones, in the new *Encounter*. Everything A. says about Jones' work is true, but the work is not poetry. "Am I dotty?" asks Auden. Dear Lincoln: Tell Wystan the answer is Yes.

Foolish rain gives me a pain.

◆

THE ORACLE OF HAZARD

Somber fellows deny the floor, distraught roars upbraid a wall, double tremblings deplore tonight, ungrateful forests disgust somehow.

Unjudged downfalls abhor the West, filial rules refine all boys, doubtful doors belie two girls, rubicund fingers adore iniquity.

Swelling failures adjust justice, winter worlds rebuke misgivings, stepping loves withstand presentiment, true walls facilitate spring flowers.

Special juices contain feast days, tuneful yellows disrupt one's liver, forlorn owners corrupt the good, fresh instability disrobes the beautiful.

◆

Scabby-assed: I knew the expression but no representatives. Now I see one in person: little Francesca. She sat in the fire weeks ago.

Shepherd Gabriele's naïveté: when I showed him the photo of the nude negress, saying, Here is my fiancée, he believed me. Another photo showed two Arabs with big cocks seated on either side of a kneeling girl (small breasts). One of the Arabs had his hand on the girl's pussy. Gabriele wanted to know if the central figure (the girl) were male or female. I had taken photos of Gabriele and when I gave him the prints they brought him such pleasure that his mouth watered—I saw a drop fall out of his smile.

◆

Laughlin was here and after lunch slumped on the couch with a big cigar stuck in his face (the house still stank the next day) ... Pavlik was reminded of a story: a woman's husband was shitting in the bushes when she passed by with another woman, caught sight (but not too good a sight) of his ass as a turd was coming out, said, "There's my husband over there smoking a big cigar." Laughlin kept saying that he couldn't get over my looking the same as I did when Kay Boyle introduced him to me in Paris in 1932. The next time he goes on like that I'll say, "Did I really look that old?"

And then I heard him saying, "... The sordid death of Dylan Thomas ..." He said he had to go to the morgue to identify the body, and the City took the brain out to examine it—a New York City custom when someone dies after being brought drunk to a hospital. It wasn't a pretty sight, the body, Laughlin said. Then went on to say, "We're getting rich [New Directions] off Dylan Thomas . . . 10,000 copies of his books sold since his death—isn't that disgusting?"

◆

The Elliott Carters and son are here. "Don't look at my pictures," Pavlik is calling to them as he dresses.

David, the Carters' son, has beautifully-shaped—long, with the shape defined by definite points at each lid's end—eyes, is blond. His mouth reveals wide-apart teeth; his ears stick out; his body is frail; he's intelligent, poised, knows what he wants, un-neurotic. He has that steady blue gaze which captures and captivates. He's eleven.

In the kitchen Peppa teased him, by asking if he weren't a Communist and he bridled. Peppa touched her nose, meaning the Communists stink, and I asked Day, as his mother calls him, if he knew what that meant. He said, "Here's what I say for the Communists," and gave the "up your ass" gesture—putting left hand in crook of arm, swinging right fist up. "You know what that means?" he asked me. "Yes," I said. "It's not very nice," he said. "I'll bet you don't do that in front of your daddy," I said. He said, "He wouldn't know what it meant."

◆

There's a handsome man spading the earth between the grapevines—he and Salvatore are doing the same thing, I think he must be Neapolitan, and I think there's a wedding ring on a finger of his left hand.

◆

Handsome man turned out to be Salvatore's brother, Carmen, and has moved in, in the basement, will be working around here for the rest of the time we're here. Salvatore, knowing I wouldn't accept, gave me a friendly invitation to eat with them, as I looked down from my window. The invitation was repeated, with a smile, by Carmen, so after they'd lunched I went out to where they were spading and gave them cigarettes, found that Carmen wears no wedding ring, was born in 1929 (looks older). He's as attractive as poor Salvatore is unattractive, well built, long straight black hair, good yellow teeth.

◆

After dinner I went down to the Royers (the French people who live on the floor below) to ask about getting some statistics and photos from the FAO office, where Mr. Royer is employed. Mr. Royer asked if we had any kerosene left, because Salvatore needed it for the stove which the Royers have lent him. I thought it would be a good opportunity to call Carmen up—which it was. I filled the kerosene can and asked Pavlik to leave us alone in the kitchen. I gave Carmen a glass of wine—he said he never drank wine at night, only at midday. I wonder if he was surprised when I kissed him on either side of the mouth; he returned the kisses—on either side of the mouth. He said he'd pose for me on Sunday. Pavlik thinks he will tell his brother I kissed him. I said, "They'll be pleased he's having such a success—" I didn't understand about his age: he was born in 1924. He's a grown man all right.

◆

Marjorie Mason came out with Parker, recently arrived in Rome. She told Pavlik she'd been at the penthouse (360 E. 55) but couldn't remember when... Those were *not* the days. These are the days. My days are always these.

◆

How I react to people, to those people who mean more to me than mere images. Each person is like a pin-cushion stuck full of pins: these pins, when touched, give off shocks of pleasure or pain, of varying intensity. This "pin-cushion" analogy occurred to me while thinking of Caroline Tate—the pins of pain (moderate pain) are more frequent in her than in Allen, I find ... In recent years the pain pins in Djuna claimed an overwhelming majority—one ceased to see her. When we lunched at the Tates' four days ago Allen told a story about Djuna and T. S. Eliot. "She just loves Tom," Allen said. "She didn't used to love his poetry," I said. "She doesn't love his poetry," Allen said, "she loves Tom." And when Tom gets to New York he always takes Djuna out to lunch. After a recent luncheon with Tom, Djuna was so "elated" that when she got to her room she fell down and broke her leg. She reached the telephone and telephoned to Cummings, in the little house across from Djuna's second-floor apartment on Patchin Place. Cummings came over but couldn't get in the door—Djuna had locked it and couldn't get to it to unlock it. Cummings went back down the steps and succeeded by various means (trees and the firescape) in getting through Djuna's window and so coming to her aid. Cummings' later comment: "I'll never answer the telephone again." ... Some time afterwards in London, when Allen went to see Tom and the story of the Aftermath of the Lunch came up, Eliot commented, "But that wasn't the day we lunched—the elation came three days later."

◆

"Charlie, what's happened to the hot water? Charlie, Charlie, there is no water in general. Charlie! No water ... Peppa! ... Peppa, no c'e acqua, niente ... Charlie, couldn't you reply ... Leaving everything for everyone to do, son-of-a-bitch ... Peppa..."

Quite a fucking wind.

MARCH

I've just found out that Pavlik was *supposed* to have been a girl, and he was named, before birth, Irene.

"They always fuck the sheep," Pavlik says about the shepherds. Gabriele posed for photographs again this afternoon—wearing a mask which I told him was a shepherd's mask—but he didn't think that it looked like the face of a typical shepherd. "Why not?" I asked ("Per che no?"). Because the nose is too long, he said. Then we put the mask on one of the sheep and Gabriele straddled it for a pose.

◆

Carmen kept his word tonight, came up dressed in his Sunday clothes. I stripped him to his waist and tried a shirt on him; it fit. He said the "Liquore" we had was "burning" when some drops fell on his hand. On his chest—growth of short hair—almost like a shadow, or if someone had dipped a hand in soot and then rubbed it across. His cazzo is not too big but it'll do. I like his joyfulness—a real pagan. If he ever heard of Puritanism he doesn't show it.

◆

"—because you're kept—"

"Why do you keep people? Why do you keep people? So you can own them!"

"I think you should buy yourself Holy Water and spray yourself day and night, it would be very good idea—"

◆

What I could unembarrassedly tell, in a conversation with a friend—that's what I want my autobiography to be.

One runs up against some hard dreams.

APRIL

Pavlik's in the hospital in Rome with a tapeworm—at least he had not been separated from the monster up until ten to nine last night, when I telephoned the Salvatore Mundi from Frascati. I took him in for an examination of the worm bits, morning of the 8th—Dr. Simeons said it was the type of tapeworm one gets in raw meat (we've had a bunch of raw hamburgers during the time we've been at Valle Violata). I'm phoning in a few minutes to get the latest bulletin.

◆

Some kind of new (American) Death-to-Tapeworms medicine was used on Pavlik and it didn't work. So the doctor is sending him home for a week's rest and he will return after Easter Sunday to recommence operations—this time they'll use the old standby (more poisonous and violent but presumably more efficacious). I went to see him yesterday around 6 P.M.—he'd been going to the toilet until four in the morning, the purge not having worked until the hours when he was supposed to be sleeping.

◆

Pavlik's back home and says he feels unusually full of energy, although the worm's head hasn't exited.

◆

My doubts about the value of the camera—as a medium for discovering poetry—no longer exist. Perhaps Cocteau's best poem is his film poem, *Blood of a Poet.*

Films. I'd like to make one which might be described with Valéry's words on Rimbaud's poetry: "Rimbaud a inventé ou decouvert la puissance de l'*incohérence harmonique.*"

◆

"... the Hare as Sacrificial Animal ... it sacrifices itself ... by leaping into a fire. Such an act recalls that of the phoenix, the mythical bird that burnt itself, whereon a new and rejuvenated bird sprang from the ashes ... The moon is traditionally 'fickle' in that it never appears two nights running in the same place or even in the same shape, and the same characteristics of surprise and variability are traditionally and actually associated with the hare . . ." ([John] Layard.)

I asked Pavlik, "What is *your* totem animal?" and he replied, "Either the turtle, or the snake."

◆

Further enlightenment, through John Layard, on the Hare: a subdivision of his book *The Lady of the Hare* (lent me by Caroline Tate) is titled, "The Hare Used as a Hieroglyph for the Auxiliary Verb 'To Be.'" *To Be*: a title I chose for an edited section of these notebooks. From Montaigne: "Nature intended us for ourselves, to be, not to seem."

◆

The plumberboys from Marino are here—watertanks on our roof have been empty since—since—when did I take a bath last? I to P. (re Ricardo, plumberboy): "He looks slightly like a monkey that's had a human face grafted on."

There may be as much difference between photography-as-poetry and commercial photographs as there is between a poem in prose and a text for an advertisement.

MAY

Pavlik has just discovered ("Yes, there are parts of the thing in it, Charlie") more evidence of his tapeworm—the head's not out.

◆

PARIS

Paris is Northern, after Rome; the buildings gray, the sky pale blue. "The people cold," adds Pavlik. But I don't find them so cold as all that—though it's true the young priest-student was Basque, not Parisian. He was short and had a hairy stomach. Had he been in Italy? Yes, but he hadn't liked Rome—"trop de curés." . . .

When I arrived at Léonor's (she was in bed with a hotwater bottle) I told her and Pavlik of what had happened to delay me—she asked for details (so did Pavlik)—so I gave them to them.

Baroness Blixen (Isak Dinesen) arrives in Paris today!

◆

I met Isak Dinesen. She was wearing a deep cloche of tobacco-colored straw. She talks rhythmically, and sounds as if she were reading one of her own stories. She said I am like what she expected me to be. I said, "You are beyond my expectations." She wore a fur jacket with longish shiny fur.

◆

This afternoon chez Jean Dubuffet. He is installed in a comfortably remodeled duplex studio, says he lives now from his paintings (one spoke of him as a "wine merchant," in the past). He is articulate, sound without being brilliant. He would be attractive in a brute way if his teeth were good. He recalled *View*, with admiration.

◆

"Heavenly," Virgil called the Genet film (*Un Chant d'Amour*) which François Reichenbach projected for us chez lui. "It's nothing to drool over," I said. Pavlik calls Genet "un moraliste—comme Sade."

◆

Vanity is often confused with generosity. A thought aroused by Francis Rose's account of the "splendid" table set by almost-penniless Alice B. Toklas. Did she really serve mangoes that cost 800 francs each?

"Professionally?" asked some vulgar auntie at Marie-Louise's Thursday, regarding my reasons for taking the photos which Cartier-Bresson was looking at and praising. "No, poetically," I replied.

The No-Purpose Photograph. With a camera one may write a visual poetry; with a camera one *reads* life, too—the poetry's already "written."

◆

I loved the Blues before I loved the Poem. Somehow the two loves were from the same source. So it was natural that I called my poetry review *Blues* (Columbus, Mississippi, 1929).

Years of work, a burst of glory, and it's all over.

JUNE

A passionate schoolboy who knew what he wanted—and got it. (In the pissoir.)

◆

My portrait of Genet, at its simplest (and what cannot be concentrated into the simple?) would be that of a man, a homosexual, full of love—and longing for love. A born poet, the outrages inflicted upon him by destiny, through "society," have made that innate large love of his take strange, perverse (chiefly perverse) forms.

I imagine myself kissing him on the cheeks day after tomorrow, saying, "Je veux t'embrasser parce-que tu existe."

"O.K.," he said over the telephone, accepting my invitation for lunch. At the Arturo Lopezes' cocktail for Pavlik I'd asked Léonor if she had seen Genet and spoken to him about doing a piece on my photos and he'd said he'd do it if he were paid—"Mais beaucoup d'argent," said Léonor.

How do we (Genet and I) compare with one another? We both have our infantilisms, our primitive likes and dislikes. He is perhaps more of the sentimentalist, in spite of having explored more thoroughly the "evil in the heart of man." I—a fortunate child, walking into the marvelous, as Genet's thief walked into an unknown house.

Léonor told Pavlik that Genet is so self-centered he's interested in nothing but getting money at this point—he needs it for lawyers to get his friend out of prison. Léonor said he could see the world crack, including her, with indifference—and that if he wrote a text for my photos he'd talk about himself rather than the photographs . . . There'll be little point in reminding him that View Editions sent him $500 for the American rights to *Notre Dame des Fleurs*—it was up to us to go ahead and publish it but we didn't. (1947.)

◆

We saw Peggy O'Brien yesterday and she gave a description of an extraordinary performance Kenneth Anger put on at a party chez Thad Lovett the night before she left Rome. It seems he appeared in the candlelit room, his face surrounded with ostrich feathers, dressed in a little girl's frock—he was on his knees, which gave the illusion of his being no taller than a little girl (he's six feet), and from under the dress, little shoes showed (a sheet or something fell down behind to hide his legs). He played with things, rolling a ball back and forth on the floor, or tossing things, pine-cones, talcum-powder, spangles, into the air—all done with little quick movements like those of a little child. He ended up by rolling on the floor, over and over.

◆

Léonor has lent me her copy of Genet's *Pompes Funèbres*, with an inscription by the author: "A Léonor en l'esprit et le coeur de qui je m'allonge me repose et m'endors confiant Jean." He told me at lunch (three days ago, when I invited him to Lipps) while eating his boeuf-à-la-mode that Léonor would fuss at him if she knew, because he's not supposed to eat too much fat.

François Reichenbach warned me that I might never see my photographs again, after putting them in the hands of Genet. The same thought occurred to Pavlik. I'm willing to take a chance.

> Fear most forever of all not the wolf in his baaing hood
> Nor the tusked prince, in the ruttish farm, at the rind
> And mire of love, but the thief as meek as the dew.
> (Dylan Thomas.)

I wouldn't call Genet exactly meek. He was subdued that day we had lunch, said he hadn't slept well, said he was still sleepy. A word comes back to me that Léonor used about Genet: "naif." I don't think he's naif, exactly. "Like a child," I said. Unworldly, yes. But not *a* naif.

And like a child, *among other things*.

He appeared at Lipps in a white shirt, first button, at collar, unbuttoned, no tie.

I am trying to sell for him a print of *Un Chant d'Amour*—Jack Newberry and Channing Hare saw it, by my arrangement, at François Reichenbach's the other night—neither was interested in buying. Arturo Lopez I haven't been able to get hold of, to talk to him about it. Genet telephoned while I was out, re-telephoned, found me in. He said that if I couldn't have an answer by tomorrow morning not to bother, that he could sell it himself. He'd told me that if I could find a buyer @ 150,000 francs, I could have 30,000 from the sale; I replied with: You will keep the

whole 150,000 and in return write me a text for my photo show. He said he'd write
the text anyway, that he wouldn't want the agreement to be "commercial." Well,
we'll see if he meant what he said.

◆

It was Sunday morning, late, that I woke up after a beautiful dream: A flock of
cows (is it necessary to say a herd of cows, a flock of sheep) were spread on a hill
(much like one of the hills of Grottaferrata), towards sunset. The sun went behind
a large cloud, which became golden all around the edges. Around the edges of the
cows there was also a golden glow, the entire scene lovely, the herd and the hill and
the cloud with the golden edge and rayons. I wanted to take a photograph and
started to search for my camera, the light was going from the sky, but fountains,
like fountains of fire, were springing up, bursting here and there from the hills.
Suddenly two cows rose into the air and their hooves clashed and gave off sparkly
balls of fire. I searched anxiously for the camera, by the time I found it at the foot
of a fence post, Marjorie Mason appeared and she was laughing at me.

◆

After the Baron de Rédé's ball last night at the Hotel Lambert, I didn't get to bed
till 4:30. I danced only with Patricia Lopez. Ned Rorem and I left before 3 A.M. and
Ned took me to the Boeuf-sur-le-toit where I found Mary Lou Williams playing
the piano. We reminisced about the goodbye ball at the Black Barn, July 4th, 1952,
where she'd made piano music in her own marvelous unique style.

◆

Pavlik's vernissage, Galerie Rive Gauche, a great success—six small things sold,
show looks, and is, beautiful. Stephen Tennant was there and I told him he looked
like a cross between Oscar Wilde and Lord Alfred Douglas, which he did.

Bettina remarked to me that the pictures were in "such good taste." "Greatness
is always in good taste," I answered back. (Sometimes it takes a *long* time to seem
so.)

◆

A schoolboy, a student-priest, a worker, an Arab—now I'd like to have a bus
conductor—

◆

And success for dear little Ghondi Kato: "Dear Mr. Ghondi, I wrote you some time
ago to the American Express here but no answer ... I am taking your sketches
(prose poems) and want to get in touch with you to pay you ... With all apologies
and good wishes ... Very Sincerely ... Marguerite Caetani ... for *Botteghe Oscure*."

◆

Genet told me over phone that he couldn't do the preface. I picked up my photos
which he left at the desk of his hotel. The one of Carmen is missing.

Marjorie M. says that Genet parades up and down the sidewalks of the St.-Germain Boulevard so often (one sees him as one sits at a cafe table) that in the end one has the feeling one has spent the evening with him. There's a lot of hollow grandeur—small doses of the grandiose—in Genet (in *Pompes Funèbres* anyway).

◆

Jacques Audiberti will write a text for my photo show. Peter Watson's arranged for it, with Roland Penrose's O.K., at London's Institute of Contemporary Art, for October. "Thirty Images from Italy." Audiberti was struck with my formulation of "Le photo sans but" as an esthétique: he'll play on that theme—varied with his own interpretation of the "photograph of love."

◆

The shapes of the head of the soul. When bell-mouthed, what is the significance?

JULY

"No 'people' in Rome?" I replied to Marjorie M. "But I like strangers!" Marjorie has the heart of a gold tooth.

Pavlik's tapeworm is showing—he announced yesterday. Wide (a finger's width), flat, ringed sections, a foot long, came out.

◆

"In the tender bedazzlement of love at first sight, Ford treats the photograph with that direct generosity . . ." No one will ever know what a tour-de-force this translating of Audiberti's text is.

◆

I'm going to spend the 10,000 francs which La Caetani sent Ghondi Kato for the prose poems (not knowing that Ghondi Kato is Charles Henri Ford) on Painter's Supplies—gouache and brushes and paper.

What to love? The painter answers with a picture, the poet with a poem, the photographer with a photograph—any lover with a loved one.

A stack of paper and a bunch of pencils, and don't look back.

◆

An enema for Pavlik, I assisting Choura; (preliminary) new assault on the tapeworm.

Pavlik's been sitting on the pot three hours and the tapeworm is not out yet. Now I go to the pharmacy to fetch some more sulphur & stuff for a second purge.

◆

Pavlik's worm-head didn't come out.

◆

"When I read about William Blake, I know what I am for. I must never be afraid of my foolishness, only of pretension. And whatever I have I must use, painting, poetry, prose . . ." wrote sympathetic sick little Denton Welch.

Is there not a difference between drawing and painting? Yes, said Pavlik: "Drawing is the construction of a world—painting is the creating of a world in itself."

◆

Italy! We've decided to go back. And tonight Italian voices come over the radio to us—Gigli singing Donizetti.

AUGUST

SIRMIONE, LAGO DI GARDA, ITALY

Towards the mountains, on the other side of the lake, the water is light blue gray golden, the gold becoming more gold towards the center, then gradually going into blue with a golden veil of very gentle ripples as one's eye follows the water down to this side . . . The far mountains and the water over there now are more purple than blue gray, the lower mountain is darker, the higher, further ridge is almost the same blue as the water, only slightly more hazy. A slab of gold, reflection of the sun down across the water, is blinding.

◆

PORTO SAN GIORGIO

Last night we slept in this house by the Adriatic sea: No. 1 via Gramsci: and we've taken the second floor until the end of September. It belongs to a fisherman (Saverio Boccolini) and his family, who live on the floor above. Pavlik has a corner room for his studio plus a bedroom with a big double bed. I have a room to sleep and work in: the front opens onto a terrace and faces the endless green blue water. One walks barefoot out the back door of the house and around in front, a dirt road is crossed and there's the beach.

There's a teenage daughter, who busies herself with cleaning the apartment— she was in a bathing suit, barefoot, though she hadn't been in swimming. And there's Bruno, with blond salty curls, pale blue eyes. He will be 13 on August 15th. He and his deafmute uncle helped bring the baggage in, assisted by a littler brother, Albertino. The mother raises flowers and sells them in the market.

◆

Rosa will come early and get our breakfast, clean, shop, cook lunch, do laundry. Her husband was killed by a truck on the main highway four years ago.

◆

O souls of flesh, feeding on vanity!
Shot in a sock (yesterday at nap time). How boring of one's balls . . .

◆

Benito showed us a garage which we may be able to rent. I've never seen a face quite like Benito's. Wide nose (not too long, fleshy at the nostrils). Green, not blue, eyes, not clear green but the color of a sandy wave. A little outbreak of pimples about the mouth today (he probably jerked off last night). He has a slightly husky voice, quite rounded chest, narrow shoulders, big flat hands, fleshy bottom, large round legs; a delightful boy, good nature oozing out—in his expression, in his movements, in the tone of voice, look of the eyes, shape of the eyelids and nose. He's going to pose in the nude for Pavlik.

◆

The elaborate workmanship of the armor with which the Knights of old clothed themselves. Are the automobiles with which we clothe ourselves any less wonderful?

"Anyone can learn to draw," is Pavlik's theory, "but to be a painter, like singing, it has to be a gift from heaven."

This Remy Martin cognac tastes nice . . .
So would Benito, I think, taste nice.

◆

Half amazed, half amused, with a dash of mepricious irritation: Pavlik's reaction to my productions in gouache.

Patterns of saffron and ox-blood made by the Adriatic sails—several ships passed this morning in front of the house.

◆

The soul is pleased to have a pleasant body to inhabit. The soul is a prisoner nonetheless.

◆

Pavlik's tapeworm is "stampeding out"—out in pieces. There's a "mago" in Porto San Giorgio (not to be called 'mago' to his face) who says he can get that beastie out completely.

◆

Clusters of friends uncluster. New clusters cluster. One never knows the reason why.

There's poetry seen, with *nothing* done about it.

I'm swatting flies to a chorus of *Dixie* coming in over radio.

I cut it off as they change to *The Battle Cry of Jesus*.

◆

Yesterday, a young lawyer, Luigi, whom we've met here took Pavlik to the mago (Pavlik wanted to know what he was going to charge so Luigi found out in advance: 15,000 lire, a special price to the famous professore—for 3 or 4 visits, which would cost someone else 45,000 lire—do you believe it?). Anyway, it was an expensive trance, because the actual tapeworm treatment will be an old housewives' standby: pumpkin seeds, quarter of a pound, at night, followed by a purge in the morning.

But the trance was something. With closed eyes, and holding on to P.'s little finger by crooking his own little finger, the Mago gave forth, supposedly not knowing what he was saying, while his buxom secretary took it all down for him to read for himself after the trance was over.

Here are a few things he "saw" about Pavlik: his prostate is in the shape of an acorn; one ball (the right one) is larger than the other; he had a fall when a child, hipbone fractured; he still has the larvae of intestinal worms he once had but the larvae will go, aren't dangerous; he will be very much more famous posthumously, he will be recognized as the greatest painter his time produced; in his work he is going back to something of very ancient antiquity; he is neurotic, his neuroticism, as well as ferment of ideas, caused by a highly developed brain lodged in too small a cranium; he needs a long rest in order to bring the ensuing serenity to his work; there is "someone" (always!) who disturbs him . . .

The Mago told Pavlik about the trouble he's had with his back (the Van Rumpt period). He told him that his work, however fantastic, always had and has a basis in reality. He told him about his gallbladder disturbances, and where the tapeworm lies.

While I waited for the seance to end, I sat on a bench on the main drag near the Gran Cafe. A young girl, untidily dressed, unwashed, unkempt hair, came along carrying a birdcage and a tray. She accosted, untimidly, women, who fished in their purses to bring out five or ten lire. She spied me, came over, I put my ten lire in the tray and, unlike the others whom I'd seen contribute, asked for my "fortune." She opened the birdcage and when the bird didn't come out she reached her hand in and set the bird (a finch) in front of the proper row of papers and it pulled forth with its beak an orange slip addressed to a "Giovanotto." It seems that I was on the point of having a disappointment due to the insincerity of a false friend, but now everything's all right. I should be more alert in future, always listen to those who wish me well. And: I shall be married within a year! The fortune ended with a rhyme:

> Amor ti tende agguato
> e tu non scapperai . . .
>   O uomo fortunato
> felice tu serai!

◆

The Mago gave me an envelope for the Professore (inside was the typewritten page-and-a-half, a transcription of his trance-analysis of Pavlik, organ by organ). He told me that he hadn't told the Professore of the existence of a little ulcer at the duodenum.

◆

"You have never heard the deafmute screaming to the chicken?" Pavlik asks. I look at P.'s hemorrhoid (burst but healing) every night with the flashlight.

◆

Pavlik is sitting on the bidet waiting for the big event: the exit of the tapeworm. Last evening he ate 3 etti of pumpkin seeds mixed with 2 etti of sugar (making a pound all together) and this morning he took a purge. The bidet was covered with a small net of gauze, before he sat down, so the monster will be netted—if and when. Doctor Nardi (the Mago) told him that if the worm is female she *can* leave behind an egg which could hatch another tapeworm months—or even years?— hence.

The purge seems to have taken effect—but no worm forth. Pavlik still sits. I pour hot water in bidet—the heat and the wet supposed to attract the animal.

P. says he's so tired, so tired, that he's been "sitting two hours—shall I sit some more?" I take him tea.

"Charlie! . . . Charlie!"

I go.

"He's coming out, he's stampeding out . . . give me tea."

He thinks it was "broken off." He says, "Look in my ass and see if there's anything hanging out."

There isn't. He gets up from the bidet, we look at the mass-cluster (unbelievable!) of slowly squirming worm—but the head isn't there, he says. The finger-width ribbon (a yard or two) is only a section. The head will be very thin.

Why was it born? "It's still there, it bites me like hell . . . I probably was nervous and it broke off, that's all."

"How do you know?"

"I know."

"Bruno has the biggest balls. He went in today in his underpants. He's all balls and no brain." I tell this to Pavlik as he sits again on the bidet. Still hope?

SEPTEMBER

A letter from Rome lawyer Marinangeli informs me that Milan publisher Bompiani wants to settle with me for $1000 for making the tactless mistake of putting a photo of me (taken by Carl Van Vechten and reproduced in *U.S. Camera Annual* during the war) on the cover of a book on juvenile delinquency!

◆

Rocco was just here—a new friend named Rocco. He's the electrician's assistant—13 years old and says he is a painter—P. and I saw several of his little oils at the electrician's. He's coming back on Sunday morning to swim, and Sunday afternoon will pose for me.

◆

Dr. Nardi in his trance yesterday told Pavlik that the head of the tapeworm is no longer there. One's first impulse is to disbelieve him, but then he could be right. He says he's going to rejuvenate Pavlik—and he may, since P. believes him.

The will to live in the tapeworm, as I remarked to Pavlik, is astonishing. It's the most fantastic animal—no two are alike and, seemingly, no two cures. "Just like us," P. said.

Benito's got a flat torso, no extra ounce of fat on it, pointed nipples sticking out from breast-plates of muscles covered with tan skin.

Did I say that Dr. Nardi has voyaged (in one of his trances) to both Mars and the Moon? Not to mention the North Pole where he saw lots of gold and other minerals deep underground.

◆

Parker writes me he's written three essays on Hamlet. I'd rather read a book on Big Bill Tilden. Big Bill, hero of a thousand boys, jailed for loving them too young.

◆

Rocco came and posed in the nude. He has a very big little thing with practically a full growth of pubic hair. But I didn't fondle him at all. I'd thought so much about him before he arrived, got so many hards on, that restraint (and restraint it was) came easy.

◆

O day.

Today is not "like" anything—it's its exquisite self. The stink from the cesspool doesn't spoil it.

Fire Game.

"The essence of an object remains as light" (Pavlik).

Flies going like crazy. "Come kill them," P. comes in my room to tell me. I go with the flyswatter to his studio-room and put out of commission several flies and a mosquito.

"Executor," he says, as I'm leaving, and makes a face.

◆

How far from reality can you get and still come? This morning's wet dream: I did a drawing of a voyou (Rimbaud) in bellhop's uniform—looking at it, I came.

I've promised Rocco to let him be the one who will do the pulling (off), next time it's done.

No, not today. But he looked prettier today than I've ever seen him. I watched him at work on a gouache. He asked me if I had "tirato" today and I said, No. "E tu?" No, he said. That's as far as the conversation went on that subject. I could have said, No, I was waiting for you—but I could tell he didn't want to do anything today. When he first came in he said he wanted to go to the beach and make a drawing, then when he came back he wanted to color the drawing, then it was time, he said, for him to go.

He asked me the other day if mine is big and when I said Yes, he said that his is too—when it "comes out."

◆

    Flew by
    A whole world of wind
  Once out of the water of poetry
      Swimming isn't

◆

Rocco came, and went (after I came) he was pleased to see the display and the shooting, didn't want to experience same, says it takes boys of his age longer, provided they haven't come very recently. For instance, he said, if he'd jerked off in the morning, then in the evening he could come quickly.

◆

One seems to bring the painting into being *with one's eyes* rather than with the brush in one's hand.

◆

There's a kind of typical vicious bad weather in Italy, with a tone and feeling all its own. Like bad Italian character, when it is bad.

◆

To see poetry is to create it.
    When the sea is churning here on the Adriatic, the waves are slop-colored. The Mediterranean stays beautiful, good weather and bad.

◆

FRASCATI (HOTEL FLORA)

To our future apartment after lunch. Nando, the superintendent, sympathetic. Marvelous views from all three sides of west, north and east terraces. King Farouk didn't take the place after all.

◆

We're in! That is to say: in Penthouse 9 at 9 via Consuelo. It's a quarter to five and the view from my room is more than wonderful, one sees every wave of the sea of the Campagna.
    The carpenter's son, Vito, is appealing.

◆

I saw Vito in his father's shop, he lent me a drill. I told him I wanted him to pose for me. His eyes are rather small but he has a large mouth with skin on the lips looking like the skin on Rocco's cazzo. That last day at Port San Giorgio Rocco drew the prepuce back to show me the raw-colored head, then *carefully* drew it up again before starting to "saw."

Before we moved out of the Flora P. was telling an American Air Force Captain, sitting at table next to ours, how his family had been Russian for seven hundred years—"without a drop of Russian blood." His ancestors, he said, were Swedes, Spanish—what else? When I said, "Tartar?" he said, "There's Tartar blood in all Russians."

◆

Gaetana, who doesn't read or write, starts to work for us tomorrow.

◆

Vito, when he saw my camera slung over shoulder, wanted to know if I intended taking "the photos" now—I'd said we'd go up on the roof, where I saw an iron sphinx sitting. When we got up there we found three sphinxes at various corners. I had V. take off sweater, shirt and undershirt, shoes and socks. He looked, as Pavlik said of him, "pretty as a picture." I told him I was sorry I couldn't take him nude (Oedipus and the Sphinx). He has marvelous legs and behind, attractive face with a pointed Rimbaud-like nose. Full of spirit, and intelligent. His father is making us a table.

Wise? Pavlik thinks all Italians from the age of 10 are wise. Italians, Italians. I think of their "centuries of childhood," as Stendhal discerned. I think Vito is becoming rather fascinated with his fascination for me.

◆

I was at a point approaching an "automatic orgasm" (something I've tried to induce before—a kind of wet daydream)—thinking of how Vito would look posing for a photograph in the nude—when Pavlik came in my room. But I still have half a hard on—

And now another hard on, just before cutting out the light. This is why men get married: hards on before going to bed alone.

◆

Vito, I found out, is "sensible" (as the French say) to the attractions of men. He was already excited (down there) while looking at my drawings—because I felt him. But he's strangely shy. After I felt him, he slipped off the bed, where he was sitting with me stretched out behind him, and sat on his haunches. I told him to undress, for the posing. He took off one thing at a time, slowly. When the underpants were finally off, I found that he was "standing" (with a nice batch of pubic hair).

"Go away," I have to tell P., who wandered around on my terrace, and peered in. "And stay away." Gaetana has noticed how demanding he is of my time, always calling me, always looking for me. He's afraid you'll escape, she said.

So I started playing with V., and discovered he has only one ball. I said, Let's do this first, then afterwards we'll be more tranquil. I took mine out and he began to manipulate it, holding it carefully as though he might pollute his hand—for his own medium-sized thing was cheesey. Then he said he didn't care about coming, would manipulate me without my manipulating him. It didn't take long for me to come, he rather withdrew his hand during the coming. Then I did a quick sketch of him in the nude.

Not long after that his father was at the door. Pavlik thinks he came probably to ask for another advance on the wardrobe he's making for us—or, possibly, to see what was happening to his son. Father and son left together. V. gave me a smile and a wink.

V. has rather a poker face when he wants to. His reaction to the whole episode was rather one of timid surprise.

What is Rome, after New York and Paris? A lot of pretty Italians.

◆

Don Giuseppe was here to bless the house (before lunch), using plain kitchen salt, and tap water, in the ritual. He read Latin from a little book, sprinkled salt in the water, using a motion which formed a cross three times, as the salt was sprinkled in the cup. Then he took the cup, dipping a kind of shaker in it, with which he sprinkled water here and there in all the rooms.

◆

Why is everyone always foolish enough to think that a sexual partner will make life happy?

I went ahead and became a homosexual—no matter what. Not everybody does that—who should (or would *like* to). All the fucked up lives—just because they weren't fucked.

A virtue of necessity? More usually a vice is made of it.

◆

One of the most attractive "sections" of the bodies of young people: from the bottom row of ribs to the pubic hair. (Pav would *include* the pubic hair.) It's so flat, and intact, so undisintegrated, unmarked with sags or superfluous fat. It's beautiful. I think of that section of Rocco, of Benito, of Vito.

◆

I enjoy life when, as Virginia Woolf puts it, "Quiet brings me cool clear quick mornings, in which I dispose of a good deal of work and toss my brain into the air when I take a walk." . . . But Djuna and I didn't thrill to Woolf's *Orlando*. Did I not read some of it aloud to her, that winter (1931–32) on the rue St.-Romain, in that lovely apartment, the heart-shaped big mirrors framed in gold, the studio bed piled high with pillows covered in a variety of "ecclesiastical" cloths, some gold-embroidered. Her big bed, in the bedroom, had lots of little lacey pillows on top of it in the daytime. She'd go once a week to get her hair curled and tinted, strawberry blond.

I was infatuated *by* her (rather than with her). And she was attracted by me—all the way to Tangier—but there I lost my charm for her because of my—selfishness—I didn't give her enough (my re-typing *Nightwood* was hardly enough, and a drunken lay now and then). I spent mornings at the beach, leaving her alone in the little Casbah house. And when she ceased being charmed, she quickly lost her charm for me. I didn't like the kind of mirror she became.

"... This ravaging sense of the shortness of life ..." (V.W.) I don't have that. I sense, rather, that life will be long—too long.

◆

After lunch, I discovered Vito in the hall, Pavlik had let him in. He came and sat in my room. I filed his nails a bit, then pulled his head over in my lap. I asked him if the pharmacist had given him any diagnosis as to what caused his left eye to swell. Too much new blood, he said the pharmacist said. "Sangue bollents," I said, and reached over and found he had a hard on ... Then Pavlik wanted tea. While the water was on to boil, I took V. up to the attic, where there's a center room, empty, another (long) room full of water tanks, and, I found, a smaller room full of boxes and stuff. We opened the door to the smaller dark room and V. went in, in front of me, I held him by the shoulders saying, in my adequate Italian, I'm going to lock you in this dark room. I let my right hand wander over his chest, down his stomach and on down to find: that he had another hard on. Then we rushed back downstairs and to the kitchen to see if the water was boiling.

NOVEMBER

I took a terrace walk and saw the most brilliant falling star—I always make the same wish: Love.

1955

OCTOBER

So I begin this diary again, after an absence of almost a year. Not from vanity. Perhaps because I want someone (besides Pavlik) to talk to. And I shall be talking here in ways that won't be like (not usually) the ways I talk to Pavlik.

Some vanity does enter in—you can't keep it out.

"Qu'est-ce que tu commence à écrire?" asks P., coming into the hall to retrieve his ink. And then, under his breath, as he returns to his studio, "Mama mia."

Vito was at the apartment after his work at new job (printer's apprentice) the evening of the day we arrived back. We found that he'd grown taller, looks less like a child, more like a boy adolescent. He'll be fifteen in December.

Nando has found us a young Maria, I'm gradually teaching her to cook. She's married, with two children, six and seven, says she's keeping it from her husband that she works for two men (he believes there's a signora in the house).

After taking my gouaches and graffiti to Paris last spring and showing them to Léonor, Ossip Zadkine and others, I was emboldened enough to make a selection (25) for a show ("cocktail vernissage") chez François Reichenbach. To my surprise, several were sold. In addition, I received offers from various galleries for an exhibition. I've already accepted, en principe, a June 1956 show at the Galerie Marforen, run by Monsieur Abesteguy, at 91 rue du Faubourg St.-Honoré.

V.'s profile (retroussé) is adorable. He's well-knit, hard arms and chest, small waist, small hands and feet. His brown eyes shine in the outdoor light.

NOVEMBER

Vito arrived this morning, as expected. How beautifully modeled he is—pink ivory, more milky than pink.

From the back, his jawbones may be seen on each side of his head. When looked at in a certain light, from above or with top lighting, slight hollows, almost imperceptible (as though shadows in a portrait by a master) appear between cheekbones and jaws.

I refer to him sometimes now—to P.—as "the Baby," ever since the woman in the photo lab spoke of the photo that I took of him (enlargement had to be made over, they cut off part of his forehead) as "il bambino."

◆

... Art, which is only found by those who seek it, and when found it flies away when neglected. (Who said that?)

Vito seems to have fallen so naturally into his destiny and mine.

I like his cat's silence. Under his chin there's that light color delicately darker than the cheeks. Looked at from underneath, his nostrils are almost round.

Frankie Lane's record is on—Vito asked me to get it: "Honey won't you take me..."

10:30 P.M. We're listening to a broadcast of *Fidelio* (Boris Christoff, Dorothy Dow) and I'm agreeing with Pavlik as to how untalented Kandinsky was.

DECEMBER

"A l'exemple des enfants et des poètes nos jeunes savants s'exercent a l'oubli voulu des rapports normaux, a marier d'une manière insolent des organismes distants les uns des autres—" says Jean Cocteau, discoursing to the French Academy on the occasion of his reception. In Paris Philippe Jullian advised me against asking Jean to write an introduction to my catalog when my exhibition is held. But I'm not so sure that I shan't ask him—he still talks and writes brilliantly. Perhaps he's written too many introductions, but—

◆

I told the Baby I'd like to give him something for his birthday. What? A medallion of the Madonna (gold, understood) to wear around his neck? Yes, he'd like that. But the next instant he said he'd rather have a wristwatch. O materialist Catholic! No, I said, "I'll look for you a watch when I come back through Switzerland . . ." I've never wanted to give more to anyone than I want to give to V. To spoil him, to buy him everything—as though he were my son.

V. looks Etruscan (P.'s discernment).

◆

Thornton Wilder just phoned, asked me to come into Rome and lunch with him tomorrow . . . It's five to four, I'll put the water on for tea. Will no one call on me today? I'll peep through the peep-hole before opening door. The new breadboy is cross-eyed, curious as a cat.

◆

Thornton Wilder met me at the elevator door yesterday, was very cordial, comfortable, entertaining, hospitable. He and a German-accented lady were having a martini (he likes to drink, he told me), I had a glass of sherry. After lunch in the Hassler diningroom, Thorton suggested we see the Caravaggios—"in what church?" he asked and I remembered: San Luigi dei Francesi. While we were gazing at the large canvases a group of young priests came up and one, hearing us speak English, spoke to me in English, asking about the paintings, what they represented, and "Are they very valuable?" "By Caravaggio," I replied—but I doubt if the name meant anything to him ... After a stroll along one side of the Piazza Navona (Xmas stalls not up yet, the sky was light and the clouds like watercolors) Thornton took me into a couple of Gothic churches, in search of "something eccentric," as he put it, then I walked him to his theater, where he was going to hear a concert of twelve-tone music, and we took warm leave of each other. He's on his way to Vienna and parts North tomorrow, wants to hear some operas, since he's writing a libretto; wants to see some snow, and enjoy his drinking in mountain air.

◆

Mother's in Taxco. She sold Baywood Park in Panama City, Fla., last July.

"Charles Henri, I wish you would clean your shoes, mon cher ami."

◆

You have to know where and how to put the shadows.

The Baby said he's going to America with me when I go but I didn't ask him to. What would you like to study? I asked. Aviation, he said. That's uninteresting, I said. Would you like to study ballet? The guitar? The piano?

"Singing," he said.

"I didn't know you had a voice ... Then you could sing with the guitar."

No, he'd sing with the piano.

◆

I've told Pavlik that he should "paint flat." (Upstart to Master.) Anyway, he told me some days later (a couple of days ago): "I would like to paint flat." I nodded my head: "Then that would be being painting instead of painting something."

"You want to know the truth?" (I to Pavlik.)

"What?"

"Matisse couldn't draw."

"That's what Gertrude Stein said."

"As for Braque—he drew worse than Matisse."

"I know that."

◆

I've asked my zio (Pavlik) to name his cafards, as the Americans name their hurricanes, with female names in alphabetical order—so I'll know which one he's in—they come so fast I don't know if he's recovering from Hortense or if it's Inez who's begun to stir.

The truth hurts—everyone.

◆

"Are you going to wait for the New Year?" P. asked after dinner (December 31).

"It'll come without my waiting," I said and he agreed.

1956

JANUARY

Pavlik insists that Vito is a born "cocotte." (The small slightly slanting eyes, the arched eyebrows, the raw-red full lips, the low forehead, the neat patch of pubic hair, the flat stomach, the curving cheeks of the behind, the full thighs, thick ankles.)

How many or how few years does it take for an Italian boy to find out that his sex is worth money, saleable? Such seeming innocence!

The natural condition of man is love. Poor creature!

◆

A black prick with a red glowing head and folded golden wings (candlewick).

◆

Phone in kitchen rang. Pavlik can't hear it with both his doors closed. I went to corridor, opened one door: "Telephone!" He moves slow. Phone rang and rang. What? "Telephone!"

He asked what number whoever was on the phone wanted. Yes, this is number 490587. "Va bene, va bene."

"Who was it?"

"At eleven o'clock they're going to call you from New York."

"Mother dead," I said.

"No-o-o," said Pavlik.

"For what other reason would anyone call me from New York?"

◆

11:55 A.M. Call not through yet. Telegram from Sister: PLEASE CALL ME IM-MEDIATELY PERSON TO PERSON TRAFALGAR 3-5254 LOVE.

◆

In the midst of lunch I got up to contact operator, wanting to find out why the call had been delayed. Frascati operator called Rome and the report was that the line had been damaged.

Now (3:10 P.M.) I receive a call from the operator saying my call is scheduled to go through at 6 P.M.

◆

A quarter to eight and the call isn't through yet.

◆

The call came through. I'm in bed now. It is just after ten. Pavlik was the first to cry. It was hard for me to talk but I stood stirring the milk until it boiled, then left Pavlik in the kitchen, sitting at the kitchen table (where we had been eating when the call came).

"I have some bad news for you," Sister said. "What is it? Why didn't you put it in the telegram?" Then she told me what it was but her voice was washed away and it was some time before I understood. "Mother," she said. "Did you hear that?" "Yes." Then I think she said, "Mother is dead." "From a stroke?" I asked. (Last letter I got from Mother, written from Taxco, said her blood pressure was gradually going up and she was planning to move to Cuernavaca, where the altitude is somewhat lower.) Then came the shocking part: "No. She was killed in an automobile accident." In Mexico.

Zach (Zachary Scott, Sister's husband) was to take care of everything—flying to Mexico—the legal things—and he's bringing Mother's ashes back to New York. She was cremated.

I waited to hear Sister's voice. She asked, "How are you?" before saying she had bad news for me. She wanted to break the news slowly.

Pavlik told me—in 1933—that I had been sent to him because his mother had died. I wonder if he remembers telling me that? I wonder if sometimes he doesn't wish I'd never been sent to him!

"We are both orphans now," I said, after he'd come to my room and sat by me on the bed in the semi-dark. I was touched by his grief.

I can't bear to think of how Mother must have looked after the accident. A violent death—for her whose life had been so un-violent ... A brave death, in a way—because she was moving, free, independent, going somewhere (even if only from Taxco to Cuernavaca!) ... Gentle Mother and the violent death—that's what's so intolerable to think about. I'll just have to keep my mind off that moment. I hope, I hope—(I put my hands over my eyes just as though I saw it)—it was only a moment. "No one will ever know," Pavlik said.

◆

I finished [Heinrich] Zimmer's book on Indian philosophies. The last line is: "The Mother is present in every house. Need I break the news as one breaks an earthen pot on the floor?"

◆

Mother in a letter to Coral, written from Hotel Victoria, Taxco (it was from there that she took the fatal car): "It took me a long time to make up my mind to spend Xmas down here and miss seeing you . . . I tried awfully hard for several weeks to find a place near New York . . . but it was impossible . . ." One goes to meet one's fate. Mathematical—"like clock-work," as Pavlik expressed it. We were speaking of destiny. And yet irony is one of its characteristics.

Pavlik thinks that some kind of underground wisdom was at work, because of Gertrude's perspicacity in getting everything wound up at Baywood and no loose ends.

And the psyche knows things that the mind does not. Pavlik thinks Mother's psyche "knew"—"nine months before."

One of the carabinieri arrived at the door this morning, wanted to know if Gertrude Ford were here—if so, she hadn't received her Permission of Sojourn.

FEBRUARY

Suffering, suffering? Pavlik had already suffered much, when I met him—a tragic face, he was never gay except as a banner waving from the castle of melancholy.

◆

We are landing at Shannon in a snowfall. It's 1 A.M.

◆

NEW YORK CITY

It is midnight and I am in bed in "Coral's room"—Sis and Zach's apartment at the Dakota, West 72nd Street. As the plane passengers waited, just after the landing, for the Health Officer to pass through and examine health cards, I hear "Mr. Ford" called out at the plane's exit, so I got up and at the exit-entrance a Panam official told me, "Mr. Scott is waiting for you outside," and I saw a tall man in a camel's hair overcoat and with a beard open his arms and it was Zachary.

I learned that Mother had not been mutilated but had died instantly from a blow to the skull. Two other passengers were killed, two escaped serious injury and the driver was very badly injured (one of his legs has been amputated). The car was a hired limousine, accustomed to take several passengers at a time from Taxco to Cuernavaca. A bus, on the wrong side of the road, ran head on into the limousine, coming around a curve, just an hour and a half out of Taxco, last Sunday morning. Zach told me he's had a mass said in a little chapel in Mexico which Gertrude admired. He's like a true brother, just as he was like a good son to Gertrude.

◆

Zach and Sister have already done a lot to put Mother's estate in order and the will is coming from Panama City.

Zach is a more complicated person than he seems at first, and I haven't "the hang" of him yet—not completely. But that's as it should be. I know I like his essence. It took me years and years to get the hang of Pavlik, and by the time I did get it (or thought so) he was another person.

◆

Why is it that somehow I have the sensation that in New York one lives rather outside of time, and in Europe—Rome, Paris, the sensation is more of being one with time (inside of time, that is)—? "Losing time" is an American feeling, Pavlik thinks.

◆

We are taking off at this moment from La Guardia. It will be a non-stop flight to New Orleans, Washington fogged out so no landing there possible. The plane, therefore, is not full, and there is a free seat between me and the Spanish-speaking woman on my right. On that seat, in a woven basket from Mexico, is the box which contains the sealed jar of Mother's ashes.

◆

On the train, "City of New Orleans." The plane did come down in Washington, D.C. after all. We got out of there about 2 A.M. While waiting for the take-off I ate a piece of the cheese (aged Cheddar) Zach gave me to bring along, packed with some rye melba in a tin tea-box. Then I took a jigger of the bourbon with which Brad had filled my flask. After a sip of tea, I dropped off to sleep. At something about 3—that is, about an hour later, I woke up, felt nauseated. I thought I was going to vomit so I undid seat belt and walked towards the rear of the plane, read the sign on one of two doors, it was the women's toilet, so I opened the door of the toilet next to it (MEN) and . . . the next thing I knew I was being held up by one of the stewardesses, and I was saying to her, "I am very sick." I had passed out!

◆

6:15 A.M. I am sitting in the bus which will take me from La Guardia airfield to mid-Manhattan.

When the train reached Brookhaven (Miss.) yesterday morning my cousin, Mathews Ard, was the first to greet me (tears in his eyes), then introduced me to others who were there and I saw Uncle Grady. Mat, as he's called, took me alone in his station wagon (an old Plymouth) to the cemetery. On the way we stopped at a florist's and I asked for all the red roses they had, three dozen, which the man, assisted by a young black Negro boy, made up into a large bouquet tied with loops of wide red silken ribbon. Those roses and a spray of white camellias, which Mat had gathered from his garden, were the only flowers.

◆

5 P.M. The motors have started, I am on board another DC7-B.

In New York I saw Djuna and took her a little bottle of perfume (Lancôme). Djuna told me over phone that she couldn't receive me for tea chez elle but perhaps they'd give us "a bun" at Luigi's. She wasn't at Luigi's when I arrived but it wasn't long before I saw an old and stooped woman walking with a stick pass by the window and I opened the door for her. Djuna's old-time snappishness wasn't there, though she tried to bare a false tooth now and then . . . She did say, when she first saw me, "You've grown hardly any older—it's disgusting!" She said various London literary lights had raved over her new play (Eliot, [Edwin] Muir, [Herbert] Read) and she's mailing the revised version to Eliot on Monday.

We may value old friends, but we can't go back to them.

And in Italy I shall be glad to be.

◆

FRASCATI

10 P.M. Pavlik looked rather worn, said he'd been sick, with cold and fever, last week. Just as we had finished dinner an explosion announced the carnival fireworks were beginning so we pulled our chairs up behind the closed glass doors leading from kitchen to terrace and watched the lovely display from the grounds of the Villa Aldobrandini. They went on for thirty minutes, from 8 to 8:30. Blinds down and we thought all was over when other booms heralded another display. Two makers of fireworks were competing and this was the second. I'd have given the prize to No. 1, if only for the long slow movement of mounting comets surrounded by bursting streamers in a faster tempo.

"Are you glad to see me back?" I asked Pavlik when I kissed him on the cheek goodnight.

"Well, I guess I am," he replied.

◆

Vito came by on his lunch hour looking so loveable—he's delighted with the model airplane I brought him. We worked together assembling it. Towards six it was getting dark, besides he'd finally had enough of working—so we started something else.

◆

P. says I spoil the Baby too much: "You can do nothing for him, you'll just ruin him."

"I don't think one ever ruins anyone."

◆

The beloved Tania Blixen writes from Denmark: "Dear Charles Henri, I have been in a nursing home for almost six months, and am only just out after a second operation. Now, you will understand, I am longing for a more pleasant side of life than the terrible sterile atmosphere of doctors and nurses! I am writing to you and Pavlik to ask you if there is any possibility that the unsuccessful plan of last year of a birthday party on my birthday the 17th of April might be carried out this year. I am thinking of flying to Rome about the 12th of April. Let me have a word to tell me if you and Pavlik will be there. I should be so delighted to see you. With my best love to you both, Yours ever Tania Blixen."

Language is sensibility. If you understand the spoken language, you understand the people.

"I'm getting [to be] an old thing, 'laid simple sans complication,' "—Pavlik. The French is a quotation from Gertrude Stein—when she once put an end (with "laide simple sans complications!") to Alice B. Toklas's attempt to describe an ugly girl without coming out and saying that she was ugly.

◆

I'm thinking of Vito ... To be burdened with possession ... or to be free to yearn. "I find him self-centered, frightful selfish." (P.) "Like all boys of his age—typical, typical." (Me.)

An animal, an animal—and, like an animal, he doesn't always obey.

Pavlik's hard to seduce completely. He thinks I'm primitive, like Vito, and that's why I like V. (he thinks). "Two makes one feel stronger."

◆

To know when to leave alone those chance happenings.

MARCH

"Painting is an illusion—how it's painted doesn't matter"—Pavlik.

◆

Sandy Calder and wife Louise came out to lunch yesterday—we'd gone to Sandy's vernissage of mobiles and gouaches at the Obelisco on Wednesday. Sandy is white-headed, though the same age as Pavlik, looks much older—"like my father," Pavlik was pleased to note (usually P. thinks *he* looks like everybody's father). Both Sandy and Louise like to drink, I gave them Negronis before lunch and Sandy poured down the wine during lunch, with the result that he started dozing during coffee—in my room—"Give him a pillow," Pavlik said. So while Sandy snored I showed Louise my gouaches and a few oils. Neither of them have much to say about anyone's painting—they were exposed to a gouache and an oil of Pav's during the Negronis, and I don't think Louise opened her mouth—Sandy referred to the (beautifully designed) spirals which form the arms of "The Golden Vase" as "bedsprings." Well, they were just being themselves, without pretensions, honest and homey.

◆

Reduced to its simplest elements, any picture is: light coming out of dark, or, dark coming out of light.

◆

Pavlik told Léonide and Sylvia Marlowe that the Gregorian chants are something to hear, sung by Greek Orthodox priests at the chapel. So we met them there; they'd brought along Prince Leone Massimo, who'd brought along his wife, who is simple and nice and has a red nose, two sons, one of whom has red hair, and a daughter who wanted to take a crippled cat home.

◆

So what about Vito? There's no real problem at the moment. Has most of the fun been in the gamble-search? Not for me. The fun has been in bed.

Don't let it go!

I have an intellectual companion—one who shares—so I'm not looking for one. I wonder if I shall ever look for another. Parker was the first, for whom I had a passion—the passion of friendship. Now when I think of companionship I think of a sexual companion.

[Vera] Zorina telephoned from Rome, where she arrived today. She's to appear in Stravinsky's *Persephone* at the Rome Opera, April 12.

◆

To start off being a poet today you have to be young and full of illusions. To end up being a poet you have to have Another Job.

APRIL

Gregorio—he's the fifteen-year-old who delivers the milk sometimes on Sunday evenings, did today—muratore's hat on, arms full of milk bottles, I stuck a piece of gum in his mouth. I must photograph those well-lashed eyes.

◆

Patience is an art too.

Pavlik's pictures for exhibition at Palais des beaux Arts, Brussels, aren't finished. He says I'm "taking away" his power to paint.

◆

V. has, as Pavlik puts it, "a difficult character." Taking him to live with me would mean transforming myself from a symbol of freedom into a symbol of discipline (what other "authority" would there be in his life?)...

"... a naked shepherd and a stranger offering him a flute to play..."

◆

Pavlik's on the phone talking to Zorina about when we can get to see and hear her in *Persephone*: "... lots of French 'M'—you know what I mean" (the French say Merde for good luck), "don't worry ... Italians don't understand anything, but a beautiful woman they can't resist . . . I know it will be all right . . . Lots of love . . . heartbroken"—meaning how sorry he is not to be able to be there tonight for her first performance.

◆

Diamonds and rainbows: Pavlik's colors.

Pavlik's "slowness" in his painting production. I think he has to put so much concentration and care in the almost incredible drawing element, in the painting as an object, that his painting as an art gets a little pushed into second place.

◆

Anyway, prose-writer, take your Vito to Paris.

◆

Today we lunched in Rome with Zorina (Brigitta [Hartwig], as we call her, her real name) and her mother and her husband, Goddard Lieberson. I went into Rome by train last evening, alone, to see the Stravinsky *Persephone* with Brigitta looking very striking in the title-role, reciting the Gide text very clearly and doing the best she could by the mediocre choreography—she still brings the "Balanchine school" on stage with her, however.

Pauline and Philippe de Rothschild were out for tea yesterday. Both of them liked the large oil of a stylized bird which P. calls *Naissance*—and Philippe would like to buy it, said he'd telephone his decision yesterday but he didn't. When Pav phoned him today, he said that he and Pauline are lunching at the Aldobrandinis' villa (which we see from our kitchen terrace) and will be by again this afternoon to look at the picture some more: they looked at it in every possible light and place yesterday. P. took a third off the American market price—it's now priced to Philippe at $2000 which he still thinks (Philippe does) is enormous.

◆

Baby's father came by before dinner yesterday. I told him to sit down and have a drink and I told him that Vito wants to study. He said Yes, he needs three more years of schooling, even to enter into a printer's métier. I outlined my plan to have V. go to a French school in Rome. He said it's Vito's mother who makes the decisions.

◆

PARIS

If I'm going to love living in Paris I'll have to get used to—even *like*—that pearl-gray sky which one sees on opening the curtains in the morning.

I talked to Jean (Cocteau) on the phone, told me to call Madeleine (his bonne) on the 5th and she'd tell me when I could come in to see him. Shall I or shall I not ask him to write preface to my exhibition catalog? Everyone's had him but me!

◆

Pavlik is in Brussels, I saw him off at the Gare du Nord. I'm going to see Cocteau in his rue de Richelieu apartment tomorrow. I shall take along my new graffiti and 2 oils and ask him to write the preface for my catalog. I was considering asking Breton until I saw his poem-preface for Man Ray's show.

◆

Jean promised to do my preface! I went to his place around noon and there were other people waiting to see him (he being busy with a visitor in his bedroom). At one point, when we were in the kitchen, he asked Madeleine, "Qui est ce Monsieur dans ma chambre?" The Monsieur had said to Madeleine that Monsieur Cocteau himself had given him the rendezvous.

Jean was in his white bath-towel robe, asked me to put my hand inside and feel how he was sweating.

◆

Jean gave me my preface! A beautiful page; I kissed and hugged him. Abesteguy, the gallery director, is delighted with it—"—il vous a gaté," he said.

◆

"Il a tout á fait l'air de putain," said Choura, after seeing the photos (nude and otherwise) of Vito.

◆

On the way to lunch chez Marie-Laure de Noailles I ran into Sherban Sidéry who told me that Peter Watson is dead. Marie-Laure had received a letter from Cecil Beaton, saying that Peter had been found "two days ago" in his bath, head submerged.

◆

Cecil is in Paris, invited me to a Dior fashion show but I preferred to see him somewhere else and I did—on the street. The edges of his gray suit, and the vest, had a border of gray material like a slip-cover. He had been to Peter's funeral which he found, I gather, unglamorous—"Peter would have hated it," he said.

◆

Pavlik came back from Brussels on Wednesday (four days ago). Choura, who was ill and irritable, irritated me that day and I left the table. She told Pavlik that she thinks I hate her, that I hadn't hated her for three years and now the hate is back. But that's not true, and I tried to explain to her: that animosities, which are natural, even towards those we love, will out. Anyway, we're buddies again.

Pavlik and I saw the Clouzot film, *Le Mystère Picasso*, which has thrilling moments (man on a bull's horns), and many incredibly inept ones.

JUNE

François Reichenbach is giving me a pre-vernissage champagne preview at the Marforen gallery, night of the 11th. He brought from the U.S. some spine-tingling Rock 'n' Roll records, said he'd make me a present of one.

◆

My vernissage is over and everyone is pleased, the Gallery's pleased, Pavlik's pleased, I'm pleased, my new friends are pleased. Marie-Laure was pleased, otherwise she wouldn't have bought one.

◆

The Soviet Ballet, with Geoffrey Gilmour last night, was worse than we thought it was going to be. The primo ballerino, a horse of a sissy, had what looked like dirty droopy drawers over his costume. Everything appeared heavy and stiff—an uncut version of *Swan Lake* . . . Truly, "trop de ducks . . ."

◆

Yesterday I arrived at the Gallerie Marforen at five, found Jean Cocteau. Madame Scarlett, who is in charge, said Max Ernst and Dorothea Tanning had just left, told how Max had been sitting down, Jean passed in front of him without looking at him; so, later, when Dorothea was ready and willing to be introduced to Jean (by Scarlett), Max shook his head. Jean told me he hadn't meant to cut him.

I learned that Jean Genet had been there earlier—with a pretty little môme; neither said a word as they looked at the pictures nor did they say anything when they left.

Pavlik's going to end up showing at Agostinci's Galerie Rive Gauche again—in November. Well (as I told him) he has nothing to lose.

◆

Boy-children I'd enjoy (and suffer with, no doubt—but does one love anything that comes too easy?) . . . Vito writes that he doesn't know what to do with himself on Sundays, looks up at the closed terrace door of my room and wishes I were there.

JULY

A Russian superstition has prevented Pavlik from packing his bags—"never pack until you know when you may go"—so there's all the packing to do before we can take off, which means that we can't possibly be ready by Monday (this is Friday); Tuesday, he says, is no good as a day of departure, so it'll be Wednesday August 1st. His horoscope has said that August is a good month for him to travel.

◆

Janet Flanner was with Dougie a week ago tonight when he died of a heart attack in a restaurant. Janet was at the bar, heard a thud, turned around and it was Dougie on the floor. He was unconscious, and dead in about a minute. Janet and Bill Taylor and Zadkine undertook the funeral arrangements, and expenses, but Zadkine was not at the funeral service, said he never goes to funerals. Pavlik was there, but hadn't been to one in years, remarked on the brevity of the Protestant service. I smell rain (miles away).

◆

Before my exhibition closed I wrote Henri Michaux a note and he came to the gallery, stayed some time, Mme. Scarlett said. Then Pavlik wrote him a note, asking him to dine, told him I would be with them—so I met him. Then he gave me an appointment to visit him in his apartment and I went, two days later. I took him one of my lithographs and he gave me a book with several black and white lithos of his own in it. I discovered that he's naturally shy, rather than stuck-up. He has a strange little laugh, often, which reveals a gold tooth on the left. He's almost bald, with pale skin—an indoor man. He's starting to paint in oils now—we talked painting. He had supposed, from my pictures, that I'd been painting as long as I've been writing; said he, "I take off my hat"—to my technique. Pavlik thinks "technique" comes natural to Americans.

◆

We are planning to spend this weekend with Renato Wild, at his villa on Lake Como (Blevio).

◆

I watched a man masturbate (tasse Pont Mirabeau).

AUGUST

Chez Renato Wild. We haven't seen him yet, the housekeeper tells us he's in Milan, will be back for dinner. I asked the housekeeper if there are other guests in the villa (which is huge—Victorian and full of things: pictures, furniture, statues, and right on the lake); she said Yes, a signora with two children. I've just heard the signora call out for one of them: "Kiki!" A little boy is calling, "Aiuto!" in the garden, playing with a dog.

In Lugano, which has a much much more charming aspect than Como, I found a watch which I wanted to buy for Vito, and bought it—he expects it. P. said I could have chosen a less expensive one. "Aiuto!" repeats the little boy. I wonder if the children will eat with us.

◆

The lady has a tic. Renato has still another guest—a Negro from Mississippi. He's a singer (non-pop); leaves day after tomorrow to give a concert in Frankfurt. His name is Charles and he's full of "nigger" (little nig) charm, laughs and all but prances, jokes with the children. The children are hardly children—the boy will be thirteen next month, the girl is sixteen or so and wears high-heeled shoes. It's the whole right side of the mother's face that gives a twitch from time to unexpected time.

The color of the lake is not pretty, nor clear—not inviting. Renato looks thin and sunburned; in contrast to the last time we saw him—in the Swiss clinic—wasn't that two years ago?—in bed, pale and plump. He brought from Milan yesterday some colored drawings by the sculptor Henghes—one is an extremely mediocre portrait of Genet: "It's going in my room," said Wild. Genet stayed here a month last December, did his writing in bed.

There was talk after dinner of a ghost in the house, supposed to haunt only the yellow room, where Charles is staying. Pavlik got wind of it and wouldn't sleep in his room, came in mine and slept in the twin bed. The signora told of seeing a black ghost here, like a long black curtain waving in the room, said it came towards her but when she got up to grasp it, it went away. This was La Pasta's villa. Chairs and tables appliqué'd with shark skin. Divulged by Renato: one seduces women with the Prick and Money; one seduces boys with Sartorial Elegance and Intelligence.

◆

FRASCATI

We're home, and Vito was here, says he will wear his watch only on Sundays and holidays. He said he'd thought of me every day. "You're in love with him!" said Pavlik to me at dinner. "In love! He's a beautiful animal, that's all."

◆

Dog woke me up at 3 this morning. Dogs barked, cocks crowed. Now trucks wail— in anguish—they want in—or out. So do we all.

◆

"You see what all those abstractions are going to be? Mrs. Nature is after them"— Pavlik, after reading about Jackson Pollock's death in an automobile accident.

◆

Baby V. never prettier. Pavlik smelled shit—it was hard to scrub all the odor off my finger.

◆

The model I want most at the moment: Dino who works in Mariano's garage. How old are you, fifteen? Thirteen and a half. The face is that square, heart-shaped kind; moth-wing eyelashes, gold lights in blond hair, soft manly voice, long long neck (every tendon shows when he moves his head this way and that), small nose with the smallest suggestion of aquilinity; as often happens with boys the development of the behind has gone before the rest.

◆

V.'s mother came to tea and brought along her sister. Mother and Aunt both pleased at my school plan for V. Mother told of V.'s long blond hair. She didn't want to cut it until his father came home (from the war) and saw how pretty his five-year-old son was, but father's reaction was: Cut it at once, what do you think he is, a girl?

◆

Tomorrow I go to Ciampino to meet Sister and Zachary and 15-year-old Coral: the child we left in '52 is now, I'm told, a well-developed maiden, taller than her mother my sister. Zachary is to make a film in the south of Italy.

◆

Coral is beautiful. "Oh, Bubu," were her first words. She is even more beautiful than Vito.

We admire other people's works, to the point of love. I admire, to the point of love, nature's work in having made Vito. I wish he had Coral's broad shoulders. But to take people as they are is the big wisdom.

◆

I dreamed of a pet mouse, this afternoon, who jumped from its sleeping place (I was just putting it to beddy) to fasten upon my lips in a prolonged kiss.

SEPTEMBER

Vito and I are back from Sicily (and Forio d'Ischia) since Saturday. Taormina wasn't it, nor was any place in Sicily.

The train ride from Rome to Naples on the 15th seemed long, and Vito was regretting the car, not knowing how much harder on me a trip by road would have been. People who don't drive—like Pavlik and Vito—just cannot understand that chauffeuring is labor; they sit there rolling along, enjoying the landscape, and assume that the driver is doing the same—a driver's tensions and fatigues are completely unknown to them.

"Do you think my child is beautiful?" I asked Auden in Forio. "Very," he replied.

When I enjoyed looking at him most: he'd be the first to get up, having slept in nothing but his white shorts, and he'd be walking barefoot about the room, would wash himself, dry himself, look at himself in the mirror. I'd lie in bed and look at him.

Pavlik thinks that I'd rather live with V., that I'm more amused by V., that I'm—(He asked me what we did on the trip, I told him there was only some M.M.)...

It's a beautiful clear day, the air is good, Pavlik is good too. "Charles Henry, don't close the doors. If you don't want to talk to me then I'm going to call up Dr. Simeons... Salvator Mundi hospital... You're in love, in love with him..."

OCTOBER

"Aren't you fucking Vito?" Pavlik tried to get out of me.

Day before yesterday I broke the little cheap mirror which rested on the shelf behind my bed—my elbow hit it as I raised the blinds. I'd heard Pavlik tell someone that a broken mirror should be thrown in water, so I planned to take it to Rome and let it fall in the Tiber—which I did, with much reminding from P. not to forget. Immediately after, on the bridge, I met a young boy, with his bird and folded "fortunes." The one the little bird picked out for me foretells a separation.

◆

Tastes change but not our natures.

Baby came in on a radio program of Louis Armstrong, didn't want to listen to Vivaldi broadcast which followed but I insisted—he spent the time thumbing through backnumbers of *Time* and *Life*, looking for pictures of James Dean, found one. I've enrolled him at the British Institute rather than French Academy. He went over the ABC's which he'd been learning in class today. I like to watch his lips (heavy underlip) pronounce English.

I bit my tongue during lunch and so Pavlik wanted me to consider myself disabled insofar as the milkboy is concerned but I'm not going to. But is he going to show up?

Vito's the one I love most ... A racing engine just raced by. Brought to mind James Dean and his racing death. We all have the desire to race towards death.

We all have that desire.

Towards life and death.

◆

PARIS

Choura asked me if I wanted to listen to Dali on the radio at 10, I said No. But she called me in her room towards the end of the interview and I listened for a few minutes. Phoney, cabotin, unconvincing, stupid … Oh Paris. Foggy tonight. If Vito lived with me here—

Being jerked off—if done by the right person—leaves no regrets.

◆

"Anyone can be mad in real life, find your folly in art." (Pavlik.)

Why was it born? What is its raison d'être? That of Paris, or any other city or humblest town. To give us the maximum pleasure, the minimum pain.

"Que c'est merveilleux de regarder! Comme c'est félin! Une nouvelle jeunesse me revenait, une des plus subtils, celle du regard." (Henri Michaux.)

NOVEMBER

As much of humanity in me as I can stand.

◆

Hiquily's studio. I hope Zach will buy the little man who turns around, holding a little mirror in his little hand. You look at it turning and see the face in the mirror at one point. It's lovely, the naked little thing.

◆

Pavlik's vernissage on the 6th: Galerie Rive Gauche never saw a more crowded one. [Pierre] Balmain and Diana Mosley bought gouaches. No new sales until now (oils bought before the show by Pauline and Philippe de Rothschild, Zachary and Sister, Gustave Leven, Lincoln Kirstein).

◆

Yesterday night there was a farewell dinner for Zev chez the Hiquilys. Pavlik's story of his adolescent visit with a schoolfriend to a Moscow house of prostitution. They asked for a big fat woman, requested her to show them all she had between her legs, took a long look, both of them, paid her and left. "We saw Africa, Asia, Australia, the Cape of Good Hope …"

◆

Chez Nicolas Nabokov met Ignazio Silone, one of my past literary heroes. He said: I wanted to be a grandmother (his grandmother seeming the most wonderful person in the world). And so one of his early disillusionments: he couldn't *ever* be a grandmother.

◆

Pavlik's exhib a virtual sell-out, only one picture left.

DECEMBER

FRASCATI

V. has the smoothest cheeks, so round. When looked at from the front, the lips seem like a lip-shaped spot from which the face-skin has been torn away.

◆

Jazz became too refined so along came Rock 'n' Roll. Same thing happens in painting, literature . . . The barbaric, the beastly regenerates.

◆

Characteristic of our age (Henry James' *The Turn of the Screw* a forerunner): more and more interest in the perversity of children. To shock now, the child must be involved—we are no longer capable of being moved-to-shock by a perverse adult. Example in painting: Balthus, more shocking than Dali. Most shocking movie: Buñuel and his Mexican boys (*Los Olvidados*).
    The child is all.

◆

Tomorrow is Zev's birthday, as well as Vito's, so we're giving a buffet-lunch and have ordered a birthday cake with "Auguri V—Z 1956" sugared on. Gertrude (Zev's wife) will also be out and that wild Frank whom Pavlik says he's going to fuck.

◆

Pav says he didn't sleep all night: has sore throat and coughed blood. But he felt well enough to join the party in the afternoon, kept up a non-stop flow of entertainment.

◆

Pav's fever was up last night, but is the same this morning as yesterday morning, though he feels worse.

◆

Design the space around: the figures the space makes. Pavlik always judges a picture this way: if the spaces make ugly cut-outs, the picture is bad.

3:30 P.M. It has just showered, I've just napped. Hope Pav slept some of his fever off.

◆

After climbing past 101 Pav's fever gone, thanks to a prescription originally meant for arthritis and the likes (Dr. Simeons).

Gregorio (milkboy) came with the milk, dressed in a Sunday jacket, jeans and rubber boots, hair slicked back with brilliantine—

◆

Tanny (Tanaquil Le Clercq) down with polio! A bitter taste of tragic irony drunk by us all—all her friends.

◆

I shall continue this document until the end of next year, then I vow to continue it no longer. It's a secret vice. Vices should be public.

The grandeur of Diogenes, jerking off in the piazza.

Don't try to be a genius unless you are one. And if you are one you don't have to try.

"My heart was always like a snail," said Pavlik. Now he finds it runs and jumps too fast—at times.

P. Tchelitchew did everything first—the mystery of dress; the Child; metamorphosis, poetry of image; the Boy, since not-since-Caravaggio. The last great painter of the XXth century—there can be no other until another century comes.

◆

It's a quarter to five this Christmas morning. Pavlik woke me up at 3:30 saying he wanted me to call the ambulance from Rome's Salvator Mundi hospital, reserve a room for him, that he was spitting blood, that his lungs might be flooded any moment and then he would "go." I phoned the hospital, the attendant woke up a doctor after fumbling about for 3 minutes trying to find "Tchelitchew" in the file. I told him to give me the doctor without waiting to find the name—"beside the point"—that we'd be cut off by the operator after six minutes. I was cut off in middle of conversation with the doctor, called back. His advice was to wait till morning, have a local doctor in, then see if Mr. T. still wanted to come to the hospital. I called the local hospital, woke up attendant to get the name of a doctor here and called him—he lives next door but could not come over, his professional duties being limited to patients in the Frascati clinic.

Pavlik's anxiety sent me towards the phone another time, to tell the S.M. hospital to send the ambulance, but then he stopped me, reconsidered, said it would be best to wait and telephone Olga Signorelli, his Russian friend in Rome, who is a doctor. Pavlik spits up blood when he coughs. The doctor I got on the phone here recommended Vitamin C!

6:25 A.M. "My nails are all blue." I have called the Red Cross ambulance in Rome—through the doctor at S.M. who opined that whatever is in the lungs is breaking up rather than beginning.

◆

It is five P.M. and I am back in Frascati after taking Pavlik to the Salvator Mundi hospital in the Red Cross ambulance which was the nearest I've ever been to being in a Frigidaire. Pavlik just wouldn't let me take him in the car, said he didn't think he could make it. But he made it down the four flights of stairs to the waiting vehicle, Nando on one side, a big attendant on the other.

The S.M. doctor whom I'd awakened twice (phone operator had said I'd need the doctor's O.K. to enter a patient in the hospital) was the first to examine P. He was concerned about the way P.'s heart was pounding—palpitating—so sent up the Heart Machine after P. had been rolled down to the X-ray room for an X-ray of his chest.

The smiling sister who manned the Heart-Reading Machine said, "Take it easy," asked Pavlik if he couldn't relax a bit more. She said his running heart would win the Olympic race. I asked the doctor what he thought—out in the hall after he'd made a personal inspection of Pavlik all over ("Are your ankles swollen?"). He was concerned for Pavlik's heart, said all the trouble, even in the chest, with the blood-spitting (which went on and on, now and then), could be caused by the heart's being out of order—"had no regular rhythm."

Anyway, the head doctor of the hospital, Dr. Randinger, was to be along and give his own analysis-diagnosis—Dr. R. is seeing to all of Dr. Simeons' cases, during Dr. S.'s absence.

Dr. Randinger's summary, made in the presence of, and to, Pavlik was this: You could be out of the hospital in twenty-four hours if—And the if was: If you'd stop upsetting yourself. "You must help me to help you. Of course, I realize that the sight of blood, your spitting blood, could be upsetting, but the blood spitting is unimportant . . . you must calm yourself, you're making yourself ill. We're going to give you a shot to put your heart back to its natural rhythm."

In the hall, I asked Dr. R. if he had anything to add to what he'd told Mr. Tchelitchew, and he said No. He added that though the heart is enlarged there's nothing *really* wrong with it—if he doesn't abuse it.

◆

Tomorrow night I've promised to dine chez Kenneth Macpherson. Nancy Cunard will be there.

◆

Opaque spaces. Not everything precious stones. Contrasts, equilibriums, disequilibriums in matière, shapes (forms); patterns of space as essential as central image.

I called the hospital. Pavlik had "a fairly good night," the sister said.

◆

I'm back (1 A.M.) where I want to be.

. . . on the train, but I didn't come . . .

◆

The hospital's heart specialist, Dr. Mattoli, visited Pavlik on the 27th: his report: Pavlik's heart condition is "grave."

◆

I recognized Nancy Cunard, Piazza di Spagna. "Nancy!" She turned, took my arm and we went on to Kenneth's. She said she thought Peggy Guggenheim would be at the dinner and she was. Peggy started reminiscing to Islay (Kenneth's friend) about the bandit-boy we picked up that night (*View* days) at a party . . .

Nancy can be awfully winning, her zircon eyes shine at you when she likes you. Peggy said I could visit her any time in Venice—"Can I bring someone?"—thinking of Vito. But I wonder if she still wants me, after I spoke out my opinion of Jackson Pollock: "Zero." Sweet, alcoholized Nancy.

◆

My dear great Pavlik is better. The oxygen tent did him good and he had a good night's sleep. He's still very weak. The coughing is less and the blood comes up less often but it still comes up. The barber shaved him this morning, while I was there.

I'm far from being at ease regarding Pavlik's condition—I'm unsatisfied with the doctor's reports.

◆

Gregorio telephoned about half an hour ago, wanted to come over, I said No, because I was expecting an American, I told him. He said he needed 100 lire for the movies, I said then come by for two minutes. We jerked each other off . . . Sometimes it's the relief one really wants rather than the actual pleasure. Gregorio has beautiful eyes, large, very white eyeballs, the longest black lashes. One nostril is always red and running.

◆

This is New Year's Eve. I saw Pavlik at the hospital this morning, he was in a rather reposed, dopey state. Dr. R. has told him that he had a heart attack. "My first heart attack," as Pavlik put it.

Gregorio's visit lifted some of the loneliness. A pin-wheel spins its sparks from a balcony across the way.

1957

JANUARY

Precious Pavlik looked and felt better than any time during the past week, he could begin to sit up in the chair a bit, while the sisters made the bed. He spoke of certain visions (half-dreams?): "Whole towns made of rags. And the rags became alive." He spoke of doors made of straw, slightly wavy, then water would come into them, from no one knew where, and make patterns.

It's New Year's Day. Vito came in while I was having breakfast, had been out shooting firecrackers and such, with the boys in his neighborhood, until 7:30 this morning; he looked it. No money left, from cardplaying.

◆

Retention versus invention. [Roberto] Matta abandons the mise-en-page to tell a story.

No better motto for any art: *moyens simples, resultats extraordinaires.*

The mystery of natural behavior.

◆

I don't know how my character will come out in these notes and memories, but I think we usually are to others what we are to ourselves.

Pavlik thinks he's not going to be "the same" when he gets out, although Dr. R. has told him his heart is better this very day than it was six days ago.

◆

Zev wanted to go see Pavlik alone so I thought this would be a good day—I gave Zev the lire from Pavlik's $150 check that I changed and he took the money to him. I've just talked to Zev on the phone and asked him if Pavlik was disappointed I didn't come to visit him today (I go every day), and apparently he was. Zev said that Pavlik said, "Charlie doesn't love me any more." Zev said it meant so much my going to see him.

◆

Vito is affectionate, but I'm afraid Pavlik's right: it's an animal only.

Not as completely an animal as Gregorio, though.

◆

Pavlik thinks he was close to death. "I myself was not I, I was outside," he said, "a little bird [like one] sitting on my shoulder: while the tissues fought."

Colors come from the soul, do they? Pavlik's morale today excellent. Their kindness is beyond praise, he said about the nuns. He isn't allowed to walk yet . . . "—when the Roman Empire comes in to wash me . . ."

◆

Zev phoned, said he'd been to see Pavlik this morning, found him walking around—but, as P. said about himself, "like a little child."

◆

Vito told me that when he was born, they thought he might not live, so baptized him at once. He didn't want to breathe. Then I read that Picasso, at birth, also seemed to be "refusing his destiny"—the father blew some tobacco smoke in the new-born's face and that brought forth breathing squalls. Is Vito to have any kind of extraordinary destiny? There's no one I know who hasn't been charmed by him, at least a little.

The affection lasts as it goes along, or it doesn't.

I'll never forget how Djuna looked, the night (before I sailed for France, 1931) she walked down those basement apartment steps on Eighth Street: slim-waisted, black-suited, high heels, hat on one side (small black hat over a short red-curled haircut), red red lips and a ruffled white blouse. We drank prune whisky, then took a taxi to the Cotton Club—one night in April.

◆

Dr. Simeons arrived at Pavlik's bedside this morning. He was serious about Pavlik's heart, says it will take years to mend. Pavlik was despondent today, said he'd cried at times. Cry a bit for me, I said, babying him. And he almost did, stopped himself. And I almost did (cry) too.

And Rome is ash-blue.
Hands in the North Wind—

◆

Pavlik coming home! I bring him in the car, day after tomorrow—the 21st. "Twenty-one, that's my number," he said.

◆

I like to live in Italy but I'm going to live in France.

Agreed, Vito is an animal. But there are animals and Animals.

◆

He isn't coming home tomorrow. Dr. S. said it may be another week. I left the room with Simeons and asked him if he had a clear picture of what condition Pavlik was in when he was brought to the hospital, if he had been in danger of death (as P. says), and Simeons said his condition had been critical, and that he *had* been in danger of death—"it was touch and go for a few days."

♦

Perhaps Gregorio's eyes sometimes have an expression which doesn't go with the eyelashes.

> Need we nought but enough
> But to reach the right line?

♦

Pavlik said that he's shakey, his hands tremble. One nun exclaimed in dismay on seeing all the puncture holes in his behind—he's had so many shots.

♦

The art followers who are on the lookout for "tendencies" and "schools," rather than for individuals, always get fooled.

♦

I saw Kot [Koteliansky] at the hospital. He finds me "looking better" than I did in Paris. Wining, worry and fucking, then, have not had such a looks-undermining effect.

If you ever start thinking that Vito isn't so pretty, just place him in the sun.

♦

The news was not good this morning. Pavlik said he'd coughed in the night, spat blood twice, Sister Catherine gave him a puncture, plus pills, but they hadn't put him to sleep—only turned his thoughts panicky—"I thought I was losing my mind."

♦

P. doesn't remember with pleasure the visit of Afro, said Afro was coughing and taking tablets, thinks he (Afro) might have infected him. I'd gone in early this morning to see our landlord (INA) about getting some action on the elevator they've promised for this building.

Of course, Pavlik will not be home this week. He knows it—though we didn't mention it—asked me to bring him his sketchbook, there's one with a few pages still blank.

♦

Pavlik vows a non-sex life from now on. He says he's just going to do without sex—purification. "I've been a dirty man," he said. I told him not to call sensuality dirty.

♦

Drugs? Yes; if one didn't have the drug of work.

FEBRUARY

"Now I'm a real Christian," said Pavlik yesterday when I'd put around his neck the little gold chain I'd bought for him, with his medals hanging therefrom, a Madonna from Lourdes, a Saint Anthony, and a Madonna of Loreto. He used to wear them safety-pinned on the inside front flap of every shirt he wore, changing the medals from one shirt to another. Sometimes they'd get in the laundry by mistake.

His complaint against Dr. S: "He won't believe I'm a dragonfly, wants to treat me as he treats the Smiths and Joneses."

I wanted to work this morning but the Baby drained my energy away (I drained his too).

Out into the night, looking for a lover? Come into the day of Italy!

◆

The core of truth is poetry.

Pavlik knew he was seriously ill, I didn't. "Je suis foutu" ("I'm finished") he kept saying that dark morning of Christmas.

◆

I started asking the Bimbo yesterday how he loved me. Like a brother, like a fiancé—? "Like an uncle," he interrupted. I guess he had the appropriate answer. Beware of uncles, I told him.

◆

Back from a rainy Rome. Pavlik was lying there, talked to me with his eyes closed, said he was weaker than ever: "It's not the dope, it's weakness."

◆

The fatal image: Vito's profile as he looked over the terrace yesterday. There it was and there's nothing one can do about it. I wasn't born to live alone.

V. is a cat-boy. Can't train cats to wait on table.

On the other hand, he's a boy, too—

◆

P. said that Dr. S. told him today: the only way to treat you is to be cruel and bully you and that's the way I'm going to treat you from now on. The only way to treat me is lovey-dovey, Pavlik told him; if you try to be cruel and bully me, watch out, you'll break your horns.

"Vito will never be anything."

"You're probably right."

But while he's on the way to being nothing—

"You want to live with Vito." "No I don't."

"Call Sister Catherine, tell her my heart is dancing."

It will be seven weeks Tuesday, Pavlik's hospitalization. Once I was optimistic as to the time it would take to get him back home. Now I say it will have been ten weeks. He improves so slowly, which impels me to say he'll never be the same man—and Dr. S. has told him so too.

◆

Well, my Baby came in and seduced me. He did, dragging at me and playing around.

I've been in poor working form lately (on my gouaches for Galerie du Dragon exhib, scheduled for Paris in May). Vito's frequent visits don't help.

"You've always had everything you wanted"—Pavlik's opinion. He was sitting up when I arrived, a little earlier than usual. I stayed my usual hour, and left him walking up and down the room with his male nurse, Giuseppe, assisting him.

◆

A pretty animal, and attached to me. What more should one ask of a mistress, aged 16? Baudelaire got the animal, but little attachment.

There are two worlds, Pavlik said, the world of the sick and the world of the healthy. But there are really three. The world of the living, the world of the dead, and the intermediate world of the Invalid.

"My future is tomorrow; I'm not making any plans," says Pavlik.

◆

Gregorio: a masculine fifteen, small-nosed; those long-lashed eyes almost like girls' eyes, coupled with the huge hands (most men's hands are less large)...

In writing as Art, there are prose stylists (Henry James) and poets (Poe). The art of painting, too, has its "prose stylists"—and its poets. Bernard Buffet, prose stylist. Tchelitchew, poet. Matta is more poet than prosateur. Klee all poet. The Douanier Rousseau, obviously a poet. Vlaminck plutôt prosateur. Modigliani, prose stylist; Odilon Redon, poet. Renoir, like Henry James, could lift prosaic things to poetic heights.

The poetry of painting? Degas, supremely. A penchant for the poetic? Chagall.

◆

Pavlik today was his slowly improving self. He wanted me to hold him while he walked up and down.

"You never spoiled your mother much, you don't spoil me, you spoil Vito."

I: "You spoil me, I spoil Vito."

Pavlik could never cease being dear.

Everything plays around. If it's not you, it's a drop of water.

Forget about sons—all right, don't forget about them. Did Hadrian have sons? No, he had Antinous.

We human animals are what we are, not great suns burning but creatures who need the dark as much as we need the light.

◆

If I were asked to criticize Pavlik's "character," it would be that he's too vindictive about people, and what they should have done and did not do for him; too ungrateful for his very genius and the success he has had. It's true that his genius has not been rewarded in proportion to its worth—but to be embittered? ...

◆

Baby went to Carnival, running around the streets and chunking confetti, with some other boys. Yesterday I found a bit of confetti in his navel.

Pavlik was in a glum fub yesterday, said Dr. S. had been rude, doesn't want to give him vitamins or shots to pick him up. Pavlik was so mad with him, said (to me) that from now on he's going to communicate with him through the sisters!

◆

Pavlik told his complaints to Sister Adelinda, so today he got his way, Dr. S. all smiles, both pills and a shot, so P. feels better. But yesterday Pavlik had decided that when Dr. S. came by on his round he'd cover up his head with a towel, be "the Turkish bride," and that's what he did, while Dr. S. examined him in his routine way. P. said he saw—through a little opening in the towel—Dr. S. turn red as a beet ... "Titian would sue anybody who sneezed in his house ... You see, Dr. Simeons doesn't understand artists."

Can't I bring Pav home next Saturday, March 2, a week from tomorrow? Then he'd see the fireworks on the 3rd.

◆

Djuna and I were sitting in a car, a Paris curb. Gertrude Stein walked by with her dog, Basket. She stopped beside the car and chatted. I just sat there, by Djuna. After a few amiable words, Miss Stein ambled on. Djuna said, Did you see the jealous look in her eyes?

◆

There go the Carnival floats around the piazza, in a slow tempo so remote from the amplified recording of Bill Haley's "Mambo Rock" blaring forth. My Pulchinello (Gregorio) is out there, supposed to be back here in an hour and twenty minutes.

◆

Best time of all with Gregorio (spots of burnt cork on each cheek)...

◆

Vito's cut-outs from magazines...Stills from Walt Disney's "The Great Prairie"; a little ciccione holding a barbell; glaciers; man coverered with huge papier-maché rooster; Picasso clowning; American Indians dancing; three carved monkeys. The one that missed was a full-page head of smiling President Eisenhower.

◆

Sonny Boy came after school (don't drool). Do I need to record every orgasm I have? All right, mark up one for yesterday.

Sunday Vito will be dressed in rose-maroon jacket, white shirt with blue lines making squares, scarlet vest with gold buttons, pink-striped tie, and cowboy Levis with a deep turn-up cuff.

MARCH

The Professore's hands tremble when he holds them out—"So how can I draw?" he asks Dr. S. Dr. S. told P.: "Charlie believes only what he wants to believe." He thinks I don't want to believe that Pavlik is as ill as he is.

◆

Pavlik is home and I'm glad he's here. It's not always easy to be patient with the patient but I am, most of the time. Speaking of the hospital: "It's unbelievable that I'm out. I stayed ten weeks all alone—you will never know ... My heart is half stone."

◆

I thought I'd locked the door but it wasn't locked and Pavlik busted in, gave an "Oh!" and went out again. He saw Vito and me—on my bed.

"You make a whore out of everyone . . ."

Vito didn't know what the Professore's further reaction would be and gave a sigh of relief after I reported, He said we could at least have locked the door!

Pavlik's summary of how I spend my time: "Fornication and fabrication." They seem to have made themselves, some of my pictures.

Last night—for the first time since Pavlik's been home—no night sweats. I told him before bedtime: "You won't sweat tonight."

And no owl screeched.

◆

Many beautiful machines—Tanguy painted. But the most beautiful machine is and always will be the human body.

◆

Pavlik: "My mind is black, black, black . . . They killed me with those anti-biotics . . . I have no desire for anything or to see anyone . . . If I arrive like that a wreck to New York, people will turn their backs. I know Americans."

APRIL

Chick Austin is dying of cancer—Kirk wrote Pavlik. Friends go so much more often than they used to—because we're older. Mary Rodgers, Peter Watson, George Platt-Lynes, and now Chick—all within a year. Chick so American, Peter so English. Am I really fond of anyone French? They're hard to get close to—even Henri Cartier-Bresson . . . Italians get nearer.

It's ten to stupid midnight.

◆

Mother and I were sightseeing (dreamed last night). Was it an open car we were in? She turned her head to look at something and lifted her tight-fitting hat which came off with her hair (false hair): underneath hat and hair was her close-cropped head. Further down the road along came a man on an enormous pig; he was wearing an Indian Chief's headdress. I wondered why Mother had had her hair clipped: I asked her but she wouldn't tell me.

◆

Sans illusions, sans amertume. Turn the glove of cynicism wrong side out.

Pavlik's bedtime words: "Nothing is in me—nothing . . . When I will be dead, you still will be shaking me, think I'm putting on—"

◆

(2:40 in the morning.) "You're barking like a sea-lion, Pavlik."

"My angel, I'm sorry to wake you up—"

"I was awake."

"—But I'm so choking here, it's simply terrible. If you could get inside my body, you'd cry days and nights . . ."

"—probably the wind from the other world—" when I said I didn't feel any cold wind blowing. His legs are terribly swollen.

◆

Pavlik finds Baby Pie "good for nothing; looking more and more like a hustler."

"La peinture . . . c'était ma seule passion; çela et la danse. C'est pour ça que je fait danser les formes. Mais les gens ne comprennent pas—"

We go to the hospital tomorrow for a cardiograph. "—Anyway—I don't want to be here—I'm not happy . . . If only a miracle would happen . . ."

◆

"I can't breathe." He says he feels ready for the oxygen tent. He's packing his overnight bag in case he has to stay at the hospital. "Je ne suis pas vivant."

2:30 P.M. Pavlik is at Salvator Mundi. The slow pulse of his that I've been feeling has not been the "real" heartbeat. And the fact that I was not able to feel the real heartbeat means that the heart is not in order. Condition "serious," said Dr. Mattoli, though not "critical."

In other words, Pavlik did not respond to the treatment prescribed for his heart on being released from his hospital bed, and this new treatment—Dr. Mattoli wants a 2 or 3 day test—should have begun days ago.

Cruel nurse (according to P., that's me). He thinks I care less for him than I do. I show less than I feel. I sometimes feel (maybe I'm wrong) that Pavlik shows *more* than he feels.

JULY

Choura and Coral are staying with me. There was Coral—just now—on the kitchen terrace smoking a cigarette. "I'm allowed to," she said.

A look of infinite, faraway sadness which crossed Pavlik's face a couple of times this afternoon . . . When I thought about it in the car, on the way back here from the hospital the tears came.

He wanted to sign a check for a thousand dollars for me to change into lire. I made the proper notations on the check stub, then wrote out the check. He studied it and studied it (the stub), he couldn't quite understand the figures. And his hands were trembling. I took the checkbook away and said we'd do it tomorrow. "Did I sign the check?" "No"—so Choura wanted me to bring the checkbook back—she thinks he's very lucid. I regretted not having said, "Yes," for P. saw that he wasn't going to be able to sign the check. So once more I folded up the checkbook to put it away, and once more he asked, "Did I sign it?" and then I said, "Yes."

Dr. Puddu, another heart specialist we called in, told us this morning that he didn't think Pavlik could resist for another week.

Sister Adelinda told us this afternoon that he'd had another "syncope" after lunch; Dora, the nurse, must have called her and she gave Pavlik the injection which helped him over the spell. She said if he hadn't been given this injection he would not have survived.

◆

I dreamed this morning, just before I was called by Marisa, that I sat in a church, looking at beautiful frescoes. They were all over the light walls of the entrance to the church, dark frescoes, I remember one figure that looked as though it had two heads (with crowns?), then I saw that the second head had a body too, but an odd one, angular like a long piece of furniture. Then out of the church came Pavlik, smiling, very gay. I was overcome with joy as I embraced him, I cried with joy. (There were real tears in my eyes, I felt them near my eyes when I awoke.) In my dream, it was as though everything else had been a bad dream, and the reality was a joyous, laughing Pavlik.

◆

10:25 P.M. When we went into Pavlik's room at our usual hour, five o'clock, he was very wide-eyed, and having the oxygen. I took my place in the chair by the bed on his left, Choura on his right. But he was breathing with such difficulty, I just had to leave the room, I couldn't have controlled my feelings. I went into the W.C., near Pavlik's room, and there I let my tears come, bathed my red eyes in cold water and went to find Sister Adelinda. I asked her if something couldn't be given to make his breathing easier and she said Yes, she'd give him an injection. She said Pavlik was very conscious today of all that was going on, and that he reads your face. Today he looked at me more than once, and his eyes were less veiled, and he seemed to be wanting to see what was in my eyes. I didn't let him see—but who knows how deeply he saw—what distress I was in.

He was calmer after the injection and his eyes would close for minutes, a little of the whites showing, then he'd open them again. His mouth looked less tired today, his face is beautiful.

◆

7:20 P.M. Pavlik was better than yesterday, not having the oxygen when we arrived, quite conscious, though he repeated questions several times. His hands were less blue, though swollen—the terrible thinness of the fingers had gone. The continual breathing through the mouth has made the insides of his lips raw.

Choura said that tomorrow we'll tell him that Coral is here. Coral says she'd rather stay here than meet her parents in Florence (Monday) for "culture." She told me she thought her mother (my sister) makes an awfully good wife. And mother? Better wife than mother: "She's just not one of us ... When did she change?"

"After she got married," I said, referring to Sister's second husband, Zachary Scott, who has adopted Coral. Coral's father was my sister's first husband, Peter Van Eyck.

Just as with Vito, it's impossible to make up one's mind about Coral—what she will become.

◆

Dora said Pavlik told her this morning that my niece is here. How do you know? she asked. I imagine so, he said.

◆

Sister Adelinda reports that Pavlik is just the same. "Sure," she said, when I said perhaps we could bring my niece to see him this afternoon. That niece of mine is something of a problem child; under a surface quiet and charm she's seething with boredom and resentment. I get little explosions out of her, which reveal her inner thoughts. Choura thinks Coral's hungry for affection. Doesn't get it from her mother—nor, says Choura, do I give it to her. It's true, I replied, I have more affection for Vito than for Coral. "Ça, c'est autre chose," replied Choura. "Le peau appele le peau." . . . Those hard stubborn lines at the corners of Coral's mouth I saw last year. She said, in a huff, last evening (referring to her parents): "I wish they'd let me be just ordinary."

◆

Yesterday at S.M. I told Pavlik that Coral had arrived. "Vraiment?" he said. "She's downstairs," I said. "Veut-tu qu'elle t'embrasse?" He nodded.

So I led her in and she was smiling, and Pavlik's sweet word, "Belleza," was spoken, she leaned over and kissed him.

◆

3:30 P.M. Dr. Mattoli told us at the hospital this morning that Pavlik's "general condition" is lower than at any time—during the crises, something could be done, an injection of some sort used to help over the crisis, but now there's nothing to be done.

Sister and Zach arrive from Venice tomorrow. Coral joins them in Rome day after tomorrow, her Frascati visit will be ended.

◆

It is after midnight. When Sister Adelinda got me on the phone a little after 8:30 P.M., she could not bring herself to tell me what we have been dreading to hear. And that's how I feel now—I cannot bring myself to write it all down. "You come here, I will tell you everything."

I knew.

I didn't tell Choura, on the way, that I knew.

Back in the apartment, Coral came towards me in the dark hall, wanting to hear. I took her in my arms, I didn't have to say anything. I just said, "I must make a telephone call."

Pavlik's great heart stopped beating at ten to eight. Sister Adelinda was with him. At almost the same moment I called the Salvator Mundi and asked to speak to her. The sister who went to the room (102, where Sister Adelinda was with Pavlik) just told her she was wanted on the phone, she didn't tell her it was I, calling from Frascati. So she didn't come to the phone. Then she tried to get my number for over half an hour. We reached the hospital shortly after nine.

Oh so cold, when I kissed him on the cheeks. Oh so cold.

AUGUST

Two hours before the end he had wanted us to go, and had not wanted us to go. He clasped my left hand (I had been stroking his left hand, Choura on the other side), holding me back a while, even after saying, "Mes enfants—partez." Choura says no use to regret not being there at the end, he wanted it the way it was. He wanted us to suffer as little as possible.

Choura has shown herself very loving to me, and I am grateful. "Je sais que c'est dur pour toi"—she came up to me on the terrace and put her arm around me. "J'espère d'être—comme un frère—pour toi," I said to her. "Tu en était toujours," she replied.

Le soir, à 8 heures moins 10. He always said that 8 was his number and 10 mine. "Che cosa terribile" were the last words that Dora could understand, during the last terrible minutes. The priest had been there that morning, said prayers and gave Extreme Unction.

We tried to think that he didn't know—he hid it so well—but he knew.

Choura says that it is a good sign when the soul is conscious of leaving the body, and Pavlik's "Che cosa terribile" was his soul speaking, at seeing the body, so sick, so changed, being left behind.

◆

I don't know who will go with me in the car to Paris.

"Vito?" queried Coral. Choura thinks she's jealous of V. and me. Choura also supposes Vito jealous of Coral and me. He doesn't seem unhappy that she's no longer here—on the contrary. He tried to show what affection he could, yesterday. His arm around me several times.

I still don't know what to do with him. He has become to a definite extent my responsibility. I suppose he will become more so.

◆

Choura asked me if I knew the story of their mother's hand appearing from the sea. No, Pavlik hadn't told me. On Pavlik's first voyage to the U.S.A., the ship

(Holland-American line) ran into such a storm, that he and Allen and others aboard did not know if they would not sink. Suddenly he saw his mother's hand rise from the waves, and they calmed down at once.

◆

Vito on back seat, after we dropped Zach & Sis and Coral-Bottom at their hotel, the Boston, on Sunday: "I'll be your chauffeur, secretary, personal friend, and, with any time I have left over, take voice lessons."

◆

When I think, as I do every day, of that last agonizing day of his, that day of agony ... I do not cry over my great loss, I do not pity myself at all.

And Vito? ... I somehow feel that destiny will decide for me ... We didn't "decide" to be born, nor do most of us decide when our death is to be.

◆

The service at the Protestant Cemetery: flowers surrounded the urn with Pavlik's ashes, in the center of the Chapel. The old priest with the white beard, Russian, speaking in Russian, calling Pavlik's first name, walking around the urn, mourned, prayed, sang—with the greatest simplicity. Infinite pathos in the humble, unpretentious ceremony.

◆

I want to do nothing but work now, with as few distractions as possible.

Vito is a distraction.

He's decorative, sweet, superficial—

A luxury.

But I shall be frugal in other ways, cannot I afford my Vito?

◆

The drug of death—that's what that veil was between us, at six o'clock on Tuesday, July 30—

◆

I don't know—I wonder if Vito doesn't love me—in his animal fashion. Anyway, until someone else comes along, I have only him. Is this a decision or a fact?

◆

Vito has become more dear during the past ten days—we've been together more. And the more I see him the more I want to see him.

No, no wife. Vito. Choose the non-pattern. "Risquez!" ... I'm not forcing anything. But some kind of love is working in me.

I want him in Paris.

Stronger than sex is sorrow
Till sorrow eats its heart away
Then along steps love and says Good day
And helps itself, if there's anything left.

There's always been a choice between what gives pleasure and what gives lasting pleasure.

As though any pleasure lasted.

When I was a Candy Kid down in Dixie
An all-day-sucker went all too quickly.
And now that I'm a grown-up man
Sweet things melt yet as fast as they can.

◆

I told him, Perhaps it's only physical, maybe I don't love you at all. He said, I think you love me.

INDEX

Because references to Pavel Tchelitchew (Pavlik) occur on almost every page of this text, they have not been indexed.

Abel, Lionel, 126
Abesteguy, Monsieur, 201, 216
Acton, Harold, 18
Adelina, Sister, 236, 240, 241, 242
Aeschylus, 86
Afro, 174, 233
Agnese (*little girl*), 90, 97
Agostinci, Monsieur, 217
Aiken, Conrad, 128
Albert (*friend of Thad Lovett*), 150
Aldobrandinis, the, 215
Alexander the Great, 22, 47
Allen, 244
Amadeo (*friend of Albert and Francis*), 150
Anderson, John Murray, 42, 112
Angelina (*Salvatore the caretaker's daughter*), 168, 173
Anger, Kenneth, 185
Anna R., 12
Antinous, 236
Antonio (*caretaker*), 175
Ard, Mathews, 211
Armstrong, Louis, 222
Artaud, Antonin, 105
Askew, Kirk, 82, 238
Astor, Mrs. Vincent, 15, 23
Auden, W. H., 10, 19, 110, 112, 135, 138, 158, 169, 170, 177, 221

Audiberti, Jacques, 187
Austin, Chick, 42, 52, 112, 124, 238

Babillée, Jean, 67
Baby, the. *See* Vito
Bachelard, 78
Balanchine, George, 9, 11, 18, 48, 109, 111, 124, 125, 127
Balmain, Pierre, 223
Balthus, 68, 224
Bankhead, Tallulah, 18
Barnes, Djuna, 12, 28, 31, 32, 34, 80, 101–2, 103–4, 122, 135, 152, 153, 162, 164, 166, 179, 196, 211, 232, 236
Barrault, Jean-Louis, 34, 68
Barry, Iris, 23
Baudelaire, Charles, 58, 60, 63, 81, 91, 100, 105, 151, 175, 235
Beadle, Ernst and Gina, 46
Beaton, Cecil, 9, 13, 20, 67, 68, 142, 216
Benedict, Brother, 39, 41
Benet, William Rose, 19
Benito (*acquaintance*), 189, 193, 196
Bentley, Eric, 123
Bérard, Christian (Bébé), 12, 13, 32, 34, 35, 67, 68, 168
Bergman, Ingrid, 29
Bergson, Henri-Louis, 117, 156

Bert (*sailor*), 13, 23–24, 29–31, 32, 34, 36, 100, 101, 109, 112, 114–21 passim, 123, 129, 165
Bettina (*model*), 186
Betty (*ballerina*), 51
Bice (*Domenico's wife*), 73, 137, 142, 168
Biéville, Anne de, 162
Bishop, Elizabeth, 19
Bishop, John Peale, 127
Blake, William, 188
Blanchard, Dominique, 13, 67
Blixen, Baroness Tania (pseud. Isak Dinesen), 6, 57, 62, 96, 127, 128, 147, 183, 212
Bobby (*acquaintance on board the* De Grasse), 47–50, 51, 153
Boccolini, Albertino, 189
Boccolini, Bruno, 189
Boccolini, Saverio, 188–89
Bompiani (*publisher*), 192
Bouchage, Luke, 49
Bousquet, Marie-Louise, 161, 183
Bouverie, Alice, 15, 16, 19, 21, 23, 27
Bouverie, David, 15, 23
Bowles, Paul, 14, 15, 53
Bowman, Wales, 150
Boyer, Charles, 20
Boyle, Kay, 148, 177
Brad, 210
Brancusi, Constantin, 63
Braque, Georges, 97, 98, 204
Breton, André, 64, 67, 216
Britten, Benjamin, 176
Browns, the. *See* Carlyle Brown
Bruno (*acquaintance*), 192
Buffet, Bernard, 235
Bulfinch, Thomas, 91
Buñuel, Luis, 224
Butler, Samuel, 170

Caetani, Princess Marguerite, 151, 186, 187
Calder, Alexander, 63, 213
Calder, Louise, 213
Capote, Truman, 30, 64, 67, 68, 99, 142
Caravaggio, Michelangelo Merisi da, 203–4

Carlyle Brown, Henri, 32, 74, 111, 138
Carlyle Brown, Margie, 111, 138, 140, 147
Carmen (*Salvatore the caretaker's brother*), 178–79, 180, 186
Carmita, 102, 103, 152, 162, 164
Carradine, John, 32
Carrie (*maid*), 32, 43, 45
Carter, David, 178
Carter, Mr. and Mrs. Elliott, 178
Cartier-Bresson, Henri, 138, 161, 169, 183, 238
Catherine, Sister, 233, 235
Cato, Ghondi, 170. *See also* Kato, Ghondi
Cato, Grandpa, 5
Cato, Mama, 38, 101, 167, 170
Cato, Marcus Porcius (Cato the Censor), 73
Cerdan, Marcel, 8
Cézanne, Paul, 5, 53
Chagall, Marc, 68, 235
Chaney, Stewart, 23
Charles (*in Switzerland, singer from Mississippi*), 219
Charpentier, Georges, 8
Chekhov, Anton, 20
Chirico, Giorgio de, 83
Chopin, Frédéric-François, 30
Christoff, Boris, 202
Chuangtse, 97
Clark, Eleanor, 135
Claude (*boy from St-Jorioz*), 17
Claudio (*friend of Franco Sereni*), 150
Clerici, Fabrizio, 76
Clouzot, Henri-Georges, 216
Cocteau, Jean, 27, 28, 29, 30, 68, 148, 181, 203, 215, 216, 217
Colbert, Claudette, 119
Colonna, Princess, 81
Conchita (*Salvatore the caretaker's wife*), 168
Conn, 135
Connolly, Cyril, 68
Cornell, Joseph, 62
Covarrubias, Miguel, 148
Coward, Noël, 119
Crane, Hart, 115

Cremonini, Leonardo, 147
Crevel, Réné, 148, 157
Cuevas, Marquis George de, 64
Cummings, E. E., 122, 123, 125, 135, 136, 179
Cunard, Nancy, 148, 149, 227

Daddy. *See* Ford, Charles L.
Daddy (*Shorty's father*), 39–40
Daisy (*neighbor*), 124
Dali, Gala, 28
Dali, Salvador, 28, 122, 222–23, 224
Dante, 56, 94
Dean, James, 222
Degas, Edgar, 235
Delamar, Alice, 4, 16, 42, 113, 127, 153, 157, 174
Del Corso, Gaspero, 74, 76, 79, 81
Dell (*cousin*), 101
Derain, André, 77
De Sica, Vittorio, 142
Dietrich, Marlene, 9
Dinesen, Isak. *See* Blixen, Baroness Tania
Dino (*garage worker*), 220
Dinsha, Edalgy, 58, 59
Diogenes, 225
Dior, Christian, 9, 158, 216
Domenico (*caretaker*), 73, 74, 89
Donizetti, Gaetano, 188
Dora (*nurse*), 240, 241, 243
Dottie (*Bert's girlfriend*), 31
Douglas, Lord Alfred, 186
Douglas, Norman, 35, 148
Dow, Dorothy, 202
Dubuffet, Jean, 183
Ducasse, Isidore-Lucien (pseud. le comte de
    Lautréamont), 100, 152
Duchamp, Marcel, 141, 164
Duff, Lady Juliet, 158
Dutourd, Jean, 167

Eliot, T. S., 169, 179, 211
Eluard, Nusch, 46
Eluard, Paul, 46
Embiricos, Perry, 21, 104, 111, 155

Emerson, Ralph Waldo, 110
Enriquez, Carlos, 77
Ernst, Max, 64, 66, 159, 162, 217
Euripides, 101

Fang, Mei Lan, 119
Farouk, King, 194
Faucett, Dean, 127
Fausto (*shepherd*), 80, 86
Feldkamp, Mrs., 19
Fiedler, Mr. and Mrs. Leslie, 141, 142
Fini, Léonor, 12, 32, 42, 51, 53–61 passim, 63,
    66, 98, 113, 119, 154, 155, 158, 174, 183, 184, 185,
    201
Fizdale, Robert, 53
Flanner, Janet, 80, 218
Florentino, Maturino, 152
Ford, Charles L. (Daddy), 4, 5, 6, 11, 14, 35–41,
    43, 167
Ford, Gertrude (Mother), 4, 5, 11, 12, 14, 17, 35,
    36, 38, 41, 43, 44, 45, 105, 109, 111, 112, 127,
    129, 167, 204, 208–10, 238–39
Ford, Grandma, 5
Ford, Grandpa, 4
Ford, Ruth (Sister), 11, 12, 18, 19, 20, 34, 35, 38,
    101, 129, 138, 207, 208, 209, 210, 220, 223,
    241, 242, 244
Fore, Lizzie, 5
Fouts, Denham, 4
Foy, Gray, 141, 142
Francés, Esteban, 127
Francesca (*Salvatore the caretaker's daughter*),
    173, 177
Francesco (*goatherd*), 88
Francis (*friend of Thad Lovett*), 150
Francis, Saint, 105
Frank (*acquaintance of Pavlik*), 224
Freud, Sigmund, 115
Fuller, Loïe, 67–68

Gabriele (*shepherd*), 177, 180
Gaetana (*housekeeper*), 195
Garbat, Dr., 35

Garbo, Greta, 28, 29, 30, 64
García Lorca, Federico, 82, 176
Garcia Villa, José, 19
Genet, Jean, 18, 51, 54, 60, 61, 99, 154, 155, 162, 183–87 passim, 217, 219
Gertrude (*Zev's wife*), 224
Ghondi, Kato. *See* Kato, Ghondi
Ghyka, 74–75
Gide, André, 87, 215
Gilberto (*Léonor Fini's lover*), 98
Gili, Beniamino, 188
Gilmour, Geoffrey, 217
Gino (*acquaintance in Lévico*), 89, 93–96, 140
Giovanni (*acquaintance*), 91–93, 94
Giraudoux, Jean, 16, 32
Gisella (*Italo's wife*), 89
Giuliano (*Sicilian bandit*), 91
Giuseppe, Don, 175, 176, 196
Giuseppe (*male nurse*), 235
Givenchy, Hubert de, 165
Goethe, Johann Wolfgang von, 162
Gold, Arthur, 53
Gordon, Caroline. *See* Tate, Caroline Gordon
Gorky, Arshile, 20
Grady, Uncle, 211
Grange, Henri-Louis de la, 155, 176
Graves, Robert, 95, 96
Greene, Milton, 165
Gregorio (*milkboy*), 214, 222, 225, 227, 228, 231, 233, 235, 237
Gregory, Horace, 19
Grimm, Jacob and Wilhelm, 114
Griswold, Mr. and Mrs., 111
Guggenheim, Peggy, 63, 65, 102, 227
Gysin, Brion, 19

H., Dr. (*Charles Ford's physician*), 39
Hadrian, 236
Haley, Bill, 237
Hanfstaengel, Putsy, 102
Hare, Channing, 150, 185

Harris, Jed, 20
Hartwig, Brigitta. *See* Zorina, Vera
Hensel, Stevie, 150
Hiquily, 223
Holman, Libby, 14
Honicutts (*apple farmers*), 128
Hopkins, Gerard Manley, 135
Horner, David, 15, 23
Howard, Brian, 138, 148
Hoyningen-Huene, George, 23
Hunt, Martita, 31
Hunter (*shopkeeper*), 110
Hutton, Barbara, 175

Inge, William, 119
Iolas, 12, 13, 34
Islay, 227
Italo, 89

Jack (*Hal Plunkett's stepson*), 39, 40
Jackson, Brooksie, 47
James, Edward, 91, 125
James, Henry, 224, 235
Jane (*girl for Bert*), 30
Jarrell, Randall, 19
Jaspers, Karl Theodor, 156
Jennings, Ollie, 28, 31
Jones, David, 177
Jonesie (*Gertrude Ford's lover*), 167
Jorgensen, Christine, 157
José (*acquaintance of Richard Thoma*), 164
Jouvet, Louis, 16, 34, 65, 67, 97–98
Juenger, 114
Jullian, Philippe, 203
Jung, Carl, 9, 77, 78, 91, 105, 106, 114, 115, 124, 125
Junod, Dr., 54, 61

Kandinsky, Wassily, 202
Kato, Ghondi, 170, 186, 187
Kirstein, Fidelma, 16, 23
Kirstein, Lincoln, 16, 18, 21, 23, 32, 47, 110, 127, 142, 148, 177, 223

Klee, Paul, 235
Kochno, Boris, 34, 67
Kopeikine, Nicholas (Kola), 50
Koteliansky, S. S., 158, 233
Krishnamurti, Jiddu, 156, 170

Laclos, Pierre-Ambroise-François Choderlos
    de, 20
Lane, Frankie, 202
Lang, Harold, 109
Lao-Tse, 59
Laughlin, James, 33, 46, 175, 177–78
Laughlin, Mr. and Mrs., 15
Lautréamont. *See* Ducasse, Isidore-Lucien
Layard, John, 182
Lea, Tom, 113
Le Clercq, Tanaquil, 47, 48, 49, 50, 109, 124,
    225
Lee, Gypsy Rose, 21, 69
Léger, Fernand, 68
Leopardi, Conte Giacomo, 89, 94
Lepri, Stanislao, 51, 58, 59, 60, 63, 76, 98, 158
Lerman, Leo, 141, 142, 147
Lesell, Philip, 63
Leven, Gustave, 223
Leven, Raoul, 54
Lieberson, Goddard, 215
Linda (*maid*), 56, 58, 59, 60, 73, 74, 75, 77, 78, 86,
    90
Lombroso, Cesare, 31
Lopez, Arturo, 184, 185
Lopez, Patricia, 184, 186
Lorca. *See* García Lorca, Federico
Lovett, Thad, 150, 185
Loy, Mina, 80
Luigi (*goatherd*), 87–88
Luigi (*lawyer*), 190
Lynes, Russell, 127

MacDonald, Dwight, 174
Macdougall, Allan Ross (Dougie), 34, 101,
    102, 218
Macpherson, Kenneth, 227

Madeleine (*Cocteau's maid*), 215, 216
Magallanes, Nicholas (Nicky), 11–12
Mallarmé, Stéphane, 94
Mamie, Aunt, 44
Mamie (*whore*), 40
Mandiargues, André de Pieyre, 51, 158
Marais, Jean, 41
Marcello (*goatherd*), 88
Maria (*Afro's wife*), 174
Maria (*housekeeper*), 141, 142, 201
Mariano (*garage owner*), 220
Marinangeli (*lawyer*), 192
Mario (*friend of Corrado Sereni*), 150
Marisa (*housekeeper*), 240
Maritain, Jacques, 175
Markevitch, Igor, 151, 176
Marlowe, Christopher, 135
Marlowe, Sylvia, 13, 23, 127, 213
Marsh, Thomas John, 169
Mason, Marjorie, 179, 186, 187
Massimo, Prince Leone, 213
Massine, Léonide, 13, 23, 213
Matisse, Henri, 156, 204
Matta, Roberto, 231, 235
Mattoli, Dr., 227, 239, 242
Mauro (*acquaintance*), 160
Mayo (*acquaintance*), 162, 165, 166
McCarthy, Mary, 21
McCullers, Carson, 119
McKay, Claude, 161
Menotti, Giancarlo, 176
Merimée, Prosper, 12
Michaux, Henri, 53, 218, 223
Miller, Henry, 99, 128
Miller, Lee, 162
Miró, Joan, 68
Modigliani, Amedeo, 235
Montaigne, Michel Eyquem de, 182
Montferrier, Florence de, 158
Moore, Henry, 111
Moore, Marianne, 19, 123, 124
Morris, Ben, 150, 162, 165
Mosely, Diana, 223

Mother. *See* Ford, Gertrude
Muir, Edwin, 211
Mussolini, Benito, 81

Nabokov, Nicolas, 158, 224
Nando (*apartment superintendent*), 194, 201, 226
Nardi, Dr., 190, 191, 192, 193
Nerval, Gérard, 12
Newberry, Jack, 185
Nicholson, Ivy, 165
Nino (*friend*), 173
Noailles, Marie-Laure de, 176, 216, 217
Noël (the "Scoot") (*friend*), 53

O'Brien, Peggy, 185
O'Casey, Sean, 135
Owen, Wilfred, 135
Ozeray, Madeleine, 67

Pace, Guerrero, 78
Paracelsus, 166
Patti, Adelina, 143
Paul (*king of Greece*), 21–22
Pecci-Blunt, Contessa Mimi, 80
Pelus, Marie-Jeanne, 11
Penrose, Roland, 187
Peppa (*housekeeper*), 169, 176, 178, 179
Petit, Roland, 67
Philippe (*barber*), 14
Picasso, Pablo, 6, 46, 67, 68, 99, 232
Pichette, Henri, 12
Pita Rodríguez, Félix, 152
Plato, 75
Platt-Lynes, George, 238
Plunkett, Hal, 39, 40
Plutarch, 75
Poe, Edgar Allan, 235
Polidoro da Caravaggio, 152
Pollock, Jackson, 63, 220, 227
Potter, Pauline. *See* Rothschild, Pauline de
Poulenc, Francis, 15, 18
Puddu, Dr., 240

Randinger, Dr., 226, 227, 228, 231
Ray, Man, 80, 148, 216
Read, Herbert, 211
Rédé, Baron de, 186
Redon, Odilon, 235
Regina (*maid*), 73
Reichenbach, François, 183, 185, 201, 217
Renoir, Pierre-Auguste, 235
Reynolds, Mary, 63
Ribblesdale, Lady, 16
Ricardo (*plumberboy*), 182
Rieti, Elsie, 127
Rieti, Fabbio, 127
Rieti, Vittorio, 13
Rikers, Georgia, 30–31
Rilke, Rainer Maria, 55, 105
Rimbaud, Arthur, 87, 114, 135, 181, 193
Robbins, Jerome, 109, 127
Rocco (*friend*), 192, 193, 194–95, 196
Rocco, Joseph, 126
Rockefeller, Mrs. Nelson, 16
Rodgers, Mary, 143, 238
Rorem, Ned, 154, 186
Rosa (*Tonino the caretaker's widow*), 169
Rose, Francis, 183
Rossignol, Mme, 65–66
Rothschild, Pauline de, 16, 215, 223
Rothschild, Philippe de, 215, 223
Rousseau, Henri (Le Douanier Rousseau), 235
Royer, M. et Mme, 178

Sade, Comte Donatien-Alphonse-François de, 82, 100, 105, 183
Salvatore (*caretaker*), 168, 178
Sand, George, 30
Sartre, Jean-Paul, 20
Sauguet, Henri, 67
Savo, Jimmy, 48
Scarlatti, Domenico, 22
Scarlett, Mme, 217, 218
Schapiro, Meyer, 123
Schippers, Tommy, 176
Schwartz, Delmore, 19

Scott, Coral, 120, 123, 127, 136, 209, 220–21, 240–44 passim

Scott, Zachary, 208, 209–10, 220, 223, 241, 242, 244

Sereni, Corrado, 73, 74, 75, 150

Sereni, Franco (Frankie), 73, 77, 139, 141, 150

Sereni, Signora, 73–74

Sergei (*bellboy*), 121

Seurat, Georges, 5, 53

Sforza, Count, 51

Shakespeare, William, 6, 109

Shorty (*Jack's friend*), 39–40, 41

Sidéry, Sherban, 58, 216

Signorelli, Olga, 226

Silone, Ignazio, 224

Simeons, Dr., 139, 181, 221, 225, 226, 232, 234, 235, 236, 237

Sister. *See* Ford, Ruth

Sisto (*shepherd*), 79–80, 86–87, 101, 140

Sitwell, Edith, 7, 14–24 passim, 27, 28, 31, 32, 35, 46, 75–76, 82, 83, 84, 91, 100, 102, 127

Sitwell, Osbert, 7, 14, 15, 16, 18, 19, 21, 23, 24, 28, 31, 32, 35, 52, 82, 84, 85, 155

Soardo, Mlle, 167, 169

Soby, James Thrall (Jim) and Nellie, 111

Sokoloff, 32

Southey, Robert, 159

Spender, Stephen, 19, 175

Stein, Gertrude, 9, 16, 102, 111, 112, 116, 124, 160, 161, 163, 164, 166, 204, 212, 236

Steloff, Frances, 13

Stendhal (Marie-Henri Beyle), 195

Stettheimer, Florine, 21, 81, 124, 125

Stettiner, Jacques, 53

Stravinsky, Igor, 158, 214, 215

Tallchief, Maria, 11

Tanguy, M. et Mme, 46

Tanguy, Yves, 46, 152, 238

Tanner, Allen, 166

Tanning, Dorothea, 64, 66, 127, 159, 161–62, 217

Taras, Johnny, 64

Tate, Allen, 175, 179

Tate, Caroline Gordon, 175, 179, 182

Taylor, Janet and Bill, 218

Tchelitchew, Choura, 50–54 passim, 65, 66, 142, 153, 161, 188, 216, 222, 240, 241, 242, 243

Tennant, Stephen, 186

Tenner, Allen, 161

Thoma, Richard, 164

Thomas, Dylan, 134, 135, 177, 185

Thomson, Virgil, 16, 19, 100, 124, 125, 183

Thoreau, Henry David, 105, 110, 117

Tilden, Bill, 157, 193

Tim (*Charles Ford's caretaker*), 4, 5–6, 14

Titian (Tiziano Vecellio), 236

Toklas, Alice B., 53, 102, 160, 166, 183, 212

Tolstoy, Leo, 13

Tonino (*caretaker*), 167, 169

Tooker, George, 127

Toumanova, Tamara, 9, 64

Turner, Mrs., 111

Tyler, Parker, 19, 21, 81, 102, 103, 117, 126, 161, 174, 179, 193, 214

Uccello, Paolo, 141

Ula (*Shorty's sister*), 40

Ungaretti, Giuseppi, 80

Valéry, Paul, 75, 181

Vanderbilt, Mrs. Cornelius, 24

Van Eyck, Peter, 159, 241

Van Rumpt, Dr., 46, 190

Van Vechten, Carl, 9, 65, 123, 139, 164, 192

Vasari, Giorgio, 152

Vidal, Gore, 19

Vincenzo (*Sisto's employer*), 80

Viola (*maid*), 23, 32

Virgil, 94

Vito's father, 215

Vito's mother, 220

Vito (the Baby) (*carpenter's son*), 194, 195–96, 197, 201, 202, 203, 204, 207, 212, 213, 215, 216, 217, 219–24 passim, 227, 231, 232, 234–39 passim, 241–45 passim

Vlaminck, Maurice de, 235

Vorisoff (*neighbor*), 29

Wagner, Richard, 13
Waley, Arthur, 93
Ward, Fanny, 42
Watson, Peter, 4, 30, 68, 154, 155, 187, 216, 238
Welch, Denton, 188
Wescott, Glenway, 28, 100
West, Mae, 35
West, Mr. and Mrs., 6
Wheeler, Monroe, 16, 18, 28
White, Miles, 112
White, Mr. (*Charles Ford's caretaker*), 36–37, 38, 40–41
White, Wanda, 36–38
Wild, Renato, 154, 162, 218, 219, 220
Wilde, Oscar, 109, 186
Wilder, Thornton, 203, 204

Williams, Mary Lou, 137, 186
Williams, Tennessee, 19, 101, 110
Williams, William Carlos, 122, 124, 136
Wind, Edgar, 19
Winwood, Estelle, 32
Woolf, Virgina, 196, 197

Yeats, William Butler, 91, 135
Young, Stark, 119, 150

Zadkine, Ossip, 201, 218
Zale, Tony, 8
Zaturenska, Marya, 19
Zev, 224, 231, 232
Zimmer, Heinrich, 208
Zorina, Vera (Brigitta Hartwig), 214, 215